Frank Coates was born in Melbourne and, after graduating as a professional engineer, worked for many years as a telecommunications specialist in Australia and overseas. In 1989 he was appointed as a UN technical specialist in Nairobi, Kenya, and travelled extensively throughout the eastern and southern parts of Africa over the next four years. During this time Frank developed a passion for the history and culture of East Africa, which inspired his first novel, *Tears of the Maasai*, which was published in 2004. *Softly Calls the Serengeti* is his sixth novel.

Also by Frank Coates

Tears of the Maasai

Beyond Mombasa

In Search of Africa

Roar of the Lion

The Last Maasai Warrior

FRANK COATES

Softly Calls the Serengeti

HarperCollins*Publishers*

HarperCollins*Publishers*

First published in Australia in 2011
by HarperCollins*Publishers* Australia Pty Limited
ABN 36 009 913 517
harpercollins.com.au

HarperCollins*Publishers*
25 Ryde Road, Pymble, Sydney, NSW 2073, Australia
31 View Road, Glenfield, Auckland 0627, New Zealand
A 53, Sector 57, Noida, UP, India
77–85 Fulham Palace Road, London W6 8JB, United Kingdom
2 Bloor Street East, 20th floor, Toronto, Ontario M4W 1A8, Canada
10 East 53rd Street, New York NY 10022, USA

National Library of Australia Cataloguing-in-Publication entry:

Coates, Frank.
  Softly calls the Serengeti / Frank Coates.
  1st ed.
  ISBN: 978 0 7322 8649 1 (pbk.)
  Adventure stories.
A823.4

Cover design by Nada Backovic Designs
Cover images: blood lily © Imagemore Co., Ltd. / Corbis; jeep by Jake Wyman /
  Getty Images; couple by Jordan Siemens / Getty Images; zebras on the Serengeti
  grassland © AfriPics.com / Alamy
Original map by Margaret Hastie, adapted by HarperCollins*Publishers*
Author photograph by Belinda Mason
Typeset in Sabon 11/15pt by Letter Spaced
Printed and bound in Australia by Griffin Press
60gsm Hi Bulk Book Cream used by HarperCollins*Publishers* is a natural, recyclable product
made from wood grown in sustainable forests. The manufacturing processes conform to the
environmental regulations in the country of origin, Finland.

5 4 3 2 1   11 12 13 14

To the people of Kibera,
whose courage, determination and
compassion for their fellow citizens were
the inspiration for this book, and to the
many legitimate and dedicated charities
who bring hope to them.

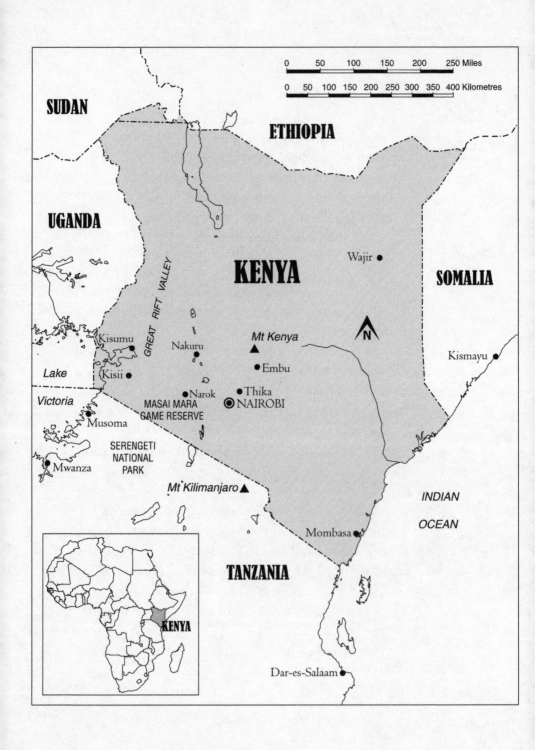

Nairobi — October 2002

It is hot and still for an October day.

A boy hurries through the alleys of Kibera. There is a storm in the air. He stops, checks the sky. Red smoke hangs above the rusted iron rooftops. Far away there is a rumble of thunder. A black kite shrieks a warning call and there is an answer from beyond the walls of rusty iron and rough-sawn timber that fashion his neighbourhood.

Urgent voices come from somewhere beyond the twists and turns of the narrow alleys. The boy squeezes into a gap as a group of young men dash past, muttering in breathy gasps.

The shriek comes again, but now it is not that of a black kite. Perhaps it never was.

An old woman, the gossip of the neighbourhood, comes scuttling towards the boy. He catches her eye. She sees him, but says nothing as she hurries by.

The scream again — not of fear this time, but of horror.

The boy starts to run. He knows these putrid narrow paths; he has played in them since he could walk. Still, he misjudges his leap across the stinking open sewer in the alley, and slimy mud and shit splash his bare legs. He crashes into a rusty wall on the other side and a protruding nail tears into his forearm. He stifles a whimper and runs on.

A cloud of acrid smoke swirls through a cross-alley. It makes his eyes smart as he plunges through it.

Another scream. A scream to halt his heart. A scream for help.

No longer can he hold to the idea of the kite. It is an inhuman sound, but he knows it's a woman's voice. He slams shut the vision that comes to mind, but the scream occurs again and the door is flung open. He knows whose voice makes those heartbreaking sounds. He knows whose throat gave flight to them.

He runs faster down the stinking path. Another cross-alley.

Flames licking through the smoke.

He stands in the mud. The screams are gone but his ears are ringing with their memory.

The grimy alleys are silent.

Thunder rolls across the blackened sky.

Flames rise and colour his stricken face.

He stares with eyes of ice at the burning remains of his home.

CHAPTER 1

NOVEMBER 2007

Joshua Otieng was narrow of hip and chest, but he had an athlete's bearing and the swagger of a young *takataka* man who had made his first sale on the streets when he was about seven years old. Back then, those sales had earned him a pittance, but it had been an important contribution to a family struggling to avoid hunger, especially when his father failed to find work as a casual labourer.

Now, ten years on, Joshua seldom failed to clinch a deal once his unerring radar had detected a mark among the stream of cars crawling towards the Kenyatta Avenue roundabout. He would engage his quarry with his compelling dark eyes and winning smile before the persuasion began in earnest. The haggling and the deal were complete and the mark's money in his bag before the traffic lights changed.

The boy had the lanky build of his Luo father and the sharp commercial mind of his Kikuyu mother. He could get by in Kiswahili, Somali and English as well as the Kikuyu and Dho-Luo of his parents. Among his many gifts was the ability to guess the mother tongue of his prospective client and use it to charm open the purse or wallet of all but the most obstinate. He had learnt his languages and also his street savvy in the alleys of Kibera, the squatter settlement situated a mere twenty minutes' walk from Nairobi's central business district.

In the mornings he sold newspapers, and later in the day it would be anything at all — usually cheap junk, *takataka*, imported from China. That afternoon he was selling little paper

3

butterflies whose gaudy wings were set frantically flapping by means of an elastic band. A dozen butterflies were cocooned in a thin plastic shopping bag hanging from his waist.

Kwazi was working the lane nearest the road divider. With his twisted spine and stiff leg, he couldn't escape to safety fast enough when the traffic column suddenly lurched into motion. Joshua didn't mind Kwazi hogging the right-hand lane. In spite of the age difference of some four years, he had been a friend for as long as Joshua had worked the Kenyatta Avenue roundabout. It was Kwazi who had loaned his younger friend the stock to make a start. And after the car accident that had crippled Kwazi a year later, at age twelve, Joshua had shared his takings with his friend until Kwazi was back on the street again.

A car had dragged Kwazi two hundred metres down Uhuru Highway, breaking bones, tearing muscle and ligaments and leaving his face distorted into a grotesque leer. Now, Kwazi sold a more basic commodity — guilt. People were prepared to pay to assuage the relief they felt that neither they nor their loved ones were disfigured like the poor crippled boy begging at the Kenyatta Avenue roundabout.

Kwazi's real name was Gabriel. *Just like the angel*, his deceased parents used to say proudly to friends. But after the accident it didn't seem to fit. The nickname came from a Frenchman who had been one of Kwazi's regular customers for the morning papers.

'What 'appened to you, Gabriel, uh?' he asked in his thick accent when Kwazi finally returned to his usual place. 'I didn't recognise you.'

Kwazi mumbled a brief reply about the car accident.

'*Merde*,' the French *mzungu* muttered. 'Quasimodo, *non*?'

The name appealed to Kwazi. Shortened, it had an African ring to it, so it stuck.

'Hey, Kwazi!' Joshua called now from his line. 'You want to finish?'

4

Kwazi pulled a handful of coins and small notes from his pocket. '*Ndiyo*,' he said. 'Let's go.'

Kwazi kept his battered wheelchair hidden among the shrubbery in nearby Uhuru Park. Joshua had found the chair years before in the mountain of rubbish he and his mother used to quarry in search of items she could sell to Kibera residents from her little stall on the main entry to the settlement. He and Kwazi had restored it using cannibalised bicycle parts, although they'd never quite mastered the wheels, one of which had an alarming wobble. But the pain-free mobility that the machine offered Kwazi made his life a little more bearable.

Joshua pulled the wheelchair from its camouflage and slipped his unsold butterflies into the carry bag hanging from the handles. He retrieved his mobile phone from his pocket and deftly thumbed through his text messages, reading some and quickly responding to others as Kwazi rolled along the pavement beside him. When they reached the incline on Haile Selassie Avenue, Joshua gave Kwazi a helping hand until their route again eased downward towards Kibera.

The Kibera squatters' settlement was the largest slum outside South Africa's Soweto, but, technically, the place didn't exist. There were no title deeds to the land. Kibera was therefore a vast collection of illegal dwellings. The situation suited the authorities. As it was an illegal settlement, they had no responsibility to provide essential services such as water, schools, sanitation, garbage collection, roads and health services. Private dealers provided water standpipes, charging twice the water utility rate in legal housing developments. Landlords felt no obligation to maintain houses in Kibera, many of which were built in dangerous or unhealthy locations amid sewers and garbage dumps. Typhoid, worm infestations and skin diseases were prevalent among the settlement's residents.

The police were rarely seen in Kibera, and never after dark. Vigilante groups brought thieves to justice, for a price.

'Have you got football training, Josh?' Kwazi asked.

'Maybe.' As usual, Joshua felt vaguely guilty about leaving his friend behind in order to attend his practice session. 'Michael texted me to say he can't make it, and he usually brings the ball.'

'You should go. Someone will bring a ball. And you need to practise every day. Next year, you'll see. The national selections. Practise hard, my friend.'

'Ah, that is for dreaming, Kwazi. Who will come to Kibera to find a football player? The selectors will be out at Nyayo Stadium or Moi International.'

'Then you will go to Nyayo.'

Joshua made no reply. They'd had the same conversation many times. He didn't dare buy into Kwazi's fantasy about a stadium brimming with ecstatic screaming fans as Joshua dashed downfield, the goalmouth beckoning. The reality of Kibera football was a generally shoeless contest, with a worn soccer ball, no referee, and with teams differentiated between 'shirts' and 'skins'. The games often ended in an inter-tribal brawl or were broken up by the administration police as an illegal gathering.

Joshua's team was lucky to have a training pitch — the one remaining open field in Kibera, which it shared with dozens of other groups. Local chiefs and greedy businessmen had progressively sold all the other sporting fields in Kibera for housing plots and *duka* shacks. Realistically, Joshua held little hope of being considered to try out for, let alone be selected to play in, a real soccer team. He was the best striker in Kibera's informal league, but he knew this would count for nothing among the elitist national selectors.

At the laneway leading to Kwazi's hut, Joshua bade his friend goodbye. When Kwazi was out of sight, Joshua began to jog down Kibera Drive towards the football ground. By the time he reached the clearing, he was running at full pace and, while his team-mates laughed and joked and kicked a ball to each other in a circle, Joshua continued to run laps, the sweat streaming from his body.

Once he joined the field of play, Joshua kicked and passed, cut and intercepted, covering all points on the pitch. At one moment he was defending; at another, he was in the forefront of the attack, using his famous curving strike to drive home a goal.

His dedication no longer elicited the ribald comments it once had. His team-mates had accepted it was just Josh being Josh — driven by his strange compulsion to be fitter, stronger and faster than anyone else who came along to kick the tattered football around the dusty field.

*   *   *

Two hours later, and thirty minutes after the last of his team-mates had deserted the field, Joshua headed for home, tired but full of the energy the game imparted to him. As he crossed the road towards Kibera he heard someone call his name. It was Gideon Koske.

'Hey, Otieng,' he said. 'Do you not know your friends these days?'

Koske was a businessman from the Kalenjin tribe, and Joshua's occasional benefactor, offering him odd jobs, usually of dubious legality.

'*Habari*, Mr Koske,' Joshua said, a little abashed. He returned to the kerb where Koske sat at a small roadside stall or *duka*, sipping tea. The *duka* proprietor eyed Joshua, then went on with his work of washing cups.

'*Jumbo*,' Joshua said as he reached Koske's table.

'*Mzuri*, my friend. Come, sit.'

Joshua sat on the offered wooden crate. 'I was thinking about something and I didn't see you,' he said.

Koske ignored the comment and took a sip of his tea.

Everyone in Kibera knew Gideon Koske, either personally or by reputation. He was a big man with large protruding eyes, and a callous opportunist who had initially made his money by claiming ownership of any disputed land in Kibera. Since titles were a rarity in the illegal settlement, he was able to intimidate or harass other claimants until they retreated from the ownership contest. This enabled him to sell the sites to the many desperate people clamouring for space upon which to erect a simple shelter. He then extracted further payments from the new owners to keep the new dwelling safe. His thugs were despised and feared throughout the settlement.

Joshua had heard Koske had used the wealth he accumulated from his illegal land dealings to buy influence in the ruling political party. There were rumours that he was backing the opposition in the upcoming elections. Joshua disliked Koske, but opportunities to earn extra cash overrode the whim of personal preference.

Koske noisily slurped his tea while Joshua waited patiently for him to speak. Joshua had noted before that Koske seemed to enjoy the power his protracted silences conferred.

'So, my friend,' he eventually said, 'I hear you are doing well in your football team. Captain! Well done.'

'*Asante*, Mr Koske. Thank you. But it's nothing.'

Joshua's false modesty concealed his pride. He had been a driving force in the team's establishment, but believed that his appointment as captain was due to his skill rather than to his organisational ability.

'No, no. I hear that you are the best striker in the competition.'

Joshua was again surprised at Koske's knowledge of the details of life in Kibera.

'*Sasa*,' Koske continued. 'I also hear that many of your team players are in need of boots. Football boots. Even you. How can you play with no boots, uh?'

Joshua shrugged. 'I can kick without boots. Others have found cheap boots in the markets.'

'Old boots. Second-hand rubbish!' Koske sneered. 'You need boots if you want to beat those fellows out by Nairobi dam. *Si ndiyo?*'

Joshua nodded.

'Here, my friend,' Koske said, producing a plastic shopping bag. Inside was a shiny new pair of football boots.

Joshua's mouth opened and closed. He was unable to make a sound. When he recovered from his excitement, he jabbered a string of thanks before Koske lifted his hand to stifle them.

'Enough, Otieng. You will find I can be very generous to my friends. I have some surprises for you. Soon. But I also may need a big favour one day, you understand?'

Joshua nodded.

'Even now, I have a little job. It's nothing, but you will help me. You and your team.'

'We will be happy to help you in any way, Mr Koske.'

'Yes. And if you do a nice job, I may be able to help with boots for your whole team.'

Joshua's eyebrows lifted in interest.

'Boots for the team, and perhaps something else for you.'

Joshua waited.

Again Koske allowed the suspense to build unbearably.

'I mean, you are a Luo, *si ndiyo*?' The question was rhetorical. 'And your man Odinga is a Luo who is standing for president.' Koske slowly stirred his tea.

Joshua could bear it no longer. 'You said boots ... and maybe something else for me?'

'Boots, possibly. And surely a Luo boy such as yourself would be prepared to do something special for Mr Odinga? I mean, to help him succeed on election day.'

Joshua nodded, unsure where Koske was leading him.

'Good.' Koske replaced his spoon on the table. 'That is all I need to know at the moment.'

He raised his teacup to his mouth, concealing his widening grin. Joshua was reminded of a hyena he'd once seen on a poster in the travel agent's window.

CHAPTER 2

Simon Otieng sat at the simple bench he and his son used as a table, pushing the remains of his *irio* around a chipped plate. From its position on the shelf above the small refrigerator, the portable TV blathered on about sorghum prices in Voi.

'There is food in the pot,' Simon said to Joshua as he ducked under the opening into the corrugated-iron-clad shack.

Joshua grunted a reply, went to the stove and spooned the greenish vegetable mash onto a plate.

'You keep strange friends these days,' Simon said as his son sat opposite him to eat. 'I saw you taking tea with Gideon Koske on Kibera Drive today.'

When Joshua didn't respond, he added, 'Is he the kind of man you should be seen spending your time with?'

'Mr Koske is a man who will stand up for people like us,' Joshua answered curtly.

Simon scoffed. 'The only person Koske fights for is Koske himself. Or else he finds others to do his fighting. People like the thugs who come to collect his tea money.'

He pushed his plate aside and placed his hand on his son's shoulder. 'Joshua, have nothing to do with that man. He can only bring you trouble.'

'He gives me work. And he will pay me for it.'

'You don't need money from people like Koske.'

'Am I to continue to sell newspapers and stupid children's toys on the streets for the rest of my life? Am I a man or a boy?'

Simon removed his hand. 'You are my son, and you will hear what I say.'

'I am a man, and a Luo. I will follow the Luo ways.'

'You know nothing of the Luo ways.'

'And who is to blame for that? Isn't it a father's duty to pass on his culture and the old stories to his next in line? I know nothing of my family. Nothing of my tribe. I should know these things.'

Simon took his plate to the plastic bucket that served as a washing receptacle.

'Now you have nothing to say,' Joshua said scornfully. 'As always.'

'There is nothing you can learn from me,' Simon replied. 'Forget Luo ways. They will not support you here in Kibera.'

'Mama told me about you when you lived in Kisumu. In Luoland.'

Simon's hand hesitated over his plate, but he made no comment and resumed scraping the scraps into the bucket.

'She told me that you killed someone, and then you ran away.'

Simon took a piece of newspaper and carefully wiped the plate.

'Who was it?' Joshua demanded. 'Why did you do it?'

'It was a long time ago. Those days are gone.'

'Was it like before? In our history? Was it a tribal war?'

'It was not a war. The old ways are dead. And good riddance. They brought nothing but hatred and death.'

'There was honour in the old ways,' Joshua said angrily. 'It is our heritage to follow them — Luo heritage.'

Simon wondered about honour and the old Luo customs. When he was a child, his grandfather had told him that the Luos' customs were very important. It was his grandfather who had taught him the dances and the Jo-Luo songs, and how to hunt and to throw a spear. And when Simon's father died and his father's brother inherited Simon's mother as another wife, as was Luo custom, it was his grandfather who had explained why Simon also had to leave his village and his friends and go to a new place.

His father's death hadn't been the last time that Luo customs had had a profound effect on Simon's life, but he recalled it was the first time he had begun to question them. He knew he could not escape the consequences of that questioning in his own life, but he had no intention of also allowing his only son's life to be ruined by them.

Looking across the table at Joshua, he could see the same glint of defiance his grandfather might have seen in him all those years ago.

'I will not have you fight for something that is so far in the past,' he sighed. 'Anyway, there is no honour in violence.'

His son glared at him. 'And is there honour in being a coward? Is there any honour in killing a man and then running away?'

Simon straightened as if his son had struck him in the face. His voice, when it came, was almost inaudible. 'You know nothing of these matters, Joshua.'

'There is nothing to know.' Joshua flung the words at him. 'You were a coward then, and you are still a coward.'

He got up from the table in such haste that the chair fell backwards. He burst through the door, which clattered against the sheet-iron wall, and continued to swing back and forth on its worn leather hinges long after he'd gone.

Simon's shoulders remained tense with anger as he stared at the space Joshua had vacated. After a long moment he let his breath slowly escape and his shoulders slump. He began to massage his broken knuckles — three on his right hand and two on his left. They always seemed to ache more when he was upset. Koske probably couldn't remember the day it happened. He certainly wouldn't remember Simon. Still, the bitter taste of utter helplessness remained vividly in Simon's memory.

*   *   *

Since arriving in Kibera, Simon and his family had always been beholden to someone, be it for the roof over their heads, water, access to sewage facilities, school fees, or the many other daily needs of a family. There was little left over from his small income so they had not been able to save more than a few shillings at a time.

Things improved when he found regular work at a new hotel site along Uhuru Highway. He was given a hard-hat and a half-hour break at midday.

Simon began to consider buying a plot to build a house of their own. For some time, he'd had his eye on a vacant site above the drain that ran through Kisumu Ndogo. It was a very small site, only enough for three rooms, but he knew it was all he could afford.

He made enquiries in the area and one day met the owner, a Nubian woman who claimed that her family had held the land all her life. Since there were no title deeds for Kibera land, Simon could only do so much to establish if the woman was speaking the truth and was indeed the owner. He consulted as widely as he was able, talking to friends, to people who knew people in the area, and to those who would be his neighbours. Of the ones who knew the situation, all agreed the woman could be trusted.

Buying the plot consumed all their money but, as he earned further funds on the Uhuru Highway site, Simon bought second-hand building materials. After work, he would hammer and saw until darkness made it impossible to continue.

One day a man arrived while Simon was up a ladder, putting a sheet of iron on the new roof structure.

'What are you doing here, my friend?' the man asked cheerily.

Simon looked at him. He wasn't the usual onlooker passing the time with idle questions. He wore a suit and an open-necked shirt.

'I am building my place. As you can see.'

'I can see that you are building,' the man said, taking a large white handkerchief from his pocket to dab at his protuberant eyes. 'But who gave you permission to build on this plot?'

'I have bought the plot. It is mine.'

'No, no. That is not possible.'

Simon, becoming agitated by the man's superior attitude, again looked down from his ladder. 'And who are you to tell me what is possible and what is not?'

'Because I am the owner of this plot.'

Simon came down the ladder on unsteady legs. The man was tall and had broad shoulders, but it was not merely his size that gave him his swagger.

'I am Gideon Koske,' he said, as if the name alone would explain the situation.

It didn't, and Simon stared at the man with a growing sense of panic. He knew enough about life in the slums to understand that a man in a suit had power beyond anything that people like Simon could match, regardless of the legalities.

'But considering you have invested so much in building materials, I am prepared to sell the plot to you on very favourable terms,' Koske said.

Simon began to laugh. He laughed until the sound grew hollow, and then stopped as suddenly as he'd started. The man's claim was just too frightful to contemplate.

'Leave,' he said through clenched teeth.

Koske considered him coldly. 'It is better that you take my offer, my friend.'

'I am no friend of yours! I said, leave! Get away from my house! Do you hear me?'

Koske shrugged and walked away.

Two days later, three men arrived at dusk as Simon was packing his tools into the old Gladstone bag he used to carry them. One of them took the bag from him. When he protested, the other two grabbed him and flung him to the ground, standing on his forearms to keep him there.

The first man, who had a large silver ring in his ear, rummaged around in Simon's tool bag and pulled out the hammer. He hefted it in his hand and smiled down at Simon.

At the time, Simon had thought the pain unbearable, but long after the agony of his broken fingers had subsided, the pain of losing his only chance to own his own place in Kibera remained.

He thought it sadly ironic that long after Koske had changed the course of his own life, he had returned to threaten that of his son.

CHAPTER 3

This Bus Runs on the Blood of Jesus! said the sign on the rear of the lumbering, lopsided Mombasa–Nairobi bus. Mark Riley peered through the plumes of black diesel smoke billowing in its wake and dared to ease his Land Rover Defender out to check the road ahead. A truck approached crablike on displaced axles, horn blaring. Riley was hungover and in no mood to have his jangling nerves tested. He waited.

On the next attempt, the road was clear, but as he passed the bus it swerved to dodge an enormous pothole, causing the mountain of suitcases and string-tied bundles on its roof to lurch alarmingly in his direction. He planted his foot to the floor and the hulking Land Rover reluctantly responded.

When the bus was in his rear-view mirror, Riley rolled down the window to empty the fumes from the cabin and rubbed his red-rimmed eyes. It had been a busy twenty-four hours, culminating in one too many lime daiquiris at the bar of his hotel. He almost always drank whisky. Why daiquiris were suddenly in favour he put down to boredom.

He reached for his cigarettes, and hesitated a moment before succumbing. *I really must give them up*, he thought as he lit up, then sucked the smoke hungrily into his lungs.

The road ran straight through a scene that he'd been warned would be endlessly repeated during the long journey to Nairobi. Here and there were scattered huts of corrugated iron. Dusty children ran behind old tyres, using sticks to steer them. A donkey cart moved precariously close to the tarmac on wobbly wheels, its load of crated chickens, bagged charcoal and baskets of maize towering above the driver. Beyond the litter-strewn roadside, an occasional ancient baobab watched over the flat, ungrateful land like an aloof and disapproving guardian.

Riley had originally planned to fly to Nairobi, but he was in no hurry and decided instead to visit two or three of the game parks between Mombasa and the capital. He was not the gawping-tourist-in-a-minibus type, and after discovering the hire costs for a four-wheel drive to be exorbitant, he'd found himself a second-hand Land Rover at a very attractive price. He had a soft spot for the old Defender as it had been the model he'd driven around rural Indonesia, which had been the setting for two of his three novels.

But he didn't want to think about his writing. Writing, or his recent inability to do so successfully, was one of the reasons he was now in Kenya. After two failures, his publisher had suggested he take a break. 'Go somewhere exotic where you can rekindle your passion,' she'd said. 'After all, it's not uncommon for a first-time author to have trouble with his next book.' She hadn't mentioned the statistics for a failure on the third.

He took the hint and decided to take a long sabbatical. He was a poor tourist and had chosen Kenya principally because it had been his wife's wish to visit the country at some stage. In the year before they married, Melissa had started supporting an orphaned Kenyan child in the care of a charity called the Circularians. Now, Melissa was dead, killed in a terrible accident. Riley wasn't sure why, but he somehow felt he owed it to her to visit the boy who had benefited from her kindness.

The Circularians were based in Mombasa and for that reason Riley had begun his visit there rather than in the capital, Nairobi. He had met with Horácio Domingues, the little Goan who ran the organisation, in a decaying stuccoed stone building on Mbarak Hinawy Road. The dark-skinned little man had brilliant blue eyes that darted about continuously as he attempted to inform Riley of the Circularian philosophy. Riley wasn't interested, and had finally convinced Domingues to simply check his files for the details of where he might find Melissa's orphan, Jafari Su'ud. When he returned with the file, Domingues explained that the boy had been adopted, but the agency had requested the details remain confidential.

This had piqued Riley's interest. Melissa's monthly contributions were still being deducted from what had been their joint bank account. If the boy had been adopted, surely they should have been notified and the deductions have ceased?

He diverted Domingues with a request for some information on the Circularians and, while the man poked into various cupboards and filing cabinets, Riley took a peep into the file. He found an address in Nairobi and copied it into his notebook.

Another belching bus blocked his path. *Road Warrior — Death Before Dishonour* it proclaimed beneath its rear window. Riley edged out to peep around it. There was just enough room to pass it before an oncoming bus reached him. He gunned the Land Rover.

Too late, he saw the pothole — it was enormous. The old Defender shook as if struck by a wrecker's ball and Riley's head hit the roof. Dust filled the cabin and there was a sickening crunch as the Land Rover bounced off the side of the bus.

The oncoming truck filled the windscreen.

Riley yanked the wheel right and headed for the bush. The Land Rover left the tarmac and became airborne. It snapped a sapling at bumper-bar level and the foliage momentarily blinded him. When the windscreen cleared, a donkey cart loaded with charcoal bags blocked his path.

The last thing he recalled as he swung the wheel hard was the cart driver's terror-stricken eyes. The Defender went into a savage four-wheel drift, throwing Riley's head sideways into the unpadded door pillar.

* * *

Riley's head rocked from side to side, sending painful darts into his brain.

He risked squinting into the light. The brightness hurt and he closed his eyes but not before he registered a bizarre scene — a man in a red dress leading a pair of bullocks that were hauling his car across the barren landscape.

He gave in to the overwhelming fatigue and slipped back into darkness.

When he opened his eyes again, the intense light was gone and he was lying on a narrow bed. His head pounded and he felt slightly nauseous. A figure in a white short-sleeved shirt appeared above him. He was Indian in appearance and had dangling from his neck a stethoscope, which glinted in the light from the window.

'Mr Riley. Welcome back.'

'Thanks.' He gingerly turned his head to each side. 'Where am I?'

The room was a small hut, like a motel room with a thatched roof.

'You are at Twiga Lodge, on a nature reserve near Tsavo National Park. I'm Dr Dass. You've had a knock on the head.'

'Thank God. I thought it was the lime daiquiris.'

The doctor looked perplexed and Riley abandoned the attempted joke.

'The car ... How did I get here?' he asked.

'David here was herding cattle near the Mombasa road.' Dass indicated a tall black man standing near the door, bare-chested except for a short red toga draped over one shoulder. 'He brought you in.'

Riley nodded, tried to smile in appreciation. His head still throbbed.

'As for the car — a few bumps and bends, apparently. I found your passport and called the Australian High Commission in Nairobi. I was trying to find a next of kin,' the doctor explained. 'Someone to notify of your predicament.'

'I see,' Riley said.

'The gentleman I spoke to said you were to contact the High Commission as a matter of urgency.'

'Why?'

'He didn't say. I hope it wasn't inappropriate for me to contact them?'

'No probs,' Riley said. *How the hell am I going to get to Nairobi?* he wondered.

'They took the car to Voi,' Dass said, inadvertently answering the question. 'By the time you're ready to travel, it will have been repaired.'

'Look, Doc, I appreciate the house call and all,' Riley said, 'but I need to get on the road again.' He raised himself from the pillow to find his cigarettes, but the thumping in his head caused him to lower it again.

'Mr Riley, you have an MTBI. It's not to be ignored.'

Riley gave him a quizzical look.

'Mild traumatic brain injury. A concussion, if you prefer. You ignore it at your peril.'

'Well, I'll get a bus, or find someone to drive me. It's no big deal. Can you pass me my cigarettes, they're on —'

'I'm sorry, Mr Riley. I believe it *is* a big deal. In this matter I'm afraid I have the last word. And I would give up the cigarettes if I were you. They're not good for you in your condition. In fact, they're not good for you in any condition. You should quit.'

Riley didn't attempt to hide his pained expression.

'I will inform the management you are under doctor's orders and are on no account allowed to leave before I see you again,' Dass finished.

Riley could see determination in the medico's eyes. 'How long?' he groaned.

'Let's give it a week and we'll see how you're progressing.'

'A week! What the hell am I going to do for a week?'

Dass was packing his instruments into his small leather case. 'Take it easy. Put your feet up. Take a break.'

Riley shook his head in dismay.

'Or find a good book,' the doctor added as he and the Maasai left the *banda*.

*   *   *

Riley wanted nothing to do with books. They were a big reason he'd run away to Africa in the first place. Books, and his need to fill the places in his brain with something less painful than the memories that had taken residence there.

It was the time between the late breakfast served after the dawn game drive and lunch that Riley found most difficult to fill. Twiga Lodge's pool was warm and gave little relief from the mid-morning heat. He swam a few laps until his headache returned and then retired to the poolside shade, but a couple of noisy, freckled children jumped and ran and splashed each other, all the time emitting high-pitched, nerve-jangling squeals. The occasional 'Now, now, boys' from their mother was ignored.

He decided to go for a walk around the grounds, and eventually arrived at the lodge's gift shop. In despair of ever relieving his boredom, he perused the library — a collection of dog-eared paperbacks dominated by Ruark, Hemingway and Wilbur Smith. He thought a biography would be safe, but there was none to be found. A book called *The Maasai — Their Land and Customs* caught his eye. The tall, colourfully dressed young Maasai guys who worked as doormen and safari guides at the lodge seemed to have an irresistible appeal for the women guests, who tended to gush when conversing with any one of them.

The summary on the back told him it was an account of the Maasai's battle against the British to retain their traditional land. Riley was a great fan of the historical novel, and hoped that Manning's Maasai history would be interesting. He signed for the book and took it to his *banda*.

Settling himself on a lounge chair in the tepid warmth outside his five-star tent, with the paradise flycatchers flitting among the acacia tree branches, he flicked open the cover. The first page held a biography and a picture of the author, Charlotte Manning. Short light-coloured hair hugged the nape of her neck and her full mouth was curled into a quietly confident smile that somehow said, *Yes, I know stuff.*

Charlotte Manning was an anthropologist, but Riley soon discovered she had a fiction writer's ability to draw her reader into the series of escalating ordeals, disasters and triumphs that made up recent Maasai history.

Throughout the saga, she painted a picture of the Maasai as a people proudly aware of their culture through their legends, or 'oral history' as she labelled it. They had been for centuries the dominant power in the region, but the white invaders brought with them diseases that decimated their numbers. Smallpox killed more than half of the Maasai people and bovine diseases killed most of their cattle — their livelihood. The ascendancy the Maasai had enjoyed for centuries evaporated in a mere handful of years.

From this devastation arose a charismatic Maasai *moran* — Parsaloi Ole Gilisho — a warrior who took up the battle for his people. Because the Maasai's military power had been wiped out, he could not challenge the British as his predecessors would have done. Instead, he studied them closely and attempted to defeat them at their own game.

As he read, Riley's excitement soared. His novelist's imagination took him way beyond Charlotte Manning's historical text to the drama inherent in such a powerful story with a ready-made hero. He was convinced that he'd found his next novel — a historical blockbuster. And the most exciting aspect of this discovery was that he had come upon the idea exactly as he'd found the thread of his first novel — by accident.

Just at the time Riley had graduated from Sydney University and was trying to convert his BA Lit (Hons) into something that could earn him a living, Eddie Mabo had begun his battle to claim ownership of his ancestral land. Riley had followed the native title court case with enthusiasm and it had led him to write his first novel — another story of the importance of the land to its indigenous owners.

Over the next few days Riley found he could not put Charlotte Manning's book down for long. The clash of cultures, the covert and overt pressure exerted on the indigenous Africans, was a very familiar story. Parsaloi Ole Gilisho was the African equivalent of Eddie Mabo; Manning had cast him as a fighter, possibly the last Maasai warrior to make a spirited stand against the all-conquering British. He was a perfect protagonist. And the story Charlotte Manning's book revealed — an amazing battle between ancient culture and modern power — shouted to be told.

Riley took a deep breath. Whether he was ready to write another book or not, here was a story he couldn't ignore. A story that would redeem his faltering writing career.

CHAPTER 4

Flight BA65 crept along the Heathrow access runway, throwing a long shadow across the grass-covered verge. It rumbled over a patch of worn tarmac and came to a shuddering halt. From her window seat, Charlotte Manning could see a queue of monoliths preparing to depart to all parts of the world. Ahead was the golden lion of Singapore Airlines, Qantas's flying kangaroo and another she couldn't recognise.

An American Airlines plane dropped to the runway with a roar and a loud screech as smoke puffed from the landing gear. The navigation lights disappeared from her field of vision long before the blast of its jets receded.

Charlotte tried to concentrate on the in-flight magazine, but the words were muddled and made no sense. She would have argued with anyone who'd dared to suggest it, but the fact was that at twenty-eight years of age, she was still as nervous about flying as she had been as a child.

Today, she felt even more nervous than usual because she'd lied to her tutor about her travel arrangements. Her strict upbringing had taught her to be truthful in all situations, no matter the cost, but getting her professor's approval for her first visit to Kenya had put the price of truthfulness too high. Regrettably, she had lied through her teeth to Professor Hornsby. The field visit in Kenya and the PhD thesis that relied upon it were too important to her, and she'd feared that if he learnt she'd changed her plans and intended to travel alone, he wouldn't have approved the funding for her trip. She needed first-hand information from leaders of the Luo community, otherwise her thesis would simply comprise a desk study and would do nothing to convince a leading research organisation that she had the stuff required for a position in field anthropology — her great obsession since childhood.

An African man occupied the seat beside her, reading a magazine under the beam of his personal reading light. His rather large wife sat in the aisle seat. Charlotte felt a familiar claustrophobia rising. *What if there were an emergency and all passengers were told to vacate the plane immediately?*

A *ding* sounded and a flight attendant began to demonstrate the safety drill. Charlotte dwelt on every word. The method of inflating the life vest, the implausible whistle. She wished she could check for the row of little lights that would guide her to the nearest exit, but her neighbour and his oversized wife blocked her view.

Her palms began to sweat. *Oh, gross!* she thought. She fumbled for a tissue, trying to calm herself as she calculated how long it would take to reach her nearest escape exit.

The cabin hummed with air-conditioning sounds and the whir of invisible equipment. Somewhere behind her a baby howled.

The British Airway's jumbo lurched forward, rumbled, and again came to a halt, this time with a faint screech that sounded like bad brakes. The thought sent a flutter through her midriff. She tried to dismiss her fear and looked out the window again. The jumbo she didn't recognise roared down the tarmac, leaving a heat mirage in its wake that caused the distant terminal buildings to shimmer.

Her plane lurched forward again, creaking as it wheeled towards the main runway, pitching her gently onto the black man's shoulder.

'Sorry,' she said.

He nodded and smiled.

The four jet engines screamed, but the plane continued to amble along. Beneath her feet she could feel vibrations, slow at first, then increasing in periodicity. It felt like a galloping horse — or, she thought with some alarm, a flat tyre! The plane gathered speed and the sound level rose, but it appeared to

Charlotte they were travelling no faster than a suburban bus. She closed her eyes and, after an interminable period, the rumbling ceased, the engines whined rather than screamed, and, after a final bump as the landing gear was stowed, the cabin became relatively quiet.

Charlotte took a long breath and relaxed, opening her eyes. The plane had levelled out and below them the French shoreline came into view. She leant back, suddenly feeling very tired from the expended emotional energy.

Even the check-in and departure process had been emotional. She had expected her mother and father to be there, but she hadn't expected to see Bradley. He hadn't changed one iota: hair immaculately in place, well-dressed, smiling as if they had been separated for only a week rather than three months.

Had she missed him during those three months? She wasn't sure. Their relationship had fallen into a pattern, one of friendship more than anything else. Their love-making — when it happened at all — had become perfunctory and predictable.

'So you're actually leaving,' he'd said.

She wasn't sure if he'd meant leaving their relationship or leaving the country. 'I am,' she'd replied. It was the correct answer to both possibilities.

'Going to Kenya. Alone. You surprise me, Charlotte.'

'There are a number of things about me that would surprise you, Bradley. Unfortunately, you've never tried to discover them.'

He'd given her his usual smile, partly condescending, partly amused, and then stood with her parents to wave her off. He was so unaware of her passions, her fears, so oblivious to her true personality, that it made her feel sad for him. Bradley the corporate lawyer, the indifferent lover, had no idea what had gone wrong with their relationship.

Inside the departure lounge, out of sight of Bradley and her family, she'd wept, not knowing why.

Now, looking out the window, her sadness was replaced by a

flutter of excitement. Below and to the left of the plane, the Mediterranean glistened like mercury on a platter. In spite of her apprehensions, she couldn't wait to see Kenya for the first time. Ahead, the rugged Atlas Mountains were visible — the gateway to an adventure that made her spine tingle with anticipation.

* * *

An elderly man with closely cut speckled black and grey hair came smiling from his office to introduce himself to Charlotte. 'I'm Paul Gilanga,' he said.

'Dr Gilanga,' she replied, taking his hand. 'Charlotte Manning. Pleased to meet you.'

She meant it. She and the director of the Institute of Primate Research had only been in contact by email so far, but even through that most impersonal of media she had felt his warmth. In person, he confirmed it.

'Please, come in,' he extended a hand towards his office, 'I have the kettle on. It's time for tea, don't you think?'

His office was cluttered with books, stacks of papers and magazines. On top of a four-drawer filing cabinet was a skull — a primate of some kind. He cleared a pile of papers from a chair and invited her to sit.

'Tea or coffee?' he asked.

'Black tea, please.'

'And how is my good friend Professor Hornsby?' he said as he fussed with the crockery.

She brought him up to date with her tutor's activities and news of the department in Oxford where Gilanga had studied. He and Professor Hornsby had been friends ever since, and now Dr Gilanga was going to manage Charlotte's bursary, which was funded by Professor Hornsby's department.

'How is your accommodation situation, my dear?' Dr Gilanga asked her when she had finished her update.

'Very comfortable, thank you.'

He handed her a cup of tea. 'Excellent! Now, before we get into discussing your work, this is your first visit to our country. What are you planning to do about seeing Kenya?'

'I … I hadn't given it much thought. I suppose I'll be seeing some of it on my field trips.'

'Undoubtedly. But that's not the best part. You and Mr Wainscote must spend some time in our national parks. There's so much more to Kenya than the villages, towns and cities. Go to any one of our wildlife reserves and you'll see the real Africa. Amboseli is quite close. Then there are places like the Masai Mara. Superb! You may even like to travel a little further into Tanzania. The Serengeti is simply magnificent.'

This was Charlotte's chance to tell Dr Gilanga that she and Bradley were not travelling together, as had been the original plan, but she was embarrassed about the lie she'd told Professor Hornsby. Now she had to keep quiet and hope that the truth didn't emerge.

'If you do want to go to the Serengeti,' Dr Gilanga went on, 'I will call my son-in-law, who is the head game warden there. He will show you around.'

'Thank you, Dr Gilanga, that's very kind of you.'

'And now, about your immediate tasks.'

Dr Gilanga had already sent her a list of resources, which they discussed. They agreed that the National Archives should be her first priority for contemporary history.

'Here are some Luo people I've arranged for you to meet,' he said, passing a typed sheet to her. 'They will be able to give you a good introduction to Luo oral literature — a very important part of your understanding of the culture, I'm sure.'

Charlotte ran her eye down the list. They were all Nairobi-based academics and businessmen. She asked if he also thought she should meet some more typical Luos, out in the Luo homeland around Kisumu.

Dr Gilanga adjusted his spectacles before replying. 'Hmm,' he said. 'Ordinarily, I'd agree. But travel can be so dangerous for foreigners.' He frowned in concern. 'I suggest we keep your interviews more structured, my dear. The people I have listed there are known to me personally. They're all very well acquainted with Luo culture and history. Let's keep it on the safe side, shall we?'

Charlotte thanked him and, shortly after, bade him goodbye, agreeing to meet again soon to plan the next phase of her study.

In the taxi on her way back to the hotel, she looked down the list of names again. In consideration of Dr Gilanga's efforts to help her, she would speak to these people, but she hadn't come all the way to Kenya to work in the constrained atmosphere of a cultural laboratory. She'd find a way to speak to the average Luo too.

* * *

Kwazi loaded his wheelchair with newspapers while Joshua sat on a nearby stack of them, reading. Beyond the lights of the distributor's storeroom, the compound was quite dark, but in the east there was a hint of pink. Kwazi knew they needed to hurry if they were to make Kenyatta Avenue by dawn.

'Let's go,' he said brusquely.

'We must register to vote, Kwazi,' Joshua said, his head buried in the newspaper.

'Why?'

'It says only registered voters can vote in the elections.'

'So what?'

'So what! So we can vote for Raila, of course.'

'Who says I am voting for Raila? Or anyone else?'

Joshua looked up from the page. 'You are joking.'

Kwazi busied himself with the newspapers, making them into a tidier stack on the seat of his wheelchair. 'Maybe I am, maybe I'm not,' he said.

He was annoyed with Joshua for not helping him load the chair, and was in no mood for one of his election rants. Since

Joshua had become involved with Koske and his campaign to promote Raila Odinga for president, he'd seen little of his younger friend. When they did get together, Joshua was a bore, bragging about how he and his Siafu friends would harass Kikuyu stall-owners, painting slogans on their *duka* walls and threatening anyone who dared to protest.

Joshua scoffed. 'Of course you are. You're a Kisii. You couldn't vote for a Kikuyu.'

'Who says I'm a Kisii?'

'You do!'

It suited Kwazi to be contrary at that moment. 'Well, what difference does it make if I'm Kisii or Kikuyu or Luhya or what? I care nothing about the elections. Now let's go — it's getting light.'

Joshua remained seated. 'How can you say that? It's very important that we boot out the Kikuyu.'

Kwazi looked at him and laughed. 'Listen to you. They are all the same, these politicians. We booted out the Kalenjin because he was corrupt. Then the Kikuyu Kibaki comes in promising to end it. All the promises about this and that. And what happened?' He stuck his jaw out, but Joshua would not respond. 'Nothing! Nothing happened. So don't tell me Odinga will do any better.'

'I am telling you he will! Raila is a Luo. He will make a difference.'

'Hah!'

'He will make a difference to Kenya and he will make a big difference in Kibera.'

Joshua was referring to the fact that Odinga was not only a presidential candidate but sitting for re-election in the Langata electorate, which included Kibera.

'What has he done for us in all these years?'

Joshua stood and threw his arms in the air. 'What can he do with the Kikuyus running the government? Nothing. But when he is president, you'll see.'

'Oh-ho. And what will I see, my friend?'

'We will have jobs. Proper jobs. We will have money. You won't have to worry about your ugly face when we have money.'

Kwazi always feigned indifference to insults about his disfigurement, but coming from his friend, who should have known better, it stung.

Joshua continued, unaware of his insult. 'When I have money I'll even take you back to Serengeti with me.'

'Serengeti, is it?' Kwazi said. 'Serengeti! What do you know about the Serengeti? You were born here in Kibera.'

'But I have chosen the Serengeti as my homeland.'

Kwazi was in no mood for another of Joshua's flights of fancy. 'You are the son of a Luo father and a Kikuyu mother. If you have a homeland, it's up in Mount Kenya or on the lake in Nyanza.'

'Everyone must have a homeland and the Serengeti is mine,' Joshua retaliated. 'One day I will be there. You will see.'

'What, are you a Maasai now? Ah? Only the Maasai can call the Serengeti their homeland. Not a point-five like you.'

Joshua spluttered, stunned by Kwazi's use of the derogative term for a person born of different tribes. He had no idea his friend was reacting to the earlier insult.

'So you can forget about Odinga and the elections,' Kwazi went on. 'They will come and go and everything in Kibera will go on as it always has. We have nothing, and from the politicians we will get nothing.'

'This time it will be different, I tell you.'

'This time will be the same. I'm older than you. You can't remember the last elections. You were just a snot-nosed kid, playing games in ...' Kwazi stopped, realising his insensitivity too late.

Joshua's mouth opened, but the words would not come. He gaped at his friend. Kwazi frantically searched for a means to redeem himself; to retrieve his unintentional cruelty.

Finally, Joshua spoke. 'I remember it too.' Then he turned and walked quickly through the storeroom doors.

Kwazi wanted to call him back, but couldn't. There was nothing to say. He watched Joshua walk out into the compound, square-shouldered and head up. He was soon lost in the golden sunrise.

*   *   *

Joshua was full of rage as he strode along the back roads of the industrial area. Taking a short cut across the Railway Golf Course, he ignored the shouts of abuse from a group of early-morning golfers. He was still fuming when he reached the Adams Arcade parking lot and scaled the stairs to the mall two at a time. It wasn't until he approached the small supermarket that he controlled his aggressive demeanour, recalling the watchful eyes of the arcade's security guards.

Inside the supermarket, he spent a great deal of time studying the shelves of canned vegetables. The guard who had followed him in tired of his procrastinations and returned to his post at the front of the shop.

In the fruit section, Joshua pulled a banana from a bunch, peeled and ate it as he walked, then tossed the skin under a display cabinet. He went to the magazine rack and fingered through the various sports titles, before choosing a popular football magazine, which he shoved down the front of his trousers.

At the register, he thrust a packet of Tic Tacs and a coin at the young check-out girl. The security guard scowled as Joshua theatrically popped a Tic Tac into his mouth and strolled out.

At the Safaricom counter he bought the cheapest top-up card and keyed the code into his mobile phone, which was held together by two bands of grubby tape. He wandered through the arcade, checking his messages. When he looked up, he realised he'd come to a stop outside the travel agent's window.

It held posters of the great cities of the world: Hong Kong and London; Sydney and New York.

They reminded him of the poster that had had such an enormous impact on him as a child. It had advertised a place so exotic, so unlike his home in Kibera, that he could barely believe it existed. The colours in the grass, which seemed to sway in an invisible breeze, were mesmerising; the immense herds of animals — outlandish creatures with stripes or horns; the unimaginable breadth of the blue sky. He'd believed he could feel the warmth of the sun on his skin; even taste the air. It had gladdened his heart to know that such a place existed, no matter how remote it might be. He remembered sobbing when his mother had dragged him away from the window.

The poster remained in the agency's window for many years, gradually losing its vivid colours in the harsh tropical light. By then he knew — because he had learnt to read English — that it showed the Serengeti National Park, located in a remote part of the neighbouring country of Tanzania.

Then, one day, the poster was gone and its disappearance left a void inside him. The poster had been his refuge — a place to go to restore his soul when life in the slums brought anger or sadness. Still, a child in Kibera quickly learns how to deal with disappointment, and soon a far greater tragedy was to occur that surpassed all previous losses.

He realised he was so angry now because of Kwazi's insult; the insinuation that being the son of a Kikuyu mother and a Luo father somehow made him less than normal. Inadequate.

The insult had stung because it touched the very centre of Joshua's pain. It wasn't so bad that he was the child of a mixed marriage, of a Kikuyu and Luo. The tragedy for him was that he belonged to neither tribe. When his mother died, he lost any chance of becoming a Kikuyu, and because of his father's stubborn refusal to share his Luo ancestry, he was excluded from becoming a real Luo. Despite that, Joshua still chose to call himself Luo. For it was a group of Kikuyu boys who had burnt down his family home that terrible night in October 2002, killing his mother and sisters. He had felt an intense hatred for all Kikuyus from that day on.

CHAPTER 5

Simon Otieng had spent the morning hanging on the gate wire of yet another building site hoping for work, but again with no luck. Now he wandered aimlessly along the rutted roads of the industrial area, kicking at stones and pondering the endless run of bad luck that continued to assail him.

The single greatest disaster in his life was the fire that had taken almost everything he had, including the lives of his wife and their three daughters. It had happened during the elections of 2002, when Kikuyu youths were howling through Kibera in support of Mwai Kibaki, their candidate for president. Much blood had been spilt that terrible, turbulent night, and Simon's shack had been set alight.

Simon felt it was not surprising that Joshua had hated Kikuyus with a passion since that night. Now he seemed to be intent on waging war on them during the build-up to these new elections. Simon knew he could change the way Joshua thought about the Kikuyu people by revealing one horrendous truth. But the truth always has consequences, and he was worried that revealing it could worsen the situation between him and his son.

The thought of death brought him back, as always, to what he believed was the cause of all his bad luck, and again he wondered about his decision to flee his Luo homeland.

* * *

In 1983, Simon and his friend Nicholas Odhiambo were just thirteen. They had been rivals for as long as either could remember. At school they competed against each other in every sport. While at play in their village they tried to outdo each other in spear-throwing and bird-catching and climbing and fire-making. There wasn't a contest or pastime that didn't incite them to a continuation of the battle for supremacy.

This time the object of their battle would be the formidable Sergeant Mutua.

Mutua was a Wakamba, a tribe more famous than any other as safari porters in the days when an eighty-pound tusk carried to the ivory markets in Mombasa could return a small fortune. Other tribes engaged in the trade, but the Wakamba were known to be able to turn around the next day to repeat the journey.

The District Commissioner had chosen Sergeant Mutua to head the local administrative police post over several more highly qualified local men because he believed that appointments from within the local community led to rampant cronyism.

Mutua was not known for his hard work, but he climbed the ranks of the administration police nevertheless. He was a dour, hard-headed disciplinarian who employed his considerable physical bulk to intimidate not only the miscreants who crossed his path but also any fellow policemen who disagreed with him.

Being an outsider, Mutua became a person of interest to the children. If he'd allowed this natural curiosity to run its course, the children would have soon tired of him, but he tackled the situation with characteristic belligerence. He scowled and threatened them, once or twice catching a child and giving him a cuff. His face went blue with anger on such occasions, giving rise to further curiosity. Just how blue could the sergeant's face become?

Most children were frightened off by Mutua's physical reprisals, but a few of the very daring continued to tease him. For Simon and Odhiambo, this was a sport demanding bravery, cunning and skill — the essential attributes of Luo warriors.

The two boys were approaching their *muko lak*, when their six lower front teeth would be removed in the ceremony that initiated them into manhood, and so were constantly endeavouring to emulate the bravery of their older cousins before joining their ranks. Instead of baiting lions to prove their bravery and readiness for battle, the boys decided to bait the next most ferocious beast in their realm — Sergeant Mutua.

Mutua was very proud of his policeman's jacket of navy blue. To keep it in pristine condition, he would remove it whenever there was a risk that it might be soiled, and always hung it on the broken limb of a tree while having his midday meal at the small *duka* near the village.

Odhiambo conceived a plan to use *siafu* ants to test the extent of the sergeant's anger. The army ant, or *siafu* in Swahili, is an extremely aggressive species that can strip meat from a carcass in a matter of hours. It is said that the soldier class of *siafu* ants prepares its assault on an enemy by waiting until large numbers are in position before launching a coordinated attack using its powerful mandibles. A *siafu* ant would be torn apart before relinquishing its vicelike hold.

Odhiambo collected a great many *siafu* soldier ants in a calabash and, on the designated date, when his friends were in situ ready to witness the event, he emptied the ants into the sergeant's coat pockets and closed the flaps.

When Mutua returned to the tree and donned his jacket with a flourish, the ants came storming from their incarceration. Within seconds, Sergeant Mutua was dancing, screaming and slapping at himself — to the huge enjoyment of Odhiambo, Simon and their friends. In his frenzy, Mutua tore the coat from his back, ripping off a sleeve in the process. His precious coat was ruined.

Some days later, Odhiambo was missing from the clearing where the boys regularly played their games. When Simon learnt he was in the mission hospital, he hurried to see him. A nurse directed him to a bed at the end of the ward.

Odhiambo lay in the hot semi-darkness under an insect net. When Simon lifted it, he couldn't believe what he saw. Odhiambo was unrecognisable. His brow had been opened to the bone, and his eyes were swollen into two slits. His nose was flattened against his face. Although his jaw was lightly bandaged, it sat at an odd angle, and when he painfully tried to smile through his swollen and split lips, he revealed a bloody mess where his six lower front teeth had been brutally removed.

Simon rushed from the ward and vomited onto the dirt.

It took him many months to come up with a plan to make Sergeant Mutua pay for the beating he'd given Nicholas Odhiambo.

He and Odhiambo agreed it was unlikely they could inflict a comparable degree of physical violence upon Mutua, so their best chance was to humiliate him, preferably in front of the entire community. Simon thought it wise to exclude any plans that involved serious injury and possible death. One idea was to hitch a bullock to Mutua's tin shack and pull it down with Mutua inside. But a bullock was a high price to pay if Mutua extracted himself from the wreck in time to seize the animal.

The harvest festival offered an opportunity too good to miss. The 1984 crop had exceeded all expectations and the Luo community planned an exceptional celebration. The council of elders, who presided over all local matters, decided to invite all the administration officers and encouraged them to wear their respective tribal costumes. For the first time that anyone could recall, Sergeant Mutua appeared not in police uniform but in the colourful paraphernalia of a Wakamba warrior. Nobody was in any doubt that it was the District Commissioner who had insisted Mutua attend.

No one noticed as Simon and Odhiambo released the old he-goat from its tether and led it away to the police compound, which consisted of a small timber-clad office where Mutua spent his daytime hours, an attached sheet-iron lockup, and a third building, Mutua's hut, where he spent the remainder of his time.

The he-goat belonged to Odhiambo's uncle. It was well known within the village for consuming almost anything that came within its reach, and for that reason it was always tethered. It was also old and useless and, therefore, in Simon's and Odhiambo's eyes, expendable to their cause.

Having locked the goat in Mutua's hut, Simon dashed back to the harvest festival while Odhiambo gathered items to set a smoky fire.

'Fire! Fire!' Simon yelled, pointing to the pall of smoke rising above the trees.

The villagers raced en masse towards what appeared to be a conflagration.

At the police barracks they gathered, wondering how so much smoke could arise from such a small pile of rubbish.

Mutua was among the last to arrive and quickly realised the smoke was nothing but a diversion. He hurried towards his hut and re-emerged moments later, rear-first, tugging on a leg of his navy-blue trousers. The he-goat came reluctantly from the hut, doggedly holding onto the other leg. After a spirited tug-of-war, the trousers split asunder, sending Mutua sprawling in the dirt.

The villagers roared with laughter.

Mutua sat in the dirt, an expression of utter mortification on his face.

Simon laughed so much, tears rolled down his face. He searched for Odhiambo but couldn't find him in the large crowd.

Turning back to Mutua, he found the sergeant's eyes fixed firmly on him. There was no longer any sign of embarrassment. Instead, the sergeant's face was suffused with fury.

*   *   *

Simon knew that Mutua might suspect him, but he could not charge him over the fire. Odhiambo reminded him that Mutua didn't need any charges to dole out brutal punishment.

'You must keep to the village, my friend,' he told Simon. 'Never be alone in a place where he can find you.'

'I am quick. Mutua is slow.'

'I am quicker than you, but he caught me.'

'Who says you are quicker than me?' Simon retaliated.

'Never mind that. We will learn soon enough in the coming games who is stronger and faster. What I am saying is to take care until Mutua gets his transfer.'

After the fake fire when Sergeant Mutua had lost his trousers and then applied for a transfer, the boys in the village had learnt that the *muko lak* had been approved by the council of elders and would be held in the coming weeks. They had decided to conduct a series of contests of their own to select a leader of their graduation group. It was necessary to keep the games secret as the council disapproved of anything that might involve injury in the lead-up to the sacred ceremony.

Simon and Odhiambo were among the six organisers who met in a grove to agree the format of the games. All were keen to include in the contests the ancient art of the spear. Target throws were the usual practice, but Simon wanted something more realistic.

'Did our ancestors prepare for battle by throwing spears at a tree?' he demanded. 'No, they fought each other in mock battles, wearing ostrich-feather headdresses and capes of leopard skin. So we must take our lead from them. We should have a mock fight with shields and blocked spears.'

'What do you mean, blocked spears?' someone asked.

'As the warriors did. We use the gum of the euphorbia to make a ball that will set hard on our spear tips. This allows you to be forceful, as in a real battle, but your spear will do no more than remind your opponent of the strength of your arm.'

All agreed to Simon's suggestion and the matches were held far from the village, in a clearing hidden within a copse of acacias.

A series of elimination bouts were fought. The fighter who 'fatally wounded' his opponent by spearing him with sufficient force in a vital part of the body immediately won the bout and advanced to the next round.

Another path to victory was to win three stones. A non-lethal strike won the attacker one stone. A defender who deflected a thrown spear with his shield or was able to avoid it in some other way gained himself a stone.

Inevitably, at the end of the day, it was Odhiambo and Simon who were pitted against each other in the final bout. The fourteen other boys watched, acting as referees and judges.

The two fighters parried and thrust for several minutes. Odhiambo feinted to his left, exposing his flank. Simon fell for the trap and let fly with his spear. Odhiambo easily batted it away with his buffalo hide shield, winning cries of appreciation from the watchers.

Simon cursed his impatience and settled down to fight more cautiously. He successfully used his spear to deflect a half-hearted thrust from Odhiambo, but in the follow-up his friend scored another stone with a glancing blow to Simon's calf muscle. He gave his lopsided grin in answer to Simon's protests that it was a contemptible tactic.

Two stones behind, with Odhiambo needing only one more lucky strike to win, Simon called on all his concentration as they circled one another. Sunlight glinted through the acacia branches, throwing pools of light onto the clearing. Simon manoeuvred Odhiambo towards one such patch, carefully concealing his strategy by making short, darting motions while remaining safely behind his shield. In the instant that the sun fell on Odhiambo's left side, Simon lunged sharply to the right and flung his spear at the glint of light behind his opponent's shield.

Odhiambo fell like a stunned ox.

The onlookers gasped, but no one moved.

After a moment of stunned disbelief, Simon rushed to his fallen friend and carefully removed the bloodied spear that had pierced Odhiambo's left eye. The block had been lost in the clash of spears immediately before Simon launched it.

His friend was dead before his body hit the moss-covered ground.

Simon had known that his life among his people was over too.

*   *   *

Simon thrust the disagreeable memories from his mind. His experience with Mutua and the later, much worse, calamity had been the reason he hadn't taught his son the ways of the Jo-Luo — the Luo people.

In the early days, he was tempted to keep to the traditions for his son's sake. He arranged to have the *muko lak* performed on him, but was afraid where it might lead. The traditional removal of the six lower front teeth would stamp Joshua forever as a Luo. Simon stopped the ceremony a moment before the teeth were removed. It was the last time he was tempted to respect the old ways.

Now, ironically, he faced the risk of his son's death in a tribal war — a tribal war in the heart of Kenya's biggest urban slum.

CHAPTER 6

Riley parked the Land Rover in the security car park and cut across the concrete concourse towards the main entrance to the Australian High Commission. He realised before reaching the building that he had forgotten to lock the car. He was about to retrace his steps, then shook his head and continued towards the heavy sliding glass doors. He felt that if a car thief dared to climb the towering walls topped with razor-wire, then drive the Land Rover through a phalanx of heavily armed security officials and over the pop-up metal spikes in front of the steel gate, then he deserved to keep the car.

The receptionist asked him to wait while she called Mr Davey. 'He's the officer designated to handle your situation,' she said.

'*Situation?*' Riley said, but the receptionist had already disappeared through a door to the back offices.

Davey didn't look old enough to handle anyone's 'situation'. He had freckles and a bristly short moustache, which waggled whenever Riley asked him a question, such as: what situation was Davey managing on his behalf?

'Registration,' Davey said.

'Registration?'

'Yes. When Dr Dass mentioned your name, I immediately went to our list of Australian residents and visitors and found you weren't there.'

'He told me you said it was urgent.'

'It is. As I said, you're not on my list.'

'So ...?'

'Every Australian is important to us, Mr Riley.'

'I'm pleased to hear it. But why the big deal about registering me?'

'The Kenyan government elections are due at the end of December. Experience suggests we need to take all necessary precautions to ensure the safety of our citizens in these potentially dangerous times.'

Davey's spiel came straight out of a Foreign Affairs circular.

'Right,' Riley said.

'You may not be aware, but during the elections in 2002 there was a great deal of violence and many deaths. We at the Australian High Commission are dedicated to protecting every Australian should that situation be repeated on 27 December.'

Riley sighed. He had already wasted an hour finding the High Commission. He might as well play along. 'Okay, what do I have to do?'

The moustache twitched. 'Well, firstly, you must fill in this form.' Davey thrust a sheet of paper at Riley. 'And secondly, you should come along this evening for a briefing by our protocol officer on the necessary precautions during the election period.'

Riley took the form. 'Since I'm here, I'll fill this in, but if you don't mind, I'll pass on the lecture.' He began to scribble down his details. 'Thanks all the same.'

'It really is in your best interests, Mr Riley.'

'I'm sure it is.'

'The talk will be held on the garden patio.'

'Nice.'

'And tonight's event will be a cocktail party.'

'Cocktail party?'

'Yes, for all our expats. Instead of our usual monthly sausage sizzle, the High Commissioner has approved a big budget to make sure everyone comes along. Drinks are on the house.'

'Hmm … What time did you say it started?'

* * *

After leaving the High Commission, Riley was at a loose end and decided to visit a few of Nairobi's places of interest. The museum was nearby, and he completed a cursory inspection of the exhibits within an hour. He ignored the adjacent snake park and headed towards Langata Road and the Nairobi National Park, but became lost among the roundabouts and found himself instead on Ngong Road.

Riley had his Nairobi map and found he was quite near Kibera. He decided to find the Circularian orphanage while he was in the neighbourhood. The address he'd seen in Domingues's file was Kibera Gardens Road. The name evoked a tree-lined boulevard and flowered verges, but the reality was a rutted, rubbish-strewn length of road with potholes the size of small lakes, which the Land Rover drove into rather than bumped over. The dumped car parts that had been thrown into the ruts to fill them reared up like ramparts against invaders.

The very modest dwellings that lined the road might have originally been white, but the reddish mud had migrated halfway up the walls, suggesting an inundation of Biblical proportions.

The road eventually petered out in a dead-end or, more correctly, met a wall of corrugated iron, cardboard and packing-case timber that emerged from the surrounding slums. It was, in fact, a collection of dwellings and small *dukas*, or shops, that appeared to have been there for a very long time.

A number of curious faces watched as Riley climbed out of the Land Rover and looked around. He noticed a sign partially obscured by a tattered-leaf banana tree and went to check it out. *Circularian Orphanage* it proclaimed. He looked at the building behind it: it had a high, flat façade into which were set tall window frames, giving it the appearance of a small church.

Riley pushed open the rusted iron gate and went to the door. It was fastened with a heavy lock and chain. He peered through the grimy windows and saw a large open space with not a stick of furniture or sign of life.

He sat on the doorstep, overwhelmed by disappointment. He hadn't quite realised it before, but he'd been pinning a lot on his hope of finding the boy who Melissa had sponsored. Somehow, in his grief, he'd imagined that meeting the boy would re-establish some kind of connection with his wife. He couldn't bear the fact that she was gone and he'd never see her again. His head dropped to his hands as the memory of that terrible night in 2002 washed over him yet again.

The Kuta night had been hot and heavy. Bali was wrapped as if in a foetid cocoon. On Jalan Legian, the earthy dank odour of open drains merged with the aromas of roasting chicken, groundnuts and aromatic spices dripping into the hawkers' smoky braziers. Fumes from bemos, minibuses and motor scooters cast a blue haze over the strip and its many bars, restaurants and food stalls. Tourists, harassed by touts and pimps, wandered among the neon lights, engaged in the never-ending search for the next diversion.

Riley and Melissa had walked hand in hand along the street. The bars were fun, but they were past all that. They had been heading home to bed and the resumption of their afternoon's love-making, when Melissa remembered she had left her cowboy hat in the restaurant.

'I'll get it,' Riley said.

'No, don't bother. I'll buy another. They're so cheap,' she said.

'Are you kidding? I love you in that hat. Wait here.' And he left his wife window-shopping at the goldsmith's display next to the Sari Club.

His wife. They had lived together for years, but Riley had felt it was important they make a stronger commitment to each other. They'd been married for a week now, and he knew that Melissa felt as he did — that their vows had formed the catalyst for an even greater love, one that they knew was forever.

He passed Paddy's Bar, which throbbed with light and sound. From the end of the crowded veranda, a dozen drunken footballers bawled boorish remarks to every passing female.

Mark entered the restaurant where they'd eaten and found Melissa's hat still hanging on a chair at their table. He picked it up and, in a sickening instant, the night erupted into an explosion of unimaginable violence. He was thrown to the floor, momentarily stunned by the blast. When he dared to open his eyes, the flash remained incandescent on his retina.

There was a fleeting and eerie silence, soon shattered by a tumult of screams, shouts and alarm sirens.

Melissa!

Shouts of 'Fire!' filled the air and everything became chaos.

People were everywhere, blocking his frantic dash to the street. Crowds jammed Jalan Legian in a mass of humanity, fleeing the devastation or rushing to help the fallen. It took Riley precious minutes to reach what was left of the goldsmith's shop.

When they pulled him from the debris and his frenzied search, his hands were a mess of shredded flesh and gore.

*   *   *

Riley stared at his hands. That memory was from another life. He knew Melissa would not want him to carry his grief around with him forever; this trip to Kenya was a final goodbye, in a way. They had talked about doing it together one day, but now he was carrying out her dream alone — and meeting this orphan boy, Jafari, was part of it. Now it seemed Melissa's money had been going into some kind of scam. He was surprised — the Circularians may have odd beliefs but they were a genuine organisation. He needed to find out more.

*   *   *

Following his visit to the abandoned orphanage, Riley couldn't shake his feelings of loss. Eventually he became sick of his self-pity and decided he needed to rejoin the human race.

The Australian High Commission garden patio was decorated with reindeer, tinsel and assorted frippery. Guests milled around the several uniformed waiters. Riley took a whisky and a skewered piece of meat wrapped in something green and dipped it into a yellow sauce. His fellow attendees — seemingly every one of the Australian expatriate residents in Nairobi — had followed the suggested 'cocktail wear' dress code. A few of the men were in black tie, and all the women were immaculately dressed, either in slinky long dresses or short, clinging creations ranging from basic black to the full spectrum of tropical colours.

Riley was the only person in the room without a tie. He was lucky he even had a jacket — he'd only packed one on an impulse. He felt conspicuous and uncomfortable, and patted his jacket to find his cigarettes before remembering he'd quit back in Tsavo. He sighed in frustration.

'Forgotten your cigarettes, huh?'

The voice was soft and Riley took a moment to realise the comment was directed at him. Turning, he found a dark-haired woman in a long red dress smiling at him. In her high heels she was only a couple of inches below meeting him eye to eye.

'Yes,' he said. 'Actually, no. I've given them up.'

'Big mistake. You should never give up something you enjoy.'

'You could be right,' Riley said, as he intercepted a passing waiter and handed him his empty glass. 'Whisky soda, please.' He looked at the woman, who was still appraising him with her smiling eyes. 'You?' he asked, indicating her drink.

She shook her head. Her long brown hair rippled under the light. 'I'm fine,' she said.

'Don't you just hate Christmas decorations in November?' Riley said.

'With a passion.'

He extended his hand. 'Mark Riley.'

She took it and held it for a moment before replying, 'Kazlana Ramanova.' Her hand was cool, her grip firm.

Riley couldn't place her accent, and her features gave

nothing away. There was a hint of colour to her skin, although it could have been just a deep tan. The light touches in her hair might have been fake or bleached by the sun.

'Why are you here?' she asked.

'I'm a writer, doing some research.' Riley didn't want to go into the more personal reasons for his trip to Kenya.

'A writer! How exciting. But I meant, why are you at this information night? Are you expecting our restless natives to attack because of all this political nonsense going on around us?' Her smile was teasing.

'No. I'm here for the free booze.'

A finger tapping on a microphone interrupted them.

'Ladies and gentlemen,' said the man at the podium. 'If I may have your attention, please.'

'What are you doing here?' Riley whispered to her as the clamour of conversation receded.

'I'm a local businesswoman,' she whispered.

'So how come the Australian taxpayer is buying you drinks?' he asked with mock seriousness.

Her smile vied with the sparkle in her eyes. 'If you don't tell, I'm sure they'll never notice me.'

'Ladies and gentlemen,' the man at the lectern repeated. 'Your attention, please.'

'What kind of business are —'

'Shhh,' she said, touching a fingertip to his lips. It was mildly exciting and for a moment he felt ridiculously pubescent.

She turned to listen to the protocol officer who had begun to cover the purpose of the meeting.

She didn't look at Riley again during the speech, but he knew she was fully aware of his sideways glances. Her plain pearl earrings matched a necklace that sat just above the chiselled line of her collarbone. Her nose had a swept-up curve that contradicted the line of her high cheekbones. Riley had a weakness for high cheekbones, and he got the feeling that Kazlana somehow knew it.

He tuned in to the speaker, who was recalling the 2002 elections. '… sadly, these incidents are symptomatic of much of Africa. I assure you that the Australian government stands prepared to evacuate our citizens in the event of any major civil or military upheaval.'

Riley turned to glance at Kazlana again, but she had gone. He slipped his hand into his jacket pocket for his cigarettes before remembering again that he had none. *Shit!* Nevertheless, there was something in his pocket. He pulled out a business card: *Kazlana Ramanova. Chief Executive Officer.*

He smiled. The very desirable Ms Ramanova had slipped her card into his pocket during one of the few moments he'd not had his eyes on her during the speech. Then he noticed the rest of the details on her card: *Ramanova and Company Ltd — Logistical Support to Kenya's NGOs.*

CHAPTER 7

The security guard took little notice of the tall, black man striding confidently towards the elevator and that was just how the man wanted it. He tucked his slim Department of Civil Aviation briefcase under his arm, pressed the elevator button and waited a little impatiently for its doors to slide open. Finally, the guard disappeared behind its closing doors and the panel light climbed towards level ten. He breathed more easily, straightened his tie in the mirrored wall, and flicked a fleck of lint from the lapel of his suit coat.

He felt a stirring in his groin as he recalled the silky voice on the telephone giving him instructions on how to find her, and to arrive at the end of the day when her secretary would be gone and the building near empty. Her final words, *I want to see you tonight*, had made him feel weak in the knees.

This would not be the first time he'd cheated on his wife, but it was definitely the first time he had been nervous about it. This woman was something special. He'd known it from the moment he set eyes on her when she came into his office to make enquiries about the details of a civil aviation accident. He had assisted her in an appropriate, businesslike manner, but when she took his hand to thank him for his help, she held it, and his eyes, for just a moment too long. She had been on his mind ever since. Even her name was tantalising. *Kazlana Ramanova*. It had the allure of the exotic, and complemented the odd juxtaposition of her grey-blue eyes and dark hair.

At their last meeting in his office she had told him that she needed more information than was offered in the official file, but he wasn't about to risk his job for a mere bribe. In response, she had made a pretence of brushing something from his suit coat and commented on how strong and firm his shoulders were. She had let her hands run down his chest to pause at the taut muscles of his abdomen. Her fingers had sent electric shocks down to his groin. He'd reached for her then, but she'd smiled and kept her hands pressed on his belly to keep him at bay. 'I like what I see. I like what I feel,' she'd whispered. 'But I can't let myself give in while there is business to be done.' She had quietly stated that business. She wanted to see the initial accident report rather than the one prepared for public release.

When he made his own investigation of the papers, he'd realised why she suspected there was more to the aircraft incident than had previously been made available. By then, he had already made his decision to do whatever he needed to do to have her — to test the promise in those seductive, grey-blue eyes.

The elevator came to a halt and he stepped out into the carpeted corridor. He paused for a moment, then walked to the door marked *Ramanova and Company Ltd.*

She was waiting for him on the sofa, a cigarette in her hand, a magazine on her lap. She stood as he approached and pressed her hands to his chest as she had that last time. His abdomen muscles clenched.

'You have it?' she asked.

'Yes.' His voice was thick with the constriction in his throat. He hesitated before handing her the leather folder.

She took it and, without looking at the contents, threw it on her desk.

'You don't want to check it?' he asked.

She pushed the suit coat from his shoulders. 'No,' she said as she began to loosen his tie.

He tried to assist her, becoming impatient with the way she slowly teased at the knot.

She pushed his hands away. 'No,' she said. 'We will do this my way.' Then her tone softened. 'Besides … you don't want to rush this, do you? I promise you, it will be more enjoyable if you allow me to do as I please. Agreed?'

He couldn't trust his voice and merely nodded.

'Good. Then you are to remain perfectly still.'

She killed the lights, leaving only the night sky and the glow of the city to illuminate the room.

She returned to him and slipped his tie from around his neck. She quickly undid the buttons of his shirt, pulling back the fabric to expose his chest. She slid her hands over his bare skin, caressing him before pinching a nipple. He groaned with pleasure and pain.

He could resist her no longer and his hand went to her breast. He grasped its fullness and heard her take a sharp breath.

She pushed his hand away. 'I said, no!' Even in the dim light he could see a flash of anger in her eyes, and then she softened. Again, the grey-blue eyes held a promise. 'Be patient. Let me have my pleasure and then I promise you can do whatever you want.'

He dropped his hands to his sides and, with a great deal of self-control, kept them there as she slipped off his shirt and loosened his trousers. They fell around his ankles and he felt a little ridiculous.

She licked his nipple and sucked it as she slipped her hand into his underpants. He gasped as her fingers closed around his erect penis. She knelt and took the fullness of him into her mouth, rolling her tongue around him, and then closing her mouth to hold him firmly there.

He could resist it no more and grasped a handful of her thick brown hair and held her to him. He knew he would continue to provide any information she asked because there was nothing as maddeningly sensuous as what he was feeling at that very moment.

The rising surge of his lust swept him up, up, up, before he groaned and fell over the edge. Down, down, down ...

* * *

53

Kazlana flipped a cigarette from the packet and tossed it onto the coffee table. She walked around her desk, trailing a finger along its edge until reaching the soft leather chair, where she paused to light the Marlboro. The flame illuminated her face, now cool and composed. As she took a long pull, the glow warmed the semi-darkness of her office. Before her was the file.

She slowly swung the leather swivel chair to the left and right as she contemplated the long and winding path she had taken to find the key man — they were always men — who could give her a copy of the incident report following her father's last flight. Now that she had it, she wondered if she really wanted to know the truth. If it were as she suspected, she knew that to pursue the culprits would mean a difficult and possibly dangerous journey that, once commenced, could not be abandoned until her father's death was avenged. The Ramanovas had always lived by that tradition and even today were sworn to observe it.

Her family had done business in Africa for generations, but had not always been agents. A century and a half ago, they were pirates, plucking rich fruit from sailing vessels plying the waters off the Horn of Africa. They had a reputation for quite imaginative methods of slaughtering those who resisted them. It served to make their boarding and looting more efficient. Merchant captains very quickly lowered their flags and sails when the most bloodthirsty pirates from Ceylon to the Swahili coast hove into view.

When the British became churlish about the piracy, sending gun boats to protect their link with India, the family changed their operations to become trading and shipping agents, working with whoever was prepared to pay a fair commission for their services. At about that time, they adopted the name Ramanova, which seemed to straddle the continents of Asia and Africa, their sphere of operation. It was deliberately chosen to disguise their ancestry — a move so successful that nobody

54

could now remember where they had originated. Kazlana's father had once told her: 'By the time anyone realised our family was important, our history had been lost in the past.'

From its early beginnings in East Africa, the Ramanova empire had expanded into the Middle East, extending into the Far East at the end of the nineteenth century. Wars, and the whims of politicians and power-brokers, had caused the family to win and lose several fortunes. But the Ramanovas had endured. In recent years Kazlana and her father, Dieter, had worked to develop separate parts of their business. She was aware that Dieter had cultivated contacts within the Department of Regional Development, but wasn't aware of the details.

Kazlana knew a little of her mixed-race heritage on her father's side, which included elements of Swahili, Indian and Arab. Her grandfather was a Swahili trader, plying the route from India to East Africa, who met a young German woman on a world cruise with her parents, and convinced her to run away with him.

On her mother's side, it was more easily defined. After her father's first wife died, he married Kazlana's mother — an Austrian — who suffered postnatal depression after giving birth to Kazlana. Two years later, unrecovered, she went back to Europe. She never returned. The only clue she had ever been in Kenya was the blue of her daughter's eyes. With no memory of her mother, Kazlana's affection was centred firmly on her father.

She looked again at the file on her desk. The newspaper report had said her father had run short of fuel and crashed the Cessna while attempting an emergency landing. Kazlana had never accepted that finding. Firstly, her father would never have been so careless as to fly without sufficient fuel. He'd been an excellent pilot with thirty years' experience. Secondly, if he had to make an emergency landing, the country around Wajir was flat. Even if the Cessna had run out of fuel, Dieter Ramanova could have glided to any number of suitable landing sites.

Sighing, Kazlana picked up the report and flipped through its pages. She found that it included the flight path, the details of the search and rescue operation conducted after the plane had been declared missing, and the coroner's report. It soon became apparent that the media reports had been fabricated.

The flight path was reported to be from Mombasa to Wajir, yet the plane was found over a hundred kilometres beyond Wajir, near the Somali border. The Cessna was completely burnt — that much of the newspaper reports had been correct — but it had not been damaged during the landing and it was considered likely that the fire had occurred after the plane had put down.

Most damning was the coroner's report. Her father's body was burnt almost beyond recognition, but he hadn't died in the fire. He'd been shot.

She could imagine why the aviation department had wanted to keep this hidden. The Northern Frontier District was an embarrassment to the government because it was obvious they couldn't police it. There was no law and order there, and heavily armed Somali raiders made frequent incursions into Kenyan territory. There was also the al-Awaab Resistance Army, always a threat to security in the area. The authorities didn't want further proof of their incompetence made public so close to an election.

Kazlana wouldn't let that stop her carrying out her own investigation. Her father's plane and his personal belongings had been left unplundered, which suggested this wasn't the work of raiders. Besides, why had her father been near the Somali border in the first place? She wasn't aware of any business dealings he'd been involved in there; not directly, anyway. She was going to find out who had killed her father, and why. And then she was going to kill them in turn.

*   *   *

'Mark Riley to see Ms Ramanova,' he said to the secretary, a slim black girl with beads in her braided hair.

'Good afternoon, Mr Riley,' she responded. 'I believe Ms Ramanova is expecting you. Please take a seat. I'll inform her you're here.'

She stepped to an adjoining door, tapped on it and waited a moment before opening it and slipping through. Riley picked up a copy of *The Nation*, and was about to take a seat on the plush white leather sofa when the secretary returned, advising him that Ms Ramanova would see him.

She came around her desk to meet him as he walked into her office. 'Good afternoon, Mr Riley,' she said, extending her hand.

'Afternoon, Ms Ramanova,' he said. He liked her grip — firm, as it had been the night they'd met. And again it lingered. 'When I made my appointment I wasn't sure you'd remember me from —'

'From the Australian High Commission? Of course I do. Please, won't you take a seat?'

She indicated a white leather armchair and sat herself on another, across a low table from him. She crossed her legs and he noticed she wore no stockings.

'Well, I would have understood if you didn't. We only had a brief chat and then you were gone.'

She laughed. 'Can you ever forgive me? I'm so sorry. I had to dash and I didn't want to be rude during the speech.' She placed a polished red fingernail to the corner of her mouth. 'Would you like a coffee? Tea?'

'No, thank you. I'm fine.'

'How can I help you?'

'I found your business card; it had somehow got into my jacket pocket,' he said, pausing to gauge her reaction.

She simply smiled and said, 'You're a writer, if I remember correctly.'

'That's correct.'

'And who do you write for?'

'For anyone who'll pay,' he said. It was true. He'd decided to do some articles while in Kenya to supplement his funds. He'd already got a couple of commissions from previous colleagues willing to do him a favour. '*Fortune* magazine, for example.'

'I'm flattered. Why would *Fortune* take an interest in my little company?'

'Little fish can be sweet, Ms Ramanova,' Riley said, smiling.

'Can they indeed?' Her smile widened. 'Call me Kazlana.'

'Mark.'

'Ah, Mark. Yes, I remember. Now … what would you like from me, Mark?'

Riley unzipped his leather folder and took a pen and notepad from it, resisting the temptation to continue the little play on words. 'Just a brief description of your business. Perhaps you could start by giving me some background and the names of the directors?'

'I'm the sole director of Ramanova and Company. It's a very old family business going back five or six generations. Trading in Africa is an informal, rambling affair, but I can tell you that the family were originally traders between the Indian subcontinent and East Africa before the time of the Omani regime. They went on to supply goods and materials to the British during the building of the Uganda railway. Later, my grandfather and his father made money running supplies to the Germans through the British blockade in World War I. Grandpa Omar was just fourteen; he manned the Gatling gun while my great-grandfather steered the dhow.'

'It seems the Ramanovas were versatile,' Riley said.

'Business is business,' she replied with a shrug. 'After the war we moved operations to the new capital of Nairobi, but we still retain some ties with the coast, dealing mainly with regional cargo. Farida can give you a copy of our company description and activities.'

'Thank you. And perhaps you can help me on a completely

separate matter? I noticed that your company is involved with NGOs. I'm hoping you can direct me to the right government department to help me.'

'What do you need?'

'I'm trying to find an orphaned child I've been sponsoring for a few years,' he said. 'I found the building I was looking for in Kibera, but there was no one there. So I went to the Department of Community Development to get the new address ...'

'... and they refused to help.'

'Exactly.'

'They said something like: it's not departmental policy to give out that information?'

'You've been down this road before?' he said.

'Have you had any other experience with the Kenyan bureaucracy, Mark?'

He smiled. 'I know what you're thinking: this guy is going to be taken to the cleaners by petty local corruption.'

'I know what it's like — even for a local like me. You could waste a lot of time jumping through hoops for no reward.'

'I've had some experience jumping through hoops in Indonesia.'

'Then you have an idea of what you're up against. What would you like from me?'

'Well, I could go back to Mombasa and start again, but I thought you may be able to put me in touch with someone in the department who's cooperative.'

'Cooperation comes at a price.'

Riley shrugged. 'I'm prepared to pay a little to save some time.'

'Are you sure this child is still with the orphanage?'

'I'm not sure of anything. All I know is the money's still coming out of my account every month.'

'I do know someone in the Department of Community Development, through my father's side of the business.'

'Maybe your father can direct me to someone useful?'

'I'm afraid not,' she said. 'He passed away late last year.'

'I'm sorry.'

'It's okay, but thanks.' She smiled a little self-consciously. 'It's strange, isn't it? It's been almost a year and yet it seems like only a week ago. I still have trouble believing he's not here, running the family business as he always did. So, this fellow in Community Development — his name's Omuga. He'll take your tea money, but you'll probably get what you're looking for.'

'How do I see him?'

'I'll make a call and let you know. How shall I contact you?'

Riley took a business card from the coffee table and wrote his mobile phone number on it.

'I'd take you to see him myself,' said Kazlana, taking the card, 'but, well, I made life difficult for a few of the senior people in the department when my father died, so if I were to introduce you, it would not be to your advantage.'

'What did you do?' Riley asked.

She took a moment before responding. 'When Papa died, I enquired about the circumstances of his death.'

'And ...?'

'Let's just say they weren't explained to my satisfaction.'

'How so?'

Again she hesitated. 'They said he died in a plane crash near Wajir.'

'I suppose aviation accidents aren't uncommon in those remote places,' Riley said.

'You're right. But my father was an ace pilot. He wouldn't have made a mistake. And the weather wasn't a factor. I knew they were lying.'

Riley could see that Kazlana was quite a strong, assertive woman, as demonstrated by her admission that she had made *life difficult for people in the department*, but he recognised a sign of grief that he shared. Rather than accept what had happened, she wanted to find someone to blame. After

Melissa's death he'd spent a lot of energy in the same pursuit. 'I guess there's nothing you can do about it now,' he said.

Kazlana stood up and moved to the door, indicating the interview was over. 'That's where you're wrong. I intend to find out who was responsible. And when I do, I'll know exactly what to do about it.'

She didn't elaborate, but Riley left her office feeling there was more to Kazlana Ramanova than just a pretty face.

CHAPTER 8

After the last of the men had departed the warehouse in the depths of the industrial area, Gideon Koske stood for a moment beside his car, reflecting upon the meeting. He had called the men together to organise a protest march, designed to cause the authorities to retaliate. The ensuing violence would make front-page news, drawing attention to the government's inability to maintain law and order. The twenty men he had recruited to incite the protesters were all very experienced operators.

He felt a little apprehensive that the police response might be lukewarm, but he had some ideas about leaking information in the right quarters to ensure that they were properly primed to take strong action. His young supporters in Kibera could be relied upon to provide the necessary enthusiasm, ensuring that the authorities felt suitably aggrieved and reacted appropriately.

He opened the car door and slid into the seat beside his driver, allowing himself a smile of self-congratulation. If this march had the desired effect, Kibaki and his supporters could be guaranteed to react vigorously to every future Odinga rally. The retaliations would escalate and the climate would be perfect for his purposes.

Everything was proceeding rather well.

*　*　*

Raila Odinga stood in the very heart of Kibera, on a makeshift platform above the bare red earth of Kamukungi and in the full heat of the sun. He was there to address his followers. His voice fluctuated in strength as he moved the portable megaphone over the many thousands who had crammed into the railway easement to hear him speak.

Joshua was near enough to feel the full volume of Odinga's words as the megaphone swept past him. It made his chest thump and his ears ring, but he was too dazzled by the great man's presence to comprehend a word he said.

Then, quite suddenly, Odinga was gone amid a flurry of personal security guards. A mighty roar of appreciation followed him out. Before the crowd had time to disperse, a man stepped onto the platform and began to address it. Joshua did not recognise him as one of the many Odinga supporters who moved among the Kibera slums promoting their leader as next president, but with his black trousers and crisp white shirt he had an air of authority about him.

His voice boomed through the megaphone in his hand and across the Kamukungi clearing. 'My friends,' he bellowed in Kiswahili. 'Do you want our brother Raila Odinga to be president of Kenya?'

'*Yes!*' the crowd roared.

'Are you tired of the police and *askaris* harassing you for tea money?'

'*Yes!*'

'Is your landlord charging you too much for your tiny plot?'

'*Yes!*'

'Do you demand that the government do something about it?'

'*Yes!*'

'Then we must march, my friends! We must march to Uhuru Park and tell the government that we have had enough of all these things. We have had enough of the police taking our money. We have had enough of landlords who cheat us. We demand the government do something about it. No more of this talk, talk and nothing happens. We want *action*!'

A general roar of approval erupted.

'Will you march with me to Uhuru Park, my friends?'

'*Yes!*' came the reply and, as a body, the crowd surged forward towards the road leading to Uhuru Park — a venue where many political wars had been fought.

*   *   *

It was Charlotte's second day of research in the Nairobi National Archives. She was tired and had difficulty concentrating. She'd allowed herself a week for research in Nairobi before heading into the field, but that time was half gone and she had barely scratched the surface. The problem was, she kept getting sidetracked by stories that were interesting, but not essential to her thesis. If she didn't put all those distractions aside, she would never get to the core of her topic.

It had been much easier with her Master's thesis on the Maasai. The Maasai had been a pet anthropological topic for decades and there was a wealth of research material in Oxford's Museum of Natural History. The Luo were another matter. Quite early in their exposure to European influence, they had recognised the benefits of that civilisation and become willing participants and early adopters of a new way of life. Consequently, their cultural heritage wasn't as widely known or documented. She felt she had formulated a good plan for her thesis, but acquiring the raw information was difficult.

An important part of a PhD was the ability to develop efficiently a line of reasoning towards a logical conclusion. She tested the words again, picking them apart and appraising them individually before reassembling them. *An important part of a PhD is the ability to develop efficiently a line of reasoning towards a logical conclusion.* Good. Very good. It reassured her that her head was clear and ready to get back to work. Then she realised they were Professor Hornsby's words, from his pep talk before she left for Kenya.

She dropped her face into her hands and let a small groan escape.

* * *

Scattered around Riley's desk was the essence of his next novel. He had thought it would be a good story when he'd first read the historical account in Charlotte Manning's book. Now, with a more complete understanding of the historical perspective, he knew it was a great story. As with his first novel, his research in the National Archives was illuminating the details of the saga; like opening the lens of a camera to throw more light on the subject. Now he comprehended the true drama of the Maasai's battle to save their land.

The young woman at the end of his table groaned and Riley glanced at her in annoyance. It wasn't the first time she'd interrupted his train of thought.

He felt his Maasai story had a lot more going for it than the 1992 Mabo native title case had. While Mabo and its legal machinations and consequences had been interesting, it had lacked blood and guts. The formidable Maasai would surely add that component. Riley had found many references to their bloodthirsty reputation. Even the Arab slave traders had avoided the fierce warriors of Maasailand for years. Somewhere, buried in the history, there would surely be accounts of fierce and bloody resistance to the British encroachment into Maasailand, perhaps even an old-fashioned massacre or two to add dramatic highlights to his story.

But he had to get a grip. History was a mine of information. A very big mine. If he were to make this story what it could be, he needed time to find the nuggets. In the meantime, he had to earn enough money to sustain him in Kenya while completing the research for his novel. He thought about the business article he was researching. It was a little dry for his taste. The political tensions in Nairobi were palpable. Perhaps there was a bigger story — an essay on politics, tribalism and corruption — that he could sell. There wasn't a lot of interest in Africa overseas at that moment, but perhaps the election would change that.

The woman at the end of his table arose, noisily scraping her chair on the parquetry floor. She seemed vaguely familiar, but he put his head down and returned to the correspondence files from the early twentieth century.

A half-hour later he collided with her in the Dewey 300–320 aisle. 'Oops. Sorry,' he said.

'I beg your pardon,' she replied.

He smiled. Then it dawned on him. She looked familiar because she was Charlotte Manning!

Here was the solution to his shortage of time and money to complete his research. Charlotte Manning, expert in all matters Maasai, could point him towards the most appropriate source documents in a trice. He could have the research component of his book in the bag and be home in a couple of weeks, ready to hit the computer. He had to find a way to pick her brains.

'African research?' he asked pleasantly.

Her glance wasn't encouraging. 'What do you mean?' she said coolly.

He smiled, innocence personified — or so he hoped — and pointed to the sign above the bookshelves: *316 — General Statistics. Africa.*

She mumbled something unintelligible, gathered her armful of books and returned to her table.

Damn! Riley thought. He was losing his touch. That response wasn't at all what he'd hoped for. Now she thought him some kind of stalker.

He took a moment to collect his thoughts. He would return to his desk and write a polite note explaining the situation, which he would place on her notepad. But by the time he returned to his desk, Charlotte Manning was heading for the door.

*　*　*

The mob poured onto Ngong Road. It had been swelled by
Kibera residents, mostly young unemployed men who had not
attended the rally but jumped at the opportunity to escape their
boredom. Joshua was in the leading group, carrying a placard
that had been thrust into his hands. It was around 5 pm and the
traffic, already barely moving in the usual peak-hour crawl,
came to a complete standstill. Joshua used his placard to club a
Volvo station wagon, while others in his group did likewise to
the cars nearest them.

The *matatus* — the ubiquitous minibuses that, so
conventional wisdom suggested, were all owned by Kikuyu
politicians — were given particularly harsh attention. Some had
their windscreens smashed; and one, whose passengers had fled,
was rocked energetically until it was overturned. The crowd
responded with a roar of delight.

When the leading group reached the Nairobi Club on the hill
overlooking Uhuru Park, they found the police waiting for
them. The hated Special Response Unit was present in numbers
— a formidable force in riot gear.

The speaker with the portable megaphone screamed almost
hysterically for the marchers to push on. 'We will not be denied
our rights!' he began to chant. The crowd joined him and, after
an initial hesitancy, surged forward.

Above the roar, Joshua heard the pop of a teargas canister.
Then another. Almost immediately the acrid smoke attacked his
lungs. At the same time a whistle blew and a score of helmeted,
shield-carrying riot police charged the leading group.

Joshua used his placard to fend off the nearest policeman —
a bull of a man in a gas mask, swinging his long riot stick like
a sword. He managed to avoid the first two strikes, but his
vision was blurred by the gas and the next caught him a
glancing blow on the side of his head.

Joshua fell like a poleaxed steer.

*   *   *

A kilometre away, on the other side of Uhuru Park, Riley collected his backpack at the security desk and hurried out into busy Moi Avenue. Charlotte Manning was nowhere in sight, but he took a punt and turned right, thinking she might be headed to the university. After a block he caught sight of what he thought was her pink and white blouse bobbing among the crowd about a hundred metres away. He dodged in and out of the heavy pedestrian traffic. Most of the shoppers had stopped, and all faces were turned in the direction of the university, their heads cocked, listening.

Riley noticed there were few cars on the normally chaotic Moi Avenue.

Then he heard it too. It rumbled like a distant storm, resembling the muted sound of a football crowd at half-time — unfocused, but able to erupt without warning. He'd heard that sound once before, in Indonesia, and it had nearly cost him his life.

The rumbling drew closer. Now he could hear the jangle of metal, and a bass drum pounding a marching beat.

Up ahead, Charlotte took the opportunity of the sudden break in traffic to cross Moi Avenue.

Riley broke into a run. He intercepted her as the mob swung out of University Way, only a block from them. He grabbed her and dragged her by the arm back to the footpath.

'*You!*' she gasped, trying to regain her breath.

'Quick! In here,' he said, and dragged her again, this time towards a café where the owner was hastily erecting boards over the windows.

'What are you *doing*?' she said as she shrugged him from her elbow. 'You're the … the *person* from the library.'

'I am. Look,' he said, pointing to the approaching mob. 'This is going to get ugly any minute and we have to get off the street.'

'Do we now?' Her eyes were blazing. 'Well, I can tell you, I've been in my share of demonstrations. It's just a simple student protest.'

'Maybe. But the riot police are most likely on their way, so it's going to get a lot uglier before it gets better.'

As if to prove his point, sirens sounded in the distance.

The shopkeeper was at his door, about to slam it. Riley lifted Charlotte into his arms and pushed past him into the café. When they were barely inside, the owner locked the door.

'*Oh!*' Charlotte spluttered, and pushed him away from her as soon as he put her down. 'What sort of Neanderthal are you?'

'Listen,' he said, pointing in the direction of the street. The shouting and accompanying cacophony of metal instruments were drowned by the screech of police whistles and wailing sirens. 'The riot police have arrived.'

'That's no reason to go dragging people off the street, is it?' she said, straightening her crumpled blouse. 'They're just students.'

'You're not at Oxford now, Ms Manning. These guys aren't just protesting for equal rights, you know. They mean business. So do the riot police. Believe me, I've seen it in Indonesia. You don't want to get caught in the middle of one of these things.'

The mob began to howl as the police and riot squad converged upon them. The sound of smashing glass came from nearby.

'I don't see what all the fuss —'

The *pom, pom* of exploding teargas grenades interrupted her. She went to the window where the hand holes in the wooden covers allowed a view of the street. Whatever she saw, it caused her to turn back to him, mollified.

'Well ... Anyway, how do you know my name?' she said.

'How do I know your ...' He took a deep breath and let it escape with a loud sigh. 'God, I'd kill for a cigarette. Let's take a seat back here, shall we? It'll be a while until the teargas clears.'

She reluctantly followed him to a table near the rear of the café and took a seat opposite him.

'I wanted to talk to you about something anyway,' he said.

'You haven't answered my question. How do you know my name?'

'I'm a —' He was interrupted by a shrieking whistle from outside. Heavy boots pounded past the window.

'I'm a researcher, just like you,' he went on.

She looked unconvinced.

'Come to think of it, I'm a fan. I've read your book on the Maasai. It got me interested in the whole field of anthropology.' It was quite a leap, but he hoped a little flattery might ease the situation.

She cocked an eyebrow at him. 'It did?'

'Absolutely. I'm a journo by profession, and it just, like, really grabbed me. You know what I mean?'

'Well, I must say there have been researchers who have inspired me —'

'Exactly. Look, let's start again. I'll buy you a coffee.' Without waiting for her reply, he called to the owner, 'Two coffees, please.'

'Tea. Black,' she said.

'Sorry, one black tea and one black coffee, no sugar.'

Fifteen minutes later, he had explained how he had recognised her from the photo in her book, and that it was an understandable coincidence that they had crossed paths as they were both researching the Maasai.

'It's karma,' he concluded.

'Hmm … Australian?' she said. Her tone suggested that, if confirmed, it would fulfil her worst fears.

He nodded. 'Accent?'

She shook her head. 'Suntan.'

'African.'

'You?'

'No, the suntan, of course.'

'Of course. But there's certainly a little of that nasally twang. So you're an Australian who's come to Africa to research a novel and a series of articles. Is that any reason to stalk a person in a library?'

'Now, hang on a moment. Sitting in a library is hardly a capital offence. I just wanted to do some research. Like you.'

'Why are you researching the Maasai?' she asked. 'You're an Australian, for goodness sake.'

'What do you mean by that?'

'Can't you do something about the Aborigines? They're your lot.'

'I've done the bloody Aborigines,' he said, becoming frustrated with the way the conversation was going. 'Now I'm onto something else.'

'What do you mean, you've *done the Aborigines*?'

'My first novel was based on the Mabo native title court case. The Maasai's land situation seems to be something of a parallel.'

'The Mabo — I'm fairly familiar with it. And you're right, there is a parallel.'

'That's what I thought.'

His confidence and enthusiasm were reignited. Even finding out a stuffed shirt like Charlotte Manning was interested in his concept helped prove his story had the legs he'd hoped for.

'Where will you start?' she asked. 'I mean, the land has been central to the Maasai psyche for centuries. Millennia.'

'Hell, this is a novel, not a thesis. I reckon I'll start around the beginning of the twentieth century, when the commissioner first started giving out leases in the Great Rift Valley.'

'Is that it?'

'Eh?'

'Is that all you plan to research?'

He sensed a touch of haughty derision in her tone — the straight-A history buff smugly polishing her gold medal.

'No. In fact, when I finish my research here, I plan to go up country to gather more grass-roots information.'

Grass-roots information? What the hell is that? he wondered, and prepared to defend it, but it went unchallenged.

'Interesting,' she said unconvincingly.

'That's what I wanted to talk to you about.'

She raised a shaped eyebrow.

'About research, I mean. Since we're both studying the Maasai — although admittedly from totally different perspectives — there's probably a lot of common ground we need to cover.'

Her expression gave nothing away, which encouraged him to continue.

'So I was thinking, why not combine our efforts? We could, you know, help each other from our respective backgrounds. You're an expert on the Maasai and I could maybe use the odd piece of advice you might offer on their history and customs. And I'm an author, so you could probably use some help in framing your thesis. We could share expenses in the process.'

She raised a clear-lacquered fingernail, tapping it gently against a row of straight, white teeth, before reaching for her shoulder bag. 'Mr …?'

'Riley. Mark.'

'Mr Riley. Two things. Firstly, I'm not studying the Maasai. As you so eloquently put it yourself: *I've done that.* I'm now studying another tribe — the Luo. And secondly, I don't need your help to frame my thesis. I have a double degree — the second in English literature.'

She stood to leave.

'Oh, one other thing. What sort of person do you think I am to agree to … how did you put it? *Share expenses* with a total stranger? I'm afraid your pick-up line needs refinement.'

At the door she looked out briefly, then slipped through it to join the crowds once again filling Moi Avenue.

CHAPTER 9

Joshua awoke among a tangle of bodies with the sound of sirens ringing in his ears and a dull ache in his head. He gingerly touched the sensitive part of his scalp and his finger found a patch of thickening blood.

Above him was a small, reinforced-glass window. The cabin — for now he realised he was in the back of a police truck — rocked and bounced as the vehicle sped around corners, no doubt on its way to the retaining cells. His heart sank. He'd heard what happened to people who were scooped up by the riot police. Around him, his fellow detainees wore sick and sorry looks. They too had no illusions about what awaited them.

* * *

He stood naked and shivering in the cool night air, fearful of what might next happen. Taunts came from behind the strong floodlights of the police headquarters' quadrangle. He knew enough Kikuyu to know they were joking about his uncircumcised penis — the cultural legacy of his Luo birth.

Icy water slammed into his bare body like the blow of a cold, steel sledgehammer and Joshua was knocked to the ground. He curled into the foetal position against the stone wall.

He became aware of the coarse concrete tearing at the unprotected skin of his back as he was dragged from the courtyard. The pain was mercifully subdued by the lingering fogginess of his mind.

The two men who had dragged him into the cell flung him face down over a high wooden bench and tied his wrists to the thick legs. Joshua jerked at the ropes and struggled, his throat constricting as his fear rose. He was very aware of his nakedness.

Someone grabbed his hair and yanked his head so he was looking into the pock-marked face of a uniformed man he hadn't seen before. Joshua searched the cold, bloodshot eyes and found not a trace of humanity there. The man was brutish, unshaven and had foul breath. When he smiled, Joshua noted a white-gold tooth glinting between thick, bluish lips.

'Ah, the sleeping beauty awakes,' the man said, before sitting back in the chair placed in line with Joshua's vision. 'And now we will have a little talk, you and I.' He lifted his belly and slid a long, black truncheon from the loop on his belt. He stroked it then began to slap it gently into the palm of his hand. It was almost a caress. The smile continued and he nodded for emphasis. 'You will tell me who your friends are. You will tell me who pays you for breaking the law.'

Joshua said nothing.

The truncheon slammed into his kidney region. He gasped in pain.

'The names. You will tell me and there will be no charges laid.'

'I don't know who was there. I am marching with many others. How can I know all their names?'

The truncheon rapped Joshua's back again.

The questions continued as the policeman repeated the *slap, slap* with the truncheon on his palm. 'I will have the name of the man who pays you to make trouble,' he said.

'So you can go to him demanding your tea money?' Joshua snapped, without a thought for the consequences.

The man's face darkened. Joshua braced for the assault and shut his eyes.

The blow didn't come. Instead, the man stood and smiled as he ran his hand up and down the truncheon.

'Now I see it,' he said, and nodded to his accomplice on Joshua's blind side.

Almost immediately Joshua felt a leather belt flung over his back. Before he could fight it, his waist was clamped to the wooden bench and the belt made painfully tight. He could scarcely breathe.

'You are what we call a convert,' the man with the truncheon said. 'A convert, just like in a church. Someone who stupidly follows a man who says he can solve all the problems of the world; or even just those of Kibera. Food for everyone.' He laughed. 'Fools, all of you.'

As he spoke, he walked slowly towards the foot of the bench. Joshua followed him with his eyes, until his position made it impossible to see further. Not knowing what was in store made the situation more frightening. He gritted his teeth, determined to resist any response that would give the thug satisfaction.

'I could make you talk, there is no doubt,' the man said. 'But why waste my strength, ah? There are plenty more who will squeak as soon as I put them in the trap. So I will let you go. But you will remember this day before you take to the streets again, my little friend.'

Joshua instinctively tensed his buttocks at the first touch of the truncheon. Then pain seared through him and, in spite of his determination to remain silent, a sound escaped his lips that was so foreign it was impossible it had come from his own mouth.

*　*　*

Simon was hanging fragments of scavenged tinsel along the rough-cut shelf above the wash bench when his son finally arrived home.

'What happened to you?' he demanded.

Joshua kept his face turned away from the harsh light of the electric bulb above the kitchen table. 'Nothing,' he said.

'You were in the riot on Ngong Road,' Simon insisted.

'I fell from a *matatu*.'

Simon moved into the light. 'Let me look at you.'

Joshua remained outside the throw of the globe.

'I said, come over here and let me see you.'

'Leave me alone. I just want to sleep.'

Simon wanted to shake his son. Instead, he put a hand to his mouth and pressed it tight so he could say none of the many angry words that came to mind. He took a deep breath and let his shoulders relax. It did no good to push the boy too far.

'The police have done this to you,' he said.

'I told you, I fell.'

Simon slumped onto his chair. He clasped his hands together on the table and stared at them. 'What has happened to us?' he asked, almost inaudibly.

Joshua said nothing. He remained in the shadows, leaning against the bench near the door.

'If your mother were alive, we wouldn't be like this,' Simon added.

He looked to his son, hoping for some sign of acknowledgement if not agreement, but Joshua's expression was sullen and closed.

'Do you blame me for the fire?' he asked.

His son shook his head.

'Then why can we not support each other? We two of the six that were our family?'

'I don't blame you for what happened to our family,' Joshua said. 'But I blame you for not avenging them.'

'But how could I? Like you, I wasn't at home.'

'I am talking of their memory. You refused to avenge their deaths. You have allowed those who killed them to laugh at you, and at me, because we haven't fought back.'

'Would finding the killers bring your mother and sisters back?'

'No, but it would prove to the Kikuyu that taking Luo lives has its consequences.'

'Oh, Joshua, Joshua. This hate will destroy you. You must let it go. You will have no rest unless you can let the innocents lie in peace.'

'That is where you are wrong, my father. It is my hate that makes me strong. Although you refuse to let me live the Jo-Luo life, you cannot deny my revenge on our enemies.'

Even in the half-light Simon could see the passion in his son's eyes. It had gone too far. Joshua must be told, regardless of the consequences.

'Son, you don't understand. On that night —'

'No! It is *you* who don't understand. Because of your cowardice, you can't see why I want my family's death to be put right. There is a tribal war coming, Luo against Kikuyu. And while you may hide from it, I will not.' He turned to the door.

'Wait! Joshua, I need to talk to you. Where are you going?'

His son paused at the open door. 'Away. Any place away from you.' He almost spat the words. 'I can't live in a house with a man with so little … courage.'

Simon sank to his chair, the sound of the slamming door still ringing in his ears. He realised he had lost any influence he'd had on Joshua. He had been stubborn, refusing the boy's requests to hear about his Luo family history, and now Joshua was rebelling.

Simon recalled that he'd been a rebellious boy himself. His actions after the death of his best friend, Nicholas Odhiambo, had challenged authority in a much more serious manner.

* * *

'But, Grandfather, if you arrange a cleansing ceremony for me, Sergeant Mutua will know about it and he will arrest me.'

'You have nothing to fear from Mutua,' his grandfather said. He had come to the village the instant he had heard of Odhiambo's death. 'It was just a terrible accident. You are a child. Nothing can be gained by charging you with the boy's death. I have spoken to the council of elders; they will speak on your behalf.'

Simon had kept the he-goat prank a secret from his grandfather. It would shock and shame him if he knew of his grandson's mischief. He also didn't know how Odhiambo had gained the injuries that had cost him his front teeth. Simon had told him Odhiambo had fallen off the train in Kisumu. Now he had no option but to tough it out, denying all and hoping he could convince his grandfather not to draw Odhiambo's death to the attention of the authorities. If he did, Mutua could legitimately bring him in for questioning. And who knew what accidents might befall a spirited young Luo boy while trying to escape custody?

'It is a greater concern that you are not yet cleansed,' his grandfather said. 'Already you have put yourself, your mother, me and everyone in the village in peril. We must act quickly.'

Simon refused.

The old man warned him that if he didn't complete the cleansing, he would be cursed with bad luck all his life. It was hard for Simon to disobey his grandfather, but again he refused.

The council of elders became involved. They asked Simon why he would not follow the tested Luo procedure to protect himself and all those close to him from the evils of an uncleansed death.

Simon couldn't answer.

The debate raged among the Luo and Sergeant Mutua heard of it. He came to Simon's house while he was absent. His grandfather told him of the sergeant's visit when Simon arrived home.

'Now, see what has happened,' he said. 'The government people know about it already. Now we will proceed. I will call on the medicine man tomorrow to perform the cleansing. We will have it as soon as possible.'

He could not be dissuaded. Simon went to stay with his mother, but when her new husband heard that Simon had refused the cleansing, he chased him out.

For two weeks, he hid in the forest, stealing or begging food from friends and relatives, until they too became concerned about the bad luck they would incur by continuing to aid him.

In desperation he went to his grandfather and confessed to his part in Mutua's disgrace.

'You cannot let Mutua come for me,' he pleaded. 'If he takes me away, he will beat me.'

His grandfather looked sad, but he could not ignore the customs. 'It is what must be done.'

Simon then told him about the ferocious beating Mutua had given Odhiambo. 'I fear he may do worse to me. Maybe he will kill me.'

Now his grandfather wrung his hands with worry. 'I must think carefully about this,' he said, but there was no doubt he was sorely troubled.

Within days the old man was ailing. It tortured Simon to be the cause of his grandfather's failing health. He felt his only option was to leave.

Within three days he was on an express bus to Nairobi. He greatly regretted leaving, but now he was on his way, he became excited by the adventure. Everyone knew the big city far to the east was full of opportunities.

* * *

Blaring horns and a cacophony of traffic noises awoke Simon shortly after dawn. The Nairobi terminal was in turmoil as he stepped down from the bus. His fellow passengers were frantically calling to the turn-boy to toss their bags from the roof. When he did, they threw themselves into the human maelstrom and disappeared like sticks in a flooded stream. They were obviously more aware than Simon of what was creating the surrounding panic. As people jostled around him, he clutched his *kikapu* to his chest, awaiting whatever disaster may be about to befall them. All his worldly belongings were in that simple straw basket.

After several minutes, he realised there was no panic. People were merely getting on with their day, although in a very different and much noisier manner than he was accustomed to in the lake province.

A boy pulling a push-cart full of *viazi tamu* bustled past him. Seeing the sweet potatoes that were widely grown around Lake Victoria gave Simon a twinge of homesickness. He thrust it from his mind as he realised he had absolutely no idea what to do next. The bus and roof rack of luggage were now empty. The passengers had scattered into the throng and another bus edged towards Simon, tooting its demand for the space he was occupying. He retreated to the sidelines, where a long row of food vendors were noisily hawking their wares.

'*Bhang?*' a voice at his shoulder asked.

'What?'

'*Bhang?* You want *bhang*? Very fresh.'

The youth, perhaps a year or two older than Simon, waved a plastic bag filled with dried leaves under his nose while nervously turning his own head from left to right.

'No,' Simon said, unsure if the boy was offering to give it to him or sell it. He wasn't even sure he'd understood the question as the boy spoke Kiswahili with a very strong accent.

The plastic bag and its contents disappeared into the front of the boy's shirt. 'Where you from? Where you from?' he demanded.

'Kisumu.'

'Jo-Luo, uh? You need a room? You need a place to stay?'

The repeated questions gave Simon the chance to decipher his odd accent.

'Um, yes,' he replied.

'Come,' the boy said, taking a few steps away. 'Come,' he repeated when Simon remained rooted to the spot.

He led Simon to a *matatu*, which the driver raced through the congested streets like a man possessed, throwing Simon about like a cork in a flood.

About fifteen minutes into their journey, the tree-lined streets and neat houses disappeared, to be replaced by corrugated-iron shacks and cheap concrete-block, two- and three-storey buildings with louvred window glass and graffitied walls.

'Come,' the boy said, alighting. He waited with a bored expression until Simon realised he was expected to pay his fare too.

'What is this place?' Simon asked as the boy led him through muddy, narrow alleys.

'This place? Mathare,' the boy said. And again, 'Mathare.'

Mathare was a place like no other Simon had seen. Although there were many cheaply built shacks in the Nyanza district surrounding his village near Lake Victoria, he'd never seen so many in one confined space. The odours of rotting vegetation and, occasionally, human and animal excrement assaulted his senses and seemed to cling to his skin and clothing. He tried to hold his breath until the stench passed, but soon his chest was about to burst and he was forced to gulp air in huge lungfuls. He would have turned back had he not already invested his thirty shillings in the *matatu* fare.

After ten minutes, the boy climbed two sets of stairs to an outside walkway that led to an open doorway into a room furnished sparsely with a sofa, a table and half a dozen chairs. There were two young men of about nineteen in the room. Without a word, Simon's guide took him through into a bedroom equipped with four double bunks.

'It's nice, uh?' he said.

Before Simon could answer, he added, 'Hundred shillings.'

Simon thought he was joking. It was a ridiculous amount. He spoke to one of the boys in the other room, who was a Luo, asking in Dho-Luo if it was true that the rent was a hundred a month.

The youth assured Simon the rent was no joke; in fact, it was a good price for a bed in Nairobi. Simon was left in no doubt that Nairobi was a very different place to his home.

He nodded to his guide, who led him out onto the landing to discuss business. A few minutes later, Simon had handed over his month's rent in advance and the boy had disappeared.

Later that day the agent arrived and Simon learnt his first lesson of his new life: trust nobody. The tout who had led him to the property held no official capacity, which meant the advance rent Simon had paid him had to be paid again. This left him with just two hundred and seventy-five shillings until he found a means of support.

* * *

Reflecting upon his past, Simon had no doubt that he had passed on his impetuous nature to his son. It was the cause of much of the trouble between them.

He wondered yet again about his decision to run away from home. How much more pain could Sergeant Mutua have inflicted upon him over what had been done since coming to Nairobi? If he had stayed in Kisumu could his suffering be worse than losing his wife and children in a fire, and his only son to misunderstanding and prejudice?

* * *

Joshua had been wandering the alleys of Kisumu Ndogo for hours, unsure of what to do. He knew he couldn't go back to his father's shack, but the only other person he felt he could impose upon was Kwazi. The problem was, he hadn't seen him since Kwazi had uttered those stinging words a few days ago, causing an open wound in their friendship.

Kwazi's place was a few sheets of iron straddling a ridge pole propped against an incomplete cement-block wall. The remains of Kwazi's cooking fire smouldered under the piece of steel-reinforcing mesh that constituted his kitchen stove, sending foul-smelling smoke drifting into the still night. Someone had found the resources to commence building but not enough to complete it. Either way, it was to Kwazi's benefit — at least in the short term, until one of Kibera's strong men moved in to claim ownership. Kwazi had lived in this semi-nomadic state for as long as Joshua had known him.

Joshua lifted the corner of the burlap that covered the door opening.

'I have a *panga*,' said a shrill voice from the darkness within. 'I'll kill you if you don't get away.'

'Kwazi, it's me.'

'*Haki ya mungu*,' Kwazi swore. 'I could have taken off your head!'

'Do you really have a *panga* in there?'

Kwazi crawled out through the burlap and peered up at Joshua. 'Why do I need a *panga* in Kibera, ah? It's not worth the stones.'

He was referring to the squatters' habit of stoning thieves to death if caught.

Joshua took a seat beside the fireplace. Kwazi sat opposite.

'You're using shit to cook your meals these days?' Joshua asked, indicating the smouldering fire.

'Ah-ah-ah. It stinks. I know. But what can I do? There was paint on the timber I found.'

Joshua waited, reluctant to be the first to speak. He'd realised after storming off the other day that he'd been thoughtless in using the word 'ugly' in reference to Kwazi's face. But it was a common expression and Kwazi should have known he would never be so deliberately cruel.

'I'm sorry about —' Kwazi began.

'No! It was me. I shouldn't have —'

'I didn't think about what I was saying and —'

'I didn't mean it,' Joshua said.

They paused, each a little embarrassed by their emotional rush for forgiveness.

Kwazi was next to speak. 'Your face ... What happened?'

Joshua could never reveal to anyone, not even to Kwazi, what had happened to him at the police headquarters. The shame would be far worse than the pain he had endured. He had heard others speak in hushed and horrified voices of atrocities such as had been forced upon him in that foul little room. He couldn't stand to be ridiculed by those who were not his friends and, worse, to be pitied by those who were. It would forever remain his secret.

He shrugged. 'The police collected some of us from Ngong Road. They took us down to Harry Thuku Road.'

He knew Kwazi would not press the matter. People taken from Kibera to police headquarters always received a beating and it was considered impolite to ask for details.

'That is not why you are here at this late hour,' Kwazi said. 'You have had another argument with your father.'

Joshua nodded, worrying the coals of the fire with a length of fencing wire.

'I heard you scored three goals against Makina,' Kwazi added.

Joshua nodded again. 'Wakamba and Kikuyus. They are easily beaten.'

'Some of those Kamba boys are big. They have a very good defence and the best goalie in the competition.'

Joshua was taken by surprise. Kwazi had a practised uninterest in football. 'How do you know about all that?' he asked.

Kwazi chuckled. 'I heard them talking in Makina.'

Joshua smiled, nodding. Kwazi was a reliable collector of Kibera gossip.

'They also say that the Siafu striker has a chance for national selection,' Kwazi went on.

Joshua shrugged, but didn't respond. It was a dream beyond imagining.

'Why did you have an argument with your father?' Kwazi asked, returning to the subject.

Joshua tried to recall. Recently, almost everything about his father tended to annoy him.

'I don't know. Nothing really,' he answered.

But he knew that was not the truth, and Kwazi seemed to sense it for he remained silent, patiently waiting for Joshua to untangle the mass of issues that spun around in his head. There was his father's annoying complacency about the upcoming elections. He wasn't interested in fighting against the Kikuyus and their Meru cousins, who had all the power while the Luo and smaller tribes had none. He thought it shameful that his father would not at least give moral support to the opposition party, which was the voice for change. It was the same attitude of indifference his father showed regarding his Luo heritage, which he refused to pass on to Joshua. As a result, Joshua felt banished from his tribe, and conspicuous among all his peers who, although not necessarily initiated into their respective tribes, at least had the comfort of learning of their roots from their fathers.

Ultimately, though, he could never forgive his father for not taking revenge on the Kikuyu youths who had run amuck that night, causing the death of his mother and sisters in that terrible fire. If his father had at least tried to find those responsible, Joshua could have forgiven him all else.

'I cannot respect him, Kwazi,' he said at last. 'He has never been a father to me. What kind of man would not teach his son the ways of his tribe? Your father and mother are gone, but I know your father taught you about Kisii customs before he died.'

Kwazi sucked his teeth. 'What do I care for Kisii customs? What good has come from knowing that old stuff?'

'It doesn't matter if there is good to come from it or not. To know it is the important thing. It's who you are.'

'I am Kwazi. If there is more to know about me, then I can say I am Kenyan. Look at the trouble the tribes are causing us right now. We should forget them. They're not important any more.'

'Ah!' Joshua spat into the smouldering fire. 'You sound like my father. There is more to being proud of your tribe than how you should vote. If he were proud to be Luo, he would have found those Kikuyus who burnt our house that night. He would have killed them all.'

Kwazi was pensive. 'I have never understood why you think they were Kikuyu. Your mother was one of them. Why would they burn your house?'

'Do you think they knew that? No. They were out to burn Luo houses in Kisumu Ndogo — of course it was a Luo house. They didn't know us. They didn't know my mother was a Kikuyu. Maybe they didn't know there were small children there. But it doesn't change their crime. They should have been punished. But they weren't.' Joshua stabbed his wire into the embers in a flash of temper. 'I will never stop until I make them pay. All of them!'

CHAPTER 10

Riley was about to leave his hotel room for the National Archives when his mobile phone rang. It was Kazlana.

'I have the correct address for your Circularian orphanage, Mark.'

'Great!' He fumbled in his pocket for a pen. 'Let's have it.'

'It's Kibera Gardens Road in Kibera.'

'But I went there. The place is deserted. Not a sign of life.'

There was silence on the end of the line.

'Hmm …' Kazlana said after some moments. 'I don't know what to say. I'm confident my information from Community Development is correct.'

It was Riley's turn to ponder the situation. He had no idea where to turn.

'Kazlana,' he said, 'I'm obviously out of my depth here. Are you able to help me?'

*   *   *

They met in a café near her office. The noise of traffic doing battle at the intersection of Kenyatta Avenue and Kimathi Street drifted to their table at the rear of the shop.

'I rang Omuga after I spoke to you,' Kazlana said. The waiter brought their coffees and she waited until he'd gone before continuing. 'He confirmed the address, but didn't want to discuss the orphanage any further. I said all I wanted was the name of the operator and a list of the children's names, but he was very nervous about giving me anything.'

'Why?'

'I'm not sure, but it took me a long time to convince him to see you. I'm afraid that means more than the usual bribe.'

'I expected to pay something. How much does he want?'

'Five thousand shillings.'

Riley did the mental arithmetic. Eighty dollars Australian. It wasn't a lot to pay for peace of mind. 'That's manageable ... if I must.'

'He said he will meet with you on Friday if you want to proceed with it.'

'Good. Why don't we set it up for Starbucks at eleven?'

She told him how to recognise Omuga. 'That orphan must be important to you,' she added.

'Aren't all kids important?'

'Of course they are. Even more so at the moment. UNICEF has set up an inquiry into Kenya's adherence to the Convention on the Rights of the Child.'

Riley nodded. He'd seen a small article in the newspaper the day before. The Convention was intended to prevent the exploitation and abuse of children and to ensure they weren't put at risk while under the care of institutions.

'What do you think has prompted it?' he asked.

'My guess is it's political. Someone in the opposition has been feeding information to UNICEF.'

'I'm getting the impression there's not much happening in Kenya right now that isn't political,' Riley said. 'Which reminds me, what's the story on these non-government organisations?'

'Government services in Kenya are pathetic. Health services are almost non-existent. There's no such thing as unemployment benefits, of course. They rely on NGOs to meet even basic needs.'

'How do people manage?'

'Family support. It's one of the reasons Kenyans have such large families. Parents rely on their children to support them in their old age. If they have no family, then they're in trouble. There's a thriving cottage industry in local NGOs — briefcase charities, they're called. Almost anyone can form an organisation, get a piece of paper from Community Development and start collecting funds. How much of the money ever reaches the needy is seldom checked. Foreign NGOs do most of the real work here, and they have to undergo audits so we know the benefits get where they're supposed to.'

'But perhaps not in the case of the Circularians,' Riley said.

'That's a question your meeting with Omuga should answer.'

'Hopefully. And thanks for your help. How much do I owe you?'

'It was nothing. But you can pay for the coffee.'

'Well, I appreciate it. Lucky for me your father had the connections. I don't know what I would've done otherwise. How did he get involved with the Department of Community Development?'

'I'm not sure. When Grandpa Omar died, Papa decided it was time to move away from our traditional role as a trading company to something better able to deal with the modern way of doing business.'

'By "the modern way" do you mean a legal operation?'

She smiled. 'Maybe. Anyway, he started a transport and logistics company specialising in areas more difficult or dangerous to access. Papa would fly into places like Rwanda, Somalia and the Congo. I suppose that's how he started doing business with the Department of Community Development — flying aid into those countries. I don't really know. Papa ran that side of the business from Mombasa. I haven't even had the heart to go through his files. It's just too difficult for me.'

'Were you involved in any part of that business?'

'Not really. I kept our trading business going here in Nairobi, and sometimes helped Papa as a part-time pilot.'

'Do you still fly?'

'I do. It's the most energising experience I know. I simply love it.'

'Maybe you'll take me flying one day.'

Her eyes twinkled over her coffee cup. 'Maybe I will.'

She gave him another of her bright smiles before she said goodbye and swung out into the busy street.

* * *

'I'm sorry, Charlotte,' Dr Gilanga said, looking over his glasses at her, 'Professor Hornsby and I are in total agreement on the matter.' They were discussing Charlotte's plans to go up country to continue her research.

'But, Dr Gilanga,' she pleaded, 'the trouble is only here in Nairobi. There's nothing like that happening in the Rift Valley.'

'That's not to say that it won't. In 2002 the Rift Valley was the site of some of the worst political violence of the campaign. And it may happen again. The issues haven't been resolved.'

'I'll be very careful. Really I will.'

She could see her visit to the Great Rift Valley fading away.

Dr Gilanga was shaking his head. 'You see, my dear, Professor Hornsby and I had the impression that you would be travelling in Kenya with your fiancé, Mr Wainscote. We might have had quite a different view on the whole matter of the bursary had we known you had changed your plans.'

When Charlotte had applied for the study grant six months ago, she and Bradley had still been together; and when they'd broken up, the last thing on her mind was the effect it might have on her field trip. The whole problem might not have arisen had her tutor and Bradley not met at a recent social function. Professor Hornsby had then contacted Dr Gilanga in a panic. But Charlotte wasn't about to let the mere matter of security interfere with her research for her thesis.

'Dr Gilanga, I hope you're not implying that I need a *male* to help me get around,' she said, stopping just short of outright indignation.

The old man let a smile creep across his face. 'We are not in Oxford now, Charlotte. You don't need to lecture me on political correctness. I'm sure I don't have to remind you that this is Africa. Even without the current political tensions, some parts of our country are not safe. And I'm not talking about the wildlife. So, yes, I am indeed saying that you need a man to accompany you on your field trip.'

'But Nairobi is the worst danger spot and I've been able to avoid any trouble here.' She pushed aside the memory of almost stumbling into the riot.

Dr Gilanga became pensive. 'In 2002 my nephew, a very bright young man who worked with us here at the Institute, was driving his family through Gilgil on his way home to Nakuru. It was a time very much like now: there had been a great deal of emotion surrounding the election campaign and the contest between the incumbent Kalenjin president and his Kikuyu opponent. But my nephew had no concerns about travelling across the Rift Valley. There had been no news of any trouble in the area. However, apparently a local Kikuyu farmer had a few days earlier shot a Kalenjin man. There was some doubt about the circumstances — there always is — but one thing led to another and a war of revenge erupted.' His hands had been resting on his desk top, but now he clasped them together, making his knuckles turn white. 'The police said that my nephew — a Kikuyu, like me — was bound and gagged by the Kalenjin mob and made to watch while they butchered his wife. He was then tied to a tree and beaten to death. His two young daughters were spared their lives, but ...'

He broke off and looked at Charlotte with misty eyes. 'In these uncertain times, Charlotte, avoiding trouble doesn't always save you. Sometimes trouble comes looking for you.'

*   *   *

Charlotte tried to get back to her research, but Dr Gilanga's veto on her up-country field trip was foremost in her thoughts. She had three options. One: forget about the field component of her work and confine her efforts to desk research. She was unsure how Professor Hornsby would view this, but from what he had said when she'd put forward her study plan, she was fairly sure that he put great store in what he called 'getting involved in the real world'.

Two: she could swallow her pride and ask Bradley to come to Kenya. She felt sure he would agree, but she didn't want to suggest any chance of a reconciliation. Having made the break, she wanted no misunderstandings about what the trip might mean. Poor Brad. He didn't really comprehend the reason for their breakup. He couldn't understand why she wasn't attracted to the idea of being wife to a partner in Stinton, Ashmore and Wainscote. Charlotte had tried to explain that such a life just wouldn't suit her; she wanted to continue her studies and one day work as an anthropologist. At some point, the idea of marrying Bradley had become just plain boring. Not that she could tell him that, of course. She'd put it down to their incompatible aspirations. She shook her head. No, she really didn't want Brad in the picture again.

The third option was her only real choice.

She stole a glance at Mark Riley sitting at the next table to her, huddled over an open collection of loose papers. He looked personable. She imagined some women might even find him attractive. He had a pleasant smile that made his green-grey eyes sparkle. Strong jaw, with designer stubble that quite suited him. He seemed intelligent. A bit of a wit — in his view, at least. Although his manner couldn't be described as refined, he seemed house-trained, if a little crude at times. He'd probably be handy in a tight situation. And once they got out to the Rift Valley, she could do as she pleased.

It might just work. But she'd have to act quickly to overcome a rocky start.

* * *

Riley couldn't work it out. Only a day or two ago, Charlotte Manning had been the ice maiden. *How dare he suggest she accompany him to the Rift Valley? What sort of woman did he take her for?* Now she was helpful, even congenial. She started by making a polite enquiry about his research, then offered a few suggestions on where he might find some information he needed. She was a practised researcher and knew all the tricks of the trade. She was a whiz on the library's computerised cross-reference system, and knew exactly where to look for those tantalisingly beyond-all-reasonable-reach details.

He was mystified by her change of attitude. What had he done or said that might have brought about this change of mood? He was fairly certain she'd been annoyed with him the first few times their paths had crossed. It got him thinking. She was quite an attractive lady, if a little reserved for his liking. Perhaps there was more to her interest in him than just their shared research? Maybe she wanted to develop their relationship in other ways?

He dismissed the idea. He wasn't at all ready for that kind of thing, and anyway she wasn't his type. What intrigued him — always had — was how a guy could ever hope to understand the intricacies of the female mind. He gave a mental shrug. An unknowable situation, and it was interrupting his concentration when he should be cramming on early British East African history.

'I'm going out for a cup of tea,' she said mid-afternoon. 'Would you like one?'

'Um ...' He ran his eyes over the books and folders on his table as if the answer might be found somewhere there. 'Yes, ah, please. I mean, no. But I wouldn't mind a coffee.'

'Fine. I'll bring you one.' She headed towards the door, then turned back, catching him staring after her. 'I've forgotten,' she whispered. 'Is it white, two sugars?'

'Black. No sugar.'

'Of course,' she said, and smiled at him as she closed the door behind her.

He sat there doodling on his writing pad for a while, before tossing his pen onto the table and following her.

She was at the dispensing machine, rummaging in her handbag.

'Need some change?' he asked.

'Oh, yes, please. I seem to be out of coins.'

'Here we go.'

He poured her black, no-sugar tea, then his coffee, and carried both polystyrene cups to one of the tables in the small alcove off the corridor.

'Thank you,' she said when they'd taken their seats. 'But I was going to bring it in to you.'

'Needed a break anyway.'

'How's the research going?' she asked pleasantly.

'Interesting. I've been into the archives on the political system here. For a long time it was a single-party democracy. A bit of an oxymoron, don't you think? Anyway, it's all here.'

He went on to explain that his idea was to follow the issue of corruption in politics and the effect that tribal associations had on the political process. Charlotte listened attentively through his whole spiel, sipping her tea in silence.

'Hmm, I think it's a great story idea. Good luck with it,' she said, picking up her empty cup. 'Well, I'd better get back to work. Thanks for the tea. It'll keep me going until dinner time.'

'You're welcome.' He stood as she did.

'Speaking of dinner,' she said with a small frown. 'Do you think it's safe to walk about at night?'

He shrugged. 'I don't know. I guess it depends. Where are you walking?'

'Not far. From my hotel — our hotel — to the Fairview. I believe there's a nice garden restaurant there.'

They were in the corridor, paused at the door to the library.

'It's probably safer to take a taxi,' he said, opening the door for her, but she hesitated, obviously still thinking about the restaurant. She frowned and tapped her fingernail against her teeth as he'd noticed her doing once before.

'It's such a bore finding taxis at night,' she said.

He remained holding the door open. The silence grew.

'Well, I guess I'll need to find a place to eat,' he said cautiously. 'Would you like me to join you? I mean, I understand if ...'

She brightened. 'Would you? I mean, that would be good. I'll be fine once I know my way around, but ...'

'No problem. What time were you thinking?'

'Eight would be perfect.'

She swept into the library ahead of him and was delving into the shelves before he had the door closed.

Now it was Riley's turn to frown. Had he just been asked on a date?

*　　*　　*

Charlotte stood at the mirror of the small vanity table, studying the faint touch of eye shadow she had just applied. It was all wrong. *What's the point of putting a vanity unit in a hotel room unless there's some decent lighting over it?* She took a deep breath and reminded herself it was just a business dinner. The make-up was merely to give her some much-needed confidence as she attempted to guide the conversation to the matter of her trip up country.

Her proposition was logical and she would explain it quite simply. Firstly, they both needed to travel outside Nairobi for research. Secondly, Mark's research for his novel could benefit from her knowledge of anthropology in general and Maasai customs in particular. Plus, there were savings in sharing travel costs. It all made sense.

There wasn't even any reason to tell him that her supervisor had refused to fund her field research if she went alone.

The tricky part was that Mark had already suggested the same thing and she had made several snide remarks while rejecting it out of hand. She couldn't blame him if he laughed outright when she raised it. It would be a monumental climb-down, but she had no choice.

They had agreed to meet in the lobby. It was time to go.

She hastily applied a film of lipstick, but then thought it too much. He would notice how different she looked, and comment on it, and she would die of embarrassment. She smacked her lips together, spreading the thin coating of lipstick even thinner. Better.

The woman staring back at her from the dimly lit mirror did not look at all comfortable. It was a business meeting, but she was so nervous it felt like going on a first date.

* * *

The evening was more enjoyable than Riley had expected. He usually felt intimidated in French restaurants: he couldn't read the menu, and French waiters always seemed to hover, making it worse. But the waiter at the Fairview was a Kenyan and quite unpretentious. He had recommended the *saucisses à l'orange* — sausages in an orange sauce. They were surprisingly good.

Even more surprising, Charlotte had been friendly, even charming. She looked a little different too. Perhaps she'd changed her hair.

During the meal, Riley wondered if he should offer to pay for Charlotte. It was an awkward situation. They were neither lovers nor workmates; they weren't even acquaintances in the strictest sense. They were merely occupying the same space at the same time: she, researching her thesis; he, his novel.

'I should thank you,' he said.

'Thank me? Why?'

'For inspiring me to begin to write again.'

'Surely not.'

'Well, that may be a little strong. But your book certainly got me motivated. How did you get into studying the Maasai?'

'Oh, I don't know. Perhaps a novel I read as a teenager — it gave me the idea of being an anthropologist. Studying the Maasai for my Master's just seemed logical.'

'Whose idea was it to have it published?' he asked, fiddling with his coffee spoon.

'Professor Hornsby's. Actually, it was his friend, Dr Gilanga, who suggested it. He's very keen to have all the tribes' folklore and customs documented before they're lost in the rush to modern ways. It's only locally published. I'm surprised you found it. So far as I know, it's only available from the university bookshop. How it got to the Tsavo lodge I've no idea. I doubt it will find a market anywhere else.'

'Anything published, or publishable, is good. Congratulations.'

She nodded, pleased.

'It's been very useful in putting together a profile of the Maasai for my book,' he said. 'By the way, I've been meaning to ask you about the Maasai's initiation ceremony. It seems to be a big deal. You made quite a mention of it in your book.'

'It's an important ceremony for a young Maasai man. You see, unless circumcised, a Maasai can't be admitted to the brotherhood of warriors, the *moran* as they're called. Nor can they progress to become elders, which they do at the ripe old age of thirty-something.' She smiled mischievously. 'So if you were a Maasai, Mr Mark Riley, I guess you'd be approaching elderhood.'

The comment surprised Riley, and the accompanying smile suited her. He noticed again that she looked different. Maybe it was a touch more make-up.

'I'd rather call it my carnal equinox,' he said with mock seriousness.

'Don't tell me you're over the hill?'

'Not quite. But I may be halfway there.'

They both chuckled.

'You were saying,' he said, 'how important the initiation ceremony is. From what I know of anthropology, which isn't a

97

lot, circumcision isn't uncommon, but this Maasai ceremony ... what's it called? Em ... em ...?'

'*Emorata.*'

'That's it. This *emorata* sounds like more than that.'

'Perhaps the procedure is a little more elaborate, but essentially it's a similar rite of passage as occurs in many other cultures.'

'Elaborate how?'

Charlotte dabbed at her lips with her napkin. 'Oh, it's probably not all that interesting to someone who's not in my field.'

'What do you mean, not in your field? My novel, remember?'

It was refreshing to be able to tease her a little. Previously, she would have become huffy if he'd attempted it. She seemed reluctant to take the conversation any further, but he persisted.

'Come on,' he coaxed. 'How am I ever going to become an expert in Maasai culture if you won't teach me?'

'Well, if you must know. It's ... well, unusual.'

'Hell, I'm no expert, but I would have thought if you've seen one, you've seen 'em all. And I'm talking about a circumcision, of course.'

'Yes, well ...' She made a small noise, almost a cough, as if clearing her throat. 'The Maasai do it differently. That's why it's so, um ... interesting.'

'Go on.'

She gave him a look as if to assess his seriousness before proceeding. 'Well, it's called a buttonhole circumcision,' she said. 'Particularly difficult when performed on a teenager. As you might imagine.'

She explained the intricacies of the slice along the sulcus at the top of the foreskin, the insertion of the glans through the new opening, and final trimming of the excess skin.

'Hmm,' he said with a smile when she'd concluded. 'I'm glad I've finished my *saucisses à l'orange.*'

This time she did see the humour. She tried to mask her smile with her hand, but with no success. Finally, she gave in to it and laughed with him until her eyes watered.

*　*　*

As the dinner progressed, Charlotte began to lose some of the tension she'd felt at the outset. Mark was relaxed and charming, and although she hadn't managed to steer the conversation in the desired direction, she did get him to talk about his research, hoping to find an opening to raise the matter of accompanying him up country.

'It's going okay,' Riley responded. Then added, 'Actually, a bit slow.'

'What are you up to?'

'I like my Maasai story, but I need a character for my background story.'

'I thought you were onto Trader Dick — the perfect protagonist?'

Dick had been a swashbuckling frontiersman whom Riley had thought ideal.

'So did I. As it turns out, he was a cattle-thieving, marauding cutthroat.'

'Oh.'

'And very soon dead. It kinda makes for a short story rather than a novel.'

'But as you said, it's a novel not a thesis. Why don't you build a fictional character around him, or better still, just create a purely fictitious character to carry your background story?'

He pondered it briefly, then shook his head. 'Nup. It has to be the real thing. I like historical novels. It has to be as close to historically correct as I can make it.'

'Oh, no.'

'What do you mean, *oh, no?*'

'Historical novels are such a pain. They simply muddy the waters. Who knows what's history and what's fiction? Historians just hate them.'

'Who cares what historians think? Let them buy a history book if they don't like the idea of historical novels. *I* happen to *love* historical novels.'

She decided to let the matter pass. It wasn't a good tactic to antagonise him if she hoped to get him to agree to letting her travel with him.

'Where does that leave you?' she asked.

'That leaves me stuck with Commissioner Eliot,' he said with a sigh.

'You don't like him, do you?'

He thought about it for a moment. 'No. Don't suppose I do.'

'Why not?'

'I don't know … He seems to be a manipulative sort. I really have a problem with manipulative people. You know the type — they appear to be considerate but in the end they're just looking out for themselves.'

Charlotte fidgeted with her napkin, her confidence flagging.

'Are you okay?' Riley asked.

'Yes. Absolutely.' She gave a soft cough to clear her throat. 'Either way, I imagine you're anxious to get up country as soon as possible.'

'Not so sure now,' he said.

'Oh … why not? I mean … I thought you were keen to get started on your research.'

'I think there might be something interesting coming out of the UNICEF inquiry,' he said. 'It could be a bankable piece. I also want to follow up on Jafari and the orphanage.'

This wasn't helping her cause.

'How are you placed for time?' she asked. 'Are you able to delay your research into the novel?'

He looked thoughtful. 'You're right. My budget *is* tight.

I could cover the newspaper article in my spare time, if any. I should just jump in the Land Rover and get on with it.'

'Hmm …' she said.

'What?'

'Nothing. It's just that at Oxford we were warned about researchers charging off into the bush only to get lost, so to speak.'

'Lost?'

'In pointless pursuit of facts rather than the real story. I assume you'll arrange a guide?' she asked, trying not to sound too manipulative.

'Why would I need a guide? I have a Land Rover and a map.'

She shook her head and smiled. 'I'm not talking about geography, Mark. Although finding a local to help with the languages would be useful. But … try to think *anthropology*.'

'Anthropology. You're suggesting I might need someone to help me with the Maasai?'

'That would be a good idea, I think.'

'I'm sure. But I asked you — the best person available — and you declined.'

'Did I? I'm not sure I understood your request. It so happens that I might have to do some research of my own in the area. I suppose I could give you a hand … if you think it would be helpful?'

He looked stunned. 'That would be great!'

She felt such a sense of relief at his agreement that she realised she must have been more concerned about the security situation than she had admitted to herself.

'Very well then,' she said brightly. 'Coffee?'

*   *   *

During the drive back to the Panafric Hotel, Riley felt a vague sense of unreality. How could he have misread their earlier discussions about travelling together so comprehensively?

He pulled up outside the foyer of the Panafric and met Charlotte on her side of the Land Rover as she stepped down.

'Thank you,' she said, as he closed the door for her.

At the hotel entrance, the doorman swept open the double glass doors, wearing his customary wide smile. 'Good evening, Mr Riley,' he said, snapping a salute.

'Evening, Henry.'

'Have you found a suitable car park, sir?'

'Yes, thank you, Henry. I have.'

'Very well, sir.' The doorman saluted again and stepped back outside.

'Are you going to the archives again tomorrow?' Riley asked Charlotte.

'Yes, maybe.'

'Me too. Plenty to do before we leave.'

'Yes. Exactly.'

'Would you like a nightcap?' He indicated the door to the bar.

'Oh, thank you, but I won't.'

'In that case, I'll have a small one for the road and say good night.'

'Yes, good night, Mark.'

He waited for her to leave. When she paused, he felt she had something to add but seemed to change her mind.

'So ... good night,' she said again.

'Good night.'

'Oh, and, Mark ... thanks for dinner. It was very nice of you to pay.'

'No problem. It was good to have some company for a change.'

'My treat next time. Well ... I'll see you in the morning, shall I?' she said, and finally left.

Riley strolled towards the bar entrance, enjoying the softness of the night air. He wondered if he'd ever work out what was going on in Charlotte Manning's head. He was going to have plenty of time with her over the next few weeks to find out.

CHAPTER 11

Mayasa had little interest in football, but occasionally on her homeward journey from her job at the Adams Arcade supermarket, she would sit on the bench at the side of the field and watch the local boys play. One of them, a tall Luo boy, was quite good. She knew from the calls across the pitch that his name was Joshua, but she also recognised him from his occasional visits to the supermarket. He never bought anything of value and she suspected he was stealing other items. Many of the Kibera boys did, and many were caught and given a severe beating by the security guards. Joshua was never caught. She suspected there was more to him than his cheeky grin.

The game ended, and before she realised it, Joshua was striding towards her, his bare chest heaving as he used his shirt to wipe the sweat from his face.

'Thank you for being my *askari*,' he said as he took a seat beside her on the bench.

'What?' she asked.

'They're not worth much but they're the only ones I have.'

She followed his gesture to the sandals under the bench. 'Oh, I see. But I wasn't really —'

He grinned at her. 'It was a joke.'

'I know that,' she said, embarrassed by her naïvety.

He chuckled. It was good-natured and she forgave him for teasing her. She searched for something witty to say to redeem herself, but her mind remained a blank.

'I was just going anyway,' she added lamely.

His back muscles rippled as he bent to unlace his boots. 'You're not waiting for your friend?'

'My ... friend?'

'Your boyfriend,' he said, straightening up to look at her.

'I don't have a boyfriend. I'm new in Kibera.' Why did she feel the need to explain?

'Since when?'

'Since ... well, it's been a couple of years.'

'A couple of years. And no boyfriend.'

He made it sound like a felony.

'I work. At Adams Arcade supermarket.'

'Oh-ho, so boyfriends are not permitted for girls at the Adams Arcade supermarket?' He was grinning at her again.

'Don't be silly. It makes no difference.'

He obviously didn't recognise her and she felt disappointed that she'd made no impression upon him.

'It's okay,' he said, obviously sensing her annoyance. 'Most of the boys have girlfriends.' He nodded towards the knot of players and their female supporters. 'Where are you from?'

'Kibera.'

'No, before that.'

Again she felt dim-witted. 'Kisumu,' she said brusquely.

'You're not Luo,' he said.

It was a statement, but one with a degree of uncertainty. She'd had many Luo friends in Kisumu and knew she could be mistaken for one of them.

'No, I'm Sukuma. From Musoma.'

'I see.'

He lifted his boots onto his lap and began to even out the length of loops through the eyes. Then he teased the laces straight before tying the boots together with a neat bow. 'Where's Musoma?' he asked, as he strung the boots around his neck and stood.

'Tanzania. Near the Serengeti.'

'The Serengeti?' He hesitated, then resumed his seat. 'The Serengeti National Reserve?'

'Actually, it's the Serengeti National Park. The Masai Mara is a national reserve.'

'You know the Serengeti National Park?'

'Well ... yes.'

'How? How do you know it? Have you been there? Isn't it too far?'

She began with a brief account of her father's job in Musoma, where he'd been a driver for the Tanzanian railways. She then described how, after her mother died, her father took her to work with him during school holidays. Sometimes they drove into the national park to eat their lunch.

The more she told him, the more he demanded to know.

She told him that her father had taken her and her three older sisters to Kisumu when he was sacked from the railway, but the job he had with the Lake Victoria Ferry Service lasted only a year or so, and they had eventually come to Kibera. Her sisters had married or moved out and she now lived alone with her father in the Kianda section of Kibera.

'You look familiar,' Joshua said. 'Have we met at the pitch before?'

'No.'

He suggested they walk together as he also lived with a friend in Kianda.

'Tell me about your visits to the national park,' he said.

'I've already told you. Papa would drive the old Bedford into the park — he knew the rangers and we didn't need to pay — and we'd park under a tree for a little while. Papa would turn the radio on, but most days it was too scratchy to hear anything.'

'But what did you see there?'

'In the park? Oh, there were always gazelle and wildebeest. Many zebra. Once we saw a huge flock of ostriches. And there were —'

'Lions? Did you see lions?'

She smiled. His enthusiasm was touching. She told him about the time her father had parked under their usual tree, but as she was about to open her door to climb the rocks they used as seats, her father had shouted and grabbed her by the arm. He'd then pointed to the lions among the rocks that neither of them had seen as he'd driven in. She laughed as she recounted the story, but it wasn't amusing at the time. She remembered her distress at her father's raised voice, his painful grip on her arm and her tears.

When they arrived at the shack Joshua called his home, he was still engrossed in their conversation. She was surprised at how basic his dwelling was. The house where she and her father lived was nothing more than an enclosed space divided into two rooms by a curtain; but, as far as she could see, Joshua had nothing but a piece of clear plastic spread on the ground under a few sheets of rusty iron.

'I live here with Kwazi,' he said, pointing to the person bent over a section of reinforcing mesh that straddled a small fire. 'Kwazi! Meet Mayasa.'

'*Habari*,' Kwazi said without enthusiasm.

It was impossible to say how old he was, and his face was so disfigured she couldn't read his features or expression.

'*Sijambo*,' she answered without thought.

Kwazi raised his eyebrows. Mayasa felt she could just bite her tongue. She had inadvertently used the more correct reply of *I'm fine*, instead of the more casual Kenyan Kiswahili *mzuri*, meaning *nice*. It was a small matter, but when she used what Tanzanians called pure Kiswahili, it tended to mark her as something of a snob in some Kenyans' eyes.

'I've seen you around,' she said in English, trying to move on from her gaffe.

'Most people have no trouble remembering me.' Kwazi's smile twisted his face and it was again impossible to read the expression behind his disfigurement.

Mayasa almost winced. She felt she was doing nothing to improve the impression he might have of her, and it seemed important that he like her since he was Joshua's friend.

Joshua came to her rescue. 'Mayasa knows the Serengeti National Park,' he said, as if announcing she were a personal friend of the president.

'*Mzuri*,' Kwazi said with perhaps just a trace of sarcasm.

'Well, I'd better go,' Mayasa said. 'I have to cook for my father.'

'Okay. Maybe we'll meet at the pitch again soon?'

'Maybe.'

They said their goodbyes, and she made a point of including Kwazi in them.

On the way home, her spirits were higher than they had been for some time. Mayasa had found it difficult to find her niche in Kibera. Many thought her too highbrow with her pure Tanzanian Kiswahili and educated ways. Apart from one or two of the girls at work, she'd made few friends. All of a sudden, and for no other reason than a few visits to the Serengeti as a child, she felt she'd made a lasting impression on the very handsome Joshua Otieng.

* * *

The Department of Community Development clerk was a short, slightly paunchy, middle-aged black man with an ill-fitting suit and anxious eyes. Riley spotted him from Kazlana's description as soon as he entered the coffee shop. When he'd taken his seat, Riley joined him.

'Mark Riley,' he said.

The man quickly scanned the restaurant. 'I am David Omuga,' he said, nervously wetting his lips.

'Thanks for coming, Mr Omuga. We can talk in confidence here.'

Riley had no idea if that were true, but it seemed Omuga needed some reassuring.

Omuga nodded, appearing not at all convinced.

Riley was unsure of the protocol, but took the envelope from his pocket and slid it across the table to Omuga, who glanced around the coffee shop and slipped the envelope into his jacket pocket.

'I believe you're worried about giving me information about the orphanage,' Riley said.

'The Circularian orphanage is very different, Mr Riley.'

'You mean there are irregularities in the way it works?'

'There are irregularities everywhere. But there is more to this orphanage than others. I want this funny business brought out. For the sake of the children. Things must change in Kenya.'

'Is that why you've come to me? To change the system?'

'You could go to the newspapers when you find out about this orphanage.'

'You've got the wrong man. I'm not a crusader. All I want is some information on the orphanage.'

'But you could help.'

Riley studied the man again. There was nothing exceptional about him. He appeared to be a typical public servant — quiet, conservatively dressed in a dark blue suit, well-spoken. He certainly didn't look like an idealistic whistle-blower.

'Why have you done this, Mr Omuga?'

'What do you mean?'

'I mean, I've only asked for information; information that your office could have given me in the first place. Now I have to pay you five thousand shillings *and* fight your battles.'

'Mr Riley,' Omuga said, 'I am a Luo. As you may be aware, there is an election in a week's time and there is a Luo candidate standing against President Kibaki, a Kikuyu. Kibaki promised to stop all this corruption, but he has failed. Everyone is affected by it. People continue to be cheated by parking officers and the police. The road contractors get the job to fix the roads, but the money goes into someone else's pockets. We are sick of it. Raila Odinga will fix all this. He will end the corruption. I can't get a telephone connected, or find a postal parcel that supposedly has been lost, without giving a little something. Money — it is always money. A little here, a little there. I have been in the department for twenty-seven years. The pay is steady, but for a man who is of the wrong tribe and not well-educated, it is not so good, and the prospects for advancement are very limited. I have eight children and an ailing wife.' He shrugged.

Riley knew exactly what the shrug meant. Just like the corrupt road contractors, Omuga wanted something for his trouble.

Riley was torn between feelings of disgust and pity. Omuga was a fraud. He claimed to hate corruption, but not enough to refuse it when offered. Conversely, he felt sorry for him, a menial, unable to avoid paying his share of the endemic petty graft, but without the power to change the system. Omuga knew, like everyone else, that change had to come from the top, and there was very little chance of that happening. He was stuck in the corruption trap like millions of others.

'It is not only the money,' Omuga said. 'This is why I have agreed to speak to you.' He pulled a wrinkled page from his pocket. 'This is the information you want.'

Riley glanced at it. It was a long list of names. 'Are these the children at the Circularian orphanage?'

'They are the ones that have passed through in the last few years. I don't know how many remain.'

Riley ran his eye down the list. Jafari's name was there.

'Where are these children now?'

'I don't know, but it is not only people in America or Europe who love children, Mr Riley. People who have no children will do anything to have them. The children come to Nairobi, and then ...' he flung a hand in the air, 'suddenly they are gone to their new place.'

'Where I come from we also have people desperate to adopt a child,' Riley responded. 'But it takes a long time for them to find a match. Boy or girl, age, so many different wishes.'

Omuga made a crooked attempt at a smile. 'Perhaps you didn't look carefully at the names I gave you. Was there nothing special about them?'

Riley shook his head. He'd only checked for Jafari's name.

'They are all Swahili boys.'

'All boys?'

'Swahili boys. I think the clients are from the Middle East, looking for a son and heir. They want a child who looks like them. Not black like me, but brown like them.'

It took Riley a moment to comprehend Omuga's theory. The Swahili were descended from the Omanis who first conquered, then engaged in trade with the coastal people centuries ago. Over time many moved to the East Africa coast. In the process they intermarried. The descendants of those unions became the Swahili people of the Coast Province whose features retain similarities to those of the Middle East.

'I think they are fortunate, these children,' Omuga continued. 'They receive everything that money can offer. Education. A good home. In time their fathers will provide them a very good wife and, after all that, they will inherit their father's wealth.'

Omuga spread his hands as if to rest his case. 'Why do you worry about them?'

'Does the organisation in Mombasa know of this ... this trade?'

Omuga shrugged. 'Again, I don't know.'

The shrug made Riley suspicious. It was quite likely that Omuga was the inside man in the department, ticking the necessary boxes to allow the kids to be smuggled out of the country — no questions asked.

'Let's say I forget about the official paths,' Riley asked. 'How could I find a child that has been at the orphanage?'

'People will want the child to be certified as healthy. Once that is done, he is taken to an unregulated border crossing. There, another organisation delivers him to the client.'

'Why would it be necessary to have the child's health checked?'

'The new parents would not want a child with AIDS, or some other hideous disease.'

'I see. So the doctor has all the records?'

Omuga nodded, his eyes darting around the coffee shop.

'And where is this doctor located?'

Omuga hesitated. 'I believe it is somewhere in Nakuru. But now I must go.'

'Where?'

'I don't know; you should ask the man who owns the orphanage,' Omuga said. 'But I must warn you to be very careful how you proceed. It could mean your life if he learns of your investigations. And mine if he discovers who gave you your information,' he added.

Riley thought Omuga had been watching too many American movies.

'Who is he?' he asked.

Omuga pointed to the name on the bottom of the page. 'He's a businessman and a politician. A very dangerous man. His name is Gideon Koske.'

* * *

Kazlana was at home when Mark Riley called her mobile phone. 'I just rang to say thank you,' he told her.

'Not at all. Did Omuga give you what you were looking for?'

'Well, I've made some progress, but he raised as many questions as he answered.' He told her that he'd found his sponsored child's name on the department's list but that Omuga knew nothing about his whereabouts. 'After he gave me the head guy's name, he refused to say any more.'

'Who is the head guy?'

'Name's Gideon Koske. Omuga says he's a businessman-cum-politician.'

'Koske ... I can't say I know the name, but if he's in the government you had better be careful. These men can be very difficult if outsiders come asking questions about their business operations. Why don't you let me do some checking before going further?'

When the call ended, she tried to remember where she'd heard the name Koske before. She thought it might have been in connection with a recent newspaper article on the latest government member to jump ship to support the opposition candidate for president. It wasn't an unusual occurrence in Kenyan politics, but Koske's name had another connection and she couldn't quite recall it. She decided to check her father's old business files.

Kazlana drove to her office. The security guard was surprised to see her at such a late hour, and disarmed the security system on her office as she ascended to the tenth floor.

She tugged the light cord in the small room where her father's files were stored. They were arranged in neat stacks on the shelves, exactly as the workmen had left them nearly twelve months earlier. Each time she had decided to sort through them, she had felt bereft and emotional. Seeing her father's signature on correspondence brought him back to mind but sadly not back to life.

She threw herself into the task now, but had trouble making sense of the filing system. She gave up after an hour, sorting the papers into stacks based upon the likelihood of success. In the *maybe* stack she found a file with a list of accounts.

Her father's bookkeeping had been perfunctory at best. At heart he was a true Ramanova — more of a pirate than a businessman — but running her finger down the list, she finally found what she was looking for.

Gideon Koske was signatory to a payment made for supplies flown from Mombasa to Nakuru. The client was the Circularian organisation.

CHAPTER 12

Gideon Koske hardened his resolve. Around him in the antechamber to the parliament were the elected members of President Kibaki's political supporters. They streamed past him, either pointedly ignoring him or giving him hostile glances. It confirmed his suspicions that the party was now fully aware of his defection to the opposition, thereby sealing his fate should Odinga's Orange Democratic Movement not win the forthcoming election.

Political party disloyalty was not unusual in the Kenyan parliament, even for junior ministers like him. There'd been far more celebrated defections than his and, although irritating to his erstwhile colleagues, it was not a matter to warrant more than the mild hostility that they now made no effort to conceal.

In Kibaki's party Koske had felt like an interloper — a neophyte among masters — and he was realistic enough to understand his poor prospects for advancement. He'd been a nobody before scrambling out of a Kibera council position to take up a fortuitous party vacancy in the Kibera electorate. It had cost him a lot to gain preselection and a lot more to buy the support needed to win enough votes to get into parliament. Having gained his seat, he was devastated to discover he was very low on the pecking order. The most he could win was his junior minister's position in an insignificant portfolio. It was then that he had decided to throw his support behind Odinga. If he could win favourable recognition from the ODM party machinery through his efforts to get Odinga elected president, then he felt sure he could secure a higher position in Odinga's new parliament.

Even then he would need funds, and, having invested in the wrong people, he had to do whatever was necessary to build them again. His acquisition of the Circularian orphanage was a wise investment, one that he knew would ultimately repay him in both financial and political capital. It was a bold strategy, but he was not a man to tolerate second-best. He had already sacrificed more than one life in his quest to succeed.

He would continue to do whatever was necessary to achieve his ambition, or die in the effort.

*   *   *

The walk to the football ground was longer from the place Kwazi called home, especially as Joshua preferred to bypass Kisumu Ndogo. He was not afraid to meet his father; he simply wanted to avoid the confrontation that would ensue. He had no reason to add anything more to what he'd already said.

He was further delayed by a large gathering of Kibera residents at a mass meeting called to protest against the restrictions on campaigning imposed by the administration police. The mood was volatile and Joshua's inclination was to join in, but he couldn't be late to training. As captain he needed to demonstrate the discipline he tried to instil in his fellow players, although deep down he knew most of them were merely involved for the fun. It sometimes appeared to Joshua that he was the only one training with a purpose.

When he arrived at the bare earthen ground used by his team as a playing field, he saw Koske, who signalled to him that he wanted to talk. Joshua trotted over.

Koske was more than usually smug. 'You see that man over there — at the rear of the goal?' he said.

Joshua nodded.

'I've asked him to come to see your team's practice game.' The smug smile widened. 'But really, it's you he has come to see.'

'Why?'

'Because he owes me a little favour. You see, he's from the Limuru Leopards.'

Joshua gaped. He looked from Koske to the man in the goalmouth and back again. The Limuru Leopards were one of Nairobi's premier football clubs.

'Yes, it's a very important team,' said Koske. 'And, as I said, if I do something for a friend, I expect that friend to do something for me. That's how I work.'

Joshua could hardly conceal his excitement.

'I've asked him to look at you and see if you are good enough to play in a trial match later this month.'

'Yes!' Joshua's heart leapt in his chest. 'I'm ready!'

Koske put his head back and laughed, but as quickly as the laughter had begun, it stopped. He grasped Joshua's shoulder. 'This I do for you, my friend.'

'Thank you, Mr Koske. Thank you.'

Koske nodded and smiled, appearing satisfied with Joshua's response.

'Now, go,' he said. 'Play your best!'

Joshua quickly stripped to his shorts and tee-shirt and bolted onto the field to join the practice game. Almost immediately, he was among the action, but it wasn't until some time later that the ball came to him on the wing. He dribbled down the flank, defeating two opponents' tackles, then lost and won the ball twice in the box before slotting it past the goalie into the top corner of the net.

After the game, Joshua searched the scattered figures around the ground but could only see Koske's broad figure on the sideline. He tried to hide his disappointment as he joined Koske. The big man made small talk until Joshua could bear it no longer.

'Did you speak to the man from the Leopards, Mr Koske?'

Koske's expression expanded into his all-knowing smirk. 'Wasn't I the one who arranged for him to be here?'

'And did he ask about me?'

The pause was excruciating.

'He remarked upon a few of the players.'

Joshua knew this was a lie as none on the pitch could match his ball control and agility, but he let Koske have his moment of control. 'And me?' he asked, hating himself for his pleading tone.

Koske nodded thoughtfully. 'He said you played well.'

'And …?'

'And I'm to keep an eye on you. He's relying on me to advise him when you are ready to test yourself against his boys in Limuru. Maybe even to play in a trial game.'

'To test myself? Did he see my goal in the first half?'

'I don't know.' Koske sucked at his teeth, then inserted a finger into his mouth to dislodge something stuck between them. 'Perhaps he did.'

'What did he say?'

'Hmm … What did he say? Oh, yes. He said he thought you had played well, particularly since you were not properly dressed.'

'Properly dressed?' Joshua repeated, searching his mind for an explanation. He dropped his eyes to his shirt and shorts before it dawned. In his haste, he'd forgotten to put on his new boots.

* * *

Mayasa had found some free time after work and headed to the football ground where Joshua and his team-mates were playing. This time she searched for Joshua's sandals and found them under one of the benches. She guessed they were his as he was on the pitch playing in football boots.

He cut an athletic figure, darting through the packs, sprinting down a wing with the ball almost on a string. His team distinguished itself by playing without shirts. She admired the long lean muscles on his back and thighs, shining with sweat.

At the end of the game she remained guarding his footwear as he had a conversation with a man on the sidelines. He seemed pleased as he headed her way.

'You are a good *askari*,' Joshua said. 'I hope you're not looking for bribe money?'

'Why not?' she said, smiling in return. 'This is the second time I have guarded your precious sandals, and look! They're still here.'

'More than that. You don't know it, but you've also been guarding something worth even more than my sandals,' he said with a conspiratorial grin. 'Look!'

He reached under the bench and from a hidden ledge produced a shiny black mobile phone.

'It's the latest-model Motorola!' she said.

'It is.'

'But you can't get them on a pre-paid plan. How did you pay for it?'

Having asked, she immediately regretted it. It was none of her business if he'd stolen it, in which case she didn't want to know.

'Mr Koske gave it to me,' he said as he pushed buttons on the new phone. 'See? I can get the internet on it … somehow. I'll have to ask someone, but I have it.'

'Koske? Gideon Koske?'

'Yes. Do you know him?'

'No … but I've heard of him. Isn't he, like … a thug?'

'He's a businessman,' he said. 'And one of us — a Raila supporter.' He peered at her intensely. 'You are a Raila supporter, aren't you?'

'Um … yes. I suppose so.'

'Good.'

'But I've heard Koske has people going around taking money.'

'He's a businessman. Of course he takes money.'

She was about to add that her father said that Gideon Koske took money for keeping people's houses safe when it was he who made them unsafe in the first place. But she didn't want to argue. Joshua was not listening anyway, engrossed by his new mobile phone.

'Listen! Here's the new one from Beyonce.'

'How did you get that?'

'My friend showed me. I can get any new song I want.'

Mayasa watched as he pushed buttons and ran through an impressive list of features, but she remained troubled by his involvement with Gideon Koske. It wasn't only her father who thought him a thug. She'd heard others say the same thing.

'What did you have to do for Koske to get this new phone?' she asked.

Joshua pushed a few more buttons before answering. 'Is there something wrong about earning money?' he asked aggressively. 'Don't you earn money at Adams Arcade?'

She was taken aback, but managed to respond, 'Yes, of course.' She was about to leave it, but decided she had to say what was on her mind. 'But I don't earn it by threatening poor people.'

'He sells plots in Kibera. There's nothing wrong with that.'

'He sells plots he doesn't own. He pushes people to pay him money to avoid getting beaten by his thugs. But you must already know all this, Joshua. Anybody who lives in Kibera knows it.'

Joshua's expression darkened. 'Yes, I live in Kibera. And so do you. But you've got a job and maybe your father has a job too, so he doesn't have to go looking, looking every day, and pay a hundred shillings to the gate *askari* even to ask for a job. And another hundred bob to his foreman if he gets work. So he can carry cement bags all day and then take home a hundred if he's lucky. And me. Look at me, selling newspapers and silly toys on Uhuru Highway. What does that buy me? A can of Coke and a Wimpy. Not now. Now I have money.'

'I know all that. Do you think I don't know about these things? My father …' She abruptly changed tack. 'I work, and we get help from my sister's husband, but still we have nothing.'

'Then don't tell me how I should get my money. You and your fancy Kiswahili. Don't tell me who I should know and what I should do. I do what I must.'

Mayasa's inclination was to fight back, but she liked Joshua and knew she was pushing him too hard. 'All I'm saying is, you should be careful around Koske. My father says he's a dangerous man.'

'Your father! Who cares about your father? In Kianda you have more than anyone in Kisumu Ndogo. What does your father know about my life? He's like my father — all the time telling me what to do. And questions, questions. All the time: what are you doing? Who are you speaking to? That's why I left home. Now you are sounding just like him. It makes me mad!'

He snatched up his sandals and stormed off.

Mayasa watched him go, wondering why he thought he was the only person suffering in Kibera.

*　*　*

Kazlana gunned the red Audi R8, fishtailing it out of the Wilson Airport car park. At the busy Langata Road intersection she dashed through a gap between a truck and a bus, earning a blast from both. She laughed. Then she planted her foot, overtaking everything before she hit the lunchtime traffic jam at Nyayo Stadium and was forced to a crawl along Uhuru Highway.

Her flight to Mombasa had been enjoyable, as flights always were for her, but a waste of time. The odd little administrator of the Circularians, Horácio Domingues, had revealed nothing of interest. The one curious fact she had learnt was that the Circularians didn't have an established meeting place but did their charity work within the local community. In particular, they provided support for local orphans until they found homes for them.

She'd also found out that her father had flown a number of missions to Nakuru for the Circularians, but never to Wajir. She'd hoped to find a link between her father's death and the mysterious disappearance of the orphanage children, but it had been just another failed hunch.

Driving was so different to the freedom she enjoyed while flying. That morning on her return to Nairobi, and on a whim, she'd changed course and flown over the blue gem of Lake Chala with the great hump of the sleeping elephant, Kilimanjaro, blocking her path. She'd tested the Cessna, climbing the eastern flank at tree-top height until the engine screamed in protest, then circumnavigated the glacial peak three times in memory of her father, who'd introduced her to flying. The glaciers had shrunk from the days she had flown over them with her father, but were nevertheless brilliant, reflecting the sun in long, dancing rays.

She could still recall the ecstasy of that first moment, at age eight, when she'd realised that she had control of the aircraft. She had made it tilt and dip, veer and climb, and felt a blast of power that sent a fire rushing through her veins. It was as though in defying the universal force of gravity, she had accumulated enormous reservoirs of energy that had to be dissipated before she could unwind. As a child she was unmanageable for hours after landing. Her father said it was the pure essence of freedom that flying gifted to some individuals. Whatever it was, the sensation had endured, and Kazlana came to realise in later years that it was closely associated with sexual arousal. She could be a ruthless and demanding lover following a flight. On the rare occasions when she had a man in her life, she would not let him rest until the pent-up sexual energy was spent. Not many men could handle her under those circumstances. Consequently, her relationships were short-lived.

At the next roundabout she veered off the highway, taking the narrow road above the Railways Golf Club. She cursed when she came upon an overloaded *matatu* lumbering up the hill. The washouts along the edges of the winding road made passing difficult, but she dropped the Audi into first, sending the rev counter into the red with the motor screaming. An oncoming sedan swung out of her way and into the ditch. The *matatu* driver trumpeted his anger or delight — it was hard to know with *matatu* drivers.

She hung an illegal right turn into Valley Road and a left down Nyerere, where she drove on the wrong side of the double lines until she reached the university roundabout, and headed for the market.

* * *

The Nairobi City Market in Muindi Mbingu Street reeked with the sickly sweet odour of decaying produce. Men wearing long colourful *kanzus* or plain white *dhotis* bustled down the crowded aisles carrying heavy shopping bags or sacks of vegetables. There were many sari-adorned Indian women with gold-studded nostrils, Swahili women in floral *kangas*, and others with eyes darting within black purdahs. Among the traditionally garbed women, chic office workers hurried to buy ingredients for the evening meal.

The stall-owners hollered prices, implored shoppers to stop, to try, to buy their produce. Boys scurried between the stalls and car park, carrying cardboard boxes for the tips. Beggars in tattered rags chose more direct methods, thrusting their grubby hands at well-dressed shoppers but seldom receiving more than a harsh word.

Kazlana, immaculately dressed in blue suit pants and a white cotton top, was not shopping. She was looking for Ahmed, one of the small band who sold information rather than goods. Ahmed's specialty was simple observation. He would follow a client's target and report on their movements. It paid to know who was doing what to whom in the shady world in which Kazlana operated.

She found him at his 'office' — beside a dumpster at the rear of the market.

'*Habari*, mama,' he greeted her.

'*Mzuri. Habari yako?*'

'I'm very fine,' he answered. 'I have what you want. You ask me to know about this fellow Koske. There are many here who know this man. He has many friends also, but not in this place.' He inclined his head to indicate the market. 'Many friends in suits. They stay in KICC building, but not interesting to you, I think. But one man, I know him. This one you maybe find interesting. I know him from the streets.' His eyes flitted about like a nervous cat. 'He is bad. Dangerous bad.'

'What has he been doing that is of interest to me?' she asked.

'I see him one day come to old Bank India building. He stays at his car, waiting, waiting. Then he watches this *mzungu* man, sometimes he has *mzungu* lady too. He follow them. Where, I do not know. I cannot follow. But one time I see them go up Valley Road.' He shrugged. 'That is all I can see.'

Kazlana would not have normally been interested in some thug stalking a rich tourist, but Ahmed's reference to the old Bank of India building piqued her interest. The building was now the National Archives and she knew Mark Riley was often there.

'What did these *wazungu* look like?'

'*Mzungu* man. Tall. Wearing blue jeans, not suit. Beard like *mbega* monkey.'

Kazlana couldn't help but smile. Ahmed's likening of the colobus monkey's short black chin-hair to the three-day growth that Riley wore was quite astute.

'And the lady?'

'Pretty like you. Same height,' he answered. 'You know them?'

Kazlana nodded. 'I think so.'

'*Tsk tsk*,' he said, shaking his head and sucking his teeth. 'You maybe tell them watch out. This bad one he follow them. Kill many people already.'

*   *   *

Sitting in the midday traffic jam, with six lines of vehicles attempting to cram into three lanes, Riley had time to reflect on Kazlana's phone call. The message was simple enough: they needed to talk, she said. But it was the way she said it, in her lilting, accented voice, that made it so irresistible.

Arriving at her office building twenty minutes later, he strode past the security desk to the elevators, his sneakers squeaking on the highly polished vinyl floor tiles. As he watched the indicator climb slowly to ten, he recalled their recent meeting. He'd felt vaguely aware of her interest in him then, but had been frequently wrong on such matters in the past. It was a long time since he'd been with a woman and he was out of practice. Nevertheless, a woman like Kazlana had all the hallmarks of trouble.

She received him in her office and went immediately to the matter she wanted to discuss with him. 'We're in the same line of business, you and I.'

'We are?' he said, watching her arrange herself gracefully in the chair next to his at the low coffee table.

'You are researching a newspaper article, and I am researching a crime.'

'What do you mean?'

'There's another thing we have in common,' she said, following her thoughts. 'Our searches are leading us to the same person.'

'Now I'm definitely confused. I'm looking for a child in an orphanage.'

'I know what you're doing, Mark. I also know something about the person who runs that orphanage — Gideon Koske.

I have my suspicions about him, and you need to be aware of the risks if you go further with your investigation of the orphanage.'

He was about to speak, but she put her finger on his lips. 'It's not important for you to know how I know about him. It is the nature of my business to know such things. Our company has often operated on the edge of the law. Many times my father crossed that boundary and, as a consequence, became involved with crooked characters. I don't know the reason he flew to Wajir, but when I find the answer to that question I will have found the reason for his death — and the person who killed him. I'm suspicious that he died because of his involvement with Koske's orphanage, but I can't be sure at present.'

She was silent for a moment before continuing. 'Koske is watching you, Mark. I'm not sure why, but I imagine he suspects you are getting too close to finding out something about his orphanage. Something he does not want known.'

Mark shook his head. 'It's too bad if he's upset. I've decided to write an article on dodgy operations like the Circularian orphanage. If I can get a tie-in with the UNICEF hearing, all the better. By the way, I was wondering if you might be able to get me a press pass into the hearings?'

'Okay, I'll help you get your pass,' she said. 'Maybe we'll be able to help each other. But remember what I said about Koske. I've heard that the man he's hired to keep a watch on you has a reputation for violence, possibly even murder.'

CHAPTER 13

In the silence of the reading room of the National Archives, Riley tried to concentrate on his research papers, without much success. The conversation he'd had with Kazlana in her office worried him in spite of his bravado.

He'd been surprised to learn that she'd gone to Mombasa to check on her father's files there and to speak to Domingues. She'd said she'd found nothing to connect the Circularians to her father's death. Riley thought it odd that she'd even considered it a possibility.

He found Charlotte and suggested they take a lunch break.

'How's the research going?' he asked once they were seated with their food.

'At this early stage, I'm pleased,' she said. 'Luo oral history is so rich. Even today, their customs have a great effect on their political and social lives. For instance, many Luos won't join the military or the police. They fear that if they kill someone and are unable to be cleansed within the required time, they'll be damned for life.'

'Even in self-defence?'

'Not necessarily. The Luos were very aggressive and successful warriors — there was no dishonour in defending someone or something personal. But a wanton attack causing death is an abomination. The killer can't return to his home until he's been cleansed. If he does, the curse of the dead will be on him and his whole family for generations.'

'What does this cleansing consist of?' Mark asked, glad to be distracted from his own concerns.

'A medicine man can provide an antidote — a *manyasi* — but it doesn't work unless the person admits he was at fault.'

'Something like a Catholic's confessional?'

'Exactly.'

'And this is what you want to study while we're up country?'

'Yes, but I really need someone who's familiar with the Luo people — a guide. Preferably a Luo with connections in the Luo homeland around Kisumu.'

Riley nodded, but he had returned to thinking about his conversation with Kazlana, which had been playing on his mind.

He knew nothing about Koske, nor the power he could wield should he seriously want to prevent Riley from carrying out his research into the Circularian orphanage.

He found it hard to gauge what credence he could put in Kazlana's opinion that he was in danger as she was obviously convinced her father's death was no accident and possibly obsessed with finding those responsible. The situation could have affected her judgement but, unlike him, she was familiar with the shadier side of business dealings in the country.

From his experience in Indonesia he understood that law and order in a developing country could be quite different from what it was in places like Australia. In Kenya he simply had his gut instinct to follow, and after Kazlana's warning it was on high alert.

*   *   *

Charlotte drummed her fingers on her knee. Three lines of traffic stretched ahead of her down Kenyatta Avenue to the roundabout at Uhuru Highway. Periodically the whole mass of shimmering metal edged forward. It would be twenty minutes before her taxi reached the city; another twenty before she was at her next appointment on Dr Gilanga's list. She wound down the window to catch whatever breeze stirred among the traffic lanes.

The taxi driver twiddled the car radio tuner.

'... *In other news, the leader of the Orange Democratic*

Movement, Mr Raila Odinga, said in Kisumu yesterday that his supporters would man all polling booths in the country to ensure that the vote rigging that has been a part of recent Kenyan elections would not —'

He twiddled the tuner again to a station playing music that Charlotte found indescribable. She tried to ignore it, instead focusing on the young vendors wending their way through the stationary traffic with newspapers and magazines. The young man in her lane was tall and slender and wore his peaked cap at an angle. She thought she saw a similarity to the Luos she'd interviewed so far on Dr Gilanga's list.

The traffic shuffled forward and he gave her a most engaging smile as she passed. A moment later he was at her window.

'Good morning to you,' he said in a cheery voice.

Charlotte nodded. 'Morning.'

'*Daily Nation? Standard?*'

'No, thanks.'

'*HQ* magazine? *Women's Health? Professional Woman?*'

'No. Thank you.'

'English, right?'

She raised an eyebrow. How could he know where she was from after so few words had been spoken? She didn't want to encourage him and refrained from commenting.

'*New Statesman? Hello!* magazine?'

'I really don't want anything to read. Thank you.'

The traffic jam moved forward thirty metres.

He was back at her elbow again. 'That's Bamboo. Great hip-hop group. You like hip-hop?'

She guessed he was referring to the noise on the radio. 'No.'

'Why you not rent a car yourself? This taxi stinks,' he said, ignoring the driver who gave him a look. 'I can get you a very good car through my friend. Save money. You English ladies need a good car. Something safe and reliable.'

She couldn't help but smile. They were the exact words Dr Gilanga had used in his email before she'd left Oxford.

'That's right,' the boy said. 'English tourists need a good car. I know you an English lady. Right? Yes, I know.'

In spite of herself, she was enjoying the diversion from the boredom of the traffic jam. 'And I know you're a Luo. Right?'

She was pleased to see her guess stopped his prattle.

The line of cars moved forward and he trotted beside the taxi until it came to rest again.

'You want culture tour?' he said. 'I can fix everything for you. Bomas of Kenya. First-class show. My friend can get a minibus for you. Not far.'

A thought came to her. She looked carefully at the young man for the first time since he'd arrived at her window. He seemed friendly. Not the usual tout with an overwhelming and threatening physical presence. Good English. Clean.

'Yes, I think I might like a culture tour,' she said.

'You would?' The smile spread across his face.

'Today. Meet me at Lemon Tree Café. Three o'clock.'

'Very good. I bring my friend.'

'No. I just want to talk to you about what it means to be a Luo.'

'Me? You want to talk to me?'

'Yes, just a short chat. I can pay a little for your time.'

The line of traffic was moving again. It appeared likely that the taxi would make the roundabout and be gone.

The young man ran alongside the car. 'You pay to talk to me about being a Luo?' he asked.

'Yes. Three o'clock. Lemon Tree.'

The taxi swept into the roundabout, dodged a jaywalker, and accelerated to beat the cars encroaching into the intersection against the red light.

*   *   *

Joshua found Kwazi sitting on the steps of the memorial in Uhuru Park.

'Hey, Kwazi! Did you see that *mzungu* lady I was talking to?'
'No.'
'The one in the silver taxi.'
'I saw no *mzungu* lady. Not even one in a silver taxi.'
'*Haki ya mungu!* You should have seen her.'
Kwazi concentrated on his Wimpy burger with cheese.
'She was beautiful, I tell you.'
'So?' Kwazi sucked the sauce from his fingers one by one.
'She wants me to meet her at Lemon Tree Café.'
Kwazi paused in his search for a fallen piece of tomato.
'*Wewe wacha,*' he said, giving Joshua a sceptical look. 'You
think I'm stupid or what?'
'I swear.'
'Ha!'
'I was talking to her. Nicely. She said she didn't want
newspaper. No magazine. And she knew I was a Luo.'
'Everyone can see that, my friend.'
'But she's a *mzungu*. A tourist.'
'A tourist?'
'*Ndiyo.* So when she said she knew I was a Luo, I said I can
find a minibus to take her to Bomas, but she said, "No, I want
to talk about you. About being a Luo."'
'*Haki ya mungu!*' It was Kwazi's turn to swear.
Joshua grinned. 'It's very good, yes?'
'Yes.' Kwazi's reply was tentative; he'd clearly never heard of
such a thing. 'What do you think she really wants?'
'To know about the Luo.'
'That is very strange. I wonder if …' Kwazi grinned, then
burst into laughter.
Joshua stared. It was rare to see his friend laugh. Ever since
his accident and his disfigurement, Kwazi was reluctant to
distort his face further, even in humour.
'What are you laughing at?' he said, annoyed.
'Do you think …' Kwazi spluttered. 'Do you think she wants
to jiggy-jig with you?'

The expression on Joshua's face showed he found the idea preposterous. Still, Kwazi laughed and laughed, until his eyes ran.

'I don't know why you think it's so funny,' Joshua said.

'You and a *mzungu* lady!' And Kwazi started to laugh all over again.

Ignoring him, Joshua speculated aloud on what he should charge her for his time.

'She wants to pay you?' Kwazi asked incredulously.

Joshua felt vindicated. 'Of course.'

'Oh, oh, oh. Now we have to get serious, *bwana*. But what are you going to tell her? You know nothing about being Luo.'

Joshua shrugged. 'I'll find something. She's a tourist. How will she know I know nothing?'

*   *   *

Charlotte had finished her tea and was about to call for the bill when she saw the Luo boy standing indecisively at the door of the Lemon Tree Café. The owner was about to see him off, but he pointed to Charlotte, who waved him to her table. The proprietor simply shrugged and went on with his work.

'You're late,' she said. 'Take a seat.'

He sat opposite her, casting a glance around the café.

Charlotte was expecting an explanation or an apology, but he just grinned at her as he waited for her to begin. She introduced herself, and discovered that his name was Joshua Otieng.

'I suppose we should start by agreeing a price for your time,' she said.

'Yes.'

'What do you think is a fair price for maybe an hour?'

'Five hundred shillings,' he said promptly.

He'd obviously given the matter more thought than she had. Her rough calculation estimated it was less than five pounds, but she'd learnt enough about bargaining to know how to play the game.

'I think fifty is closer to a fair payment,' she countered.

'Okay. Three hundred.'

'A hundred. And another hundred if you have anything worthwhile for me.'

She held up her hand to show it was her last price, and pulled a hundred-shilling note from her purse and slid it under her empty teacup.

Joshua nodded solemnly.

'Now, to begin,' she said, opening her notebook. 'You're a Luo. And your parents are both Luo?'

'Of course.'

She made a note. 'And where were you born?'

'Serengeti.'

'The national park?'

'Um, quite near.'

'Curious,' she said, making another note. 'Where was your home?'

'Oh, it is such a small village.'

'Yes, but it must have a name.'

'A very small village.'

She waited, her pen poised.

A persistent fly buzzed around him and he swatted at it. 'It's called Lwang'ni Fuyo,' he said, spelling it for her.

'Lwang'ni Fuyo,' she wrote. 'And how old were you when you and your parents came to Nairobi?'

'I was, um … fourteen.'

'Fourteen? So you must remember your early life in Lwang'ni Fuyo quite well. I'm interested to know how your life in Nairobi differs from your childhood in Kisumu.'

He stared at her for some time.

Charlotte wondered if he'd understood. Perhaps he was reluctant to give out personal details.

'What I'm saying is, you must have been closer to Luo customs and traditions in Kisumu than in Nairobi, in which case, what has changed the most?'

He fumbled with the tattered cuff of his shirt and said nothing.

'For instance, social gatherings. How was your music there?'

'Oh, yes, music.'

'Tell me about it.'

'Yes. Plenty of music.'

'What instruments did the Luo people have?'

'We had the, um … the thing with the strings.'

'Its name?'

'We called it the *kum dudu*.'

'The *kum dudu*.' She made a note. 'And any drums?'

'Yes, we had the *mbongo*.'

'Anything like a flute?'

'Oh, yes. We had the *wafluti*.'

Charlotte then engaged him in a wide-ranging conversation about life in the small village of Lwang'ni Fuyo. She learnt that Joshua had been very active in his childhood. Much of his time was spent hunting with his father and uncles. Their quarry included lions, which they hunted to protect their cattle and sheep, and game — warthogs and zebra. He also recalled hunting antelope, but became confused when she asked him what species of antelope.

The village sounded idyllic. It was built on the banks of a swiftly flowing stream where fish abounded. Joshua was given the task of catching fish for the family of six. He was generally successful. On the hills behind the village was a thick forest where most of their hunting was done. Above the forest, at the very top of the hills, was a clearing and in the distance was a large lake.

'Lake Victoria?' she asked.

Joshua agreed.

She learnt that Joshua and his many friends in Lwang'ni Fuyo had enjoyed sport, particularly football.

'Do you still play football here in Nairobi?' she asked.

'I do. I am captain of the team.'

While he had been shy, even hesitant, when describing his life in his home village, football was obviously a keen interest. He explained the finer points of playing as his team's striker, their successes against all challengers, and his prospects for selection to join the national squad.

Charlotte had filled several pages of her notebook. She gave Joshua his hundred and another as a bonus. 'Thank you, Joshua, that was very helpful.' She flipped through several pages of her notes. 'You know, I may need to speak to you again. Would you be interested?'

He beamed. 'Of course!'

'But how will I contact you?'

'I have a mobile phone,' he said, digging into his pocket. 'It's new,' he said proudly.

'Well, let me have your number, and I'll call you if I need you again.'

'Also, if you need a guide, I am very available.'

'A guide?'

'For Nairobi. I can take you any place. I know Nairobi very well. And I am also your … how you say it? Your interpreter, if you want it.'

'You speak other languages?'

'Of course. English, Kiswahili, Dho-Luo, Kikuyu. Anything.'

'You can speak Kikuyu?'

He grinned. Turning to the proprietor, he rattled off a quick succession of words.

The proprietor nodded.

Charlotte asked him what Joshua had said.

'He asked me to tell you he can speak perfect Kikuyu.'

'Well … can he?'

'Yes.'

'What else did he say?'

The man looked a little embarrassed and then shrugged. 'He said you're a very pretty lady and also a smart lady to employ such a clever Luo boy to be her guide.'

*   *   *

Joshua marched down Kenyatta Avenue with a smile on his face, a double Wimpy in one hand and an ice-cold Pepsi in the other. The remainder of his two hundred shillings bulged and jingled in his pocket. He could hardly wait to tell Kwazi of his success and, more importantly, the joke he'd played on the *mzungu* lady.

The name he'd given to his invented musical instrument, the *kum dudu*, was based on his guess that she knew no Kiswahili. It could have been a costly prank had she known it meant 'insect'. He was also quite pleased with his completely imaginary *mbongo* and *wafluti*.

But his masterstroke was the name he'd given his mythical home village, which at least was a Dho-Luo phrase. Although he knew nothing of the Serengeti, he imagined that Lwang'ni Fuyo, or 'buzzing flies', was perhaps a more appropriate name for Kibera than for a village on the outskirts of the national park.

CHAPTER 14

The chairman heading the inquiry into Kenya's compliance with the Convention on the Rights of the Child, Judge Bernhard Hoffman, recently retired from the Austrian Constitutional Court, called the hearing to order with a rap of his gavel.

He ran his eye around Conference Room One in the Kenyatta International Conference Centre and waited for the whispered conversations to end.

Riley sat with the press corps, feeling slightly out of place among the raft of black journalists. Being the first of such hearings in Africa, the proceedings had attracted interest from neighbouring countries, where many thought similar scrutiny could be applied.

'Ladies and gentlemen,' the judge began, 'this is day three of our preliminary hearings in accordance with our charter to monitor the implementation of the Convention on the Rights of the Child by its state parties, in this case the Republic of Kenya. I ask the counsel assisting to call the first witness.'

When the lunch recess was called, Riley decided to call it a day. The morning had been interesting, but the afternoon session was set aside for procedural matters, during which the various government departments and agencies were expected to engage in turf wars.

As he entered the car park, he noticed a couple of men climbing into a blue Peugeot parked near the gate. The same men had arrived exactly when he had earlier that morning.

He shook his head in dismissal. Kazlana's paranoia was getting to him.

* * *

Charlotte and Mark had developed a routine of meeting for a sundowner in the Panafric's combined coffee shop and bar. It was a leafy space, sufficiently removed from the noise of nearby Valley Road to enjoy some peace.

Mark emitted a long sigh after taking a sip of his whisky soda. 'Ahh … now if I could just have a cigarette …'

'Oh, please — just have one if you're so strung out.' Charlotte found his simulated martyrdom irritating.

'No, I'll be good. I can keep a lid on it most times. It just gets really tough when I'm having a drink,' he said.

'Perhaps there's a message there.'

'Huh?'

'Maybe you're drinking too much.'

'Is that possible?' he asked, grinning.

'All I'm saying is you always seem to have a glass in your hand.'

She wondered if she'd gone too far, but he answered her mildly enough.

'I haven't seen you refusing the odd glass of wine.'

It was her turn to grin. 'That's because you've corrupted me, Mark Riley. I barely drank at all until I came to Africa. Now I'm clinking glasses almost daily.'

'At least you're not craving a cigarette.'

She rolled her eyes. 'Put it from your mind. Tell me about your research. How's it going?'

'It's going very well. I spent the morning at the UNICEF hearing. It's given me an idea to expand the scope of my article about Jafari and this possible adoption racket into an investigation of crimes against children in the whole region. This morning I heard about children being smuggled over borders to work in brothels, and I spoke to a Ugandan journo who told me about the Lord's Army — they've been kidnapping kids for more than a decade and forcing them to fight. Nothing's being done about it.'

'That's awful,' she said, although she was wondering if the

article was taking over from the novel. Maybe he would change his mind about accompanying her up country. 'But I was actually referring to the research for your novel.'

'Oh! I see ... Well, I think I'm done at the National Archives. I've found a great link connecting the Maasai characters, the colonial administration and the settlers.' He explained how he'd discovered that the warrior in her thesis had been involved in a situation that brought him into contact with the British system of justice. 'He's the character I need to carry the narrative of the great battle between the settlers and the tribes. Parsaloi Ole Gilisho will be my protagonist, just as Eddie Mabo was in my first novel.'

'I see ... So does this mean you don't need to do your research in Maasailand?'

Mark shook his head. 'There's no way I'll get any idea of Ole Gilisho's life from what's in the National Archives. As far as I can see, he's a man virtually unknown outside his own people. He's hardly mentioned in the protectorate's history. That means it's even more important to talk to the Maasai elders who know the tribe's oral history — they can fill me in.'

Charlotte felt relief wash over her. 'That's good to hear. And the timing couldn't be better. I'm ready too.'

'When do we leave?'

'Well, I was thinking about what Dr Gilanga advised.'

'Which is ...?'

'To take a short break before getting into the real work. He's suggested we do a few game parks. Even the Serengeti.'

'How would that fit in with what we have planned?' he asked.

'I've worked out a possible itinerary.' She hunted inside her backpack and opened her diary. 'Our first stop could be Lake Nakuru National Park. Then through the Great Rift Valley, picking up the first of your Maasai reservation sites on the way. Then through the Masai Mara to the Serengeti.' She checked to see how he was receiving the idea before continuing. 'On the way back I can visit Kisumu and other places in the Luo country.' She looked at him. 'How's that sound to you?'

'Sounds good,' he said.

'And I think I have a guide for us.'

'A guide?'

'Dr Gilanga says it's pretty important to have a local translator. Someone who knows the area. I've met a Luo boy — I'd say he's about eighteen or so — who speaks a number of languages fluently. And even better, he was born and raised near the Serengeti. I think he might be interested, for a small fee.'

Charlotte filled him in on the details.

'A street kid?' Mark said.

'He lives in Kibera. But he seems quite well-behaved.'

* * *

Joshua gathered the thirty or so young men around him in the centre of the football pitch. It was Sunday morning. He had sent a group text message calling his team-mates, reserve players and the handful who acted as sundry helpers on game days to an important team meeting. They had won their game the previous day and so the turnout was better than usual. Everyone was in good spirits.

Joshua spent some time recalling the high points of their victory the day before, and by the time he'd finished there was a buzz of enthusiastic camaraderie among the group. It was exactly as he'd planned, for he had matters other than football in mind.

He held up his hands for silence, and, like an orchestra leader, waited until there was complete hush before he began.

'*Sawasawa*. All right. It was a good win. A good victory. We Luos showed the others how to play football. *Si ndiyo?*'

'*Ndiyo!*' they chorused.

He let the self-congratulatory clamour run its course.

'Yes, we played well. We tried hard and we can be satisfied

with our victory. But there is more to do. And I am not talking about football now.' He ran his eyes around the group. 'It is not enough that we Luos can prove ourselves on the football pitch. There is much more to do. We must find a man who will stand for us in the high places. We need someone to speak for us in the government — a Luo man. How many Luos do you know who have money?'

The group exchanged glances. Many shrugged.

'That's right. Not many. But what about the Kikuyu? Who runs most of the stalls in Toi Market? Who owns the biggest businesses in Nairobi? And who has the biggest farms in the Rift Valley?'

Joshua had no real knowledge of these matters, but it was Koske's words he used. And they seemed to be working. The young men were grumbling among themselves.

'How many times have you seen a job come and each time it is a Kikuyu who gets it?'

The rumblings of discontent grew.

'Are you happy with this?'

'No!' they chimed.

'That is why we — all of us — must take action!'

The group was animated now, crowing in support of Joshua's every suggestion.

'We will make changes happen in Kibera. More work for the Luos. More prosperity for our people. More money for our people!'

The young men hooted in agreement.

'To do this we must see that a Luo is our leader, not only in Kibera but for all of Kenya. Raila Odinga is our man. Our Luo leader. We must help him beat the Kikuyu Kibaki. We will go and talk to everyone here in Kibera. We will tell everyone that our only hope is with Raila.' He ran his eye over the group. They were excited.

'Raila for president!' Joshua said, raising his fist.

'Raila for president!' they said.

'Raila for president!' he repeated, punching the air.

'Raila for president!' they yelled, and a host of fists punched the air.

* * *

Joshua was at the head of his Siafu team-mates. Their name came from the fiery ants that overpowered their quarry by sheer weight of numbers. It was Saturday and the press of shoppers in the tight pathways between the tiny iron-clad stalls of busy Toi Market made for slow going until they began their chanting.

'No Raila — No Peace ... No Raila — No Peace ...' they sang.

People pressed back out of their path.

'No Raila — No Peace ...'

Many of the stall-holders were intimidated by the show of strength, but a few told the young men to be off. They said there was no need for politics in the Toi Market.

Koske had prepared Joshua for such an outcome.

'You Kikuyus have taken too much from us. No more!' he yelled. 'No Raila — No Peace!' And he immediately charged to the nearest stall and upended its entire stack of fruit.

His Siafu friends whooped in joy and joined him, tipping racks of clothes and shoes into the mud. Many of the stall-owners resisted, but with little effect. Soon there was a mêlée, with the young footballers beating up the Kikuyu and tearing down their displays.

A whistle blast pierced the clamour of voices. Joshua noticed the Maasai security guards forming in numbers among the stalls surrounding them and called to his Siafu team members to retreat. More stalls were upset in the chase through the market that followed. The Maasai *askaris* shouted threats and waved their heavy wooden *rungus* in the air, but they could not catch the Siafu boys.

Back in Kisumu Ndogo, the young men joked with great bravado about their adventure. Joshua was delighted with the exercise. Koske would hear of it and be pleased. In time, the Siafu would be offered more interesting assignments and receive more rewarding payments than a few pairs of cheap Chinese football boots.

CHAPTER 15

Simon sighed as he lowered himself to the broken cement block that his friend's customers sat on while awaiting their shoe repairs. Behind Dede, the cobbler, was a sheet-iron wall holding racks of decrepit shoes. Above him, but not high enough so he could stand under it, was another sheet of corrugated iron to shelter him from the rain or scorching sun. The *duka* was no more than three metres by two and filled with the tangy-sweet smell of leather and glue.

'*Habari yako?*' Dede asked around a mouthful of tacks.

'*Mzuri,*' Simon replied desultorily while rubbing the knuckles of his right hand; the old break still gave him trouble after all these years.

The cobbler looked up from his work. 'Hmm ... You sound like you are carrying a stone on your shoulders.'

Dede had been Simon's friend for years. He had the typical Luo build, only his was generally described as long, rather than tall, as there were few who had seen him unfurled from his crouch over somebody else's shoes. Dede was his nickname, derived from the grasshopper he resembled while squatting over his last, the knees of his long legs around his ears.

'What can I say?' Simon replied. 'Would you hear a long story about a stupid man who has chased his son from his house?'

Dede spat the tacks into his hand. 'Joshua?'

Simon turned his hands up in a gesture of acquiescence.

'He's always been a strong-minded boy.'

When Joshua was seven and Charity five, Nellie had been born. Patience, Simon's wife, had decided she needed to earn money so they could find a larger place. She had begun to collect discarded items from among the comfortable houses of Kileleshwa and Lavington estates and, with Joshua's help, sold them outside the markets or at the side of the road. Faith had arrived two years later and Joshua, at age nine, having ignored his two sisters to that time, suddenly assumed the role of protector of all three. He fussed over them and scolded them if they didn't take care. When out with their mother, it was he who kept them in sight and shepherded them along like a sheepdog with three little lambs. The neighbourhood never referred to the Otieng children by name. Because they always seemed to be together, they became known collectively as 'Joshua and the girls'.

'But a good boy,' Dede continued. 'Didn't he organise a *harambee* for the football team? And that was when he was just a *toto*. The money he raised bought beautiful football boots.'

'Tee-shirts.'

'What?'

'He raised money for football tee-shirts. So the team would look more professional in their competition games.'

'Yes! I remember. A good boy, I tell you.'

Simon's silence made Dede shake his head. He dropped the spit-coated tacks from his hand into an old tobacco tin. 'What troubles the boy?' he asked.

'The same troubles. We share the same terrible memories.'

'But you know more about those things than the boy does, Simon. You must try to explain things to him.'

Simon looked into his friend's grave eyes. They were bloodshot from many years of fine work in poor light.

'I've resisted telling him for so long. Now, when I realised my error and tried to tell him, he wouldn't listen.' Simon absent-mindedly pulled at strands of his hair as if he were plucking a chicken. 'He ran off in the middle of the night.'

'Then you must find him and speak your mind. Where is he?'

'I don't know.'

'Where have you looked?'

'Kisumu Ndogo, of course. This morning I didn't go looking for work; instead, I went to Mashimoni on the other side of Kibera. I don't know why. People there are not talking to strangers. Now that the elections are starting, there's so much suspicion about people from our side.'

'He'll be around somewhere,' Dede offered in encouragement.

'He's around, yes. People have seen him. But no one knows where he sleeps.'

'Maybe he stays with a friend? Someone will know.'

Simon shook his head in despair.

'Mama Hamza,' Dede said.

'What?'

'Mama Hamza will know. She knows Kibera. She'll know where your boy is.'

'Who is this Mama Hamza?'

'A Nubian, of course. And she knows every woman in Kibera.'

At Simon's look of incredulity, Dede added, 'Well, she knows many. And if you want to know what's going on in Kibera, you must ask the women. Does any man doubt how much they can talk?' The cobbler nodded his head by way of emphasis. 'Mama Hamza, I tell you. She listens to the women. She knows everything about Kibera.'

* * *

Simon had met many people in Kibera whom he'd assumed to be old but had later been surprised to learn their true age. Years of poor hygiene, inadequate food, misfortune and escalating hardships showed in the skin of most residents of the slum: it became grey and lustreless and deep lines appeared, like crevasses on a water-worn hillside. Eyes clouded and hair became lank. Those who had no spirit to continue the daily battle succumbed.

Mama Hamza was old in years, but she was far from beaten. When Simon introduced himself, her agile eyes searched his face and then his soul as she probed him with questions. They seemed to be more about Simon himself than his missing son, but his concern about Joshua encouraged him to press on.

He answered quickly — too quickly, it seemed to him — but in his search for her he'd heard so much of her work helping others that he worried that she might have little time to spare for him, a person with such trivial problems.

There was no doubt that Mama Hamza was a Nubian. Her shining jet-black skin, her silver loop earrings and colourful headscarf, her bold-patterned white dress with the big red rose motif — all these were the colourful trademarks of her people. Her age showed in the gaps between the few large teeth that still adorned her generous mouth.

The Nubians were the original landholders of the area now known as Kibera. After the Great War, the Nubian soldiers were demobbed in what was to become the colony of Kenya. They reminded their British leaders that they had faithfully served the mother country against the Germans in Africa and elsewhere, and would it not be reasonable to expect a stipend in the form of some land where they could settle? They were, after all, British servants and, under the colonists' own definitions, 'landless natives'. The administrators were forced to agree.

To the south-west of Nairobi, where the railway tracks first rose from the swamplands surrounding the new township, was a forest. It was land totally unsuited for farming and therefore of no use to the settlers the British hoped to attract to the colony. The Nubian soldiers were told they could have the forest — the *kibra* as it was called in Nubian. However, no title was issued to formalise the bequest and the Nubians never thought to ask. Fifty years later, the colony of Kenya gained its independence and the *kibra* became Kibera — a desirable piece of land on the very edge of the burgeoning capital. But still there was no title and all two and a half square kilometres of the area remained without administration and largely unmanageable.

Those with connections to the new positions of power began gradually to acquire control over Kibera. The Nubians were warriors before they became foot soldiers for the British; they had never been businessmen and didn't realise the value of their estates. They preferred to exchange their surplus land for more useful things like money or goods. Soon they were reduced to tenants on an ever-diminishing portion of their original forested inheritance.

'Why have you come to me?' Mama Hamza asked after Simon had finished telling her about his runaway son. 'What would you say to him if you found him?'

'There is so much ...'

'What would you say?' she persisted.

'I would tell him the truth.'

The old woman's eyes twinkled. 'What is the truth?'

He began to explain what had happened in 2002, but she waved her hand at him.

'We all have our idea of what is the truth,' she said. 'I know this much. There was madness in Kibera that night. Rape. Looting and burning. You would do well to remember that madness before you ask your son to understand what you call the truth. Do you know what happened that night, Simon?'

He had thought he knew exactly what had happened, but the way she posed the question made him wonder if in fact he did. Perhaps his memory had caused him to misinterpret the events of that unforgettable night. Even now, after five painful years, his recollections were too horrible to relive. He was old enough to know that time could distort the truth, particularly if the memory was painful. Surely, he couldn't be mistaken, but there could always be doubt.

'I think so,' he said at last.

'Then you should find your son and tell him what you believe to be the truth.'

'Do you know where I can find him?'

'Kibera is still a very large forest. A forest of people. Who can

146

say where one boy can hide if he chooses to remain hidden? There are more places to hide than leaves on the trees.' Her wrinkled eyes creased, revealing the many smile lines. 'But I will ask the women for you.'

* * *

Mama Hamza followed Kibera Drive as far as she could before entering into the maze of narrow, unpaved alleys that snaked among the slab huts, lean-tos and shacks that comprised the majority of housing in the slum settlement.

Kibera Drive was a useful pedestrian highway, but the people whom Mama Hamza needed to talk to were not to be found there. They were in the alleys where the brief greeting became a chat that almost always led on to more weighty matters. Was it true that the police had rounded up dozens of Odinga supporters? Had she heard about the carpenter with seven children who had been shot during a demonstration in Makina? Courtesy decreed that none of the gossip was treated as trivial.

Occasionally she met folk who gave her more useful information — like Jared, a short-order chef at a local hotel, who had bought buckets, squeegees and sponges for a group of local youths to form a car-wash service on Ngong Road. Like many within the slum, Jared was a good-hearted person who did what he could for the community. He had noticed that a few of the local boys were getting into mischief, and worse, and had decided to do something about it. Although struggling to raise his own young family, he took no share of the boys' income; instead, he distributed it among them, keeping a small portion for future improvements. Mama Hamza had been helping Jared to get council approval for a power outlet so the young men could operate a steam carpet-cleaner to improve their services. As usual, the council were less than helpful. Jared was loath to use the youths' hard-earned cash on a bribe, but that appeared to be the only way to go. Mama Hamza had promised to speak to someone on his behalf. She gave Jared an account of her meetings, which appeared to be achieving some positive results, and hurried on.

There was more talk as she went, much of it about the forthcoming elections. Would the counting be conducted fairly this time? What did Mama Hamza think of this or that candidate? She tried to keep her replies non-committal. It paid to be discreet in such matters. Her community consisted of women from all tribes and political leanings.

The underlying concern was whether the election process could be completed without the violence of 2002. Mama Hamza was careful to be reassuring, but her true thoughts were not so confident. The broad network that extended from her own Kibera Women's Association to the larger Kibera population formed a barometer of local public sentiment. In 2002, the women had expected violence during the election campaign and polling. When it was so, they were shocked but not surprised. Now, it seemed history may be about to repeat itself. Last week, Mama Hamza had heard that a *duka* used by a Kikuyu man to sell second-hand clothing had been set alight during the night. Two days later, a Kisii hairdresser's shack had been robbed before it too was burnt. It had begun again. She could only pray to Allah that the end results would not be the same this time.

She crossed the railway line and followed the path down the hill. It hadn't taken her long to find where Joshua Otieng was living. A Nubian friend — one of the women on the community security committee whose duty it was to know about the itinerants in the area — knew Joshua's friend Kwazi. Kwazi had been a recipient of the women's charity when he was orphaned at age four and again when he received his disfiguring injuries at age twelve. When Joshua moved in to share Kwazi's shack in Kianda, the Nubian woman knew of his presence.

Mama Hamza was weary by the time she reached Kwazi's shack, and disappointed when she received no response to her calls of *habari*.

She poked her head into the opening. A voice that came from behind startled her.

'There is nothing in there to steal, old woman.'

She swung around to find a fine-looking young man grinning at her.

'It would not be Kibera if you had something to steal, young Joshua.'

His smile was quickly replaced by a frown. 'So, my father is sending old women to talk to me?'

She ignored his tone and said, 'I am Fatima. People call me Mama Hamza.'

Joshua nodded. 'I have heard of you.'

'I was hoping I'd find you here, but I am sorry I looked into your shelter.'

He nodded, remaining aloof.

'I know your friend Gabriel,' she said. 'You call him Kwazi.' Ignoring his silence, she went on. 'I see him from time to time. He often speaks of you.'

Again he made no response.

She would not relent. 'He is very popular in Kibera. He can go anywhere; speak with anyone. Kikuyu, Kisii, Luo, Kamba.'

'Kwazi says tribes make all the trouble. He says we should forget all our tribal things.'

'Hmm … Maybe Kwazi is correct. But, I think, also wrong. It's good to know about our customs and heritage. We should be aware of our dances and songs. We should enjoy them. There is much to respect and be proud of among our many tribes, but it is bad if we cannot respect one another's customs. It is bad if this brings about hatred of the people who celebrate them.'

Mama Hamza fell silent and appraised the young man standing before her. He was exactly as she had imagined him following her discussion with his father: proud, determined, confident. Like many of the young men she now saw leading the gangs in Kibera, he was probably full of his own opinions, ignoring all others. She could see the difficulty his father would have trying to encourage any discussion with him. Like many in this modern age, he had no respect for the wisdom of his elders.

'Your father is worried about you, Joshua,' she said simply.

'He cares nothing for me.'

'How can you say that? What father does not care for one of his own?'

'My father is a coward who will not fight for what is right.'

She nodded that she understood his feelings.

'If you know me, if you know what we do in the Kibera Women's Association, you will understand that I mix with many, many people who come from all over Kenya. I know all the tribes. I know their customs, their stories, their history. There is nobody who can say one tribe's customs are better than another's. We try to teach people to understand one another by knowing something about the other person's customs and by sharing them.' She paused. 'I know a lot about the Luo people, Joshua.'

For a fleeting moment Mama Hamza caught a glimpse of interest behind Joshua's stern defences, but he quickly concealed it with a sarcastic sneer.

'Nobody can know about all the tribes,' he said. 'There are too many.'

Her gaze didn't falter under his surly expression. 'I know things about the Luo that your father and your father's father know.'

He stared at her before turning to look at the smouldering refuse heap some way down the alley. He studied it to avoid her gaze, but she could see she had piqued his interest.

'I have heard something about the Luo,' he said, keeping his attention on the fire. 'I have heard that it is important for a Luo person to be cleansed after the death of another.'

'Cleansing is a very important ceremony. Without a proper cleansing the person will suffer very bad luck throughout his life. He will have no peace in this life or the next.'

'But it is just a children's story,' he said with a dismissive gesture. 'Isn't it?'

'I have only heard about it from Luos. You would need to ask a Luo about the truth of it.'

'Is this cleansing ceremony important even if the person is a boy at the time of the death?'

She shrugged. 'I believe so.'

Although he continued to stare into the smoke, she could tell he wanted to know more but couldn't ask.

'Your father was responsible for the death of a friend,' she said.

It was a guess, but over the years she had learnt to see into people, particularly those with a troubled past. She had looked into Simon Otieng's eyes when they met and seen in him something that brought trouble to his heart.

Joshua nodded.

'He worries about you, Joshua,' she said. 'Perhaps he worries that you will be involved in violence and suffer the curse of an uncleansed death as he has.'

Joshua turned from the smouldering waste. 'He *should* worry. There will be violence, yes, but it will not fall on me. It will be on people who refuse to defend what is important. It will fall on the cowards who reject their duty.'

He started to go, but turned back to her. 'And if you are not careful, it will also fall on you, old woman. You and your women's association are foolish, because it is not possible to be a friend to all people, all tribes. Not these days. You must choose your friends and stay close to them. All others are enemies. You cannot try to remain in the middle. You will be cut to pieces.'

CHAPTER 16

Joshua had slept poorly and felt vaguely troubled all morning. Mama Hamza's visit had annoyed him more than it should. She brought an unwelcome reminder of his father and had stirred uncertainties that Mayasa had earlier kindled.

He roamed among the alleys, chatting to friends until mid-afternoon, then became irritated by his inability to make a decision about the plan he'd been hatching all day.

He marched along Ngong Road, gathering his thoughts. Ten minutes later he was walking boldly through Adams Arcade as if he were a regular customer, refusing to make eye contact with the security guards. He strode through the auto swing gate of the supermarket and grabbed a plastic shopping basket from the stack.

Once inside, he wasn't so confident. He moved around the aisles mulling over the speech he'd prepared in his head. It didn't sound to him quite as eloquent now that he was about to deliver it. Nor as succinct. It had to be brief as he would be in a line of shoppers and he didn't want to attract the attention of the guards any more than usual.

He stood in line at Mayasa's register, a packet of Tic Tacs the only item in his basket, and watched her as she served the women ahead of him. She was very efficient, swiping the items under the barcode reader while her fingers flew over the keys. He gained confidence by his anonymity. He would have the advantage of surprise when he reached the register. He would be able to get his message out before she was able to gather her thoughts.

The woman ahead of him collected her receipt and pushed her shopping trolley out into the mall.

Mayasa slid Joshua's basket towards her and said, 'Is that all, Joshua?'

'Yes ... um, no.' She hadn't even looked up at him. 'About the other day —'

'That'll be five shillings fifty.'

'I just wanted to say —'

'Five shillings fifty,' she repeated, and under her breath whispered, 'I get off in fifteen minutes. Wait for me at Java House.'

Joshua was out in the mall with his Tic Tacs before he really understood what had happened.

* * *

Mayasa found Joshua sitting at an outside table at the far end of Java Coffee House. He saw her coming and smiled sheepishly as she sat down beside him.

'*Habari*,' he said.

'*Mzuri*.'

'You are finished working?'

'I finish early on Thursdays; later on Fridays.'

'I see,' he said, toying with the sugar packets.

The waitress came to their table and asked if they wanted to order. They said no. She fussed around them, cleaning and straightening tables.

'We'd better go,' Mayasa said.

'I'll walk home with you.'

'I'll come to your place,' she said, trying to sound offhand. 'I'll say hello to Kwazi.'

'He's gone to visit a friend,' he replied, and explained how the man had been seriously burnt while trying to extinguish a fire. 'They set alight his *duka* in Siranga.'

'That's awful,' she said. 'Who are "they"?'

He shrugged.

'There's so much violence like that,' she said. 'I hear about it all the time at Adams Arcade. They say it's just like the last time, in 2002.'

'No. We are in control now.'

She hesitated a moment, unsure if it would be safe to raise the matter that had led to their previous argument. Then she decided she couldn't continue to be concerned about him if he couldn't see the danger he was in.

'Who is this "we"?' she asked, knowing he meant Koske and his thugs.

'I know you don't trust Koske, and neither do I,' Joshua said.

'Then why do you deal with him?'

'I don't like the way he gets his money, but he's on Raila's side. He helps us get supporters for Raila and the ODM.'

'But why do you have to be so close to him? Can't someone else do his work?'

'Koske helps our football team,' Joshua explained. 'He looks after us.'

Mayasa gave him a quizzical look.

'He also has contacts.'

'Contacts?'

'In the National Football Association. He knows people who make selections for the national squad.'

She knew little about football, but enough to understand that Joshua had some skills in that regard. 'So you believe he can get you selected for the national training squad?'

Embarrassed, Joshua retreated a little, but left her in no doubt that national selection was his goal. She was surprised and pleased that he had ambition. Perhaps it would get him away from his obsession with politics and the dangers that entailed.

'You're good, Joshua. Very good. If anyone can get selected, you can.'

Upon seeing her enthusiasm, he brightened. 'You think so? Koske said he might be able to arrange a game in front of the national selectors. I'll get my chance.'

'That's wonderful. And if you get selected, what happens then?'

He told her about the training camps, usually conducted somewhere outside Nairobi — the food and accommodation provided by real hotels — and the chance to play trial games against teams from other countries.

'And if I get picked for the national team, I get paid to play football!'

'You'll do it,' she said. 'I know you'll do it.'

They continued to talk all the way to Kwazi's shack.

'We're here,' Mayasa said.

'But I was going to walk you home.'

'There's no need. I can get there myself.'

'Yes, but I'd like to know where you live. I'll walk with you.'

'No.'

She knew she'd said it too hurriedly. And it came out far more vehemently than she'd intended.

Joshua was silent.

She tried to cover her rudeness. 'Will I see you tomorrow?' she asked.

He mumbled that he would probably be around.

They continued to make an effort at conversation, but it was strained. In the end she gave up the pretence and said goodbye. She paused for a moment, wanting to kiss him if for no other reason than to undo her tactlessness, but he kept his eyes averted.

She walked home, hating herself for not revealing as much of herself as Joshua had of himself to her.

* * *

Fridays were always difficult — Mayasa had a long shift at the supermarket, finishing at ten. Today, it had felt extra long, and miserable. Joshua had said he would come to see her and he hadn't.

She walked wearily up the hill and reached the alley that led to where she and her father shared their shack. She peered into the alleyway's forbidding gloom. It was her home neighbourhood and she had walked down the alley late at night many times before. Yet tonight she felt nervous about entering its confined spaces.

She summoned her courage and entered the darkness. Chinks of light escaped the shuttered window openings and closed doors. Muffled voices came from within the shacks but otherwise it was quiet. Kianda seemed to have shrunk into itself at night since the political campaigners had begun their exuberant marches through Kibera. Perhaps it was the same in other parts of the settlement too.

Mayasa became aware of faint footsteps behind her. She peered into the murkiness but could see nothing. She hurried on, using the remembered stepping stones of daylight hours to avoid the filth. The footsteps hurried too. She turned again and glimpsed a tall figure as he passed a slanting column of light. He was approaching fast.

Her heart leapt in her chest. Her house was only a minute away. But then she recalled it was Friday and her father was visiting her sister as was the custom. She could make it home, but she would be alone there. For a brief moment she considered banging on a door, any door, but she was afraid that door might be slammed in her face. She didn't know what to expect from people any more. Even family members had become distant after learning about her father.

At her door, in the darkness, she fumbled with the key. In her panic it almost slipped from her trembling fingers. The key wouldn't fit into the padlock, then she realised she had it the wrong way around.

The man rounded the bend, fifty metres away. She could hear his footsteps pounding in the mud.

The padlock clicked and she ripped it open. Inside the shack, she slammed the door and slid the bolt into place.

She could barely hear anything above the beating of her heart, but she knew the man was nearing the house.

At the door — knocking.

'Mayasa!'

The realisation that he knew her name terrified her.

'Mayasa, it's me. Joshua.'

She almost collapsed with relief. Regaining her composure a little, she opened the door. It was dark, but she knew it was Joshua. His voice, his build, the outline of his body, all had become familiar to her. She flung her arms around him and buried her face in his chest. It felt good to hold him.

He grabbed her shoulders and pushed her from him. 'What is it? Why are you hiding from me?' he demanded.

'Hiding? I'm not hiding from you.'

'Yesterday I told you I was sorry for what I did, but you didn't forgive me at all. You ... you pushed me away.'

'But I did forgive you. It wasn't that. I —'

'I thought we were friends,' he said. His voice was lower but there was still an edge to it.

'We are friends. Aren't we?'

'Then why didn't you let me walk you home? Are you ashamed to be seen with a Luo?'

'No. I'm not ashamed of you. How could I be ashamed of you? I ... I like you.'

It was dark, but her eyes were becoming accustomed to it. She tried to read his face. His breathing subsided and she sensed the heat of his anger fade.

'You like me?' he asked, his voice now just a whisper.

'I do. Very much.' She put her hand on his chest. His heart thumped against it.

He moved tentatively towards her. She slid her arms around him and felt his muscles ripple under her hands. His body was hard against her and he lowered his face and kissed her.

She drew him in, pushing the door closed behind him. He almost fell on her as they stumbled together into the darkened room. She muffled a giggle. He laughed. They kissed again, more urgently.

'Your father …?'

'He won't be home,' she said, barely able to take her lips from his to answer.

She felt a rush of excitement as Joshua's hands went to her breasts. But even as the excitement rose and he was undressing her, she felt torn. She knew she should reveal her secret, that it was unfair to let him go on, but his hands were now on her bare skin and she could feel his excitement through his jeans.

In the darkness he fumbled with her clothing and his, muttering as he stumbled to remove his obstinate shoes. When he returned to her arms she felt the thrill of his naked body press against hers. She helped him remove her jeans and panties and his trembling hands explored her.

'Come,' she said, leading him towards her bed.

'Oh!' he muttered as he stubbed his toe.

They giggled together.

She pulled him down beside her and, too soon, his hands were gone and his body was over her and then his weight was on her.

She gasped as he entered her.

*   *   *

Joshua lay beside her in sleep, his arm across her belly, his mouth close enough that she could feel the soft caress of his breath on her ear — like whispers from his soul. But they revealed nothing of what he might feel when she told him her secret.

He had fallen asleep quickly, confirming her belief that he had no worries to trouble his mind. Mayasa had no such luxury. She lay in the silence, staring into the hovering darkness that threatened to smother her. The more she gave thought to her worries, the more they seemed to have no solution.

What would he do when he learnt the truth? Most people couldn't understand it, and everyone she met feared it. Maybe Joshua would be fearful too. And unforgiving about her dishonesty.

Mayasa was now trapped in her deception. She should have taken the time to explain at the beginning. How could she now reveal that her father had AIDS — a truth so terrible that it had kept friends and even family at bay?

She felt she could be happy with this proud, impetuous Luo boy, but because of her weakness she might lose him. If she had told Joshua about her father at the outset, he might have gone his own way before her feelings for him had grown stronger. Before she had realised that she loved him.

CHAPTER 17

'What time was he supposed to be here?' Mark asked.

'I said around five.' Charlotte glanced at her watch for about the third time since five o'clock. For some reason she felt responsible for Joshua's behaviour. 'I'm sure he won't be long.'

She had the impression that Mark didn't really agree they needed a guide. If he were anything like Bradley, he probably thought it reflected poorly upon his masculinity.

'I hope he's a bit more reliable if we find ourselves treed by a Serengeti lion,' he said.

'You know quite well he's not that kind of guide. He has my mobile number. I'm sure he'd ring if — oh, there he is.'

Joshua, looking a little apprehensive, stood in the opening to the Panafric's garden. He searched the tables and when he spotted Charlotte his expression brightened. Grinning, he came towards them with a loping, swaying motion. He might have been acting the part of a hip-hop artist on MTV. She was pleased to see he wore a clean pair of jeans and sneakers. His hanging tee-shirt reached halfway down his thighs, and when he arrived at their table he stood loose-kneed with his hands on his hips as Charlotte made the introductions.

Mark shook his hand and then sat back to study him. Charlotte placed an order for a round of soft drinks.

Before they arrived, Mark took charge of the discussion, as Charlotte had hoped he would.

'Charlotte said you were born in a small village near the Serengeti. What did your father do for a living?'

'My father was a worker for the Serengeti National Park. A driver.'

'That's interesting,' Mark said. 'What was his job?'

'He drove a Bedford truck. He would take the truck for deliveries.'

'I see.' Mark tapped his fingers together thoughtfully. 'Do you mean he was a driver employed by the rangers to bring materials into the park?'

'Yes.'

Charlotte sensed Mark was testing the boy. She thought that Joshua might have realised this too because he answered carefully without the Nairobi–Kiswahili inflections he had used when he'd spoken to her in the traffic jam on Kenyatta Avenue.

'Are you familiar with the national park?' Mark asked.

'Oh, yes. I went often into the park with my father. He would drive his old *rukwama* — sorry, I mean the Bedford truck — into the park. We would stop maybe on a hill and take our lunch. You should have seen the animals there. It was such a beautiful place with so-o-o many animals. We would see gazelle — there were always gazelle. And zebra. And many, many ostriches. And there were —'

'Charlotte probably told you we want to take a tour of the Serengeti before we go to Kisumu. Do you know Kisumu?'

'Oh, yes. It's my homeland.' Joshua paused to take a long drink from his creamy soda.

Charlotte intervened. 'Do we really need Joshua to be our guide in the park, Mark? We have maps. I think what we really need is someone to be our translator. Joshua, tell Mark the languages you speak.'

Joshua recited his impressive credentials.

Mark seemed appeased, but Joshua had warmed to his subject. 'And do you know, Mr Mark, one day we parked under a tree and a lion jumped out. It was very exciting, you know.'

'I'm sure it must have been. Now, can we discuss money?'

'And another time, we saw ma-a-a-ny elephants. Oh, so many.'

'Great, now about payment.'

After a little haggling, Joshua seemed surprisingly content with the fee Mark suggested. It made her deal for an hour of his time quite preposterous.

Charlotte confirmed she would call Joshua when they had a departure date in mind and he loped off the way he'd come.

'Not a bad kid,' Mark said. 'I'm glad we decided to take a guide.'

Charlotte let the comment go. There was something about men and the way they had to lay claim to all the good ideas that she found extremely irritating. Instead, she focused on achieving her objective of travelling up country. So far, all was proceeding well.

* * *

Joshua was delighted about the upcoming trip. Not only would he be able to visit the Serengeti National Park — a dream he had held since childhood — he would be paid to do so while sitting in a car feeling important.

He told Kwazi about the trip. He told his football team-mates and supporters. He would tell Mayasa when next he saw her. It would have pleased him to tell his father, but he would not lower himself to knock on his door. He thought it most probable that Simon would hear about it eventually anyway.

Koske was furious at the news. He called Joshua a coward for running before the battle had begun. He said he showed great disrespect for Koske himself — a man who had spent so much of his valuable time and money on the football team that Joshua represented. Hadn't he always had Joshua's welfare at heart, even sending one of the leading football scouts to see him in action? Koske said he was hurt to see how little loyalty he received, considering all the good things he'd done for Joshua.

'Yes, Mr Koske,' Joshua replied.

'Yes, what?' Koske demanded.

'Yes, I think you have been very good to me.'

'So what are you going to do about this — what do you call it? This guide's job?'

'But you see ... the Serengeti is my homeland. Everyone has a homeland.'

'Hah! *Takataka!* Rubbish! You're a Kibera boy. Born here. And you'll die here.'

Under Koske's indignant barrage, Joshua was losing his resolve.

'It's such a beautiful place, the Serengeti,' he offered lamely.

Koske changed tack. 'Listen to me, Joshua. The elections are coming. We want Raila to win, don't we?'

Joshua nodded.

'And when he does, that's the time to take your holiday in the Serengeti.'

Joshua made no response.

'Look. I myself will see that you go there. I have a friend in Kisumu who can arrange a visit for you. You'll see. And it's better to do that knowing that our man is the president. *Si ndiyo?*'

Joshua nodded again.

'That's better. And I tell you one more thing. That football scout that came to see you? He wants to see you in the trials.'

Joshua searched Koske's eyes for any sign of truth in his statement. As usual, he was unreadable. But he wanted it to be true.

Koske could read his thoughts. 'I swear,' he said, putting his hand on his heart. 'I promise you. It's your big chance.'

Joshua felt he couldn't threaten that chance, even if it were an unlikely one. 'I'll be here, Mr Koske.'

'Good boy!' Koske slapped him on the shoulder. 'Good boy.'

Joshua watched Koske walk away before turning towards the railway line and making his way home to Kwazi's partially completed sheet-iron shack in the depths of Kibera. Only an hour ago he had felt euphoric. The Serengeti. A job. Money to spend as he chose, and the prospect of living like a *mzungu*, even if ever so briefly. Now, the alleys he passed through suddenly seemed more putrid; the houses more ramshackle.

He knew Koske was lying about getting him a trip to the Serengeti after the elections. He wasn't so sure if he was lying about the football scout. If he had to forgo his safari to the Serengeti, he had to cling to the elevating thought of playing football with the Limuru Leopards. It remained strong as he crossed the railway line to Mombasa. It was still there as he jumped over the putrid drain running through Kisumu Ndogo and it almost lasted until he arrived at Kianda. But then it faded.

Even if Koske stood by his promise, Joshua could not relinquish his one and only chance to see the Serengeti. Not for Koske. Not for the football scout. Not even for Raila Odinga himself.

*　*　*

They held each other in the darkness at the door to Kwazi's shack. Mayasa could feel his breath hot on her neck, then he pressed his lips there and touched her skin with his tongue. A slight shiver ran through her body. Slowly she ran her hand down the ripple of his ribs to his hip, then inched it across to his groin to feel the heat of him there.

'Wait until I go inside,' Joshua whispered to her. 'Let's pretend we are the only people in Kibera and you are trying to find me.'

He slipped through the door of the shack and she waited a few moments before following him.

She felt her way along the inside wall. With her other hand, she searched for the low overhead beam in the one room that Joshua and Kwazi had managed to complete. The unfinished section of the corrugated-iron wall was rough with rust.

The window shutter was propped open, letting the faint glow from the muddied sky fall on the bed. As her eyes adjusted to the darkness, she could see Joshua's naked body outlined against the pale sheet that covered the bed base — the most expensive item in the shack. She could sense his hunger, almost feel his urgency, but she wanted to extend the delicious time until he was on her and in her. Her skin tingled with anticipation. She let her shift fall to the floor, unclipped her bra and stepped out of her panties.

He lifted his hand to her and moved to allow her space on the firm, narrow base. His hands were so gentle on her breast and he placed soft kisses there as he whispered how much he loved her.

From her nipple he moved to her nape and nibbled and kissed her there before moving to cover her mouth with his. She drank in his sweet breath and searched for his tongue with hers.

His long, lean body pressed against her side and she could feel his hardness against her thigh. He softly moaned when she held it in her hand. She pulled him to her and sighed as he pressed his body into her.

* * *

Joshua lay in the darkness with Mayasa's head resting in the crook of his shoulder and her hand on his bare chest. They were both breathing heavily. He stared into the sky through the unshuttered window. The quarter-moon was a smudge behind the smog and smoke from Kibera's thousands of smouldering rubbish dumps and cooking fires. Stars were seldom visible, and there were nights when even the moon was hidden.

'When will Kwazi be home?' Mayasa asked softly.

Joshua fumbled for his mobile phone in the dark. It was ten thirty. 'Soon,' he said.

'I'd better go.'

'In a moment. Lie with me for a little longer.'

Mayasa was not his first girlfriend but there was something special about her. Unlike any of the previous ones, he wanted to keep her close to him after they'd made love.

'When I come back from the Serengeti,' he whispered, 'I will have money, and the *wazungu* will give me a reference so I can get real work. Maybe in a factory or where they are building something. And we can find a place together.'

'I'd like that, Joshua, but are you sure you should leave Nairobi? Koske is not a man to anger.'

'He will be angry for a time, but I can keep out of his way until he cools.'

'But in Kibera … he owns so much. He will make it difficult for us.'

'Maybe instead of coming back here, we can both return to the Serengeti. We could live there together. I might get a job as a tour guide. Maybe I can even buy a Land Rover. A very, very old one, but it will be enough to start.'

She remained quiet.

'Mayasa? Would you come with me?'

'I would … but my father …'

'I will speak with your father. Tonight.'

'No.'

'Why not? I must meet him. It's not right that we are together and I haven't met your father.'

'But I haven't met yours.'

Joshua had not seen his father since leaving home. He felt bad, but couldn't weaken. 'You know I am not speaking with my father.'

'Yes, but why?'

'He has no … qualities.'

'What do you mean? Of course he has qualities. He's your father.'

'Yes, but … Anyway, I will meet your father tonight. We will talk like men together.'

'No … He … he will already be asleep. He must be up very early to look for work.'

'Then when?'

'Soon.'

Armed with Koske's megaphone, Joshua worked the roads and alleys of Kibera, cajoling, harassing and encouraging people to vote for Raila Odinga on election day. Accompanying him were more than a score of his football team's supporters and players, who blew whistles, beat metal cans and waved flags. As they moved around Kibera, their numbers swelled with other Odinga supporters. Many of the marchers used their mobile phones to send messages to their network of friends. Soon there were hundreds — mainly unemployed men and youths — in the crowd. As their numbers grew, they were forced onto the wider roads.

Joshua was elated by the demonstration of support for Odinga and excited at his success in rallying such a crowd. He saw Kwazi standing on a corner watching the parade. Kwazi's opinion of such political demonstrations was well known to Joshua. He called them 'tribal gatherings', and thought them divisive, and his current expression of derision told Joshua his opinion hadn't changed. Still, Joshua was euphoric and signalled to Kwazi to join them. Kwazi gave him a disparaging gesture with his finger.

A dozen or more young men at the head of the procession, the most vociferous and fervent among the throng, saw what they thought to be an insult directed at them. They flew into a rage and, before Joshua could react, descended on Kwazi, whooping and yowling like wild animals. They knocked him to the ground and rained blows and kicks on him.

Joshua was momentarily stunned by the sudden violent turn in events. Recovering, he raced to where Kwazi was pinned to the ground and, roaring at the top of his lungs, threw himself into the mêlée, pulling at the bodies piled on Kwazi. His efforts were useless. The pack had become possessed by blind, mindless vengeance.

Eventually, at some invisible and unheard signal, Kwazi's assailants fell away, leaving his battered and bloody body on the hard, dead earth of Kibera.

*   *   *

Kenyatta National Hospital sat on the hill above Nairobi, a bleak, grey, high-rise concrete monolith on the border of the Kibera slums. In the early days of the settlement, the hill had been the most desirable location in town, housing the governor's residence and the prestigious Nairobi Club. A collection of fashionable stone dwellings had risen in the club's vicinity, but many years later fashion had moved on and the stone houses on the hill had fallen into disrepair. Those that weren't demolished became low-cost lodgings or communal housing.

Joshua ascended to the hospital's sixth floor in a steel elevator that wobbled alarmingly. He wandered the corridors until he found Kwazi's ward, but he couldn't see his friend. He continued to search, peering into overcrowded rooms and seeing things he really didn't want to see. Suffering was apparent on many of the stricken faces that stared back at him. Joshua had always been appalled by sickness of any kind, for in his experience it usually led to death. Here, in the corridors of Kenyatta National Hospital, death was all too palpable; he could almost smell it.

He returned to the admissions desk, where the nurse confirmed the ward number he'd already been given. He went back and thoroughly checked each bed, including the trundle beds covering much of the floor space. He again failed to find his friend. It was Kwazi who saw Joshua and raised a hand to him.

Kwazi's head and arms were swathed in gauze, much of it smothered with black bloodstains. He smiled at Joshua through swollen, split lips, revealing broken and missing teeth.

'*Habari,*' he croaked.

'*Mzuri,*' Joshua mumbled, stunned at the sight of his friend. 'How are you?'

It was a pathetic effort, but he could think of nothing more constructive to say.

'Broken nose,' Kwazi said. 'I've lost some teeth. See?' He pointed the finger of his unbandaged hand towards his mouth. 'No more pretty smiles for the girls.'

Joshua remained sober-faced.

'*Haki ya mungu,*' Kwazi said. 'Will you look at you? Have you forgotten how to laugh at a joke?'

Joshua made a feeble effort at a smile.

'Doctor said I've got some broken ribs,' Kwazi continued.

Joshua nodded.

'And a ruptured spleen.'

Joshua nodded again.

'What's a spleen?' Kwazi asked in a whisper.

'I don't know. What did the doctor say?'

'He said if I don't have money for the operation, they can do nothing for me.' The pain showed as he attempted to swallow. 'He said I can stay for a few days. Maybe the spleen stops bleeding. Then I must go.'

'Where is this ... spleen?'

'Down there.' He nodded towards his abdomen.

'Is it your *mbolo*?' Joshua asked in a hushed voice, darting a glance towards Kwazi's crotch.

'No. Idiot. It's here.' He raised his hand to indicate his ribcage. 'Somewhere in there. It's painful to touch.'

'I'm sorry about what happened,' Joshua said after a moment.

'Stupid fools! What were they doing? Marching along like anybody cared about politics.'

'But ... I'm sorry they beat you up.'

Kwazi said nothing.

Joshua glanced around the ward. A few patients were being fed by their visitors.

'I'll bring you food,' he said.

'Why did they attack me?' Kwazi asked.

Joshua considered a moment before answering. 'They thought you were making bad signs at them. They thought you were against Raila Odinga.'

Kwazi had his eyes closed, but nodded. The answer seemed to satisfy him.

'You should sleep,' Joshua said. 'I'll come back with food,' he added, but received no response.

* * *

On his way down the six flights of stairs — he did not want to risk the elevator again — Joshua tried to rationalise his lie to Kwazi. It was true the marchers may not have been happy that someone on their route did not approve of their message or did not agree that Raila Odinga should be president. But what had worried Joshua, and had made him lie to his friend, was that he had seen many that morning who had indicated their disapproval of the marchers and their sentiments. Some had been far more outspoken than Kwazi. The difference was that none of them had looked like Kwazi.

Joshua had witnessed something that morning that made him feel uncomfortable. He'd glimpsed an ugly side to these people with whom he agreed on many matters; people whom he admired for their courage in supporting Odinga against a brutal administration that was determined to silence them. But now he realised that these people could be brutal themselves. He had seen their brutality turned on Kwazi, and only because he looked so different from them.

Joshua worried that in other circumstances he might also reveal an ugliness such as he'd witnessed that day.

CHAPTER 18

Nicholas Omuga turned off his office lights and walked among the empty desks to the dimly lit corridor. The elevator carried him to the twelfth floor and the office of Gideon Koske — the chief executive officer of one of the largest NGOs assisting the Department of Community Development. As requested by Koske in his phone call, it was exactly seven o'clock.

A solidly built man with a large silver ring in his ear sat at the receptionist's desk. When Omuga approached, he looked up from his newspaper, took his feet off the desk and, without a word, slipped through a door into the adjoining office.

Omuga scanned the office, trying to settle his nerves. It was very well decorated, but a wheeled canvas-lined litter trolley had been left behind by the cleaners, detracting from the fine paintings and fresh flowers.

A few moments later the man returned. 'Go in,' he grunted.

Omuga swallowed, and tried to smile, but couldn't. Deep in his gut he felt an emptiness caused by his misgivings. He feared the only reason Koske would summon him to his office was because he no longer required his services. The monthly contribution he accepted from Koske to keep his NGO registration from prying eyes helped to put food on his family's table. What if Koske had heard of Omuga's treachery? Omuga had received his five thousand shillings, but what was that if he lost Koske's benefits? Or worse, lost his job?

'Omuga,' Koske said. 'Thank you for coming.'

Omuga nodded, smiled nervously. 'Thank you, Mr Koske. Thank you.'

'Please, sit. No, not there. This chair is better.'

Omuga sat where he was told, his back to the door. He drummed his fingers on his knees and crossed and uncrossed his legs.

'I suppose you are wondering why I've asked you to come to my office this evening, Omuga.'

'Well ... yes, Mr Koske, I —'

'You see, I have a policy of recognising people who are doing a good job. People like you, Omuga, who might not be noticed by their bosses.'

'Th-thank you, Mr —'

'So you have been singled out for a little special bonus. Credit where it's due is what I am saying.'

Omuga's face muscles twitched as his smile made an effort to overcome their tension.

'You have eight children, Omuga.'

It was a statement more than a question. Omuga was amazed at Koske's awareness of the personal details of one of the menial members of the department.

'They must be very proud of their father — a faithful employee of the Department of Community Development.'

'Yes, Mr Koske,' Omuga replied, feeling much better. It appeared he had nothing to be nervous about. His secret was safe.

The office door opened behind him and Omuga heard the clatter of the litter trolley. He thought that Koske would be angry that the cleaner had come at such a bad time, but Koske was still smiling.

Suddenly someone grabbed his arms, pulling them painfully around the back of his chair. In surprised panic he tried to free himself, but the man holding him was too strong.

'Your reward for your good service is a long holiday, Omuga,' said Koske. 'A very long holiday. It's a shame you won't have time to say farewell to those eight children of yours.'

Koske pulled a large white handkerchief from his pocket and untangled a short springy piece of thin wire from it. He smiled as he took hold of the little wooden handles at the ends of the wire and snapped it tight.

He moved swiftly to the side of Omuga's chair and flipped the garotte over his head, pulling the handles until the wire cut deeply into Omuga's neck.

Omuga kicked and struggled.

The last sound he heard was Koske's demented laugh.

*　*　*

Riley left the UNICEF inquiry's hearing room and marched through the Kenyatta Centre's main door, heading to where he'd parked the Land Rover on the far side of River Road. He was running late, and he knew the jam through the city would be bad at that hour of the afternoon. He'd formed the opinion that River Road was something of a boundary between the controlled chaos of the city and the complete anarchy of the squalid area around the Nairobi River. It was also close to the long-distance bus terminal, which attracted swarms of darting *matatus*, each one driven by what appeared to be a homicidal maniac. For both these reasons, Riley seldom parked near River Road, but on this occasion, he'd ignored all his well-founded resolutions and succumbed to the convenience. Time had slipped by and now he was late for his next appointment.

At the cross-street he broke into a trot, hesitating only a moment to glance to his right as he crossed the bus terminal concourse.

A shout. He turned.

A car careened towards him from the wrong side of the road. Riley dodged to the left. The car swerved to meet him. He took a precious moment to judge his next manoeuvre, but now the car was almost upon him and he had few options. He launched himself at the nearest object — a push-cart — landing among a load of sweet potatoes.

The car, a blue Peugeot, clipped the wheel of the cart, ripping it from the axle and dumping Riley and the sweet potatoes onto the road.

*　*　*

Riley sat at the Norfolk's Lord Delamere Bar, nursing his bruises and a long cold Tusker beer while reflecting on his near miss. In the moment he'd taken to determine whether the driver was taking evasive action, their eyes had met. Riley could still see the man's dangling silver earring, his fists clamped to the steering wheel, the determined glare. There was no way it was an accident. The driver had meant to run him down. He was on a deliberate mission to kill or maim.

No longer could Riley consider the blue Peugeot's earlier appearance as a coincidence, or Kazlana's warning to take care an overreaction. He had to believe the incident in River Road was connected to his search for the orphaned boy, Jafari, and that someone wanted to stop him discovering what had happened to him.

He felt the stirring of his journo's instincts. A missing child, a vanishing orphanage, corruption, politics, perhaps even a mysterious plane crash in the desert. They were the elements of a classic investigative piece.

The research for his novel had uncovered an increasingly exciting storyline and his desire to complete it was powerful, but here was a story with greater immediacy. The attempt on his life had merely made it more personal. Intensely so.

*　*　*

It was Christmas Eve and the *Standard* was pathetically light on news. As Kazlana was flicking through the pages, a photograph caught her eye and made her flip back.

The photograph appeared to be from Omuga's security pass.

It showed him in the ubiquitous dark blue suit of the public service, with a smile that was fading as the photographer snapped after dithering too long with camera adjustments.

Death and Funeral Announcement, the text below it read. *It is with profound sorrow and acceptance of God's will that we announce the death by misadventure of Nicholas Jeremiah Omuga, Section Head of Non-Government Organisations in the Department of Community Development, on 19 December 2007. Husband to Nellie, father to Elizabeth, Jacob, Elphalet, Rose, Kennedy, Abner, Malath and Milka. Son of the late ...*

Kazlana stopped reading. *Death by misadventure*. It could mean accidental death, but her suspicions were aroused.

She rang a contact at the *Standard*'s crime desk and learnt that Omuga had been found floating in Nairobi dam, his head almost severed and his wallet, watch and personal effects intact. It was not misadventure, but cold-blooded murder.

*　　*　　*

Riley and Charlotte had agreed not to make a big deal out of Christmas Day. They decided to join the merry crowd at the hotel restaurant's buffet and then spend the rest of the afternoon by the pool.

When the waitress appeared at Riley's shoulder and discreetly told him he had a call, he asked Charlotte to excuse him for a moment, leaving her with her tea while he took the call in the hotel lobby.

It was Kazlana.

'Hi,' he said. 'Merry Christmas and all that. I was going to ring you later. I forgot to fill you in on my meeting with Omuga. What a guy!'

He laughed as he told her of Omuga's paranoia about being discovered.

'He told me some weird stuff about the orphanage, but I'm not sure if I can put too much confidence in —'

'Mark.'

'Yeah?'

'Mark, there's been some news about Omuga,' and she told him of the funeral announcement.

After the initial shock, Riley felt bad for being unable to immediately recall Omuga's face, but then a vague image of him came to mind — lumpish, sweating. A crumpled blue suit.

'How did it happen?' he asked, dreading the answer.

There was a moment's hesitation at the other end of the line. 'It wasn't an accident, Mark. People who know the details leave me in no doubt. The only reason I'm telling you this is so that you'll take care.'

'How do you know it wasn't an accident?' he asked.

'He'd been ... Well, I have it on good authority.'

He insisted she tell him everything she knew and, as she recounted the gruesome nature of the crime, he felt the cold clamminess of nausea spread from the pit of his stomach.

'It's very sad,' she added. 'Apparently he had quite a sizeable family.'

Eight children and an ailing wife.

'Mark, people like Omuga are into all manner of dirty dealings. You can't assume that his death had anything to do with you.'

He thanked her and hung up.

In the washroom, he splashed cold water onto his face. The image staring back at him from the mirror was ashen. Regardless of Kazlana's reassurance, Riley felt sure his inducement to reveal confidential information had been the cause of Omuga's death.

Mr Koske is a very dangerous man. Be very careful how you proceed. It could mean your life ... and mine.

He patted his cheeks and took a deep breath. He decided to keep the matter from Charlotte; it was pointless to concern her. Anyway, they would soon be gone from the city and out of Koske's reach.

CHAPTER 19

'You will be at Kasarani on Friday night, Otieng,' Koske said in his usually cryptic fashion. It was his way of putting people off-balance.

'Do you mean Moi International?' Joshua asked, only daring to hope Koske was referring to the football stadium and possibly the trial game he had previously mentioned.

'Yes.'

Training had ended and the playing field was empty apart from him and Koske.

'Why is that?' he asked. 'I mean, what can I do for you there, Mr Koske?'

Koske merely nodded, letting the knot in Joshua's stomach build. Finally he said, 'You will play in a game against a training squad. The Red Top Buffalos.'

'Is it the trial game? The one you arranged with the Limuru Leopards?'

In spite of himself, Joshua couldn't keep the excitement from his voice. The Red Top Buffalos were the reigning premiers, owned by Kenya's largest brewery.

'Yes. It is something they put on for some charity or other.'

Joshua was almost dancing on the spot. 'I see. Very well.' He had difficulty controlling the excitement in his voice. 'I'll be there. Of course.'

'But this time you must play for me,' Koske continued. 'I have asked that you be a striker in the Leopards' line-up.' Koske raised his hand, silencing Joshua before he could interject. 'It will be a small game, nothing much. You will play well.' His smile became malevolent. 'But sadly, your team will not win. I want the Buffalos to win.'

'But —'

'It's for some friends, you see. They like to make wagers on football games.' Koske shrugged.

'But what if someone else scores a goal? Or maybe the Buffalos' goalie is too good?'

'Do you think you are the only pebble on the beach, my friend? It is not for you to worry about anyone but yourself.'

Koske took a large handkerchief from his trouser pocket and dabbed at his eyes before noisily blowing his nose. 'I myself ... I don't gamble,' he said. 'But people ... friends of mine, do. And they use big money, even on little games like this one on Friday night. So you will help me, and I will help my friends.'

Joshua was stunned, wondering how he could demonstrate his skills as a striker while not scoring a goal. Koske seemed to read his mind.

'You are thinking how can you display your many talents if you, the striker, cannot shoot a goal, *si ndiyo*?'

'Yes.'

'Then you will not think like that. You will do this for me because I am your friend, and as your friend I will take care of you — as I have already promised. There will be other opportunities, but this time you will not play well.'

Joshua's mood had fallen from high to low. He waged an internal battle to control his anger.

'She is quite pretty,' Koske said.

Joshua followed his eyes to where Mayasa sat waiting for him on the sidelines.

'Yes, your girlfriend is very cute, Otieng,' Koske said, almost wistfully. 'You'd better look after her. There is so much violence around these days. It would be terrible if such a pretty one was hurt.'

* * *

In the late afternoon, with the long shadows of the grandstand falling like huge slabs across the pitch, the Moi International Sports Centre appeared enormous. Joshua had only seen it from the cheap seats during the season proper, but from the middle of the arena, it was huge.

'It's very big!' he whispered to himself, scanning the whole circumference of the stadium. It held sixty thousand — the biggest capacity in Kenya. He had been allowed onto the pitch two hours before the game commenced to familiarise himself. According to the manager of the Limuru Leopards, this would help reduce first-game nerves.

It didn't.

Joshua had prepared all his life for this moment, but now that it had arrived, he was consumed with doubt and immobilised by gut-wrenching, choking, panic-stricken fear.

The Leopards' manager watched from the sidelines.

'You're nervous,' he said when Joshua trotted back towards the gate to the locker rooms.

'No, I'm not!' Joshua responded immediately, then added, 'Well, only a little. It's very big.'

'You'll soon forget about the stadium and the people. If you don't, you'll not play well.'

Joshua's stomach tightened further.

'And you must play well. This might be just a trial game to you, but —' The manager seemed to change the direction of his thoughts and sighed. 'I owe Mr Koske a favour. That's why you're here. Do you think I don't have a hundred boys like you? You only get one chance with the Limuru Leopards. And this is it.' He smiled to soften the impact of his words. 'Now go and get ready. I'll bring you on after the start to have a look at you.'

Joshua stood rooted to the spot. He wanted to assure the manager that he had the talent and wanted the position on the squad more than life itself, but he was afraid he might say the wrong thing.

The manager frowned. 'Go!'

Joshua turned and trotted down the player's race on rubbery legs.

*   *   *

Gideon Koske sauntered into the locker rooms, condescendingly nodding to players and officials. He stopped to exchange words with a few, laughing loudly and slapping some on the back. After a while he came to where Joshua sat fidgeting with his laces. He couldn't seem to get them at the right tension.

'Otieng,' Koske hissed.

Joshua lifted himself from the bench to stand beside him.

'So ... your big chance, ah?'

'Yes, Mr Koske.'

'And you remember what we discussed, ah? Don't disappoint me, my friend.' The smile was cold, more like a sneer.

Joshua swallowed and nodded.

'*Sowa sowa*. Okay. Play well.' Koske's malevolent smile lingered. 'But not *too* well, ah?'

*   *   *

Mayasa had been grateful for Kwazi's company on the journey to Moi International, but now that they were there, seated high in the grandstand awaiting the game, with nothing to discuss that they'd not already discussed during the long *matatu* ride from the city, she felt decidedly uncomfortable.

Kwazi still bore the signs of his beating at the hands of the mob. His face, already distorted from his childhood injury, was blotchy with bruises. A strip of grimy plaster ran along his jaw from his chin to one ear, which remained mottled with dried blood. He had not been openly antagonistic to her as he'd appeared to be during their first meeting, but there was a polite but cool screen between them that made conversation difficult. She tried a new tactic.

'Joshua says you have been friends for many years,' she said.

'We have. Since he was little.'

'Has he always been interested in football?'

'Of course. It's all he's ever wanted to do.'

'Then you must be very happy for him tonight.'

Kwazi remained silent.

She persisted. 'I mean, here he is, after all this time. I don't understand football, but if this is what he's always wanted, I imagine he will be very keen to play well.'

'He hasn't told you,' he said.

'Hasn't told me what?'

He was again silent.

'Kwazi? What is it?'

'I'm not here because I enjoy football. I think it's a stupid waste of energy. No, I'm here to see if my friend is foolish enough to play to win.'

'Of course he's playing to win! As you said, he's waited his whole life for this chance. And I know him well enough to know that he will give everything he has. He wants to win.'

Kwazi shook his head despondently. 'Yes, you're right. Football *has* been his whole life. But if he plays too well tonight, it might be the end of it. Koske has told him he must lose and Joshua has agreed. But I know him better than Koske does. And I think I know him better than you do. He says he will do what is sensible, but there's something in that head of his that will not let him lose the chance he has been waiting for all his life.'

She leapt to her feet. 'I must speak to him. He mustn't —'

There was a tumultuous roar from the crowd. Mayasa looked down at the arena. The players were emerging from the race. Near the end of the line of men was Joshua — tall, proud and looking magnificent in his gold and black guernsey.

* * *

Joshua felt sick. In horror, he imagined vomiting in the middle of the pitch where he stood with his team-mates as the national anthem played through distorted speakers. Somewhere in the grandstands was Mayasa, among forty or fifty thousand fans — die-hards not able to wait for the start of the season proper before seeing their first game of the year.

The pre-game warm-up was a confusion of lights and movement. A football flashed past him, he took an ineffective stab at it, and then a siren sounded and he was on the bench beside the manager, fidgeting and willing one of the Leopards' players to be injured.

This continued until the manager sent Joshua on as a substitute for one of the defensive players. As he ran to take his position, the crowd erupted in response to a goal attempt at the far end of the field. The sound set a flock of small birds fluttering in Joshua's chest cavity. The remainder of the half was a blur, including his only touch of the football as the siren sounded half-time.

At the start of the second half, he was again on the bench, watching play while keeping an eye on the clock. The Leopards' defensive squad was skilful, deflecting every Buffalo charge. On the other hand, the Buffalos' defenders were sloppy, but the Leopards' strikers were failing to take full advantage of that. They passed back and forth before ultimately losing the ball.

In the thirty-ninth minute, with the score nil all, the key striker in the Leopards' attack went down from a brutal tackle in midfield. He was in the hands of the trainers for some time before the manager signalled to Joshua to take the injured player's place on the field.

Joshua ran onto the pitch, unable to feel the ground beneath his feet. Around him the night pulsed with energy. The spectators — a seemingly single organism whose raw emotions electrified the air — roared and hooted. The glaring lights blinded him. How could he possibly see?

And then the ball was in his half. He took a poorly directed pass on his non-preferred left side, but quickly managed to gather it under his control before he was tackled. He fended off the Buffalo challenge and passed to a midfielder. Joshua broke into an open space that offered a clear path to goal, but the ball didn't return to him, going instead to the other wing where it was lost to the Buffalos.

Another ball came into the attack. Again he received it wide and in good position, but he was bailed up with nowhere to go. He passed to another player, but the ball didn't return and was soon sent downfield again.

Joshua gratefully took the respite, but noted that the game was now into injury time. He moved into the defensive part of the pitch and stole a well-directed Buffalo pass, dribbling it into his attacking zone while defeating a number of spirited challenges.

The Leopards' midfielders offered support. Joshua ignored them, realising that he was not the only player not playing for a win. He was in full flight, charging into the forward half. Thirty metres from goal, a vicious kick from a brutish Buffalo defender caught him on the right ankle, taking him to the ground. He was winded and in pain. The mercury-vapour lights drilled into his brain. The referee hovered above him, yabbering that he had won a direct free kick. A trainer stood over him, yelling at him to let a substitute take it. His team-mates and opposition players crowded around.

He was somehow on his feet. The referee took the ball and placed it in position for the penal foul.

The crowd was whistling and yelling. Joshua could see nothing because of the glare, but his thoughts went to two people in that vast crowd: Mayasa, who would be praying for him to score; and Koske, who would damn him if he did.

Thirty metres. The referee held up his hand and blew full-time. Opposition defenders shuffled into position in the wall, and there was much shifting and changing while they strengthened it with additional men.

Joshua knew he could make the shot if he could use his right foot, but he was barely able to stand on it.

The referee sounded the whistle to signal that the shot could proceed.

Nil all.

Joshua studied the defensive wall. There was no way through, and even a high top-spin shot, if it were able to avoid the goalie, would be unlikely to get under the bar. There was clearly no disgrace in missing such a difficult shot. He could make an honourable attempt, satisfy Koske's orders and hopefully keep his chances alive to join the regular Leopards' squad.

Do you think I don't have a hundred boys like you? You only get one chance with the Limuru Leopards. And this is it.

Joshua started his approach, setting up to take the ball on his left side, but in mid-flight he changed to his right, punching the ball hard and wide. It careened off in a wide, sweeping curve.

A bolt of pain shot up his leg and burst in his brain.

* * *

Mayasa climbed out of the overcrowded *matatu*. Joshua followed, taking care to keep the weight off his injured ankle. When he offered to hold Kwazi's sticks as he alighted, his friend ignored him and stumbled down with them under his arm.

At the turn-off towards Mayasa's house, Kwazi said goodbye to her, but ignored Joshua. They watched him hobble down the alley with his painful, jerky gait until he was out of sight.

'Kwazi's annoyed with you,' Mayasa said, feeling sympathetic with at least some of his sentiment.

'Yes. He's an old woman.'

'And am I an old woman too?' She had been torn between sharing his elation and fearing the outcome. Now the cold reality of their situation displaced the last of the euphoria. 'When he told me about Koske, I couldn't believe you would shoot that goal.' She looked into his eyes. 'What are we going to do, Joshua?'

'I leave tomorrow for the Serengeti.' He turned to her. 'You will meet me there?'

She chewed the inside of her cheek. 'I … I can't.'

'But why, Mayasa?' he pleaded.

She wanted to tell him it was because there was a serious matter they needed to discuss, but she couldn't handle the expression she imagined she'd see if she told him about her father's condition. Certainly not at that moment, when he was so happy about his achievements on the football field.

'There are things I have to do,' she said. 'Then I can come.'

Mayasa had spoken to her sister about taking over the responsibility for their father's care. She was hopeful that something could soon be arranged, but regardless of the practicalities, her first duty was to inform Joshua that her father had the dreaded disease.

'Then if you can't leave Nairobi, will you be safe when I'm gone?' he asked. 'Can you stay at your sister's house?'

She nodded. 'I can. And you must keep out of the way until tomorrow. You know that Koske has his thugs everywhere. He'll kill you if he has the chance.'

Joshua nodded, but she could tell his mind had drifted away.

'Joshua?' she pressed. 'You will be careful, won't you?'

He smiled. 'It was a great goal, wasn't it?'

CHAPTER 20

Simon sat surrounded by ecstatic Limuru Leopards' fans. He was probably the only man in the *matatu* who wasn't a football fanatic. And probably also the only one who didn't actually care who'd won the game. Simon was happy because he'd seen his son shoot the goal of his life. He couldn't keep the grin off his face all the way from Kasarani stadium.

It was fortunate that he even knew about the game. A parent of one of Joshua's team-mates had mentioned it, never suspecting that Simon knew nothing about it. In fact, Simon was probably the only Kibera resident who hadn't heard about Joshua's debut well in advance of the game. He'd made it to the stadium in the nick of time.

Although Simon wasn't a fan, he naturally knew of the Limuru Leopards — one of the best football teams in the competition. He also knew that Joshua had for many years dreamt of playing with the Leopards.

Simon had often been tempted to moderate his son's idealistic aspirations, but he recognised something of himself in his boy. Joshua had the right amount of nerve and audacity to make a good sportsman. And in Kibera, dreams were a lifeline that had to be nourished at all costs.

It was a dream that had drawn Simon Otieng and his young wife to Kibera in the first place. He should have realised at that early time that no matter how hard he tried to make a life for them, Kibera would refuse to yield for him.

* * *

1989

Like ghosts they moved through the cool mist and pre-dawn darkness to be first in line at the factory doors and construction site gates, all seeking a day's work. Simon often failed to find work and wondered if it were because of his Kisumu accent. Try as he might to lose it, it unerringly returned to give him trouble — even after five years in Nairobi. It was a source of great amusement for many, and particularly troublesome as it marked him as an outsider, possibly naïve and therefore an even better target for exploitation.

'And how are things in Nyanza Province?' they'd ask soon after he opened his mouth to speak. Or, 'You'll have to talk a little slower. I can't keep up with you.'

None of these comments was particularly humorous or original, but each aspiring comedian would ensure everyone within earshot could hear him. If the comments came from a potential employer, Simon could do nothing but smile at such dazzling wit. It was difficult enough to find a labourer's job in Nairobi without giving vent to his anger or making it worse by standing on his dignity.

The battle for work began at the entrance to the premises. Building sites had gatemen; factories had security guards. There was always more than one step to win a job, and there was always someone demanding a little something to allow a man to the next step. And then there was the foreman. Any man who could lift a bag of wheat, or push a broom, or carry a crate of beer, was a potential employee for the day. The foreman therefore expected something for his trouble.

Simon would typically have to hand over a hundred shillings to the man at the gate, and another hundred to the foreman for the privilege of carrying cement bags from seven to five. At the end of the day, he might take home one hundred shillings for ten hours' hard labour.

He was nineteen, and might have given up and returned home if it hadn't been for Patience.

* * *

Simon was shy in the company of women his own age and would stumble over his words when attempting conversation. He felt awkward, and his few bumbling attempts to find a girlfriend came to nothing. In despair, he put women from his thoughts. When his testicles ached, and he used his hand for relief, he had no particular girl in his mind as he raced towards his mind-numbing climax.

When he saw the girl in her tight jeans and snug white tee-shirt, she was sweeping the dirt outside a *duka* on the alley that ran down to the putrid Mathare River. His greeting fell from his mouth before he had time to think. '*Habari*,' he said, and when she looked up she had the eyes of a gazelle — deep brown pools framed by long lashes. She smiled and he couldn't find words to speak again. She was more beautiful than anything he'd ever seen.

Although she hadn't spoken, her smile gave him courage, but before he could recover she completed her sweeping and moved inside.

He looked at what the *duka* had on display on the outside shelves. There were a few canned goods, toothpaste, a jar of rubbery snakes for the children, cigarettes in singles or packs, and a row of dog-eared magazines and newspapers. And a sign that said *Fresh Tea*.

He chose a seat at one of the three small tables and agonised over his next words. His mind was a blank. In that moment, it appeared that *Habari* was the limit of his entire vocabulary.

Suddenly she was at his table, wiping it with a damp cloth.

'*Habari*,' he said, inwardly cursing himself.

'*Mzuri*,' she replied, and the steel bands on his chest made it difficult for him to breathe.

'Would you like to order something?' she asked.

He nodded.

She smiled and raised an exquisite eyebrow.

'Oh! Tea ... please.'

'Milk and sugar?'

He marvelled at her command of words.

'Yes.'

She was still smiling at him. 'Milk or sugar or both?' she asked patiently.

'Milk, please,' he stammered. 'And sugar.'

She turned and her bottom wobbled as she returned to the *duka*.

Haki ya mungu, he whispered to himself irreverently.

After his second cup, her father appeared at the doorway with a face of stone.

A further two cups forced him to move on with a bursting bladder, but not before he knew her name. It was Patience.

He also knew he wanted her more than anything he'd wanted in his whole life.

* * *

It took Simon many days and countless cups of tea while dodging her father's scowls to gather the courage to ask Patience to go out with him. When she readily agreed, he wondered why he'd taken so long.

'I thought you were never going to ask,' she said, recalling his tentative early approaches.

'I wasn't sure.'

'I was.'

It was Sunday, and they were in City Park, which was either a long walk or a cheap *matatu* ride from Mathare. The matt grey sky, typical of Nairobi in July, kept the temperature down, so they had walked there.

The park had once been the pride of Nairobi. The city planners had set aside a generous portion of the wooded slopes above the town as a recreational area. It was some time, however, before the park was safe. For many years, lions and other predators continued to occupy their traditional territory, making a visit to the park a hazardous activity.

From its heyday in the mid-twentieth century, the park had fallen into disrepair. It had again become the hunting ground of predators, but this time it was foreigners and the wealthy who were the prey as the predators became more interested in cash than flesh. But the thieves recognised Mathare residents when they saw them, and Simon and Patience knew they could stroll the overgrown paths with impunity.

In a deserted corner of the park, they found a small clearing among the overgrown shrubbery. It was concealed from the path in the unlikely event of an intruder entering their domain. Simon smoothed away the leaves for her to sit down.

'And, of course, there's your father to think about,' he said, sitting beside her on the grass.

'He'll get to like you when he knows you as well as I do.'

'I don't think so,' he said, and a brief cloud of uncertainty threatened to spoil the happiness he felt having her by his side.

'But how about you, Patience?' he said, teasing her with feigned seriousness. 'Do you like me?'

'You know I do,' she replied, before stealing a kiss. 'There, I've shamed you in front of all Nairobi.'

He looked up into the trees and laughed. There was only a troop of Sykes' monkeys for company. 'I don't think the monkeys will mind,' he said, and took her into his arms.

Her lips were soft and full. He tentatively touched his tongue to her open lips. She responded. It made his head spin.

'*Ninakupenda mingi*,' he said, hovering over her. 'Patience ... I love you very much.'

She pulled him down on her and he kissed her, long and hard.

'Simon ...' she whispered into his ear.

Her hands went to his belt and he fumbled with the zipper of her jeans. In a tangle of trouser legs and underwear, he pressed his body into hers.

It had never crossed his mind, neither then nor previously, that she was a Kikuyu and he was not. And that their love might offend people of both tribes.

*　*　*

'You are a Luo,' Patience said. 'We are Kikuyu.'

'I know that,' Simon said with some exasperation. 'But that's no reason for your father to hate me.'

'He doesn't hate you, he just —'

'He just wants to take that *panga* he keeps under the counter and cut me into small, small pieces with it.'

She smiled. 'In time he will learn. What I mean is, you are a Luo and I am Kikuyu. We are different.'

'What does it matter? We love each other.'

'Of course we do, Simon. What I am trying to say is that when we marry, well … Some people don't like to see mixed marriages. They will tease us, or … maybe they'll make it difficult for us.'

'We know what we are doing.'

'I know what I'm doing, Simon. But do you?'

'Of course I do.' He lifted his cup and dabbed his finger into the puddle of tea on the laminated table top. 'It sounds like you've changed your mind about getting married.'

'I haven't. I'm just trying to think of everything we need to think about. Things that you don't know about. You haven't seen how things can be. It's different in the smaller towns. People are among family there. They know everyone in town. But here in Nairobi, we're all strangers.'

'What do we care about strangers?'

She reached a hand across to him, and he stopped finger-painting the table to meet her eyes. She stared at him for some time, then smiled. 'Maybe you're right,' she said. 'Maybe I worry too much.'

He covered her hand with his. 'I won't let anybody say anything about you ... about us. I will never let anyone hurt you.'

*   *   *

'I'm sorry,' Patience said, dropping her head to her chest. 'I should have ...'

'What could you do? Ah? It is my fault. I should have used something.'

She nodded. 'Perhaps.'

Simon glanced at her, feeling bad now. 'Can you take something?' he asked.

'Like what?'

'I don't know. I've heard there are medicines ...'

'That's stupid talk. Witch-doctor stories. You can't believe what those boys in your building are saying. They know nothing about having babies.'

They were silent for a few moments.

'What will we do?' he asked. 'Will your father help us?'

She shook her head. 'It's going to take all my courage to tell him. When Fiona told him, he was so angry I thought he would hit her. He gave her nothing.'

'He will not hit you. I will be there with you.'

'Then he will hit *you*. It is better I tell him. I can be sweet with him. And Mama will help me.'

'Have you told your mama?'

She nodded. 'She cried.'

Simon nodded too. 'Now that the baby is coming, I will find us a place.'

He felt her eyes upon him. He knew the question that sat on her lips. He knew that she desperately wanted to ask it, but she also knew he had no answer. There seemed to be just no way they could survive with a baby.

*   *   *

As life became increasingly difficult for them in Mathare, Simon looked further afield to find a house and a means to support Patience and the baby, when it arrived. He made a few visits to the Kibera slum — the sprawling metropolis on the other side of the city — where plots were cheap. Many were of the opinion that Kibera was a place of great opportunity; so large that it generated an industry all its own. There were jobs to be found in the many small *dukas* and stalls in the markets. People needed labourers to build the small houses and huts.

Simon saw for himself the building activity as the Kibera population expanded with immigrants from up country and as people extended their houses to match their own growing families. Here was a place to raise a family and make enough money to buy a plot. There was even an area within Kibera called Kisumu Ndogo — Little Kisumu — where the Luo people had congregated. Although he had left his Luo traditions at home with his grandfather, Simon felt Kisumu Ndogo would offer his small family the security denied them in the disorganised communities of Mathare. It was the right place to settle.

Late in Patience's pregnancy, Simon packed their belongings into a rickety push-cart and headed out before dawn. An hour later they'd reached the other side of the city. They pushed their cart up the hill to Kibera, into a scattering of people coming down towards them. Soon there was a vast river of people flowing around them, buffeting them and their cart, mumbling apologies and stumbling on into the dawn. It seemed as if all of Kibera's enormous population had decided to abandon it. Simon realised they were headed for the same industrial area that he had often approached in the opposite direction from Mathare. The promise of a new life in Kibera suddenly became as intangible as the pre-dawn mist.

Simon had known then that his run of bad luck was unlikely to end in Kibera.

CHAPTER 21

Kazlana kept the nose of her Cessna pointed at the two broken teeth of Mount Kenya. When Lenana's brilliant glacier-capped peak filled her windscreen, she banked the Cessna into the rising sun and commenced her glide path to the small private airfield outside Embu.

She was unconcerned about the authorities knowing of her destination. Nobody would question her onward journey to Wajir from Embu. The region was famous for *miraah* — the semi-narcotic stems and leaf of the *Catha edulis* plant, very highly prized across the Somali border, which was just an hour or so from Wajir. *Miraah* was not illegal in either Kenya or Somalia, where it was called *kyat*, and many pilots owning planes small enough to land on rural airstrips, and patient enough to haggle with the irascible Somalis, could make good money for their efforts.

She taxied to the small hangar that served as a terminal. As soon as she cut the engine, she was surrounded by a press of growers thrusting samples of *miraah* leaves into her face. She waved off the first few, who were trying to offload yesterday's leaf onto her, obviously assuming a woman would be a naïve buyer. She picked a couple of leaves from a more promising bunch and examined the stems. They were freshly cut. She tucked a sample into her cheek and almost immediately felt the gentle rush. She spat out the *miraah* and quickly concluded her negotiations for the remainder of the farmer's plastic bag. Her contact in Wajir would appreciate the gift.

In the air again, she levelled off and sat back to enjoy the savage scenery of the Northern Frontier District.

Flying came naturally to her, as it had done to her father,

Dieter, who had been her instructor. He had been reluctant to teach her at first, saying she was too young, but, as was the case in almost everything she really wanted from him, he couldn't deny her once she put her mind to it. And she had loved him for it.

Since her father's death, Kazlana had become increasingly intolerant of the male companions she had once enjoyed. Other men paled into insignificance against the memory of her father, even though she knew her recollections of him glossed over his many faults. Such as his insistence that he build the NGO side of their business alone — a decision that had led to his death.

Wajir appeared in a sea of sand, still gilded by the morning sun. The airstrip shimmered as she circled closer to gauge the condition of the surface. It wasn't unknown for a warthog to dig a burrow in the baked earth. All was clear and she made a perfect landing in the still morning air.

Again a crowd gathered, this time to purchase her cargo of *miraah*, but she told them she had nothing for sale. The men melted away, disappointed.

One robed figure remained where he'd been standing, waiting for the crowd to lose interest and disperse. He wore a *futa* — the traditional white, wrapped skirt — but because of his height, most of the lower half of his long, nut-brown legs remained exposed. The upper body-wrap covered most of his torso while leaving his lower arms free. A chequered turban crowned his head and a trailing length encircled his face except for his eyes, which twinkled darkly at her.

Kazlana walked towards him and he loosened the headscarf to reveal his smile.

'Ah, God is good that I see you once again,' he said.

'You've been out here too long, Antonio. You sound like an Arab. Anyway, what would an Italian Catholic know of God?'

He laughed aloud, his white teeth contrasting with his deeply tanned skin. 'Just as irreverent as ever, *cara mia*.'

'Of course I am. Now, are you going to offer a girl a drink?'

Aside from the low outer wall, made from local stone in the shape of a boat's prow, only the bar inside the Royal Wajir Yacht Club remained intact as a reminder of the club's glorious and improbable past. Antonio told Kazlana that, in 1932, the white fort, like something out of *Beau Geste*, had been established by the British as a bulwark against the continuing incursion of lawless Somali raiders. When the area was flooded in a rare rainstorm, the district commissioner, Mad Freddie Jennings, set sail from his residence in a tin bath, declaring himself the founder and first commodore of the Wajir Yacht Club. Inspired by boredom or too much gin, the expatriate soldiers had embraced the idea of a clubhouse and a tradition was born. Even more improbably, it was said that His Royal Highness the Prince of Wales had intended to visit Wajir during a trip to Kenya, but was called home due to his father's illness. He authorised his emissary to bestow the title of *Royal* on the yacht club by way of consolation.

Antonio had, years ago, made enquiries and found that the club had been derelict since the 1960s, before an enterprising Somali had restored the thatched *makuti* roof and, with a prayer of forgiveness to Allah, opened a small bar in one corner. In this setting, leaning back in a canvas deckchair, with his dark good looks and a gin and tonic in hand, Antonio Diconza might have organised the whole affair in order to play the desert prince in a Hollywood movie.

Kazlana smiled and shook her head ruefully. 'What a waste,' she said. 'Why you spend all your time out here in the desert I'll never know.'

'But I thought you did know, my darling.'

'Hmm, yes. I suppose I do. And as I said, what a waste.'

'But tell me all your news. What brings you out here? To see me, I hope.'

'Of course. And to go over some of the information on Papa's death.'

Antonio's face saddened. 'Kazlana, *cara mia*, how much longer must we chase these old ghosts? The trail is long dead. You should get on with your life.'

Kazlana bristled. 'I will get on with my life when I have found who or what ended Papa's life.'

He shrugged. 'As you will.'

She took a sip of gin to calm herself. 'When we first began to trace the events of his death, you said he had no reason to fly to Wajir.'

'That's correct. At the time, business was slow. Dieter only had a delivery contract from Mombasa to a customer somewhere near Nakuru. I believe they were medical supplies.'

'But he landed near here.'

'*Si*, the burnt-out Cessna was found about a hundred kilometres north-east of here.'

'And since it was north-east of here, he wasn't coming to Wajir either.' She was thoughtful for a moment. 'What haven't you told me, Antonio?'

He raised his eyebrows.

'Don't give me that innocent southern European look. I know you better than that.'

He sighed and took a long pull on his gin. 'Kazlana, remember what happened to your father. He was probably coming here to ask the same questions. It is not good for you to know those answers.'

'You must let me decide that.'

'It will only trouble your heart, and for what?'

'Tell me.' Her voice had an edge like flint.

He shrugged, forgoing the last vestige of resistance. 'I don't know why he flew to the Somali border, but he told me he would come later to Wajir to speak to me.'

'Why?'

He hesitated. 'To tell me something about the medical deliveries.'

'The Nakuru deliveries?'

'I believe so. Something was troubling him, but he wouldn't tell me anything over the telephone. You know how unsafe these open lines are. He said he would leave Mombasa at nine to give the ground mist time to lift. But, of course ...'

'... he never arrived,' she said, finishing his sentence.

Kazlana took another sip of her drink.

During the '90s, Antonio had been an important middleman between a group of corrupt rangers in the huge Tsavo East National Park and ivory dealers in Somalia. He had arranged to transport the ivory across the border into Somalia where it was sold into Asian markets. The money was laundered through the Ramanova company's offshore account in the Jersey Islands and paid to the poachers, less the company's commission. Kazlana had only learnt of the poaching operation after her father's death. She knew Dieter would have had no interest in the poaching itself, but the old-time trader in him would have loved smuggling the contraband goods across the border, to a Somali war lord, Faraj Khalid Abukar.

'What does your friend Abukar know about it?' she asked Antonio.

'Nothing.'

'I know the organisation Papa was working for in Mombasa,' she said after a moment's thought. 'There's something strange about them. Do you know what strip he used for the Nakuru deliveries?'

'*Si*. I think so.'

'Then I think I should go there to find out where those medical supplies were going.'

* * *

The morning was exceptionally bright, swept clean by an overnight shower. Mayasa stood with Joshua on Ngong Road, awaiting the arrival of the Land Rover that would take him far from her. She was feeling downcast and sad, but Joshua was excited although he did his best to conceal it.

Last night Mayasa had again tried to tell Joshua about her father, but had failed. He was so affectionate after they made love that she just couldn't bear to spoil it.

'Will you call me, Josh?' she asked in a small voice.

He took his eyes from the road to smile at her. 'Yes. I will.'

'You can just text if you don't have credit.'

'I will.'

The minutes passed. Joshua was absorbed in his study of every approaching Land Rover.

'Joshua,' she said.

'Hmm?'

'Joshua, I need to tell you something.'

'Is that them?' he asked.

The car sped past.

'No.'

'Joshua, are you listening?'

'I am, Mayasa, but I must watch for them.'

'I need to tell you something important before you leave.'

'Okay.'

'It's about my father.'

'You've told him about us?' He glanced at her.

'I have, but that's not what I need to tell you.'

'Did he ask why I haven't come to see him? I knew I should have done it.'

'No, it's —'

'Ah! There they are.'

He waved at the approaching Land Rover. The headlights flashed an acknowledgement.

'What you need to know is that my father ...'

Joshua lifted his backpack and slung it over a shoulder.

'Joshua ... look at me.'

The Land Rover stopped at the kerb. The following cars immediately began to toot.

'I must go, Mayasa,' he said, stooping to kiss her quickly on the lips.

'My father has AIDS!'

Joshua froze at the open car door. He studied Mayasa's face intently. She tried to hold her nerve, but she bit her lip and blinked back the tears.

An impatient voice from the Land Rover dragged his attention from her. He clambered into the car and shut the door.

The Land Rover roared off along Ngong Road and Mayasa watched until it disappeared from sight.

*   *   *

'We'll be right back with top of the pops music in ten short minutes. Right now it's 8 am and time to cross to our news desk with John Muya. Good morning, John.'

'Good morning, James, and good morning, listeners. Here is the news for this Thursday, 27 December 2007.

'The chairman of the Electoral Commission of Kenya, Mr Samuel Kivuitu, has called for calm at polling booths throughout the country ahead of today's civic, parliamentary and presidential elections.

'Mr Kivuitu released the statement following reports from the Rift Valley of increasing numbers of political clashes reminiscent of the situation during the 2002 elections when hundreds of people were injured and many were killed in violent clashes.

'In Kisumu, home of the presidential candidate Mr Raila Odinga, a group of young men chased and beat officers of the administration police whom they said were in Kisumu to rig the election results against their candidate. Two police officers were killed in the attacks and six more are in Kisumu Hospital, two in a critical condition.

'Meanwhile, the latest polls show that Mr Odinga now appears to be in a close race with the incumbent, President Mwai Kibaki.

'In other news ...'

Charlotte turned off the radio. Joshua didn't mind; the news was no more than a distraction from his thoughts about Mayasa and what she'd revealed to him as they said goodbye.

In Kibera AIDS was everyone's living nightmare. He was well-informed about the disease — it had been part of his education at school — but street-corner experts said it could be contracted in more ways than the authorities would admit. The talk in Kibera was that a person sharing a house with an AIDS victim could catch the disease; that kissing someone with AIDS was as dangerous as having sex with them.

Joshua had already lost four people he knew to AIDS. He'd heard that three in ten Kibera residents were HIV-positive. Numbers meant nothing to him. It was the faces that told of the tragedy. And now all he could think about was Mayasa, as sweet and as beautiful as anyone could be. He couldn't reconcile that vision with what he saw on the streets and alleys of Kibera: the stick figures with sharp, angular faces and haunted eyes.

To take his mind from these disturbing thoughts, he pulled out his mobile phone. He had a text message waiting. The label told him it was from Mayasa. He stared at the name, but left the message unread.

Instead, he tapped out a text message to one of his friends in Kibera, asking that he keep him informed about Gideon Koske's movements and if Koske was still looking for him.

Joshua's initial apprehension about defying Koske's demands to stay in Nairobi for the duration of the elections was now massively overshadowed by his defiant goal during the football game. Although Joshua had been fortunate to avoid Koske's anger to date, it was well-known throughout Kibera that nobody could defy Gideon Koske with impunity. He knew that his fate, whatever it might be, was only temporarily suspended for the period he was out of Nairobi.

But it worried him that Mayasa was still there.

CHAPTER 22

The crudely painted sign, *Vantage Point — Refreshments*, gave Riley the opportunity to pull off the road for a break. The Land Rover came to a sliding halt in the narrow parking lane at the edge of the Great Rift Valley.

He was conscious of the fact that he'd been subdued during the drive towards the Great Rift Valley and Nakuru — their first overnight stop. He had much on his mind and now regretted agreeing to leave when they had. The novel could wait, but he'd barely commenced his article on briefcase NGOs. His time would have been better spent attending the UNICEF hearings.

Omuga's death continued to torment him. The more he thought of his amateurish attempts to prise information from the Community Development man, the more he regretted it. He shouldn't have tried to play detective with Omuga. What did he know about detective work? He'd made a fundamental mistake with Omuga — a professional would not have met his source in a coffee shop, of all places. Star-*fucking*-bucks. Why not a goldfish bowl and be done with it?

He forced his mind back to the scenery.

'Wow,' he said. 'Beautiful, eh?'

Below them stretched the Great Rift Valley, golden in the late afternoon sun. Cloud shadows added texture to the coloured patchwork of grasses that shimmered in undulations towards the distant escarpment that rose grey-blue through the heat haze — a rampart thwarting progress to the west.

Charlotte followed his gaze over the escarpment and into the valley below. 'Breathtaking, yes. But I'm not sure I'd describe it as beautiful,' she said. 'Perhaps more like *magnificent*.'

'Beautiful? Magnificent? What's the difference?' Riley asked.

'Sodas!' Joshua said from the back seat, and slipped out of his door. 'We need a drink.'

Charlotte fished a small note from her purse and Joshua headed to the *duka* at the edge of the road, which was doing good business with sightseers.

'Maybe I'm being pedantic,' she said, 'but beautiful is how I'd describe a floral arrangement or a colourful parrot. I'd even go so far as to describe a valley somewhere in the Swiss Alps, with pretty little cottages peeping through the autumn leaves, as beautiful. But this is none of those.'

The land dropped away just beyond the bitumen roadside. Riley ran his eye over the edge into the heart-thumping leap of the escarpment. Studying the middle distance more closely now, he found grey-green islands sprinkled sporadically among the ochred waves: a curl of white smoke; the dots of a cattle herd; the smudge of a maize garden. The minutiae added a grander perspective to the scene. It was something to challenge the imagination, but Charlotte was right, it was not beautiful. The valley had many of the attributes of an Australian landscape — wide, challenging to the eye — but essentially it was more impressive because of its magnitude than its beauty.

Riley turned away. He thought that beautiful things, even magnificent ones, were better enjoyed in the presence of a loved one. Without someone important to share it with, the scene somehow lost some of its lustre.

'Kuta at sundown is beautiful,' he said.

'Is that in Bali?'

He nodded. 'Uluwatu Temple on the cliff, silhouetted against a red sky. On the beach, it's like standing at the door of a blast furnace: hot and still and there's hardly a ripple on the ocean. You can almost drink the air, it's so heavy and hot. And when the sun touches the water, it sends out a long golden finger that seems to point right at you.' He caught her expression and shrugged. 'So they say.'

He knew he was on dangerous ground now. He should stop. A deep valley, like the sea, can pull the guts out of a man if he allows himself to be drawn into it. Riley today was a different person from the man who had stood on the golden beach at Kuta almost exactly five years ago. He'd been happy and full of optimism for the future back then. His first novel had been a critical success and had hit the heights in sales. And there was Melissa and all that love; it had surrounded him like a bubble.

'You know Bali well,' Charlotte suggested.

'I thought I did,' he said.

'What do you mean by that?'

He studied her for a moment, regretting the lapse in his resolve. Bali and its many memories were to be denied. Down that dark path was nothing but trouble. He couldn't even answer Charlotte's question so he simply turned the Land Rover's ignition key and revved the motor.

'We'd better keep moving,' he muttered, tooting the horn for Joshua, who was at the stall, soft drink in hand, talking to the boys working there. Joshua hurried to the car and climbed into the back seat, soda bottles clinking together.

Riley swung the car into a gap in the traffic. The diesel roared.

*   *   *

Joshua stayed in the car while Mark and Charlotte were at the reception desk of the Sarova Lion Hill Lodge. From his position in the back seat, Joshua could see them signing papers. The receptionist gave them each a key, which surprised him as he'd assumed they were sleeping together.

'Our rooms are up the hill,' Mark said when they returned to the car to collect their luggage. 'You'll be staying with the other guides and drivers. If you ask that guy sitting in reception, he'll look after you. We'll be spending a day or two here, so take it easy until we're ready to go.'

The person Mark indicated was a smug young Kikuyu who looked Joshua up and down as he stood before him. Joshua disliked him instantly. They traded thinly veiled tribal insults until the man finally gave him directions to what he called the dormitory.

'You'll be staying with the drivers. They're Kikuyus of course,' he added with a smirk.

The setting sun sent long shadows through the acacias as Joshua carried his bag down the path to a sprawling, low-roofed structure hidden from the other lodge buildings by a long line of enormous old bougainvilleas. Their brilliant colours glowed in the sun's sloping rays.

Five middle-aged men sat around a low table playing cards. They barely glanced up as Joshua entered.

'Not there,' one said as he put his backpack on an unoccupied bunk.

Joshua looked over the eight beds and could see that five were rumpled or had personal items on them. The one he'd put his pack on was clearly not in use.

'Why not?' he asked.

'It squeaks,' the man said around a cigarette hanging from the corner of his mouth. 'You will keep us awake.'

Joshua moved to the next vacant bunk and tested the bed. It didn't squeak, and was far more comfortable than the second-hand springed base in Kwazi's shack.

'I'm Maina,' the card player said. 'And this is Henry, Jamleck, Samuel and Jonathan.' He took a long puff on his cigarette and adjusted his cards. 'And what's your name, Luo boy?'

Joshua was tempted to retaliate in a similarly rude manner, but he knew he would be sharing with these men for some time. In a rare display of self-discipline, he said, 'Joshua. Joshua Otieng.'

'You don't sound like a Luo,' Maina said, taking his eyes off his cards to give Joshua a glance. 'And you're not missing any teeth.'

The others chuckled.

Joshua kept his lips tightly shut.

Undeterred, Maina continued. 'What brings you to the Lion Hill Lodge, my friend?'

'I'm a guide for two *mzungu* tourists,' he answered as nonchalantly as he could. 'I'm taking them to the Serengeti.' He fiddled with the catch on his backpack.

'The Serengeti?' Maina removed his cigarette and appraised him more thoroughly. 'You know the Serengeti?'

'I usually go through Kisumu and Musoma.'

Maina nodded thoughtfully. 'How's the road out that way?'

Now it was Joshua who nodded thoughtfully. 'It's not bad. It's not bad at all.'

The men played on, only occasionally muttering if someone played a card that didn't suit them. Joshua had no idea how to play the game, but watched as if he did.

'Do you want to play cards, Luo boy?'

'What are you playing?'

'Rummy. You need a hundred to get into it.'

He shook his head. 'I don't like rummy.'

'We can play something else. We like Luo money.'

Again the others laughed.

Joshua searched for a plausible excuse. The silence grew. All five card players were now studying him with interest.

'Oh!' Joshua said, pulling his phone from his pocket. 'Look, I've missed a couple of calls from the office.' And he hurried outside.

* * *

Joshua stood at the door of the dormitory, staring into the darkness. Strange noises came from the invisible beyond: scuttling sounds among the dead leaves of the garden and squeaks and twitters from the trees overhead.

He took a tentative step from the reassuring light of the

doorway. His breath caught in his throat. Above him were stars — millions more than he'd ever seen or imagined were possible. They formed a translucent dome of light above the trees and hills, so close he thought them almost reachable. And the air was so different he initially had difficulty identifying its unique character. It finally dawned on him that it was not what the night air had but what it lacked. It was crisp and clean and, apart from the slightest hint of sweet wood smoke, it contained little else to define it, but he felt he could drink it rather than breathe it.

In Kibera, there was nowhere he could go without the powerful taint of decay and filth. The open gutters were foul with decaying food and putrid water. There was always smoke in the air; not the sweet scent of wood, but the stink of smouldering plastic, rubber and the detritus of hundreds of thousands of people with no other means to dispose of their waste. In troubled times, when many were afraid to leave their doorways at night, they relied on Kibera's infamous flying toilets — human excrement in plastic shopping bags was flung into the night to land wherever misfortune determined. The stink of this foul litter was at times overpowering for even the most hardened residents.

An animal's roar filled the night — a nameless sound from the far side of the hill, made more threatening because of its anonymity. The short hairs on the back of Joshua's neck tingled. The roar hushed all others and there followed a period of utter silence — a unique experience in Joshua's life — leaving nothing but the soft beat of his heart and an indeterminate hiss in his ears.

The sound came again — one long, moaning grunt followed by a succession of staccato encores before it dwindled to nothing. After a moment's respectful silence, the lesser creatures resumed their positions on the night stage: twittering, scuttling, sniggering, barking, howling and squealing.

It was hard for him to imagine that Nairobi was only two or three hours away. Kibera was further — an eternity, surely.

He pulled his mobile from his pocket and clicked open Mayasa's text. *Ninakupenda*, it said. *I love you* was far more poetic in Swahili than in English. *Call me*, she'd added. She seemed so far away she might have been in another universe. Only her text message, carried across time and space, remained of her reality. He felt lost in a fog of loneliness.

Muffled sounds of conversation drifted from the drivers' quarters. How he envied them their nonchalant acceptance of the beauty outside the stuffy confines of the dormitory. How could they remain indoors when such a magnificent night lay untouched outside their door? It implied they had experienced even greater beauty elsewhere, beauty he couldn't imagine; or they had seen so much beauty that they'd become bored with it. In either case, he resented them immensely. Just a small portion of the purity contained in that single night could gladden the hearts of half of Kibera.

He edged away from the dormitory a step at a time. Five metres. Fifteen.

A three-quarter moon was rising, throwing a silver wash over the landscape that transformed it from a world of highlights and deep shadows into a two-dimensional image of reality. He wanted to plunge into that silvered scene; to become part of it; to know what being silvered felt like; and to look back to where he stood, rooted in wonderment. But the very thought of moving into the open made his skin prickle with fear and excitement. In Kibera he could recognise the dangers; he could avoid or confront them depending on his mood and the circumstances. But here he had no idea where danger lay. Indeed, it could be lurking at close quarters, even behind the huge bougainvillea bush a mere five metres from where he now stood. He had been drawn fully thirty paces from the dormitory. The umbilical cord of light that had kept him connected to the building ended ten metres away. He felt adrift in the night, unaware of the new world he now occupied.

A terrifying screech of unimaginable savagery shattered the silence. It came from the tangle of bougainvillea. It had such force that he doubted any living creature could create it. A comb scraped across a highly sensitive microphone came to mind.

He dashed to the dormitory door, sending a chair clattering into another on the small porch, and entered the room owl-eyed and blinking.

The drivers looked up from their game.

'It's a tree hyrax, Luo boy,' the fat one spluttered as the others howled with amusement.

*   *   *

The shower stung Riley's back with its icy darts. Turning, he endured its full force on his face until he was unable to catch his breath, then turned it off.

He grabbed the towel and, in front of the bathroom mirror, ran it vigorously over his back and legs to warm him. His reflection stared back, and he moved closer to the mirror, turning this way and that, studying his features as he'd not done for a long time. It was as if he were in front of a vaguely familiar portrait. Tiny crow's-feet clung to the corners of his eyes. As had been the case for some years, his dark brown hair was thinning on each side of his crown, but now it was slightly more obvious. The grey, sometimes green eyes stared back.

Out there on the Great Rift Valley escarpment, Charlotte must have thought him demented. The only excuse he could find for his moment of weakness was the memory of Omuga and his eight kids.

Now he had to get dressed for dinner and face Charlotte again, with those sympathetic eyes.

He screwed the towel into a ball and tossed it into a corner of the bathroom, then pulled on a tee-shirt and ruffled his hair to make it sit.

He suspected that dinner at the lodge was a casual affair, but it was the holiday season and dear Charlie would probably be dressed up. He wondered if there were ever a time when she had not been in control of the situation or had ever let her hair down.

* * *

Charlotte paused in the doorway of her cabin. She'd been preoccupied with her thoughts and now ran her hands over her pockets until she found her key.

She flicked the light switch and walked in darkness down the path from her *banda* towards the main building. The light fittings mounted every few paces on low posts threw yellow pools at her feet but did nothing to reveal the surrounding bush, which was in almost total darkness. The occasional spotlight at the foot of the fever trees turned their trunks an eerie green, and there were unnerving rustles in the shrubbery.

She'd been worrying about the wisdom of her suggestion that she and Mark share a short holiday before commencing their research. Mark had been decidedly uncommunicative on the drive from Nairobi and she was concerned how she was going to cope with similar moods over the days ahead. She wondered if her wish for a holiday showed a lack of dedication to her work, but soon dismissed the thought. She was aware she was often too harsh on herself, expecting excellence in her every activity. Surely a brief excursion to experience the wonders of Kenya was permissible.

Laughter came from the dormitory where Joshua was billeted with the tour bus drivers.

She entered the brightly lit reception area with a sigh of relief and sweating palms. The head waiter greeted her at the door and led her into the dining room. The candles sitting in glass bowls on each table made for a quite intimate atmosphere. She found Mark already seated with a drink in his hand. Thankfully, he was wearing jeans as she was.

'Evening,' he said, half rising to his feet. 'Would you like a drink?'

'Hi. A drink?' She had planned to avoid alcohol at dinner. It had become too easy to follow Mark's habits, which couldn't be healthy. But the night was warm and somehow special. 'Hmm ... What shall I have?'

'Wine? A gin and tonic?'

She nodded. 'A gin and tonic, please.'

He gave the order to the waiter. 'And another whisky,' he added.

The waiter nodded and left.

'How's your *banda*?' he asked.

'Very pleasant, although it's a bit, um ... remote.'

'Me too. And they don't call it Lion Hill for nothing. Did you hear the roaring?'

'No! Was that what it was? A lion?' She had been in the shower when she'd heard what she'd thought — hoped — was the rumbling of the hot-water service.

'Apparently.' He shrugged and smiled, looking a little abashed. 'I thought it was the hot-water system, but the guy who came to turn down the bed told me about the lions on the hill.'

'Really? And you didn't recognise it? I thought all you Aussies were outback types.'

'We certainly didn't have lions in my hometown.'

'Which was where? Sydney?'

He paused for a moment before answering. 'Wagga Wagga.'

Charlotte tried not to smile. She failed. 'Wagga, um ... Wagga?'

'I knew it,' he moaned good-naturedly, shielding his eyes from her with his hand.

'I'm sorry, but it just seems so ... well, redundant. And why, if you must call a town Wagga, compound the problem by repeating it?'

'Nobody but an Aussie can understand,' he said.

'Do any of you understand the double names?'

'Generally, no. Not unless you're from Woy Woy.'

This time she burst out laughing, as much from relief as amusement. He seemed to have come out of his pensive mood. She liked him when he joked around, but there were times when he seemed to be on his guard in case he revealed too much of himself. *A man of many moods*, she thought.

They chatted for some time before helping themselves at the buffet. Over dinner, they discovered a mutual interest in primitive art. She told him she'd read that there were cave paintings near Lake Victoria, and he said he'd like to see them when they were in the area later that week.

During dessert she asked him about life in a country town.

'I wasn't there all that long. My parents moved to Sydney when I was twelve, and when Dad's job made them move again a few years later, I stayed on to finish school and uni.'

'What did you study at university?'

'BA Lit at Sydney.'

'So did I. Well, not at Sydney University, of course, but at Oxford.'

'I know.'

'You do?'

'*The Maasai — Their Land and Customs* by Charlotte Manning,' he reminded her. 'M Sc (Oxford), BA Lit (Oxford).'

'Oh.'

'No need to be shy about it. In your line of work you need impressive credentials. A popular fiction writer, on the other hand … well, publication is credit enough.'

'How did you get into fiction?'

'I worked as a journalist for a few years before making a start on my first novel. Part-time.'

'A journalist. That must have been interesting.'

'Not really. Endless column inches on petty theft, social events and stock sales. My boss owned and ran the *Sunshine Coast Sun*. Had done for years. His idea of investigative journalism was a good lost dog story.'

She laughed.

Mark became more thoughtful as he talked about his path to writing his novel. 'Queensland, in fact all of Australia, was focused on Eddie Mabo's native title claim at the time. Mabo's home — an idyllic speck of an island in the middle of nowhere — became the public's perception of Eddie Mabo's cause — to win ownership of his ancestral land. After a ten-year battle, he won the case in the High Court.' He explained that the key point in the court's decision was the Murray Islanders' strong relationship with their land. 'In my mind, I believed they regarded their island as a paradise lost. It inspired me to make a start on my novel, based on Eddie Mabo's personal story.'

'Was the book a success?'

'Amazingly, yes. It was published in 2001 and the Australian sales took me to number twelve on the bestsellers list.'

'Congratulations! And did you follow up with another?'

He folded his napkin and placed it before him on the table. 'No. I mean, yes, but it was a totally different novel.'

'What was it about?' she asked, leaning forward.

But Mark seemed to have lost his enthusiasm and Charlotte's question hung in the air. She wasn't sure whether to press the issue. They'd had an enjoyable conversation and she didn't want to spoil it.

'It must have been so difficult to hold down a day job and tackle the second novel,' she offered sympathetically.

He was holding her gaze, but his mind was far away. He seemed to be debating how much to tell her. It was similar to their exchange on the edge of the Rift Valley earlier that day; he was there, but strangely disconnected.

She tried to ease the situation for him. 'I can understand if you don't —'

'Melissa and I decided to follow up on our luck,' he said. 'We married the year after my book was published and decided to go to Bali for a holiday.'

His mention of his wife came as quite a surprise.

'You're married?' she asked.

'We met in Surfers in 1999. I wasn't bad, but she could really surf. And a good tennis player too.' He was absorbed in his recollections. 'It wasn't a honeymoon as such — we'd been living together for three years — it was more of a working holiday, for me at least. I was researching my second book, which would be set in Indonesia. And I loved the place,' he said, reliving the memory. 'Can you believe that? Loved it. I'd taken Bahasa at uni. Learning a language gives you such an insight into a country's psyche, don't you think?'

She nodded, unsure if any other response was needed.

'The Balinese are very friendly people. Who could have imagined such an atrocity happening on Bali?' He stared into the candle flame, which was struggling to stay alight in a pool of wax. 'The death of a loved one is always incredibly painful. Their death in such freakish circumstances — a one-in-a-million chance — is like ... like a theft. My wife ... my life ... just disappeared in the instant my attention was diverted.'

The candle light succumbed to the wax with a waft of smoke.

'A bomb, for chrissakes! A bomb in paradise. It was an impossibility.' He ran both hands through his hair and dropped his eyes towards the table to collect himself. 'The blood. Body parts in the debris. The stench of burnt flesh. Nobody could understand.' He slowly shook his head. 'Melissa didn't deserve to die. We weren't over there fighting for a cause. We were on holiday. Why did they do it?' He looked up and gazed intently at her. 'Why?'

The mood of the evening changed as Mark was drawn back into the past and a time that had plainly been devastating for him. He talked about his wife as if she had only just died. It had been five years, but the pain was clearly still raw. In his uncharacteristic frankness, Charlotte glimpsed a side of Mark that she never would have suspected existed. He had obviously loved his wife dearly, and Charlotte felt moved by his need to explain his life with her.

When Mark had finished, there didn't seem to be anything Charlotte could say. Conversation flagged, and shortly thereafter Mark left, saying he needed to sleep. Charlotte remained at the table alone, touched by his confidence, by his faith, in her.

CHAPTER 23

It wasn't Joshua's wish to succumb to sleep, but he did. When he awoke with a start about an hour before dawn, he lay on his bunk listening. Beyond the snoring and grunting of the Kikuyu drivers arose the indistinct sounds of a world he had never heard before, where the wildlife fought or fed or did whatever creatures of the night did. He invented an unlikely menagerie of beasts to fit the myriad sounds. Between the grunts and shrieks, there were periods of profound silence.

He slid out of his bunk and pulled on his trousers, shirt and sneakers.

Viewed through the sparse foliage of the fever trees, the stars had lost a little of their immediacy and a hint of dawn colour suffused the sky above Lion Hill. Free of the bungalow's fusty air, the delicious scent of foliage dampened by dew filled Joshua's lungs. He took a dozen steps and the hair on his arms bristled with the excitement of just standing there, feeling like the only person on earth.

The scrunch of gravel under his feet seemed deafening as he made his way down the driveway towards the lake circuit road. He paused to listen. Silence. It was as if all the gathered dawn invaders held their breath preparing for the departure of the night. The intense silence rang in his ears until, minutes later, a faint whispering came from the hill. It was the sound of birds, surely thousands of them, on the other side of the rise — the first to sense the coming of the sun, singing like a multitude of angels in their faraway heaven.

He picked his way across the stock grid, where a sign forbade guests to proceed beyond that point on foot, and was soon on the circuit road where he padded in silence on the soft dirt.

He'd walked only a hundred paces when he heard a very slight sound from the grassy area at the side of the road. Through a break in the bush he saw a large animal. His heart stopped. It was an antelope of some kind, watching him. The word 'impala' came to mind, although he had no idea how he knew it. Its long, curling horns drew the eye. Joshua tried to imagine how it would feel to wear such a beautiful crown; the power it would confer. As he watched, barely daring to breathe, the animal sent a shiver down its flanks, rippling the rich russet felt of its coat. It turned its magnificent head and trotted away.

Suddenly there was the *woof* of a car engine and through the foliage came the headlights of an approaching car. Joshua slipped into the bush, taking delight in the idea that he and the impala shared the same need to be hidden from the impositions of the outside world.

* * *

Riley eased off the handbrake and let the Land Rover roll silently from the car park until it came to a stop at the lake circuit road, two hundred metres from the lodge. On the hill behind the collection of bungalows the sky was dusted in lavender-pink.

Riley wasn't intending to go anywhere in particular. The only reason he had for leaving his bed at such an ungodly hour was to put an end to the nightmares that had troubled him for most of the night. In the most recent, he'd been seated at a table under a cherry red bougainvillea drinking coffee with Omuga. His wife and eight children were gathered around. A horseman wielding a wicked scythe came galloping along the road and removed Omuga's head with a vicious swipe as his wife and children screamed hysterically.

Through the thin stand of lanky acacia trees he could see Lake Nakuru — a sheet of black glass reflecting the shadowed line of hills bordering the far shore.

A troop of vervet monkeys crossed the road to his left. When he drew alongside, they scampered off, watching him pass from the safety of the scrub at the side of the road.

After some time driving through the forest, the road with its covering of crushed quartz became a luminous pink. He came out of the acacias onto the grass flats along the lake shore and saw a squadron of flamingos skimming low over the water, stirring the morning air and setting up tiny ruffles in the silver-grey shallows. They wheeled and banked, catching the dawn sky's colour and turning their feathers from pastel to fuchsia pink. They landed, almost in unison, on the water's edge. A moment later, the water was still again.

Riley cut the motor and sat watching the wading birds, their lowered heads skimming the caustic soup for the small crustaceans that comprised their food source. Their number grew as more came wheeling in to join the flock. Soon there was a multitude lining the banks in both directions.

Riley became aware of a low, trilling sound that puzzled him for some time. Eventually he realised it was the sound of perhaps a hundred thousand flamingos sluicing the bitter waters of the lake through their beaks. It had a soporific effect and, to clear his mind, he opened the car door and stepped onto the soft mud of the lake shore, which was now coming to life as the eastern sky shifted from red to golden.

There was a muffled sound like the muttering of an enormous football crowd as a pink cloud lifted from the warm alkaline water. A rush of foetid lake air hit him in the face as the sky filled with thousands of flamingos ascending in panicked flight, leaving behind a large hole in the pink frieze that a moment ago had skirted the lake.

Riley wandered along the edge of the water, sending more and more flamingos into the air. He also startled a number of gazelle and other grazing animals unaccustomed to the sight of a human on foot. They galloped off into the taller grass towards the trees. He passed within a hundred paces of a rhino without noticing it, only seeing it when it trotted away, having caught his scent on the wind.

The sun was well above the confinement of the surrounding hills before he became sufficiently uncomfortable to realise it was burning into him like a blowtorch. He had let his thoughts carry him too far in time and space. The Land Rover was now so far away it was out of sight. When he reached the car an hour later, he was in a lather of sweat and feeling quite light-headed.

He searched for the water canister and cursed himself. He had taken it to his bungalow the previous night for a refill and had forgotten to put it back. He wasn't ready to return to the lodge, but now he had no choice.

He turned the ignition key. The starter motor gave a plaintive snarl and fell silent. Riley turned off the ignition key, waited a moment and tried again. This time there was only the alarming click of the solenoid, indicating the battery was flat. He checked the instrument panel and found he had forgotten to turn off the headlights before he went for his walk.

He slapped both hands onto the steering wheel before flinging the door open and stepping out of the cabin. The sun's heat immediately assaulted him. It seemed to have doubled in intensity in the few minutes since he'd returned from his walk.

He was reasonably sure the lodge was not too distant, but the warning made to every cross-country traveller in Australia's dry heart came to mind: don't leave the vehicle. He decided to ignore it, believing that a vehicle from the lodge taking guests on a pre-breakfast safari would find him before he went too far. He had no container, but as a precaution he removed his shirt and clambered under the car to soak the cotton in radiator water.

He pushed along the grassy verge of the lake, expecting to find the road before too long and a safari vehicle. With nothing but his hot, soaking shirt and the poisonous water of Lake Nakuru to quench his raging thirst until he reached the lodge, he hoped his prediction was accurate.

The shrill, melancholic call of a fish eagle caused him to look aloft to find it, but his eyes burned under the blazing sunlight.

* * *

Kazlana checked her bearings and looked below to confirm she was now over the Great Rift Valley. The huge Menengai caldera was to her left and beyond it lay Lake Nakuru.

She flipped on the plane's internal intercom. 'There's our destination,' she said to Antonio, who was sitting beside her.

He smiled and gave her a thumbs-up. 'Well done. What happens when we land?'

'I've arranged some transport to take us to the lodge. Tomorrow I begin my search for the person Papa visited.'

'I should go with you, *cara mia*.'

'No, I can do this alone. And you have family to see.'

Antonio had been born and raised near Nakuru — the son of an Italian prisoner-of-war in World War II. With his many comrades, his father had built the road that crept down the Kikuyu escarpment to Kijabe, on the floor of the Great Rift Valley. After the war, Antonio's father had returned to Kenya with his new wife, where they set about raising a family of four on the fertile hills above Nakuru. The Diconza vegetable farm was still there, now run by Antonio's three brothers.

'I should come with you,' he insisted. 'You never know what you will find.'

'It's an orphanage, Antonio. Don't be so dramatic.'

He shook his head. Kazlana knew what he was thinking. He had never won an argument with her after she'd made up her mind.

She lowered the Cessna's nose and they glided in over the lake towards the airfield at the southern end of the park. On the west side, she saw a Land Rover with the door open and nobody within sight of it. She thought it curious as it was strictly illegal for a tourist to leave a vehicle.

She skimmed over the strip to startle off a herd of zebra and checked the condition of the half-kilometre she needed to land the Cessna. When she was satisfied all was well, she banked to again approach from the north.

On her second pass over the lake, Antonio nudged her. 'What's wrong with this guy? Is he crazy?' He pointed to a man below them, walking through the grassland between the lake shore and the road.

Kazlana shook her head in disbelief. 'Some of these tourists think they can just go for a walk in the park. I saw an empty Land Rover down there. That must be his.'

Antonio shrugged and ran his forefinger across his neck in a cutthroat sign. 'He's looking for trouble, no?'

She nodded. 'And if he's not careful, he'll find it.'

Kazlana gave the man one last glance before she turned her attention to the landing strip. Tourists were always taking stupid risks, but she and Antonio would have to pass the southern end of the lake on their road to the lodge. They would try to find him before a buffalo or lion did.

*   *   *

Soon after leaving his car, Riley's throat was so constricted that he could hardly swallow his own spit. A short time later there was no spit to swallow.

He knew the lodge was on the hill on the other side of the lake so he had no concerns about the direction he needed to take, but the ignominy of arriving at the lodge, whether by foot or in one of the lodge's vehicles, dishevelled and thirsty would be an extreme embarrassment.

A boggy reach of the lake forced him to take a diversion into the taller grass beyond the alkaline foreshore. It was heavier going and the grass trapped whatever slight breeze played from the lake. He sweated profusely.

A pair of waterbucks bolted from a thicket, stopping a short distance away to peer back at him in wonder before they again moved off. Riley paused to reassess the wisdom of proceeding on foot. The rhino he'd seen had given him a wide berth, but he wondered if the other animals in the park would be so obliging.

He ran his eyes over the terrain ahead and to the landward side of the lake. Stunted, drab shrubs pock-marked the blond grassland, but on closer inspection he realised that some of the shrubs were in fact antelope of some kind. *Wildebeest*, he said to himself hopefully.

When he checked the shapes again, they appeared to have grown in bulk.

Remain calm, he counselled. *Whatever they are, they're not in your path and they're some distance away. At the moment.*

In his mind he searched for all the information he'd ever heard or read about buffalo. Just in case.

* * *

Joshua looked into the white-hot sky. Not a single cloud offered relief from the cruel sun. Around him was a sea of grass and, somewhere beyond that, the lake, which had seemed tantalisingly attractive in the early hours of morning, but an hour later had become the door of a furnace. He vaguely recalled from his primary school geography classes that the Great Rift Valley was much lower than Nairobi and therefore much hotter. The knowledge gave him small comfort now that he was hot, thirsty and quite possibly lost.

When he'd left the grassland surrounding the lake to seek the shelter of the acacia forest, he'd felt he could quite easily retrace his steps, find the lake and return to the lodge. But once he'd reached the trees, he came upon a herd of zebra, which he followed for a time before they led him to a small group of giraffe. They were impossibly tall on their long, elegant legs, far taller than any he'd seen in the tourist posters and far more graceful. They sailed through the tall grass like fishing dhows with gold and black sails. In every shaded alcove among the acacias were many more golden-brown impala, who watched him pass with wide-eyed curiosity. Guineafowl dashed, head down and serious, into the security of the reeds.

In the process of these discoveries, he'd somehow managed to misplace the lake.

He was now out of the forest and in tall grass, which was reassuring since it was the landscape that he'd initially followed when he'd taken his meandering path from the lake. There was no shelter. Only a few stunted shrubs poked above the metre-high grass.

Suddenly one of the shrubs moved and a large, dark head with angry brows knitted beneath an enormous spread of horns loomed from behind it. The beast was ruminating when Joshua first spotted it, but when he stopped to stare at it, its jaw became still, it lifted its wet and running nose in his direction, sniffed and then let out a low, assertive grumble.

In the next instant, Joshua heard the grass crush behind him. 'Don't move!' came a rasping whisper at his shoulder.

Joshua had no intention of moving. His legs had become jelly, but he turned his head without taking his eyes off the buffalo.

'Mr Mark?' he whispered.

'Yes. Now just back up. Very slowly.'

Joshua did as he was told.

The buffalo snorted and shook its head irritably.

'Keep moving,' Mark said, guiding Joshua with a hand on his shoulder.

From some distance came the low rumble of a diesel motor. Joshua turned towards the sound and stumbled backwards over a clump of grass.

As he scrambled to his feet, the buffalo gave one flick of its tail and, without a bellow or a murmur, charged directly at them.

'Run!' Mark yelled, and he and Joshua dashed towards the approaching vehicle, leaping grass tussocks and vaulting stones and mud wallows. Neither dared look behind, but the thundering hooves of the buffalo drew nearer.

Joshua drew level with Mark as the utility appeared through the scattered scrub and swung around to allow them to vault into the back of the vehicle.

No sooner were they on board than the driver gunned the motor, spraying dirt into the buffalo's face as it attempted to gore the tailgate.

CHAPTER 24

It was around nine when Charlotte passed the reception desk on her way to the dining room for breakfast. The desk staff chatted idly among themselves. One couple was settling their bill with the cashier. The surrounding gardens were empty, except for an old man shuffling around the courtyard and sweeping leaves into a long-handled dustpan.

She wondered if most guests were out on a morning game drive. She'd suggested the idea to Mark at dinner, and they'd agreed to defer breakfast until after their morning safari. The plan had been to meet in the car park at dawn — the earliest departure allowed by the park authorities — but when she'd got there, the Land Rover was gone.

The waiter who'd served them the night before greeted her and escorted her to a table. She was the only one there.

He asked, 'Is madam dining alone this morning?'

'Ah, yes, I am.'

He eased the chair in behind her as she took her seat.

'Has my friend been in this morning for breakfast?' she asked.

'No, madam.'

'Hmm, perhaps he went on the early morning game drive.'

'No, madam. There was no game drive this morning. Nobody was interested.' He smiled. 'Maybe everyone has too much beer for holiday party last night?'

She returned his smile. 'Maybe.'

Curious, Charlotte thought. It seemed out of character for Mark to change his mind about an early start — he was far too organised for that.

After breakfast, she walked down to the guests' car park again, wondering why Mark had gone out alone. She thought through all possible explanations without coming up with one that was feasible. They'd been getting along fine last night, and even though the evening had ended on a sombre note, she was sure that wasn't enough to make Mark want to exclude her from the safari.

She made her way back to the lodge. As she was about to enter the reception area, a small pickup truck came roaring up the driveway and stopped abruptly at the foot of the reception office steps. An attractive woman dressed in beige slacks and what seemed to be — improbably — a Versace leather jacket over a lemon blouse climbed out from beside the local driver and went to the rear section of the utility.

Sitting with their backs propped against the front cabin were a deeply suntanned man wearing what appeared to Charlotte to be a Bedouin's flowing robes and Joshua and Mark, the latter's face, neck and arms resembling raw steak.

Mark's cracked lips parted into a smile. 'Charlotte,' he said in a painfully brittle voice. 'I'd like you to meet Antonio ...'

The man swung down from the utility, his robes swirling around him. He was stunning. 'Antonio Diconza,' he said, making it sound like an Italian aria. 'Delighted to meet you, Ms Charlotte.' He plucked her hand from her side and kissed it.

Charlotte wanted to giggle.

The woman in Versace joined them as Mark and Joshua climbed out from the back of the truck.

'And this is Kazlana Ramanova,' Mark said. 'Kaz, I'd like you to meet Charlotte Manning.'

As soon as the women had exchanged greetings, Kazlana turned and clapped her hands. '*Wasili tafadali*,' she said, hailing a bellboy. '*Upesi! Upesi!*' she added impatiently as the boy hesitated. She soon had three staff members at her disposal, to whom she quickly issued a number of orders.

'Now,' she said, turning to Mark, who looked quite unwell.

'You are probably dehydrated and have a touch of sunstroke, so I've told the staff to set up the daybed on your veranda and to bring cold towels and iced water.'

She ran her eyes around the group. When there was no comment, she shrugged and added, 'So ... shall we go?'

Fifteen minutes later, Antonio had excused himself to check in, Joshua was last seen heading towards the staff quarters, and Mark was lounging on the daybed, a wet towel draped over his head and a glass of iced water in his hand.

'Any chance of some whisky and soda to go with the ice?' he asked.

Kazlana tut-tutted. 'Not at this time of day,' she said, filling his water glass again.

Charlotte, who had stood back during Kazlana's whirlwind of organisation, was surprised by the familiarity that existed between her and Mark. She wondered how they knew each other, and found the opportunity to ask when Kazlana enquired about the progress of Mark's magazine article.

'I take it that you and Mark are collaborating on the article about the UNICEF inquiry?' she said to Kazlana.

Kazlana took a sip of her Coke. 'You could say it's something like that.'

She looked pointedly at Mark, who nodded, but said nothing for some moments. Then: 'Kazlana has a number of contacts within the various NGOs — non-government organisations — and has been kind enough to arrange interviews with ... some key people.'

'I see.'

Again, there was a gap in the conversation, as if neither wanted to further explain their relationship. Charlotte felt as if she were intruding.

'Well, I think I'll go for a swim,' she said, standing. 'Mark, I'll call in later to see how you are.'

She said good day to Kazlana and headed towards her *banda*, more than a little miffed. As she changed into her swimsuit, she wondered about her annoyance. It wasn't as if Kazlana and Mark had been secretive, but there was something between them that indicated they had more than a passing relationship. Why she cared was another puzzle. Perhaps it was because she had been touched by Mark's admission of his love for his wife. Now, the connection she had felt with him last night seemed illusory.

By the time she reached the pool and sank into its tepid water, she'd decided it was none of her business how they knew each other. Perhaps they were lovers. Perhaps not. It really didn't matter to her at all.

*　　*　　*

Kazlana sat back in the cane chair on the veranda of her *banda* and took a sip of her gin and tonic. Below her, the Lion Hill Lodge bungalows spread down the slope to the main building and pool. It had been many years since she last stayed here. Fortunately, it had changed little.

Antonio came out the door, the bottles and glasses he carried clinking. He had showered and changed from his Arab attire and was now looking magnificent in white cotton drawstring slacks and a striped Italian sailor's shirt. He was one of that rare breed of men who always looked good in whatever he chose to wear.

She often teased him with the name *chameleon* because of his ability to change his persona to suit his situation. In Wajir, and across the border, he was a Somali in dress, religion and language, but on his home visits he reverted to Western clothes, Catholicism and English. It was his Muslim side that had been most useful to the family business. He was their contact in Wajir and beyond to Somalia. He was an entrepreneur, operating — as she did — with a wink and a nod at the letter of the law. They had worked together on various projects over recent years.

Antonio Diconza had been a friend of the Ramanova family for as long as Kazlana could remember. At age forty-three, he was twelve years older than she, and had joined the family business when Kazlana was just five. Her father had treated Antonio as a son, and Antonio, who had lost his own father at an early age, loved Dieter Ramanova almost as much as Kazlana did. Although he later developed business interests of his own, he and the Ramanovas had remained close associates; and in 2006, with the death of Dieter, it became an association strengthened by tragedy.

Kazlana had always adored Antonio. As a child, she had followed him about like a puppy, employing all her spoiled-child antics to get his attention. When she was unsuccessful, she'd sulk, but he would tease her by mimicking her long, sad face until she laughed.

As Kazlana matured, the many boys who filled her orbit tried to seduce her, but it was the handsome, manly Antonio who had captured her heart. To her great chagrin, he ignored all her best efforts to attract his attention, even though it was he who shepherded her through those troublesome teen years. Even her father couldn't control her wild nature, but Antonio could.

She had become increasingly bold in her pursuit of him, and one night watched him undress from outside his bedroom window. She was determined to catch him at his most vulnerable moment, and, when she guessed he had fallen into the first stages of sleep, she had slid open his window and slipped into bed beside him. Her fingers had trembled as she reached under the sheet and ran her hands over his chest, feeling the warmth of his flesh and the tautness of his muscles. She felt him responding to her caresses and, for one delicious moment, imagined he was aware it was she. Then he awoke with a start and pushed her from him.

He must have decided it was time to set matters right, for he turned on the light, pulled a sheet around his nakedness, sat beside her on the bed and told her he was gay. Kazlana, at age sixteen, had no idea what he meant; had never heard the word. Even after he had explained that he preferred males to females, she had thought he was making a sick joke at her expense. Concealing her tears, she'd rushed from his room and wouldn't speak to him for days.

Her father, while unable to control her behaviour as he might like, was close enough to his daughter to see what was happening and guessed that the besieged Antonio had at last explained his situation to her. It was her father's patient and kind words that helped Kazlana to understand. Antonio continued to treat her as his little sister, and she transferred her affections to others, although the night she had almost had his body remained among her most secret fantasies.

Antonio took his seat across the table from her now, facing the lake and the distant hills, and sighed. 'I sometimes forget what it is to enjoy the comforts of our beautiful country.'

'You're away far too often, but welcome home,' she said.

'Thank you, *cara mia*.' He raised his glass to her. 'To the success of your next conquest.'

'Conquest?'

'Or should I say, your next love adventure?'

'What are you talking about? Mark's a journalist and I'm helping him with his story.'

'You forget, my dear Kaz, I used to chaperone you when you were flinging yourself at those callow idiots who thought they would steal your little cherry.'

Kazlana remembered how she had so wanted to please Antonio that she would reject any prospective boyfriend whom he thought unworthy of her.

'I don't forget that you chased away more than one by threatening to cut off their *cojones*,' she said.

Antonio raised his eyebrows in mock surprise. 'Ai-yi-yi! What are you accusing me of?'

'You know very well, big brother. I was seventeen before I was able to get past your security system.'

'Jesus, Mary and Joseph! I thought you were still a virgin!'

They laughed together.

'But my toast remains. Good luck on your next conquest.' He raised his glass to her again and this time she met it with hers. 'You do have eyes for the fellow Mark, no?'

'I notice you're still on security duties. Can't you see he has a girlfriend?'

'That fragile English rose? She is no match for you, *cara mia*.'

Kazlana laughed. 'I have a toast,' she said. 'To our success.'

'*Si*. Our success. Ah, we need ice,' he said, and took both glasses inside.

She heard him in the bungalow, rattling ice in the bucket, and began to mull over the details of their plans. She had some lingering concerns.

When he returned with their drinks, she asked, 'How am I going to find this place where Papa delivered the medical supplies?'

'I know he used the landing strip inside the park, so the house must be close.' He drummed his fingers on the arm of his chair. 'I remember when I was a boy, before the park was created, my brothers and I would ride our horses right around it. There was a house somewhere on the west side of the lake, I think. I'm not sure, but maybe you could make a flight around the perimeter and see what you can find.'

She sighed, wondering if this were yet another tenuous clue that would come to nothing. There had been many of them in the previous year and she'd devoted her energy to each one, often to the detriment of the business and certainly of her personal life.

'I sometimes wonder if we'll ever get to the bottom of this matter,' she said.

'You've always been a very determined lady,' he said. 'I love that about you. I believe we have the best chance of finding the facts here in Nakuru. All the events seem to point to it. But if this turns out to be another, how you say, wild-goose chase, I believe it is time we put the whole matter to rest.'

He noticed her frown of annoyance. 'Before you cut my head off, let me say I believe we will find the truth here, if for no other reason than because you have set your mind to it. You know, there's never been a time when you've not got exactly what you want.'

'You know very well that's not true,' she said, smiling at him. 'You, of all people.'

'Well, that's another issue,' he said, smiling broadly before again becoming serious. 'But you must be very careful, Kaz. If this is connected to your father's ivory trading, it will be very dangerous. The Somalis are something to worry about, yes? But if there are also people in Nairobi involved, I am sure they will want to keep their operation a secret. Dealing in ivory is now forbidden. So we must remember they are dangerous. Maybe also very powerful.'

She nodded, the steel returning to her voice. 'That will not save them, my darling.'

CHAPTER 25

Koske waited for his call in the courtyard outside the Kenyatta International Conference Centre. A large crowd was gathered in the car park and surrounding streets, hoping to hear news of the election. Inside, the Electoral Commission of Kenya was counting votes in the ground-floor auditorium.

Koske thought it ironic that in the neighbouring conference room, the Austrian judge was hearing matters to do with the so-called Rights of the Child. Koske had been concerned that he might be called to testify to the committee, but now that Omuga had been silenced, he felt at ease. Even if he were called to make a statement, he could do so with complete confidence that he could not be challenged.

His mobile phone rang. He pressed it hard against one ear and jammed a finger into his other ear. Still he had difficulty hearing above the noise.

'What?' he asked. 'I can hardly hear you. Too much noise.'

'I said, how is it at KICC?'

Koske moved further away from those around him before replying. 'Our people are doing their best, but everything is going bad here.'

'What about the loading dock where they bring in the boxes? Are our people there?'

'Yes. We know the ballots are going straight to the counting room. So there is nothing going on in the KICC. They must be doing their work at the polling stations.'

'That's exactly what we see out there.'

'And Langata, ah? The ODM people are saying the boxes haven't come in. The counting is going slowly, slowly. You know what this means?' Koske asked.

There was a delay at the other end of the line. 'So Odinga could win the presidential election, but lose his own seat?'

'Exactly. In which case, it is impossible for him to be president.'

Silence again, then, 'I'll call the executive together immediately. You stay there and call me as soon as the Langata results are known. I hope your Kibera plans are in place. Maybe we need them sooner than we thought.'

*   *   *

Join us at kicc. The text message, marked *Siafu*, meant it was a mobile broadcast to Joshua's football team and other Odinga supporters.

Joshua's thumbs flew deftly over the keypad: *Wot happening kicc.*

The reply, a few minutes later, came from his team-mate David. *Trouble. Raila result not in. Can u come.*

No but go kicc. Fight strong.

*   *   *

Joshua walked into the drivers' dormitory while sending off another text message. His contacts in Kibera, many of whom had gone to the KICC, had kept him busy for hours with the facts, figures and rumours on the progress of counting. As far as the poll results were concerned, the reports from his many sources were mixed. The consensus appeared to be that the ODM was doing very well. The main concern was the situation regarding Odinga's own seat. Under the Kenyan constitution, a presidential candidate must stand for and win a parliamentary seat before becoming eligible for the presidency.

'Oh-ho,' one of the Kikuyu drivers said. 'Look at this boy now. Is he a reporter from KTN? Busy sending messages every time you see him. My, my.'

'No,' said Maina. 'He's just a spy for Raila Odinga.'

The other drivers, lounging on their bunks, chuckled.

Joshua had initially been very wary of Maina. He was fat and jovial and always keen to find a new way to tease the latest arrival. But Joshua had found his measure, and gave as good as he got. Maina was delighted at the sport.

'*Haki ya mungu*, Maina,' Joshua said. 'It's you! I thought a baby hippo had come from the lake and gone to sleep on your bed.'

The other drivers laughed.

'Listen, my young skinny friend,' Maina said. 'If you had a *mbolo* as big as mine, you'd need some muscle behind to give it a good pumping.' He lewdly simulated copulation with the vigorous thrusting of his hips.

'Maybe muscle,' Joshua replied. 'But a belly full of *ugali* is no help.'

'What would you Luos know of *ugali*, ah? All you do is drop a string in the lake and hope that an unlucky fish will bump into it.'

'Soon we won't worry about fishing. It's our turn to eat, *bwana*. *Kitu kidogo*, a little something. For the Luos this time.'

'So you think your man will win this one, Luo boy?'

'Even if the votes drop like rain, Kibaki cannot win. I guarantee.'

Maina laughed. 'Listen to him. A guarantee from the Luo. What price is your guarantee worth?'

'What do you mean, what is it worth?'

'I mean, what do you wager that your man Odinga will win the election? No, that's too long to wait. Let's make it interesting. What do you wager that your man Odinga will be leading in the counting by tomorrow night?'

Joshua felt all eyes on him. Maina probably suspected that he had no money to wager and was calling his bluff. He couldn't back down.

'Hmm ... You want a bet that Odinga won't be leading on Saturday night ... How much does Kenya Allover Tours charge for a morning game drive?' he asked.

Maina smirked. 'For an exclusive, guided game drive by an expert like me? A thousand shillings.'

'Then that is our bet. A thousand shillings that Raila Odinga will be winning the election tomorrow night.'

'Okay. It's a thousand shillings.' He turned to his audience. '*Ati!*' he said, using the Kikuyu question word. 'Am I crazy? Ah? What chance has he of paying me?' Turning back to Joshua, he said, 'I don't think you have a chance to win, my friend, but if you do, you will be seeing one thousand shillings for the first time in your unlucky life. *Si ndiyo?*'

'If I win ... when I win ... I don't want your thousand shillings.'

'No? Then what are you saying?'

'When I win, I want a special, personal game drive by you, Maina. And I want it for free.'

*   *   *

Koske's anger had been brewing for hours. Days. The vote count for Odinga's party had been swinging wildly. Everyone knew the votes were being rigged up country where the practicalities made scrutineering difficult. The answer was to keep public pressure and media attention on the situation, but he was having difficulty mobilising sufficient numbers of his Kibera foot soldiers to maintain the required awareness.

Again he cursed the unreliable Joshua Otieng. His first fatal mistake had been to defy Koske in the football trial he'd so generously arranged for his benefit. Then he had callously deserted him on the eve of the elections to go on some pointless safari. Koske's only consolation was his plan for revenge, but he put such thoughts aside. There was work to be done first.

At least he had the consolation that his other source of annoyance had been effectively disarmed. The UNICEF committee had become a nuisance. They were threatening to call him before their hearing to question him on the whereabouts of some of the children from the orphanage. Apart from the children themselves, Omuga was the only person who knew enough details to cause him embarrassment. With his elimination, Koske could attend the UN's pretentious hearings with their *aforementioned this* and *thereby that* without fear of exposure.

His rage eased and he let his mind drift back to Otieng and his crimes. It was just too bad that the Limuru Leopards had called Koske rather than Joshua himself to ask the boy to attend another trial and to discuss a possible contract. Otieng would never hear of that now that he'd turned against Koske. But that loss would be the least of his worries once Koske got his hands on him.

*   *   *

'This is Valley Radio, top of the Rift right here in Nakuru. It's 10 pm, and time to cross for our Friday night special report on Kenya's national elections presented by Valley Radio's own Jesse Chege. Over to you, Jesse.'

'Thank you, James. Yesterday, Kenyans turned out in record numbers to select the people who will govern them for the next five years. Long queues formed at polling stations from dawn until the official closing time. Many were turned away without the chance to exercise their vote.

'Most interest centres on the presidential race, where President Mwai Kibaki is fighting to avoid being the first post-independence leader to be voted out of office. After their landslide victory in 2002, Kibaki's Party of National Unity could have had every reason to be confident coming into this election, but Kibaki's election promise to clean up corruption has come to nothing. Voter dissatisfaction has been growing for some time and opinion polls midway through this year had Odinga's Orange Democratic Movement well in front of Kibaki and the PNU.

'*The present situation is that polling booths closed more than twenty-four hours ago, but the Electoral Commission of Kenya has released results from only sixty-nine of the country's two hundred and ten electorates, giving rise to claims from opposition supporters that Kibaki is trying to steal the election. Even so, these early results show Odinga to have fifty-eight per cent of those votes.*

'*There are riots breaking out all over Nairobi — nowhere worse than in Kibera. The mood of the people is turning, and tensions are building.*'

Joshua turned off the Land Rover's radio and sat in the dark. He should have been delighted with the news, but the election victory was not enough to dispel the two thoughts that troubled him.

The news report presented a picture of escalating violence in Kibera. He wondered how his friends and team-mates who were involved in the protests were faring. There would be trouble all through the settlements. People like his father and Kwazi, who were not involved in the struggle, were not immune from danger.

The problem that concerned him most was that somewhere in the chaos of Kibera and all its turmoil was Mayasa. He had dared to hope to live happily with her somewhere else, anywhere but Kibera. But that bubble had burst with her shock disclosure of her father's illness.

Her text message glowed in the dark: *I love you. Call me.*

He hadn't called her, but he hadn't stopped loving her.

CHAPTER 26

A light rain was falling on Lake Nakuru at dawn; now, an hour later, it showed no sign of weakening. Kazlana knew there was no point going aloft. It would be impossible to find where her father had delivered the medical supplies until the cloud cleared.

She paced the short length of her veranda until Antonio, sipping the pungent black coffee he preferred, complained.

'You invited me to join you for coffee, but I cannot stand you stalking about like a lion. It will not stop the rain.'

She puffed hard on her cigarette, tapping the ash into the garden. 'I hate this waiting. It seems like I've been waiting a lifetime.'

'Soon enough, *cara mia*.'

She continued to pace, then abruptly sat at the small table opposite him. 'This friend of yours, Abukar ... He says he knows nothing about Papa's plane ... I don't believe him. Can he be trusted?'

'What can I say? Faraj Khalid Abukar is a war lord at the end of a long line of warrior chiefs and war lords.'

'But can you trust him?'

'I know him quite well, Kazlana. He is a very charismatic man. His grandfather joined the British side to fight the Italians in World War II. The Allies conquered Italian Somalia in 1941, then won back British Somalia. But the Somalis never regained all their lost territory. Abukar's family — his whole clan — has been fighting to regain it for many, many years.' He paused to sip his coffee and consider the question again. 'But you ask, can he be trusted? When you asked me to speak to him about your father's death, I asked myself the same question.' He shrugged. 'I say he can, but we must remember that he and his people are very determined. They may say one thing and do another. That is not to say they are not honourable people. They are. But they are also desperate people and they can take desperate actions, no? Perhaps the question should be: do we have a choice?' He smiled at her. 'In which case, the answer is quite simple. No, we do not.'

* * *

Riley shifted his head and, through his sleepy vision, made out a window. Beyond it was a monkey in a tree. A yellow tree.

He was in his bungalow and he was safe. He'd slept well, although he still felt an unsettling embarrassment at the fuss he'd caused the day before. It didn't help that he'd underestimated the distance involved, nor that he was just dead unlucky that there were no game drives that morning. The fact remained that when Kazlana and her boyfriend had come along in their utility, the buffalo had been gaining ground and he'd been on his last legs. It had taken all his remaining strength to fling himself into the back of the ute beside Joshua. Thereafter he'd lain there like a stunned mullet.

He swung his feet over the side of the bed and sat up. His head spun, but he padded out onto the veranda and squinted into the brightness of the morning.

Charlotte was coming up the pathway, carrying a tray.

'Good morning,' she said. 'I've brought you some breakfast.'

'Thank you. I'm starving.'

'Are you okay today?'

He ran his fingers through his hair and stretched. 'I am. Just needed a good night's sleep.' He pulled out a chair for her and she placed the tray on the table.

'You've brought me breakfast,' he said, smiling. 'That's something my mother would do.'

'I'm sorry,' she said, sounding a little annoyed. 'I imagine you're able to look after yourself.'

'Charlie, I'm sorry. Thanks for everything you've done.'

She remained standing.

'You're very kind. Please … let's sit down out here.'

'Well … the morning's too beautiful to argue,' she said, taking a seat.

'It is. Reminds me of mornings in Surfers Paradise.'

'Is that where you met Melissa?'

'Yes.'

'How did you two meet?'

'Melissa and I were destined to meet. As soon as I saw her I knew we would spend the rest of our lives together.'

He smiled self-consciously, embarrassed by allowing his emotions to show. Keeping his memories and emotions under a tight rein had been important over recent years.

'I love stories about destiny. Tell me about it.'

'Oh, well …' He cleared his throat, uncertain whether to proceed. 'Are you sure you want to hear this?' he asked.

'Please.'

'Okay, well … I was batching in this cheap flat out the back of Surfers. It didn't have much of a kitchen, which didn't matter as I wasn't much of a cook. But it had only a small fridge so I was constantly down at the supermarket buying one of this and two of that. The day I met Melissa, I was supposed to be surfing off the heads at Burleigh with a mate, but the nor'wester had gone, and an onshore breeze made for an ugly chop, so we cancelled and I went to Woolies instead. She came in while I was wrestling with a trolley. You know how they get stuck together? I was getting kind of annoyed and then I saw her. Her hair was piled up on her head — it was about your colour, only a little longer. And she had on this sleeveless white blouse with crinkled bits around the shoulders.' He paused, a smile playing on his lips. 'God, she was gorgeous.

'Anyway, I caught her eye. She seemed to be staring right at me and I was taken by surprise. I mean, she was a vision … And she was just so obvious; staring at me like that. At least that's what I thought. Later she told me she couldn't remember seeing me there at all, that she was probably preoccupied with other things. You see, she wasn't supposed to be there either. She was in a hurry, and only dropped in because of some changes to her plans that evening.

'So there I am, thinking this beautiful creature's keen on me, so I kind of hover around her — discreetly, I thought — waiting to catch her eye again. I was still under the impression that she was staring at me, so I was full of confidence.'

'I can't imagine you any other way,' Charlotte said with just a touch of sarcasm.

'Confident? Are you kidding? I would never have said a word to her if she hadn't given me what I thought was that lingering look.'

'Okay, I believe you,' she said, sounding unconvinced. 'Go on with your story.'

'I go to the fish counter and I know Melissa's just behind me, waiting her turn, so I make it clear to the attendant that I only want a small piece — just enough for one, I say, to let her know I'm single. Subtle, eh? After that, it became a bit of a game to manoeuvre my trolley so it was coincidentally beside hers. Buoyed up by my impression that she had this burning interest in me, I engaged her in small talk. I said something about cooking and perhaps we should swap recipes.'

'You didn't!'

'Sadly, I did. But it gets worse. I'm not sure how I managed this, but, to my shame, I told her I was an author.'

Charlotte began to chuckle. 'Oh, Mark …'

'I know. In fact I used the words "published author".'

'Oh, no!'

'Why she allowed me to go on after that, I'll never understand.'

'What then?'

'I introduced myself. She said that Mark was a popular name in her family. Somehow I got the courage to ask if I could call her, and she gave me her mobile phone number.'

'Nice going.'

'I couldn't believe it. We went our own ways then, but I still couldn't believe my luck, so I called her before I left Woolies.'

'Before you left the supermarket?'

He nodded. 'As I said, I knew we'd be right for each other, and I didn't want to waste a moment.'

'What made you so sure?'

'I believe in fate. Some people call it synchronicity. Neither of us should have been there on that day. It was a one-in-a-million chance.'

'It's a lovely story, Mark. You must have loved her a great deal.'

He looked down. 'Melissa's the only woman I've ever loved. And then ... well, as I told you the other day ...'

'I'm sorry,' she said. 'I didn't mean to bring back bad memories for you.'

'No, it's okay. Since I got it off my chest last time, I've been able to face things a lot better. It used to hide in the back of my head and hurt like hell when I let it out. I think I'm getting better at handling it now.'

'That's a good sign, don't you think?'

He smiled at her. 'Thank you. I think it is.'

'Oh, look,' she said. 'You have another visitor.' There was a slight edge to her voice.

Kazlana came strolling up the path.

'You live!' she said. 'I've come to make sure of your survival. And Charlotte ... so nice to see you again. Have you been nursing your boyfriend back to good health?'

Charlotte blushed.

Riley jumped in. 'Charlie and I are just, well ...' He looked at her for help but she didn't seem to have anything to offer. 'Friends,' he said. 'And business partners, in a manner of speaking.'

Charlotte avoided his eyes and he had the feeling she wasn't pleased with his description.

'Perfect!' said Kazlana. 'I think it is good that a man and a woman can be friends.'

'Where's Antonio?' he asked.

'Poor darling, he had too much to drink last night, and now he's resting before going to see his brothers on the farm. I said I must check on how you're recovering, and I can see you are already better, so ... that's excellent.'

'I have some matters to attend to in my bungalow,' Charlotte said as she rose to her feet.

Kazlana turned to her. 'Before you go, I'd like to invite you and Mark to join me on a joy flight over the valley as soon as this cloud clears. Would you like that?'

Charlotte seemed to barely give the invitation a thought. 'No, thanks, Kazlana. You're very kind, but I ... I have to do some work before we leave for Lake Victoria.' She gave them both a wave and a smile and strode off up the path to her bungalow.

Riley felt as though he'd said or done something to offend her. It wasn't the first time he'd felt that way around her. She seemed to be a woman with strong opinions on how one should conduct oneself.

Kazlana remained standing.

'Oh, please. Won't you make yourself comfortable?' he said.

'I always do,' she responded, flashing him a broad smile.

* * *

It wasn't until early afternoon that the low cloud finally burnt off, allowing Kazlana to deliver on her promise to take Riley for a flight over the Great Rift Valley. She climbed into the Land Rover beside him and they headed towards the small airfield.

'I spoke to Charlie in the garden just now,' he said. 'I tried to convince her it's a great way to see the national park, but she still said no.'

'Pity.'

'Yes. She says she has work to do, but I —'

'Let's not worry about her,' Kazlana cut in. 'Why don't we just relax and enjoy the day?'

Riley felt concerned about Charlotte — she'd seemed a little out of sorts at breakfast — but had to agree with Kazlana's sentiment. 'What are you flying?' he asked.

'A Cessna 182.'

'Hmm … Nice little buggy.'

'You know the plane?'

'I learnt to fly in a Cessna after I finished university.'

At the airstrip he helped her ready the Cessna for take-off. Inside the cockpit, she reached over him to check his seatbelt. He was very conscious of the heady combination of perfume and tobacco that came off her skin. It was almost irresistible.

'Would you like to take the controls?' she asked. 'They say you never forget your first one.'

'So I've heard,' he said, smiling at her *double entendre*. 'But I'm not current. I didn't bother keeping up my hours. Thanks anyway.'

'Okay. I'll take her up, then you can try your hand. Are you ready?'

'Ready.'

Kazlana flew north, before climbing to the east out of the valley and circling Mount Kenya. They continued to the north until she told him they were over Rumuruti and the Laikipia Plateau. From his research Riley knew Laikipia was the northern extent of the Maasai's traditional territory — the homeland that was taken from them by the British in 1911. Even from a thousand metres he could see it would be prime grazing land.

They flew back to the national park and Kazlana circumnavigated the lake several times, intently studying the terrain below.

'Have you lost someone?' he asked, reminding her of the previous day when he'd been the person lost.

She smiled. 'No, just interested in that house down there. It's almost in the national park.'

After another circuit during which she again studied the farmhouse below, Kazlana levelled out and offered Riley the controls. He hesitated a moment and then grinned.

The Cessna was a joy to fly and his experiences flying in the cattle country of west Queensland came vividly back to him. It was a job he'd taken to build his capital so he could take time off to write. Life had seemed so simple back then. He would rent a shack out the back of Surfers Paradise, do a little surfing in the morning and write into the wee small hours. But then he met Melissa — a life-changing event.

He touched the right rudder and it responded immediately, dipping a wing and easing them off to the west over the Mau Escarpment. The Cessna ploughed into an air pocket as they turned back over the Great Rift Valley and the brief sense of weightlessness took his breath away.

Kazlana must have shared his exhilaration. She reached to where his hand rested on his thigh, laid her hand over his, then patted it. The gesture might have been intended as platonic, but, as had happened on the night they'd met at the Australian High Commission, the simple touch sent a ripple of pleasure through him. He turned towards her. She was smiling, but her eyes, hidden behind her silvered sunglasses, were unreadable.

'We're running short of fuel,' she said, breaking the tension. 'I'd better take us back to the strip.'

She took the controls from him and banked sharply before nosing the aircraft into a glide towards the lake.

On the murram strip, she made no move to leave the aircraft. He could hear her breath coming in short, soft pants. She pulled a water bottle from her pack and, after taking a long swallow, offered it to Riley.

'Thanks,' he said. 'What made you take up flying?'

'My father taught me when I was very young.'

'He did a good job,' he said, taking a mouthful from the bottle.

She was silent for a long moment. Riley glanced at her, thinking she'd not heard him. A mix of emotions played over her features. Her eyes, now without the inscrutability of the sunglasses, burned. The change from the soft, even amorous expression she'd worn in the air was dramatic. It was almost as though she'd shed one mask to don another. She was transformed.

She sensed his eyes on her and immediately suppressed whatever thoughts had possessed her. The mood fell from her like an unwanted robe.

'I can't stop wondering about the plane crash that killed my father,' she said without emotion. 'Some say I should forget about the circumstances, but it's difficult.'

'I'm sorry. Maybe we should —'

'Don't be sorry.' Her words cut the air like a knife. Her persona had changed again. Riley watched, fascinated by the metamorphosis.

Kazlana's easy smile returned. 'You should never be sorry for your good intentions, Mark.'

She searched for a tissue and, finding one in her pack, dabbed at the tears that had suddenly appeared, seemingly embarrassed by her display of emotion.

'He gave me this,' she said, sliding a thick gold ring around her finger to allow the light to catch the facets of the large blue stone it held. 'It's tanzanite — the world's newest gemstone.'

The stone might have been eight or ten carats and was remarkably blue.

'It's very lovely,' he said.

'Yes. It changes colour slightly depending on the light. At this time of day, when the sun is a little lower, it has yellow and orange tinges. See?'

She held her hand higher. He took it in his and studied the flare of the sun in the stone's blue depths. Her hand was ice cool.

'They say that at midday the stone becomes true blue — what some say is its real colour.' She continued. 'But I think it's at night, when it's shot with violet, that it comes to life. It's very mysterious.' She was silent then, studying the ring, before she added, 'Shall we go?'

'Sure.'

Riley went around to Kazlana's side of the aircraft and opened the pilot's door. She looked down at him with red-rimmed eyes, the tissue held to her nose. She appeared unwilling or incapable of climbing out of the plane. Riley coaxed her, holding his arms up to her. She unclipped her harness and swung her legs out of the cockpit. He caught her under the arms and allowed her to slip to the ground, supporting her weight against his body. She remained there with her cheek against his chest. Her warmth, her scent and her vulnerability made for an intoxicating combination. A woman's body against his was a rare experience since his wife's death.

Riley had returned to the Gold Coast from Bali in a fog of grief, depression and helpless rage. His friends had tried in their various ways to assist him in his recovery, but he'd been incapable of applying himself to what seemed the trivial business of meeting people and having fun. When the attentions of a well-meaning ex-wife of a friend had become more than purely sympathetic, he had been aroused at first, but then stricken with an overwhelming sense of betrayal of Melissa. After that, he'd found himself unable to have a relationship, even a one-night stand, with anyone. He'd thrown himself into his writing and refrained from any further sexual encounters. In time, he'd come to accept his life as a celibate.

Now, with Kazlana so invitingly close, to his utter dismay he felt himself becoming hard. The more he willed the erection down, the more insistent it became. He gently tried to move away, but Kazlana was leaning her body against him. He put his hand on her shoulder, gently allowing the weight of it to press against her, but she remained there — an unbearably sexual being.

He needed a diversion. Anything.

He reached into his pocket, giving him an excuse to move away from her body. 'Here, you can use my handkerchief.'

She looked at her tissue, which was a sodden mess, and took the handkerchief. A smile fluttered at the corners of her lips. 'You're very sweet,' she said.

Riley didn't feel sweet at all. He felt like a bastard.

'Why did I think of this ring?' she wondered aloud. 'I was telling you about my father ... Yes ... He died in the Northern Frontier District — a place of red dust and sand that suffocates you when the wind blows. A desolate country ...'

She became lost in her thoughts, perhaps revisiting the scene again.

'He went to the desert country near Wajir,' she said eventually. 'The aviation authority released a version of events that I refused to believe. It was ridiculous to suggest my father would make such a stupid mistake. But I feel I am missing something. Why would my father put down in the middle of the Northern Frontier District? It just doesn't make sense.' She dabbed at her nose and put the handkerchief in her jacket pocket. 'The only other flying he did at the time was here to Nakuru. Some kind of medical facility.'

'Medical facility?' Riley said. 'Omuga mentioned a medical facility that the Circularians use in Nakuru. I couldn't quite get the gist of it, but he said the children had to be checked out before they were offered for adoption.'

She stared at him.

'I think we need to take a closer look at that house,' she said.

CHAPTER 27

The afternoon dragged on. After tea and too much chocolate cake, Charlotte went to sit beside the pool, but she grew bored with that and decided to go to her cabin and read her book.

She noticed rainbow-coloured lizards on the rock-lined pathway. With the remainder of her chocolate cake, which she retrieved from the dining room, she tried to coax one of the lizards to eat. It gave three quick little flicks of its head, as if nodding in agreement, but ignored her inducement.

The lizards remained unimpressed with her and, after playing their game for some fifteen minutes, Charlotte had a similar feeling about them. She stood and brushed her jeans down and tried not to imagine Kazlana and Mark flying together. The very thought of it turned her legs to jelly.

It was too late for a nap and too early for dinner. To fill the time, she decided to take a walk to the fence below the lodge's grounds.

As luck would have it, the Land Rover came rocking up the road as she was returning from her walk. She stepped from the road and remained concealed as they drove past. She didn't want them to think she had been waiting anxiously for their return.

* * *

Riley walked around to Kazlana's side of the car and took her hands in his as she stepped down. She looked up and thanked him, all traces of the emotional roller-coaster she'd ridden gone.

'And thank you for your kindness back there at the strip,' she added.

'Losing someone close is tough,' he said. 'I know the feeling.'

'You know the feeling?' She studied him for a moment, then said, 'I can see you do. Every loss hardens the heart, but you have to find a way around it, otherwise the pain of loss can diminish you. In the end we can only help ourselves when bad things happen. But you see, I have an advantage.' The softness of her tone was quickly displaced. 'I have experience in these matters. You can't live your whole life in Africa without seeing evil, and you have to find a way to deal with that. I've decided that my father is the last loved one I'll lose.'

'How can you be so sure?'

She smiled. 'It's simple. I don't intend to fall in love.'

'You said you have to find a way to deal with the evil. What's your way?' he asked.

'The only way I know how. I let the hatred burn until it becomes an anger so hot it gives me energy. It would be easy to be consumed by it, but, knowing those responsible are probably within reach, I take care to control myself. It's amazing what a person can do if he or she can channel hatred. It has such power.'

Kazlana's moods flickered between daylight and darkness, like the fall of sunshine through the branches in a dark and menacing forest. Riley wondered how such a feminine woman could harbour such ominous passion. In Kazlana's darkness he recognised some of the characteristics he'd experienced after his own loss. Following Melissa's death, he had become a very angry person. But unlike Kazlana, he doubted that anger alone would ever allow him to get over the loss of his wife. It only seemed to torment him further. But the similarities were sobering.

'It's an interesting philosophy,' he said. 'In my case, I'm not sure I have enough hatred there. It's my anger that I have to control, and I can't say it gives me energy. I sometimes feel it's just dragging me down.'

'Maybe it works for some and not others. All I know is that it works for me.' She paused to reflect. 'Only ... I don't know what I'll do when I've had my revenge. Maybe I'll just deflate. Like a balloon.'

'Somehow I can't see you doing that.'

Kazlana shrugged and smiled. 'Perhaps you're right. We'll see.'

She took his hand and squeezed it before reaching up to kiss him gently on the lips. Then her mood changed again. 'We should get moving if we're going to find the house today,' she said in a businesslike manner. 'Let's meet up again in half an hour.'

*   *   *

Charlotte watched as Mark helped Kazlana out of the Land Rover. She paused to dab at her eyes with a handkerchief, then they spoke earnestly for some time, before Kazlana kissed Mark and walked off towards the lodge.

Charlotte remained in her hideout, a voyeur hidden among the shrubs. Having witnessed the tender scene she felt a sense of guilt; as if she had intruded into something that should have remained between these two.

Suddenly Bradley came to her mind. *Odd*, she thought. It had been her decision to break off their engagement, but she now felt a trace of regret. Regret, guilt, tenderness — a mix of emotions.

Could it be that seeing Mark and Kazlana together had reminded her of how comforting it had been to have someone to care for her? Someone to dispel the loneliness?

Or was it something more primitive?

*   *   *

Kazlana had noted the landmarks well and was able to guide Riley towards the house she'd viewed from the air. He stopped the Land Rover at an overgrown track leading from the national park road. A locked gate blocked their path; Riley helped her to scramble over it. In the tall grass beside the gate was a chipped and faded sign. In large letters were the words *Nakuru Safe House*; and in smaller, barely legible letters underneath: *Circularian Organisation, Mombasa.*

As they walked towards the house, an African boy of about fourteen came wandering down the track towards them.

'*Habari*,' Kazlana said.

He looked at her, then at Riley, but said nothing as he continued towards the gate. He seemed absorbed in his own thoughts.

'*Kesi!*'

The voice came from the direction of the house and a man wearing a white dustcoat came into view. He was of southern European appearance with grey-flecked hair and rimless spectacles. When he spotted Kazlana and Riley he paused ever so briefly, then smiled.

'Oh!' he said. 'I'm sorry, but did you see Kesi go by?'

Riley said a young man had passed them moments before.

The man hurried past them.

'Please wait there,' he said over his shoulder. 'I'll be back.'

When he returned, he was leading Kesi gently by the arm.

'Is the boy all right?' Kazlana asked.

'He's just awoken. Half asleep,' the man said. 'He's supposed to wait for one of us to take him.' He eyed them suspiciously. 'How can I help you?'

'I'm Kazlana Ramanova,' she said, handing him her card. 'And this is my assistant, Mr Mark Riley.'

He lifted his eyes from her card. 'Pleased to meet you, Ms Ramanova. Mr Riley. But I have no need for a public relations company.'

'Oh, I do beg your pardon,' Kazlana said, wearing a radiant smile. 'I should have explained. With all of the poor publicity coming out of the UNICEF hearings, we've been retained by the department to put a more positive perspective on organisations such as yours.'

The man wasn't convinced. 'Who in the department told you we were here?'

Kazlana mentioned three names who she said were her departmental contacts. They were obviously familiar to the man and, somewhat mollified but still reticent, he introduced himself as Dr Agousi.

'As you can see, Dr Agousi,' Kazlana continued, 'my company does work in the NGO area. We all know that organisations such as yours do some wonderful work, but the department is concerned about the flood of bad publicity that's coming out of the UNICEF inquiry. So, can you describe what facility you are operating here, please?'

'We are a safe house for drug-affected children,' he said. 'We have street kids like Kesi here, and others, little ones, who have acquired a dependency in vitro.'

'Are you a private company?' Kazlana asked.

The doctor smiled. 'No, no. We are a charitable institution.'

He explained that the members of their organisation working in the Nairobi slums identified children at risk and sent them to the safe house for rehabilitation. They'd found that the old house near the national park was suitably isolated, keeping the older children from harm's way — safe from the drug pushers.

'And there are other benefits of our position,' he went on. 'Being so close to the park discourages any of the boys who might want to go wandering into the town. There are enough scary sounds around us, particularly at night, to keep these city boys indoors.'

A canvas-covered truck was parked beside the house, which appeared to be an ordinary farm residence with a number of outhouses, which Agousi said were bungalows.

'We can accommodate about a dozen boys at a time,' he said. 'Only boys. We tried a mixed program about a year ago, but ...' He shook his head. 'Hormones, ah? It was impossible.'

Agousi led Kesi up the steps to the veranda, where he opened the front door to let the boy enter. Kazlana got a glimpse of a handful of other boys of a similar age, sitting quietly at tables.

When the doctor came back to them, he began a lengthy overview of the organisation's methods of raising funds and covering costs. 'Now, if you'll excuse me,' he finished. 'I have work to do.'

They thanked Dr Agousi, who watched them retrace their steps to the car.

'A strange man,' Kazlana said.

'He did everything but put his hand out for a donation, but didn't offer to show us inside the house.'

'Do you believe him? Could this be a safe house for drug-affected teenagers?'

'Maybe. It's just ... being out here, so far from everything ... it's an odd place for rehabilitation. And what's the connection with the orphanage — if any?'

'You heard what the doctor said. The location keeps them away from drugs.'

'It just doesn't seem right,' Riley repeated. 'How do you know those names in the department?'

'Contacts,' she said.

They climbed the gate and returned to the car.

'Do you think that boy, Kesi, was still suffering from drug use? He was so ... out of it,' she said.

'I've seen quite a few kids on drugs,' Riley said. 'Kesi was definitely affected, but it may have been from something else.'

'What do you mean?'

'He looked as if he may have been waking from a strong sedative rather than street drugs.'

* * *

The lodge management had placed a notice in every bungalow to advise guests that a state of emergency had been declared in the nearby town of Nakuru. It was short on detail, but said that guests were advised to remain in the safety of the lodge until the present short-term situation was resolved.

'Until the present short-term situation is resolved,' Charlotte said from her seat on the edge of the sofa, a copy of the memo in her hand. 'What does that mean?'

Nobody answered. Riley was fiddling with the TV remote, trying to get some news. Although the guests' TV room could comfortably seat about ten, Kazlana paced the floor, unable to relax.

'Try KTN,' she suggested.

The screen flickered to reveal a scantily clad group of women and men climbing rope ladders and crawling through large plastic barrels.

'*Survivor!*' Riley said in disgust.

'KBC then.'

A Swahili soap was on the national broadcaster. He flicked through the subscription channels — CNN, Discovery, MTV — then sank into the chair beside the TV. 'If there's nothing on the local channels, pay TV won't have it.'

'Let's try the radio,' Kazlana said.

'*Here is the main story again. Counting continues in polling booths around the country. The presidential results of Thursday's national elections indicate that the opposition candidate for president, Mr Raila Odinga, is polling well ahead of President Mwai Kibaki.*

'*In a stunning turnaround since the most recent opinion surveys, the figures indicate Mr Odinga has a lead of some 1.5 million votes.*

'*Meanwhile, in the Rift Valley electorate, tensions are at boiling point as police and administration police try to control the continuing violent protests over land rights in the Naivasha and Nakuru regions.*'

Riley watched Kazlana fumble in her purse for a packet of cigarettes. She held a match to the Marlboro and inhaled. The episode that afternoon came back: Kazlana's closeness; the strong emotions liberated by their conversation about personal loss; her perfume. And, yes, the tantalising suggestion of tobacco on her lips. He suppressed a groan.

'The problem is not knowing,' Charlotte said. 'If it *is* just an isolated event, then surely the police will handle it.'

'It's not that easy,' Kazlana said. 'I've seen all this before, in 2002. Every cause. Every small insult. Every family feud.' She took a long draw on her cigarette. Riley watched the smoke hang at her open mouth for an instant before she sucked it in. 'What's the word? Opportunism? Some of them don't even need a cause.' She exhaled a stream of delicious blue smoke. 'Thugs. Thieves. Rapists. When something big happens in Kenya, the police can't handle it. And the thugs, the thieves and the rapists know it.'

'Surely there are decent people around to keep the nasty elements in check?' Charlotte said.

'There are. But out in the bush, on the open roads ...' She shrugged. 'There's nobody around.'

'I think we should listen to Kazlana, Mark,' Charlotte said, turning to him.

Riley said he wasn't so sure. 'The situation is still evolving — we could get out now. But if the trouble gets worse, we could be stuck here for days. Weeks.'

The thought of being confined to the lodge for so long when he should be doing something constructive on his article as well as the novel put him in favour of an early departure.

'You're in the safest place you can be,' Kazlana said. 'Nobody's going to come storming into a national park. Even lynch mobs are afraid of lions. Anyway, the park rangers are armed. Nobody comes in here.' She thought for a moment. 'If you wish, I can fly you out. Leave the Land Rover. You can come back and collect it when it's safe.'

'Fly out?' Charlotte's eyes widened and her voice rose in pitch. 'I don't think that's a good idea at all,' she said, shaking her head.

'Why not?' Kazlana asked.

Charlotte didn't answer.

Riley hadn't been able to understand Charlotte's odd refusal to take the joy flight Kazlana had offered. Now he understood. She'd shown no timidity in dealing with rioting students, she wasn't intimidated by the aggressive touts that preyed on bewildered tourists, especially females, nor the maniacal drivers on the treacherous Rift Valley roads, but self-assured, sophisticated, intelligent Charlotte Manning was afraid of flying! Suddenly she seemed delightfully vulnerable, and somehow infinitely more interesting. Instead of the consummate, know-it-all professional, she appeared more ... human. Riley looked at her with different eyes.

'Why not?' Kazlana repeated.

As Charlotte floundered about for a reply that might make some kind of sense, Riley cut in.

'I agree with Charlie. It's a generous offer, Kazlana, but we're okay here. And it's all likely to blow over in the next day or so.' He exchanged glances with Charlotte. 'I say let's stay put.'

Kazlana shrugged. 'As you wish. But I have to leave. After Antonio comes back from visiting his brothers, I'm taking him back to Wajir, then I'm off to Nairobi.' She stood and wished them good luck.

At the door, she turned back with a final warning. 'Be very careful if you leave the park. The highway's not a safe place. The thugs erect roadblocks and if you stop you'll be robbed.' She looked pointedly at Charlotte. 'Or worse. And if you try to run it, you're liable to become a moving target for someone's home-made pistol or handgun.'

CHAPTER 28

Mark was waiting at the junction of the pathways to their respective *bandas*. 'I thought it might be you picking your way down the path in the dark,' he said, offering his arm.

Charlotte took it. 'Thank you. It is a little tricky in high heels.'

In the lodge's foyer he lifted from her hair a jacaranda blossom that had fallen there in the darkness.

'Violet,' he said, holding it against her cheek before placing it in her hand. 'It's beautiful. The colour suits you.'

It was such a gentle gesture, Charlotte was momentarily taken aback. 'Um, well …' she stammered. 'Thank you.'

'I'm no expert, but I reckon that colour's just about a perfect match for that blue-grey blouse you're wearing.'

She was at a loss how to reply. He seemed so different. The touch of his hand on her hair. The jacaranda flower. She looked down at her sleeveless top with its high neckline. She was glad she'd chosen it, a variation on the very practical jeans and tee-shirts she'd been wearing.

The head waiter arrived and swept them towards their table. When they were seated, Charlotte felt her stunned silence needed to be filled and mouthed the first thing that came into her head.

'I'm … wondering what your impressions of the countryside are? I mean, now that we're out of Nairobi for the first time.'

It was a lame attempt, but it worked. Mark gave it some thought and Charlotte was able to gather her composure.

'It reminds me of the outback in some ways. Except for that,' he said, indicating the distant roar of a bull hippo.

'I've never been to outback Australia,' she said. 'I went to Melbourne once, for a conference, but I had no time for sightseeing. Bradley didn't like me to be away for too long.'

'Bradley?'

She felt annoyed with herself. She hadn't meant to bring Bradley into the conversation. 'My fiancé. *Ex*-fiancé.'

'Ah, a boyfriend. Tell me about him.'

'It's a long and boring story. You don't want to spoil your dinner, do you?'

'Don't you want to talk about it?'

She shrugged, smiling self-consciously. 'Oh, it's not so bad, I suppose, nor so unusual. Boy meets girl. Girl gets bored. Girl runs away to Africa. The end came quickly and it felt right.' She shrugged. 'It's done.'

'Was he a control freak, this Bradley of yours?'

She smiled. 'Maybe. He's no longer *mine* though.'

'How long were you together?'

'Four years. We broke up four months ago,' Charlotte said.

'I'm sorry to hear that. It must have been tough after being together so long.'

Charlotte wondered about that. Was it tough when she and Bradley broke up? At the time, she'd been quite upset, but, upon reflection, that was probably more to do with the inconvenience she'd caused everyone.

'How amazing,' she said.

'What?'

'I've only just realised that, in my mind, I'd left Bradley quite some time before the actual separation. It was almost … well, subliminal.'

'How does that happen? Presumably you loved him at the outset. How do you one day realise you're no longer in love?'

She thought it a curious question from a thirty-five-year-old. 'It happens.'

He offered to top up her wine glass, but she placed her hand over it.

'You said you knew things weren't working between you and Bradley,' he said, clearly not willing to leave the subject. She was starting to feel as if she were being interviewed for one of his investigative articles. 'How did you know?'

She took her time before answering. She hadn't discussed the end of her relationship with anyone before. Or thought about it much herself, she was realising.

'This may sound a little callous, but I think a person's love life is a little like a balance sheet — a balance sheet of emotions. There are pluses and minuses as you go through your lives together. You can carry a deficit for a short time, but if it's not corrected, sooner or later the relationship becomes bankrupt.'

'Hmm ... That's sad.'

'It is. In fact, it's quite painful for a time. And then someone else comes along and sparks your interest and you move on.'

He nodded thoughtfully. 'Moving on ... I reckon that's a really healthy sign.'

He seemed more reflective and somehow more at peace. She studied him as he filled his wine glass. Her instincts in these matters were seldom wrong. Mark was different that night — very different.

* * *

Riley stayed to chat to the head waiter at the desserts buffet before following Charlotte back to the table.

'Something's brewing, all right,' he told her. 'Things in the Rift Valley are apparently very threatening. Three Kikuyus were beaten to within an inch of their lives in a town further up the highway.'

'Perhaps we should make a dash for Nairobi?' she said.

Riley nodded. 'It's probably for the best. And the sooner the better.'

'Tomorrow?'

'Okay. Will you tell Joshua?'

She said she would find him in the morning. 'He'll be very disappointed. He was quite excited about going back to the Serengeti.'

'I'm disappointed too. I probably won't get there at all now.'

'What will you do about your book?' she asked.

'Oh, I guess I can write the book without seeing every site the Maasai occupied. And there's plenty more to keep me busy. For one, I'm going to complete this NGO article. I can't let Omuga's death stop me.'

'Omuga? Isn't he the man you interviewed about the orphanage?'

Riley winced. He'd wanted to keep the more sordid details of his story from her. 'I didn't want to upset you,' he said, before recounting the basic facts of the murder.

Charlotte commiserated, and chided him for his feelings of guilt about his incompetence. 'How were you to know?' she asked.

He had to agree he couldn't have foreseen the murder, but felt guilty regardless.

'You must finish your article,' she said. 'Which is all the more reason for us to get back to Nairobi as soon as possible. And which reminds me, thanks for understanding my reasons for not wanting to fly out with Kazlana.'

Riley was tempted to act dumb, but nodded. 'That's okay. More wine?'

'Thank you. Just a little.'

'And thanks for keeping it to yourself,' she added as he topped up their glasses.

'I didn't know you were afraid of flying.'

'It's silly, isn't it?'

'I don't know. Fear's one of the most primitive emotions; it's not always possible to overcome it. But if it begins to affect your life too much, then yes, it's silly not to try to do something about it.'

'Oh, I've tried, all right. Therapy, hypnotherapy, pills,

alcohol. Nothing seems to work and it makes me so cross. I say to myself, *You can beat this*, but as soon as I get on board I become a mental and physical wreck. I'm so afraid, I literally can't think.'

'But you still fly.'

'I won't let it dominate my life any more than it already does.'

'Sometimes things just are what they are and can't be changed.'

Charlotte smiled at him. 'That sounds very philosophical, Mr Riley.'

'Maybe.'

'And, if I may say so, it also sounds like you've got it all together.'

'Me? Not likely.'

'How so? Here you are, a published author, working on book number four.'

'After crashing out — twice.'

'Why weren't those books successful? Do you mind me asking?'

'No, I don't mind.' He thought about it for a moment. 'I guess it's a little like what you said about flying. You can't think because of your fear. For a long time, I couldn't think because of my anger. I don't want to go over all that old ground again and I must apologise for getting so maudlin the other night — but I think that's been my problem for the last five years.'

'There's no need to apologise,' she said, placing her hand on his.

The gesture touched Riley. When she removed her hand, he wanted to reach out and take it again.

'And you weren't maudlin,' she added. 'Grief is a healthy part of the healing process.'

'Maybe you're right. I feel I've had enough grief. Maybe it's time to feel better about myself.'

'That makes two of us.'

Riley waited for her elaboration, but it didn't come. Instead, there was a long pause in the conversation.

'I've really enjoyed our dinner tonight, Charlie,' he said.

'You keep doing that …'

He raised an eyebrow. 'What?'

'Calling me Charlie.'

'Do I? I'm sorry. Just a habit. Shortening everything, I mean.'

He didn't want to admit that in his mind he'd been calling her Charlie for weeks.

'My father used to call me Charlie,' she said.

He nodded, wondering if he should apologise again.

'I think I'll call it a night,' she said.

'Me too.'

She placed her hand on his once more. 'Thank you again for being so understanding.'

This time he reached for her hand, but she was on her feet, collecting her purse.

He rose with her, and together they climbed the path to her bungalow. He waited at the door until she found the light switch. It clicked, but nothing happened.

'Oh!' she said. 'The globe must be blown.' She moved from the entrance to the sitting room, feeling along the wall to find the light switch. 'There's another light here somewhere.'

'Can I help?' Riley followed her inside.

A familiar perfume came to him out of nowhere: *Beautiful*. It instantly took him back to Melissa and their first night in Bali when she'd worn her new duty-free purchase. It scented the room then as now. But the feelings rising in him now were no longer about the past.

He found Charlotte's hand on the wall and covered it with his. She made no move to draw away from him. He slid his hand up the smoothness of her arm to rest on her shoulder. He felt it rise as she took a deep breath. In the darkness he moved his face closer to hers. He sensed her proximity and felt the soft warmth of her breath on his face. His lips brushed her cheek, tingling, and he moved them along the firm line of her jaw. His head swam.

He waited for the jolt of guilt that invariably supplanted desire. But the irrepressible sensation of *woman* — a sensation he'd denied himself for so long — came so forcefully from the darkness that it caused him to breathe in sharply. It was all the more amazing because, after the initial memory induced by the perfume, it was Charlie rather than Melissa who filled his consciousness, enveloping him.

Euphoria swept over him. Nothing seemed to be beyond his capabilities. His feeling of hopelessness about his writing vanished. The mental cage that had imprisoned his emotions for five years was broken open. He allowed the elation to linger for a moment, and then again became aware of the sensation of Charlie, so close, so enticing. He moved his lips slowly down to her neck, where he nuzzled her and took her intoxicating fragrance into his soul.

'Mark,' she whispered.

Her voice drew him back to the bedroom, the darkness. 'Mmm?' he asked.

'Mark ... I think I should use the light on the coffee table.'

'What?' He took a step back. 'Oh, good idea. I'll get it.'

He stumbled across the room, knocking his shin against the solid wooden coffee table. 'Oh! *Jeez!*' he spluttered, swallowing the words he would have preferred to use.

'Are you all right?' she asked.

'Yeah, I'm ... I'm okay.'

He fumbled and found the switch. The room, almost identical to his own except for the position of the coffee table, appeared in the soft glow of the table lamp. He rubbed his shin where a bump was already forming.

'Can I get you some ice for that?' she asked.

'No. I'll be fine. Just a bruise.'

He searched for something else to say to ease his embarrassment. He had completely misjudged the situation with Charlotte. Of course he had. There was nothing between them. The touch of her hand in the dining room had been just an expression of sympathy; what any woman would do under the circumstances.

'Well ...' he said with a bright smile, 'I'd better let you get to, um, bed. I'll just ... um, go.'

She returned his smile. 'Oh,' she said. 'I suppose so. It's late, isn't it?'

'Yes.'

He walked to the door, resisting the urge to rub his throbbing leg.

'Good night, Mark.'

'Yes. Good night, Charlie.'

She closed the door behind him.

'*Shit!*' he muttered as he picked his way through the shadows to his own bungalow.

*   *   *

Charlotte heard Mark's muffled curse and sighed. It both pleased and saddened her to know that he felt as awkward as she did about their blundering attempt at romance in the dark.

The touch of his hand on her shoulder, his lips on the very sensitive skin on her throat, had thrilled her. She'd sensed his shortening breath, could feel his excitement growing. In the darkness there'd been an unmistakeable and mounting energy between them. Why then had she caused it to end? She wasn't even sure she had wanted it to end. Her suggestion to try the table lamp had been a stalling mechanism. She'd needed time to think. But why?

If she were quite truthful, she'd have to admit that for some time she'd felt a growing attraction towards Mark. Her need for time, therefore, had nothing to do with wanting to know more about him or to work out if she had any feelings for him.

Maybe it was that after four years with Bradley, she felt unsure of how to manage a budding relationship. Was that the case? Or was it simply that she couldn't contemplate a romantic entanglement while attempting to write her thesis?

Whatever the reason, one thing was clear to her. She liked Mark Riley very much.

CHAPTER 29

'*And now for some late breaking news on the election results, we cross to Samuel Muthami at the Kenyatta International Conference Centre.*'

'*Thank you, Desmond. I'm with Mr Nicodemus Ogwan'g, who is chief scrutineer for the Orange Democratic Movement here at the central tallying room at KICC. Mr Ogwan'g, are you able to bring our listeners up to date on the current situation regarding the presidential elections?*'

'*I am, indeed. We believe that most of the polling stations across the country have now completed or are near to completing the counting for the presidential ballot. Our people at those centres have kept us informed of the count and we now believe our candidate has an unbeatable lead.*'

'*Are you saying, Mr Ogwan'g, that Raila Odinga has won the presidential election?*'

'*I am.*'

'*But we've heard nothing from the chairman of the electoral commission to that effect. How have you come to that conclusion without hearing the official count?*'

'*Our people at all the polling stations have made it clear to us. Mr Raila Odinga will be our next president.*'

'*On what basis do you make your claim?*'

'*The people have spoken. They have voted overwhelmingly in favour of change. They have chosen Raila Odinga to be their champion for change.*'

'*But, Mr Ogwan'g, aren't you —*'

'*It therefore gives me great pleasure to announce that the Orange Democratic Movement declares Mr Raila Odinga winner of the presidential election. Thank you. Thank you.*'

'There you have it, Desmond. The Orange Democratic Movement, through its official spokesman, Mr Nicodemus Ogwan'g, has claimed victory for their candidate, Mr Raila Odinga, who is set to become the first Luo president of Kenya.

'This is Samuel Muthami at SKY FM, reporting to you from KICC in Nairobi ...'

The green text on Joshua's mobile phone glowed in the dark. He jabbed awkwardly at the keys with his thumbs. *My darling mayasa. No credit. Good news odinga wins. Love you too. Will call soon. Josh.*

*　*　*

Joshua bounced out of bed at the first chime of his mobile phone alarm and went immediately to Maina's bunk and gave him a rude shove.

Maina didn't like being woken so early on his day off, and he hadn't liked being woken very late the previous night to be told he'd lost his bet and it had to be paid at dawn because Charlotte had sent a note advising Joshua they would depart for Nairobi in the morning. Joshua had guessed it was because of the violence sweeping the country. He'd half expected it, as stories of violence, death and destruction thundered from all news outlets.

He paced the gravel as he waited beside the Kenya Allover Tours's safari car. He simply loved the still, cool, liquid air of morning in Nakuru, with the last of the stars winking farewell, and the hush as the night predators gave way to the faintest stirrings from the creatures of the day.

Just as Joshua was thinking about returning to the dormitory to rouse Maina from his bed, the Kikuyu stumbled out, scratching his behind.

'Harrumph!' he said in reply to Joshua's cheery greeting.

Joshua fidgeted impatiently as Maina stood outside the car to hitch his trousers around his ample girth, tuck in his shirt and rebuckle his belt.

'So, Luo boy — I hear you're leaving, ah?'

'I am. My ... clients are going back to Nairobi.'

'And that means no Serengeti for you this time.'

'No. Not this time. Maybe later.' He couldn't hide his disappointment. 'I don't know.'

'You've never seen it, the Serengeti, have you?'

'No.'

'Of course not. That Kisumu–Musoma road is terrible.'

Joshua could only smile with him. His bravado had been outrageous and Maina had seen through it from the start.

'Ah, the Serengeti,' Maina said, leaning against the vehicle, arms folded across his chest. 'That's the place to go. You think this is nice around here?' He flung an arm to indicate the lake and its surrounds. 'It's nothing, *bwana*. The Serengeti ... that's the place. The smell of it. The sounds ... soft. Quiet like a church.' He fell silent as his thoughts carried him away.

Joshua tried to imagine something better than what he'd seen here in Nakuru, and couldn't. He had so many questions he didn't know where to begin, or even if he should try — Maina's ridicule could be ruthless.

'Are there lions?' he tentatively asked.

'Lions? So many lions. You can get sick of seeing them hunting, I tell you.' Maina pulled a handkerchief from his pocket and noisily blew his nose. 'They follow the migration. Wildebeest and zebra and antelope. So many you couldn't believe.' He shook his head for emphasis. '*Haki ya mungu*. And so, maybe I'll do the seeing for both of us this time.'

'You're going to the Serengeti?'

'Of course. After Kisumu I cross to TZ and into the Serengeti. It's not the best time, but it'll be okay.'

Joshua tried to imagine. Again, he failed.

'*Sowa sowa*,' Maina said. 'Let's go.'

Once on the circuit road, Maina began reciting many of the features of the park, as if conducting the usual spiel he gave all his clients. 'More than four hundred bird species ... sixty-two square kilometres ... over a million flamingos ... the most fabulous bird spectacle in the world ... many animal species ...'

Then he nodded to the right. 'We're in the acacia forest now. There ... under that mopani tree — a bushbuck.'

Joshua stared into the grey, misty middle distance. 'Where is it? I can see nothing.'

'Take off your city eyes! At the edge of the clearing. See it?'

The bushbuck moved. Not in a panic, but by its movement became visible.

'It's beautiful,' Joshua said.

He could have studied it for an age, but Maina moved on.

'Olive baboons.'

Joshua gawked. There must have been forty or fifty of them. A large male strutted belligerently along the road not twenty metres away. He stopped to pick daintily a small item from the roadside and tested it by touching it to his lips. He discarded it and moved on.

'That fellow could fight a leopard,' Maina said.

'There are leopards here?' Joshua couldn't keep the awe from his voice.

'Of course.'

'Can we see one?' he pleaded.

'Maybe. This is not a zoo, Luo boy. But we might get lucky.'

Joshua was unsure about the reference to luck. He ran his eyes around the open vehicle. Apart from a couple of roll bars that served as support for clients wishing to stand for a better view of the surroundings, there was nothing to fend off a pouncing leopard. Or anything else.

'Are there lions here?'

'Plenty.'

It was an offhand reply that did nothing to calm Joshua's nerves. He began to examine every possible place a lion or leopard could conceal itself. Maina continued to spot the most obscure creatures at the same time as he avoided potholes. Joshua was immensely impressed. For a fat Kikuyu, Maina was undoubtedly savvy.

'How did you learn such things?' he asked after Maina had rattled off a number of facts about a bird he pointed out called a red-chested cuckoo.

'I joined Kenya Allover Tours after working for some time as a KWS ranger.' Before Joshua could ask, he added, 'Kenya Wildlife Service. But the tips are good for a driver. And if you can answer clients' questions and tell a few jokes, then even better. Now I've been doing this driving job for twelve years. Rothschild's giraffe.' There were seven among the acacia trees. 'These fellows came to the park in 1977. They are not so common as the other species. The giraffe can have two, three or five horns.'

'How can anybody know so much about one animal?' Joshua said, shaking his head in amazement.

'I could tell you a lot about any animal you might find in Kenya, my skinny friend. And a lot more about giraffes too, but I know you Luos are a little slow. For example, the giraffe is what we call a browser — he eats the leaves of trees and shrubs. He can even strip the leaves off a thorn tree without sticking himself on the thorns. And the female, she gives birth standing up. So the baby giraffe falls nearly two metres on his birthday.'

He turned to Joshua. 'Maybe that happened to you, Luo boy, ah?' he laughed. The sound rolled around his generous girth. 'You think I'm joking? It's true!'

He caught Joshua's expression and laughed again. 'Look at you! You look like you've swallowed a fly.'

They circumnavigated the lake, stopping at times to study animals in their acts of hunting, feeding or sleeping. Maina was an inexhaustible source of facts.

'Oh-ho,' he said, drawing the car to a halt. 'We are very lucky.'

'What?'

'Shh …' he hissed. 'Will you look at that …?'

Joshua followed Maina's gaze, through the acacia forest into a sea of grass. Nothing. He couldn't contain himself.

'Maina! What is it?'

'Can't you see it? Probably from the forest pride. A year-old cub. We are very, very lucky.'

He engaged the clutch and edged the safari car off the road into the grass.

'Where is it?' Joshua pleaded.

'Straight ahead.'

The car crawled forward, hissing through the thick tussocks.

'Look for the ears — lion's ears,' Maina whispered, 'and you'll find her.'

Joshua immediately spotted the young lion, and another.

'Yes! I see two.'

'That's it! You have it, city boy,' Maina said, giving Joshua a rush of satisfaction at the unexpected praise.

The lions — almost fully grown, but still with the gangly appearance of teenagers — were stalking an outcrop of the flamingo flock that had gathered into a tight bay among the grass.

'Ha, ha,' Maina chuckled. 'They have no chance. But let's watch and see.'

The pair parted, each approaching the flock from almost opposite directions. From their vantage point, he and Maina could see the whole strategy unfolding. At a certain point, both lions halted, as if following an agreed plan. A moment later, the lion on the left raised its head. It was enough to send the flamingos into a paroxysm of panic. They turned and lifted en masse towards the lion concealed in grass on the right-hand side of the inlet. The hidden lion leapt more than two metres from a standing start and snagged a flamingo with its outstretched claw, making a full back-flip as it came to land. The second of the pair galloped through the shallows to reach the prize.

The flamingo had died instantaneously, giving pause to the young lions' enthusiasm. It was a thin, pink string of feathers, insignificant in size beside the capturing lion. After a couple of sniffs and a desultory attempt to pluck feathers, the lions yawned and wandered off.

Maina swung the wheel, returning the safari car to the lakeside road.

'This fellow is a cousin of the giraffe,' he said when they stopped at the northern end of the lake.

'A giraffe? It's a hippopotamus, isn't it?'

'Of course it's a hippo! But it's also an even-toed ungulate.'

'*Haki ya mungu,*' Joshua sighed. 'I don't understand.'

'Order, family, genus. It's been too long since I knew all that. But lucky for me, my clients don't care. If I can just put a name to everything, they're happy. And I get my nice *kitu kidogo* — my tip.'

Maina swung the car onto the lodge's access road. 'End of the tour,' he said. Joshua knew he'd been acting like a schoolboy, hanging on Maina's every word. He wasn't so naïve that he couldn't see that although the Kikuyu had lost the bet, he was enjoying a victory nonetheless. Demonstrating his knowledge to the Luo city boy would be worth a thousand shillings. Joshua didn't care. If Maina's safari had been nothing more than a hasty spin around the lake, he could have legitimately claimed to have delivered on his wager. But by taking a more leisurely pace and so unselfishly sharing some of his knowledge with Joshua, he had made what might have been merely an interesting experience into a life-changing one.

A car horn bleated from the other side of the car park as they drove in.

'I have to go,' Joshua said.

'*Sowa sowa.* Okay.'

'Maina, when you trained as a game warden …'

'Yes?'

'Well, is it easy to find a position? I mean, what schooling do you have to have?'

'Nothing special. Just the eight-four-four.'

Joshua felt an emptiness in the pit of his stomach. He'd only completed the eight primary school years.

'But in TZ I hear you only need to read and write English and Kiswahili,' he said.

The horn sounded again; this time, more persistent. Mark's voice followed it.

'I have to go,' Joshua said again.

He extended his hand and Maina shook it African-style, with the alternate gripping of thumb and palm.

'*Kwaheri,*' Maina said.

'*Kwaheri,*' Joshua replied. '*Mzuri safari.*'

As he hurried to join Mark and Charlotte in the Land Rover, Joshua struggled with a huge dilemma. From an early age he'd wanted to be a champion footballer, playing in front of thousands. But now a new objective intruded. Now he desperately wanted to become a game warden in the Serengeti National Park.

CHAPTER 30

In the morning hours of Sunday, 30 December, the people of Kibera filled the streets and alleys. Those who had not heard the declaration of victory by the ODM soon did. Luos celebrated throughout Kisumu Ndogo, in their homes, in the markets and at the homes of friends and family.

It was not only the Luos of Kisumu Ndogo who celebrated. Luos all across Kenya knew their time had arrived at last. Over the many decades since independence, they had seen their brightest lights rise only to be struck down by unknown assassins. The deaths of Tom Mboya, Robert Ouko and many others remained a mystery too deep for the police or government to resolve. Conspiracy theories were legion.

And it was not only the Luo people who celebrated. So did the Luhya, the Kalenjin, the Maasai, the Kisii and many of the Kamba. And on the coast it was the Giriama, the Taita and the Wadigo who danced and sang.

Most of the Kikuyu and their cousins, the Meru, were disappointed, but there were many among them who had become disillusioned by their man, and were also ready for change.

Wherever Raila Odinga supporters lived, there was rejoicing. And even greater hope. A new man was about to enter State House and a new order was about to begin. Everyone in Kisumu Ndogo knew that Kenya's first Luo president would change their lives — would change everything — for the better.

The years of frustrating lethargy following the last election, when President Mwai Kibaki had promised the world but had changed nothing, were over. Although a Kikuyu, Kibaki's victory had been universally popular in 2002. His platform was to end the long period of corrupt government that Kenyans had endured for many years. But his promises had amounted to nothing. Over the five years since his election, the excitement had flagged. For most Kenyans, there had been little change. In Kibera, nothing had changed.

Simon Otieng had seen it all before. The majority of the revellers were youths whom he thought were more interested in a party than in the details of the new president's platform. He scrutinised every young face in the good-natured crowd, trying to find his son.

'*Habari yako?*' a voice asked from his side.

'*Mzuri*, Mama Hamza.'

The old woman's brilliant white teeth illuminated her tar-black face. 'Why are you not running the streets like these boys, *Bwana* Simon? Are you not happy that Raila Odinga has won?'

Simon sighed. 'I have seen too many leaders come and go to think any one of them will change our lives here. What are your thoughts of these happy days?'

She shook her head. 'I am thinking the party is starting too early.'

'What have you heard?'

'I hear that Kivuitu at KICC has been given some interesting numbers. He is wondering how he can release them without causing trouble. Very big trouble.'

'That is not possible. Odinga has won by —'

'There is no winner until the Electoral Commission of Kenya speaks. Kivuitu has yet to open his mouth.'

Simon thought about the consequences should Odinga not be declared winner after all this celebrating.

'Have you seen my son? Have you seen Joshua?' he asked.

'One of my women saw him getting into a Land Rover on Thursday.'

'Thursday? Polling day? Was it the police?'

'No. It was a *mzungu*. A man and a lady. They went down Ngong Road.'

Simon sighed with relief, but he was puzzled. 'A *mzungu*?'

'You have heard nothing of him?' she asked.

'No,' he said, shaking his head slowly. 'Nothing.'

'Then he is gone from Nairobi. And safe.'

'But ... where?' he asked.

'No matter. You should be pleased he's out of Kibera. If what I've heard is true, it is better for all of us to run away from here. But since we can't, we must stay close to home.'

Simon studied her face. 'Will it be as bad as 2002?'

'Look at this,' she said, indicating the youths waving flags and dancing. Their singing was loud and discordant. 'Do you think these boys will be happy to roll up their flags if their victory is stolen from them?'

* * *

Although disappointed at missing his chance to visit the Serengeti, Joshua had the consolation of Odinga's election win and the more immediate and exciting prospect of being with Mayasa. She had been in his thoughts since he'd left her at the side of Ngong Road. At night he couldn't get her out of his mind and the days since they'd made love felt like weeks.

What was it about time? When waiting for bad things to happen the time flew by, whereas while waiting for good things to happen it simply dragged. He remembered as a child his mother informing him early one day that his father had managed to hold a job for the whole week and there would be special food on the table that night. They would have chapattis, rice, curried goat, sweet potato and his favourite — lima beans. His mother had even hinted at a treat beyond belief — a bottle of Fanta for him and each of the girls. The day had been interminable.

Still, the time away from Nairobi had worked in his favour by easing his initial alarm about Mayasa's father's condition. Joshua's logical side could accept the illness was not necessarily a risk to Mayasa or himself, but it was hard to forget the horror stories learnt from his street education. He realised he had not handled her news about her father very well, and he was anxious to have her back in his arms where he could reassure her of his love and support. With his newly won skills as a guide, he would make *mzungu* money, white people's money, and they could leave Kibera together.

He therefore started the journey to Nairobi feeling very positive about the day ahead, but they hadn't travelled far before he became aware of something strange. Even for a Sunday morning, the road was eerily quiet.

He sensed that Mark and Charlotte had also noticed it. Their conversation dwindled until all three drove on in silence.

They passed no vehicles, and on the outer fringe of Nakuru, where the market stalls had been a throng of shoppers and traders the day they'd arrived, there was no one. A few mangy dogs sniffed among the empty stalls, and one old woman scuttled down an alley and out of sight as they approached.

Nobody in the Land Rover appeared willing to give voice to their thoughts.

They passed through town and joined the highway where the railway passed overhead, then continued towards Naivasha.

The roads on the outskirts of Naivasha were as quiet as those of Nakuru, and continued to be so until nearer the centre of the town where they saw a tight knot of people gathered at one of the taverns. There was music and dancing. Joshua recognised some traditional Luo songs.

'They're Luos,' he told Mark. 'A party for Raila.'

'A very big and boozy all-night party by the look of them,' Mark said as he swung the car left into a side street.

'Do you know where this takes us, Mark?' There was apprehension in Charlotte's tone.

Mark glanced at her. 'I'm guessing I can take a right somewhere along here and rejoin the highway further across town.'

Her silence suggested she remained unconvinced.

'We'll be fine,' he added.

Now Joshua picked up on her nervousness. Away from the Luo party on the main street, Naivasha remained deathly still.

Mark took a turn to the right after a few minutes only to find the whole street blocked by a mob of young men.

Charlotte gasped.

It was too late to turn in the narrow street and retreat. Mark stopped the Land Rover at the head of the mob.

'Charlotte, it's okay. Let's try to stay cool,' he said. 'What's going on, Joshua?'

Joshua's heart thumped in his chest. The mob was obviously agitated and probably headed towards the Luos' party. They carried clubs and garden tools. Some had pieces of timber with nails hammered right through to produce a very vicious weapon.

'They are Kikuyus,' Joshua whispered. 'And looking for trouble.'

The scene reminded him of the worst of his nightmares from 2002, when the thugs had run amuck in Kibera.

'Well, they'll get none from us,' Mark said. 'Be calm, everybody. Let me talk to them.'

He wound down his window. 'Good morning,' he said to the angry faces closest to him.

'Where you go, *mzungu*?' one asked.

'We're going home. To Nairobi. Do you mind if we pass through?'

But the leader was not looking at Mark; he and his allies stared with angry eyes at Joshua in the back seat. Others crowded around Charlotte's side of the car. One tried the door. It was locked, but Charlotte let out an involuntary gasp. Others rattled the door handles in anger.

'We want to speak to him,' the leader said, pointing to Joshua.

'Why? He's just our guide.'

'Shut up, *mzungu*. We want him out here, or you go nowhere.'

'Okay, okay,' Mark said. 'But let me out so we can talk in private. Just you and I.'

'Mark, *no*!' Charlotte said in a harsh whisper.

Mark gestured for her to remain calm. 'It's okay, Charlie. I'm just going to talk to this young man. I know what I'm doing.'

Joshua was quite sure he didn't. The mob was in no mood to talk. The leader smirked and took half a step away to let the foolish *mzungu* out from the relative safety of his car.

Mark opened the door halfway and, grabbing the leader's shirt, pulled his head into the door before slamming it on him.

In the same instant as the man let out an angry howl of pain, Mark gave a blast on the horn and the Land Rover roared forward.

Those nearest the car reeled away, except for one, who was scooped up onto the hood and bounced off the windscreen before falling back onto the road.

They sped off amid a shower of rocks.

*   *   *

'Papa, no. I won't leave you here alone,' Mayasa said.

Her father placed both hands on her shoulders and gave them a gentle pat. 'Mayasa. You know very well what happened in '02. You will go to your sister's house in Langata.'

'Then you must come too.'

He shook his head. 'Enough that one of us will be crowding into that *kadogo sana* house.'

'Maybe it will not happen like 2002. Maybe things will become quiet. The elections are over.'

'Yes, the elections are over, and this is when the real trouble began last time. Do you not remember? These Kenyan people are always fighting, Mayasa. Not like us in Tanzania. We don't care about this tribe or that tribe. If a man wins the votes he is president. It is simple. But here, *mungu angu*, that is when the mother of all trouble begins.'

Mayasa stepped away from her father's hands, angry at his stubbornness and unwilling to accept the truth in his argument.

But she knew he was right. The vast majority of Kenyans were irreparably tribal. Even when confronted by imminent disaster as they were now, they refused to see the danger in it. They had identified with tribe long before the concept of *nation* appeared. It had been their way for decades.

She wrung her hands. She had always cared for her father, and now he would be alone in Kibera — the worst place to be when a tribal war was in the air.

* * *

About fifteen minutes after leaving Naivasha, Mark pulled off the road at a quiet section of the highway. He climbed out of the car and began to inspect the damage. Charlotte and Joshua joined him.

'That was close,' Mark said, putting words to Charlotte's own thoughts.

'We were very lucky,' she agreed, wondering what she would have done had she ignored Dr Gilanga's warning and ventured up country alone. 'How's the damage?'

'A few small dings,' he said. 'Nothing to worry about.'

'Then there's nothing stopping us from going on.'

'What?' Mark stared at her, then broke into a smile. 'You're joking, right?'

'Not at all. I've found another route — I'll show you.'

She dived into the cabin and pulled a road map from the glove box. 'See? We can take this road west to Narok, then on to Kisii, then —'

'Charlotte, we're not going into the Rift Valley again.'

'Why not?' she demanded indignantly. He was being a typical male, taking control. 'Naivasha is just a hot spot. We'll be safe if we keep away from the big towns.'

'Excuse me, but when did you become an expert on Kenya?' he said.

'Don't be so stubborn. Just because you've found a more important project than your book —'

'This isn't Oxford. We're not going anywhere but back to Nairobi until this blows over.'

'And how long will that take? We don't have time to sit around. If I don't get some work done in Kisumu, I might as well forget my thesis.'

Mark glared at her, but she didn't care. He was being totally unreasonable. He had completed most of his book's research in the National Archives, and now he was so consumed by his story of the lost children, he didn't care what happened to her work.

Joshua, who had been silent throughout, asked, 'Why do you want to go to Kisumu?'

Charlotte stared at him, realising she'd never informed him of her reasons for needing a guide. His only expressed interest had been in their side-trip to the Serengeti.

'Well, it's to interview some Luo people for my thesis — the paper I'm writing to gain my professional qualifications.' She explained briefly that she'd interviewed a number of academics, but she wanted to speak to what she called ordinary Luo people too.

'Then come to Kisumu Ndogo,' Joshua said. 'There are many Luo people there. Just like Kisumu, but in the slums.'

Charlotte was stunned. How could she have missed it? Surely she should include in her research a study of how Luo culture could survive in urban communities? Taking the idea further, why not examine translocated Luo communities in the ultimate urban climate — Kibera, the largest slum in Africa? It was brilliant!

'How can I get to see Kisumu Ndogo?' she asked, barely able to contain her enthusiasm.

'Easy,' Joshua said with a shrug. 'Come with me.'

CHAPTER 31

'Charlotte,' Mark said, before she climbed from the Land Rover, 'is this a good idea? You're still a little shaken from what happened in Naivasha. Why not leave this until tomorrow?'

Charlotte's annoyance with Mark had diminished during the journey back to Nairobi, but she was in no mood to concede his point.

'I'll be fine,' she said coolly. 'It's just a quick tour today. Joshua will take care of me.'

'Well, I guess you know what you're doing.'

Charlotte climbed out of the Land Rover and joined Joshua at the side of the road.

'Take care of Charlotte, okay?' Mark told Joshua.

'Everything is okay, Mr Mark. She is safe with me.'

'See that she is.' Turning back to Charlotte, he said, 'What time do you want me back here?'

She looked at her watch. 'It's one now, so let's make it around five.'

'Five it is. I'll be here on the dot.'

He said goodbye, and she watched as he spun the wheel, taking the Land Rover into a U-turn, over the far kerb and bumping down again into Kibera Road.

'Now, Joshua,' she said. 'Let me see this Luo village you call Kisumu Ndogo.'

* * *

As Riley drove down Kibera Road, his mind roamed around ideas for his article, which was seldom far from his mind. The various themes were now in place and he was increasingly drawn to the personal aspects. He knew his search for Jafari would be prominent among them.

The Circularian organisation was central. It seemed to Riley to symbolise the dichotomy between the compassion of the legitimate charitable institutions and the greed of those such as Gideon Koske, who he suspected was using his political position to scam funds for a non-existent charity.

He was approaching Kibera Gardens Road and decided to refresh his memory of the dilapidated orphanage, which he would feature as an example of how foreign funds, sent from private donors, were not being used as intended. He drove down to where the slab-built huts sat in mute witness to his arrival and studied the building, etching the details of its structure in his memory. The oblong window openings in the bleak façade gave the place the appearance of a mournful clown.

He thought back to Melissa's suggestion of visiting the orphanage and the child they helped to support. His memory was a little hazy, but he seemed to recall they were standing on the beach at sundown, as they often did in Bali.

'Why don't we just up and go somewhere?' Melissa had said, wrapping her arms around his neck and resting her head on his chest.

'Good idea. Where?' he'd replied.

'Somewhere we haven't been.'

'That leaves quite a wide field, my darling.'

'How about Africa? We could go and see little Jafari.'

'Who?'

'Oh, Mark! Our little waif, of course.'

'In Kenya? Oh, yeah. We could do that.'

They were silent then, and he'd remarked that he thought the sunset was beautiful.

'Beautiful? I'm not sure I'd describe it as beautiful,' she'd said. 'Perhaps more like *magnificent*.'

But they weren't Melissa's words. They were Charlie's, spoken only a few days ago in reference to the Great Rift Valley, not Kuta Beach.

As he turned to leave, his eye was drawn to a corner of the garden where a metal sculpture of a child stood with hands and feet within the rim of a wheel or large circle. It was quite tall, about the actual height of a five-year-old, and he wondered why he couldn't remember it from his first visit. Then he noticed the grass had been cut — not mown, but hacked into shape, probably with a machete as was the practice in many gardens around the city.

The windows had also been cleaned. He could see a figure moving about inside.

He was stunned, and quickly went to the door and knocked.

A woman wearing a plain white pinafore over a pink blouse answered. She had a rounded, matronly shape and her shining black face was illuminated by a surprised smile. Another woman was standing over a cot in which a child lay among a clutter of plastic toys. There were four children in the room, all little more than toddlers.

Riley stood in the doorway, speechless. He didn't know what he had expected to find, but this scene of domestic accord was not it. His surprise must have been obvious.

'Can I help you, brother?' the woman in the white pinafore asked. 'You seem to be looking for something.'

'Yes. No. I mean, I am. Is this the orphanage?'

It was a stupid question.

'I mean, is this the Circularian orphanage?'

'It is. And I am Sister Veronica and this is Sister Margaret. Can we be of assistance, Mr ...?'

'Riley,' he said, and took a deep breath. 'I, um ...'

'Please,' the woman said, 'won't you take a seat, Mr Riley?'

'I think I should,' he said, pulling a chair out from the table.

He looked around the room he'd previously seen as derelict. It was now spotless, with lightweight cotton draw-curtains on the windows, a half-dozen neat cots, chairs and the table, which was long and looked like it might have once been a conference table. One corner of the room was set up as a kitchen with a bench-top stove, microwave oven and a set of shelves holding a range of white crockery with animal cartoon motifs. The floor was covered with cheap but clean vinyl tiles.

Sister Veronica placed a cup of steaming tea before him and he thanked her.

They began to chat and he asked her about the Circularian religion. And why, for instance, they were in the orphanage business. Very soon he realised his mistake. The Circularians had at least one thing in common: boundless enthusiasm for extolling the principles of their belief. Sister Veronica began with *two-pi-r* and went on to explain the many incidents in history that demonstrated its power.

'Do you know, Mr Riley, that as soon as mankind discovered the world was round, we entered the most fruitful period in human history? All the great mathematical theories, scientific discoveries, magnificent inventions, followed.'

When he managed to drag the conversation around to the orphanage, Sister Veronica insisted it was all part of the same philosophy.

'The circle is the symbol of family life,' she said. 'When we see an orphan, we know we must complete the circle for the helpless child, so we find a home for the little ones, like these,' she said, indicating the babies. 'But the older children, well ... sadly, no one seems to want them, except for the older boys. Mr Koske is particularly successful in placing the difficult ages after about seven. The other organisations are quite envious of our successes.'

'So, how does he manage it?'

'Mr Koske has an arrangement with people in Somalia who find homes for them.'

'And you don't mind that he sends the children to an unknown future?'

She shook her head. 'The children are known to God. We are happy that they are able to begin their journey to happiness.'

'Happiness? How do you know? They may become child labourers, or worse. Don't you have some follow-up?'

'No, Mr Riley. Completing the circle is all that's required. To … follow up, as you call it, would mean we are distrustful. We trust in God and the circle. All who do are favoured in the eyes of the Almighty.'

'So you don't know where the children go?'

She shook her head and smiled. 'We simply know they go on to complete their circle of life. These little ones commence that journey tomorrow.'

Riley sighed. It was pointless to continue the discussion. He was beginning to understand the term 'blind faith', with all its limitations. He gave up, but some questions remained unanswered.

'I was here a couple of weeks ago,' he said, 'and the place was deserted. More than that, it looked as though it had never been used.'

'That's correct, Mr Riley. We close the orphanage when we have no children to place. These items wouldn't last long in an unoccupied house in Nairobi,' she said, indicating the various appliances. 'We have them put into storage until Mr Koske takes another group of children from our headquarters in Mombasa.'

'I see …'

'Mr Koske is simply wonderful the way he can find homes for our children. They come in for a few days and then they fly away like butterflies to begin their new lives.' She was beaming with pride. 'In between times, Sister Margaret and I work with other organisations in Kibera.' She peered into his teacup. 'More tea?' she asked.

'No, thank you.'

'So tell me, Mr Riley, now that you know about us, are you interested in joining the Circularians?'

'I have to admit, it's not the reason I'm here,' he said.

'Then why are you here, if I may ask?'

'I was hoping to find one of your children, by the name of Jafari Su'ud — a boy of about twelve or thirteen by now, I suppose.'

'Long gone, I'm afraid. As I said, the older boys are always quickly placed. I believe Mr Koske has a contact in Wajir who is always looking for Muslim boys to place with Arab families. But you've come from so far away — how did you hear about us?'

Without a thought of where the conversation might lead, he told Sister Veronica about Melissa and their discussion in Bali, but became diverted and found himself talking about their meeting in the supermarket; of how he'd loved her at first sight.

'Oh, that's so sweet,' Sister Veronica said. 'Did you hear that, Margaret?' she asked her colleague. 'Love at first sight.'

The other woman nodded and, smiling, took a seat beside Sister Veronica.

Riley became immersed in the details: the wedding photos on surfboards, their marriage ceremony. He roamed into recollections of other happy days in Australia, and smiled as he recalled the fun they'd had learning to windsurf; how Melissa would shriek with delight when she finally remained upright for long enough to catch the wind and run with it. The story meandered back to Bali and the day they'd discussed travelling to Kenya to see their foster child.

'It's the reason I'm here today,' he said. 'Melissa and I had been talking about coming here to find Jafari for some time.'

'And I can see it was the love you share with your wife that brought you here. But where is she? Where is your wife, Melissa?'

As usual, he found a way to avoid the question. He strung more memories together, but soon he was recalling that terrible night in Bali: the forgotten hat; the ear-shattering explosion; the horror of Jalan Legian.

Sister Veronica's hand went to her mouth.

He recounted the long moment of shocked disbelief; the mad, blind dash to where he'd left Melissa, and his frantic search for her among the ruins. And suddenly Melissa was in his arms — a lifeless, broken body.

Tears brimmed and he forced them away. His story was finished but he felt unsure if he'd told the sisters how much he'd loved his wife. He told them anyway.

The two nuns sat side by side, tears tumbling down their cheeks.

He was exhausted. Empty.

But it was over.

*　*　*

Kazlana sat in her empty office, reading the civil aviation report again. It all made sense now. Her father would never have landed the Cessna near the Somali border unless he had a compelling reason to do so. He had arranged a meeting with Abukar to get details of whatever he suspected was going on at the Nakuru medical facility, and Abukar had murdered him. Which meant she could never avenge her father's death — Abukar was beyond her reach.

She dropped her head into her hands and groaned in frustration.

Her mobile phone rang. She ignored it.

A moment later the telephone at her receptionist's desk buzzed. Who could be calling her office on a Sunday? She pressed the answer button.

'Antonio!' she said. 'How are you? Is everything all right?'

'*Cara mia*. You are a very difficult person to find, no? Everywhere I am calling you, here and there, and now I find you in your office! Never mind. I have some news about your father.'

'You do? I've been going crazy here. I can't understand what —'

'Kazlana. Stop. Listen to me. I do not have a lot of time. Your father had a rendezvous north of Wajir. That is why he landed where he did.'

'Yes, I know. It was with Faraj Khalid Abukar.'

'No. It was not.'

'How do you know?'

'Because … I was with Abukar that day. Neither he nor his men were involved.'

'Then, who?'

'Ah, that is the difficult part. I don't know this person, but my information is that he's — how you say? — a big noise in Nairobi.'

'Antonio, wait. What are we doing? We shouldn't be discussing this on an open line. You know how it is.'

'There is no time. I leave for Somalia tonight.'

'I don't want to hear the name. For your own sake, hang up now.'

'I don't have the name, but maybe you can find it yourself. This big noise came here in a government helicopter. They arrived on —'

'Antonio! For God's sake, stop. I'm hanging up.'

Shaken and annoyed by Antonio's recklessness, Kazlana went immediately to her computer. Logging on to the *Daily Nation* website, she drummed her fingers while the archives page took an age to download. There was another agonising wait after she'd searched for news reports for the day her father's plane crashed.

She perused every article on that day and every day of the following week, but there was nothing about a member of the government arriving in Wajir. Maybe it just wasn't newsworthy.

She was about to close the site, but on a hunch called up the page covering the day before the crash. There it was. A small piece in the *Gossip Around the Nation* column:

Wajir. Thursday. Despite all the chest-beating the government is doing about the need for economising, our spy in Wajir has informed us that a government helicopter with one official aboard arrived in Wajir today. Junior government minister Mr Gideon Koske was on a flag-flying mission. Anyone would think there was an election in the wind!

* * *

Henry, the doorman, met Riley as he was parking the Land Rover and took the suitcases from him. 'Would you like me to help you to your rooms with them, Mr Mark?'

'Don't bother just now, Henry. Put them in the luggage room. I need a drink.'

The talk with the Circularian nuns had shaken him. He felt exhausted, but strangely relieved, as if a huge burden had been lifted from him.

He entered the bar and, when the waiter asked, ordered a whisky and soda. Then he changed his mind. 'Better make it a coffee,' he said. It was a first, but Charlotte was right: he *was* drinking too much.

He took a newspaper to a table and flicked through the pages. A small headline on page five caught his eye: *UNICEF Hearings Off to a Shaky Start.*

The UNICEF committee meeting now in session at the Kenyatta International Conference Centre has heard that Kenya is neglecting her responsibilities under a UN agreement to protect the rights of children.

The chairman, Judge Hoffman, has requested a witness protection program to overcome the apparent reluctance of people to come forward with important information.

'I have been given a number of first-hand accounts of matters clearly at odds with the UN's Convention on the Rights of the Child,' Judge Hoffman said today outside the KICC. 'But most witnesses have refused to go public,' he added.

A spokesman for the Justice Department said that it was unlikely that a witness protection program could be set up before the hearings are due to end.

Meanwhile, the Chief Inspector of Police said that it would be most irregular to establish such a program for an international authority such as UNICEF. 'Witness protection programs are seldom established, and when they occur are exclusively the prerogative of the Kenyan police force.'

Riley folded the paper and took a mouthful of coffee. If Judge Hoffman's committee could nail a few big names it would be the perfect vehicle to launch his article.

He called the committee's secretariat. Hoffman wasn't available but he left a message for him. Then he called Kazlana to fill her in on what he'd discovered about Koske's orphanage and his supposed success in placing orphans in Somalia. If she agreed to testify with him, together they could offer the committee information on Koske's links with the Circularians in Mombasa who collected orphaned children from its streets, his orphanage in Kibera and the supply line of children to Somalia. He was sure there was some link to the Nakuru medical facility as well; if that were so, then Kazlana's paper trail showing Koske had financed the delivery of medical supplies to Nakuru could be vital evidence.

But there was no answer on either Kazlana's office or mobile phones when he called. It worried him, and he decided to check that she was okay.

* * *

Riley had taken a taxi to avoid the need to find a parking space, but he needn't have bothered. Nairobi's central business district was quiet. In fact, he thought it abnormally quiet, even for a Sunday, and vaguely ominous.

Iron grilles barricaded most of the shopfronts and office buildings appeared deserted except for nervous security guards who peered from alcoves. He could not recall a time when he hadn't seen throngs of people crowding the footpaths and roadways. Even the ubiquitous traffic police were missing.

He took the elevator and made his way along the tenth-floor corridor, where not even the hum of the air-conditioning plant broke the silence.

The entrance door to Kazlana's office suite was unlocked.

'Hello?' he called.

There was no response.

He slowly opened the door to Kazlana's office. The diffused light from the curtained window made it difficult to see, but the scent of fresh tobacco smoke hung in the air, and a moment later the red-hot tip of a cigarette glowed in the dimness. She was sitting on the sofa that occupied the best part of a wall.

'Hello,' he said. 'I was beginning to wonder if I had the right office.'

'Would you care to join me?' she said, and indicated a bottle of whisky and a pitcher of melting ice. Condensation had left a puddle on the timber coffee table. He noticed a near-empty highball glass in her hand.

'Thank you. And you?'

She held out the glass and he poured in a measure of whisky.

'More,' she said.

Her voice was hard and he looked at her, but she was smiling.

'Please,' she added.

He filled it. A drop of condensation fell from her glass onto her bare knee, but she ignored it.

He sat at the other end of the sofa and turned half-on to face her. 'Cheers,' he said.

'To love and glory,' she replied, and took a long pull on her drink. 'Why are you here in Kenya, Mark?'

'I think I've already told you. To find a boy I used to support through one of your local charities.'

'Is that all?'

She was drunk, but her eyes were bright and acutely focused on him, and her voice was crisp and concise.

'To find the boy and to do a little sightseeing,' he said.

'Really?'

'Kazlana,' he said, 'I came here to tell you what I've learnt about the orphanage and the Circularians. It seems Koske may be smuggling kids into Somalia. God knows what happens to them there. Don't you want to hear about it?'

'Oh, poor Mark,' she said, placing a hand on his thigh. 'Of course I do. Please go on.'

Mercifully, as he started to relate the story of the Circularian sisters, and the religion's odd beliefs, she removed her electrifying hand to light a cigarette. She didn't appear to take any interest in what he was saying until his mention of the distant Kenyan town where many of the children were sent before crossing the border into Somalia.

'Did you say Wajir?' she asked.

'Yes. Apparently it's quite a frontier town.'

'Outside the law,' she said, almost to herself. 'Even for Kenya.'

She took a long pull on her drink, emptying the glass. She held it out for more. Riley filled it.

'Aren't you interested in finding out more about the Wajir connection?' he asked.

She slowly shook her head. 'Thank you for your help. I only wanted to find out why my father was murdered. And now I know.'

'Tell me.'

'No.'

'Kazlana,' he said, trying to keep the exasperation from his voice, 'this racket is a crime. Kids are involved. It needs to be exposed.'

She turned to face him, expressionless. It was as if having discovered the circumstances of her father's death, she had already put a distance between herself and the fact.

'And I need to know what happened to the boy my wife and I sponsored,' he added. 'It's ... important. And personal.'

'I don't know what happened to your boy,' she said at last. 'But I can tell you what happened to my father. The rest is up to you.

295

'Papa was lured to the desert beyond Wajir. He had found out something about Koske's racket, I suppose, but was keeping quiet about it until he knew the whole story — the story that you also want to know. He must have thought the meeting in the desert would give him what he needed. The problem was, he didn't know that the man behind the scheme already suspected him. It was Koske. That explains why Papa didn't immediately take off at the first sign of trouble — he *knew* the person who met him out there.'

'I'm sorry about your father,' Riley said. 'But what about the children?'

Kazlana looked quite composed now; far more peaceful than he'd ever seen her.

'Maybe it would be better not to know about the children,' she said.

'What do you mean? I must know. And UNICEF needs to know too.'

He told her about the UNICEF hearing and the call for more information to help prosecute those involved in the abuse of children. 'If you tell the committee what you know about Koske's connection to the Nakuru operation, the police can do the rest,' he said.

She began to laugh. 'The police? Mark, don't be so funny. Of course the police won't help. They were in Wajir to investigate my father's death and did nothing. Don't tell me about the police. Someone has been filling their pockets for years to keep this quiet.'

'Then give me the papers you have. I'll take them to the UNICEF hearing.'

'Antonio suggests I forget the whole matter,' she said, ignoring his request. 'He says I should get on with my life.' She looked at him. 'What do you think?'

'I say he's wrong. We have a duty to the innocent to avenge their deaths.'

She didn't reply.

'Don't you agree?' he asked.

She replaced her cigarette in the ashtray. 'I do,' she said, and put a hand around the back of his neck, drawing him to her. She kissed him, lingering on his lips for a long moment. Her closeness and fragrance drove him mad. He took her in his arms and covered her mouth with his. Her tongue explored him and he tasted the delicious spicy flavour of her tobacco.

Then he moved away from her, breaking the embrace. 'Kazlana, this is … I can't do this.'

She smiled. 'You know me too well. I frighten you.'

'Look, I only came here to get your agreement to testify —'

'You will never catch Koske by any of these legal tricks,' she said. 'He is too smart and has too many corrupt people in his pocket. The children are gone. They cannot come back from where they are.'

'Maybe, but we can stop what Koske's doing and make him pay.'

'There is only one way to make him pay.'

'How?'

She rose unsteadily to her feet and went to a filing cabinet and unlocked it.

'Here. Here are the papers you want.'

He took them. 'Thank you,' he said. 'Is this what you meant by the only way to make him pay?'

She smiled again. 'No.'

He stood and put the papers in his pocket. He thought about saying something like, *Be careful. You know how dangerous Koske is*, but he knew he'd be wasting his breath. Kazlana Ramanova was incapable of being careful.

CHAPTER 32

Joshua took Charlotte to a high point called Kamukungi to see the extent of Kibera. Surrounding her was two and a half square kilometres of bustling, dirty, crowded tangles of ugly buildings, smoking rubbish heaps and foul odours where Joshua said over a million people lived, most of them without toilets and running water. They loved, they laughed, they ate, squabbled, prayed and ultimately died there. Very few had experienced any other home.

On the western horizon the sun peeped from behind a fragment of cloud, sending piercing shafts of gold through the smoky atmosphere to highlight the vast fields of rusty iron roofs. She could see thousands of them, but knew there must be tens of thousands more in the squalid alleys and laneways, where children played in mountains of garbage or in foetid drains with odours of excrement and filth.

A few substantial buildings, like churches and a government centre, poked above the sprawling shacks. There was a radio mast and scores of power poles, some leaning at alarming angles. Telephone cables radiated from any high point, including trees and tall struts attached to roofs. In some places they hung in coils like dead snakes.

Charlotte was enthralled. Kibera had a vibrancy like no other place she'd ever been.

People stared at her, but there was no animosity in their glances. Far from being populated by indolent layabouts, Kibera was a hive of industry with most people too busy to gawp.

By mid-afternoon, Charlotte had spoken to a dozen people and was regretting having allocated so much time to her excursion. It was hot — too hot — and the afternoon too long.

She was debating whether to ring Mark and ask him to collect her early, when Joshua introduced her to Mama Hamza. The old lady's smiling eyes were piercing. Charlotte felt Mama Hamza could plumb the depths of her soul with those eyes, but she had a warm and welcoming manner.

Charlotte heard of Mama Hamza's work with the women in Kibera; how she had managed to transcend the tribal barriers to address the underlying problems that the women of the slums had to contend with daily. But she said she was not interested in wasting time talking of her achievements; she was more interested to hear why Charlotte was in Kibera.

'I'm studying all aspects of Luo life,' Charlotte said. 'Even in the slums.'

'Do you believe that a Luo in Kibera can be the same as a Luo in Nyanza Province?'

'I don't know. What do you think?'

'All of my work has been with women. Women of all tribes. In Kibera, we are bound by common problems: poverty, domestic violence, drunken husbands, greedy and aggressive landlords. In this case it doesn't matter if you're a Luo or a Luhya or a Kikuyu. I try to tell my women we are all Kenyans, and if they must feel a part of a tribe, then we are members of the Kibera tribe.'

They discussed her community support group, one of the many, Charlotte discovered, that had been established by concerned Kibera residents and without outside funding or official support. Many, like Mama Hamza's Kibera Women's Association, became so successful that non-government organisations wanted to become aligned with her. The KWA provided family-planning information, health education, remedial classes for children who had dropped out of or been forgotten by the education system, and a range of microfinanced assistance packages.

'So you see,' Mama Hamza concluded, 'we help people in many, many small ways. We are small and we want to remain small. I have seen too many people come into Kibera with briefcases. They have money, but do nothing.'

'I'm only here to study. I have no briefcase and no money,' Charlotte said.

'Why come to Kibera to do your research?' Mama Hamza asked. 'Why not to Nyanza, the Luo homeland?'

'I'm interested in speaking to Luos who have seen Luo life on both sides, Kibera and Nyanza. That's why Joshua is helping me. He's seen it from both sides.'

Mama Hamza looked curiously at Joshua, who turned away as his mobile phone bleated an incoming call. He took it, and his face fell as he listened.

'What is it, Joshua?' Charlotte said.

'It's ... There's something happening at KICC.' He swung his head around as if searching for an immediate escape. 'There is trouble coming. You must get out of Kibera!'

* * *

Henry snapped to attention and gave his usual friendly salute as Riley climbed out of the taxi. It was after four o'clock and he didn't want to be late to meet Charlotte in Kibera.

'Good afternoon, Mr Riley,' Henry said as he swung the hotel doors wide.

'G'day, Henry. Nice day.'

'Yes, sir, it is.'

Instead of entering the hotel, Riley headed towards the hotel car park with a brisk step.

'Mr Riley, sir!' Henry called after him. 'Excuse me, sir, but may I ask where you're going?'

Riley smiled at Henry's odd question and worried look. 'I'm just going out again for a bit. Why, what's up?'

'I don't know if you've heard about it, Mr Riley, but there's some trouble in town.'

'What kind of trouble?'

'To do with the elections. The GSU is there.'

'The GSU?'

'The General Services Unit. If the GSU is there, it always means trouble. There may be rioting.'

'Well, I'm not going into town, Henry, but thanks anyway.'

'That's a relief, sir. If you stay away from town, you'll be fine. And Kibera, of course.'

Riley was almost to the garden when he caught his last words. 'Kibera?' he said. 'Did you say Kibera?'

'Yes, sir. But that's not a place you'd be going. It's the slum area out on —'

'Henry. What about Kibera?'

The doorman saw Riley's worried expression. 'It's off Ngong Road, sir.'

'I know where it is, Henry. Tell me what there is about Kibera that I need to know.'

'W-well, if there's trouble anywhere in Kenya, it always flies to Kibera. Those people there, they —'

Riley dashed through the garden gate and sprinted to the Land Rover.

* * *

'Hurry, Miss Charlotte,' Joshua said, leading her down one alley and into another.

'What's going on?' she asked. 'If the trouble is at the voting centre, why are we worried about it here?'

He wasn't sure why he was concerned. There was no sign of any problems yet. He only knew that Kibera could be a very changeable place and there was an all too familiar electricity in the foetid air. He remembered the atmosphere immediately following the last elections: the explosion of violence; the looting; the rapes. He wanted to take no chances. A *mzungu* in Kibera with him as her guide was one matter. A *mzungu* woman in Kibera during a riot was quite another.

301

'What time was Mr Mark to meet you?' he asked.

'Five. But he won't be there yet. It's only about four.'

Joshua frantically tried to come up with a plan. He needed a safe haven until five o'clock. His father's little house was the safest place in Kibera that he could think of.

* * *

Less than fifteen minutes later, they were standing outside a door made from a patchwork of various timbers with a strong slide bolt aligned against a sturdy timber upright.

'This is my father's house,' Joshua said.

Charlotte nodded and waited.

'He may not be home,' he added.

Still they waited. Joshua seemed reluctant to enter.

The door opened. A tall, lean man in a clean white shirt and long grey trousers stood there. His sad eyes saw only Joshua, and as he stared at him an awkward silence grew.

'This is my father, Simon Otieng,' Joshua said to Charlotte.

Simon seemed startled to see her, but took her outstretched hand. She found his callused fingers quite gentle, holding her hand as he might a bird.

'Father, this is Miss Charlotte.'

She said hello and Simon nodded, still looking bewildered by her appearance at his door. He spluttered an apology and invited her to enter.

The shack was dimly lit from a small, high window above a packing-case cupboard. There was just one chair. Simon brushed the seat and offered it to Charlotte, then sat on a box on the other side of a narrow bench that served as a table. Two thin, cotton curtains were strung on wires along the edge of the beds. A dog-eared poster of Michael Jackson hung from a nail above one of them. A TV with what looked like a fencing-wire antenna sat on a small fridge beside the cupboard. Joshua remained standing, leaning against the fridge, arms folded.

302

'I'm pleased to meet you, Mr Otieng,' Charlotte said, wondering why she had never asked about Joshua's family.

The tension in the room was almost tangible. She stumbled on as best she could in a one-way conversation, but soon realised the tension was not due to her presence. It was clear that father and son were as strangers.

Eventually, Simon asked Charlotte if she would like to have tea. She said she would.

'Miss Charlotte,' Joshua said, 'can I leave you here with my father while I try to find out what is happening?'

'Of course,' she answered.

He turned to leave.

Simon stopped him at the door. 'Joshua,' he said. 'My son, there is trouble coming.'

It was the first time Simon had addressed his son since they'd arrived.

Joshua looked at his father and nodded. 'I know. That is why I must find a way to get Miss Charlotte out of here.'

* * *

When the afternoon sun lengthened the shadows in Kisumu Ndogo, Simon turned on the kitchen light, which flickered and finally glowed yellow.

'They say it's the voltage,' he explained when Charlotte asked about the dull glow. 'Not enough to make it white, as it should be.' He shrugged. 'It's just like that.'

Charlotte said she understood and asked if Simon would mind telling her a little about his childhood. 'I am doing a study on the Luo people,' she said.

He appeared reticent and asked what she'd like to know.

'Anything. Everything. Why not start by telling me about the customs around your birth?'

'Oh, we Luos don't worry about birthdays. But as far as I know, I was born in 1970.'

As he warmed to his subject, Charlotte pulled out her notebook and began to scribble down what he told her.

He described how, in the Luo way, a son was 'the centre of the home'. It was an expression of love, but also of recognition that to the Jo-Luo a son ensured the family's cultural heritage and oral history would be carried on to the next generation. A boy's birth, especially that of a firstborn, was a most joyous occasion, invoking praise for the mother and congratulations for the father.

The first act after the birth was the burial of the placenta, which bound the child to his ancestral land. The new mother was treated to a special gruel made from finger millet, and fed the stewed meat of a goat or even a bull to rebuild her body. When the mother emerged from her confinement, she and her baby wore headdresses of woodpeckers' feathers so that the birds, whose calls were considered a bad omen for the child, would be kept at bay. The parents and the newborn were shaved to end the birthing cycle, then joined with their extended family in days of celebrations and self-congratulatory announcements to the wider community.

And so it was for Akoth Otieng and his wife, Ayira, when their son, Gero, was born. He was a lively baby, which didn't surprise many of their friends and family. What could the parents expect, the elders said, when they had tempted almighty Nyasaye with such a name? Gero meant 'fierceness' and if the child were later to become a warrior, then all would be well. But if the British continued to uphold the peace by means of a gloved fist, a fierce boy among the warlike Luo could only lead to anger and confusion for the child. Fortuitously, according to those who predicted disaster, before the child reached the age where he must be formally named, Ayira had a dream, and in that dream her beloved and long-dead grandmother visited her.

Ayira's grandmother had been an important member of the Luo community and in the dream she cautioned against the name, saying that she saw a cloud over the child and it would be wise for Ayira to choose another name. The old woman had been an early convert to the new Christian ideas spread by the eager missionaries and she suggested the parents turn to the New Testament for a more calming name. Akoth was not pleased but had to concede that it would be prudent to heed the voice of such a wise woman.

On the rolling hills outside their village, where the wind off Lake Victoria blew hot and strong in the weeks before the rains, the extended family gathered for the *juogi* or naming ceremony. There, Gero became Simon in the first of what would be many ceremonies that mark a Luo's life.

But, as Simon explained, that was not how it turned out for him.

*   *   *

Riley was at the top of Valley Road, at the end of a traffic jam that extended around the corner and beyond the roundabout. He spun the wheel and roared back the way he'd come. Ten minutes later he was bumping down a muddy, unmade suburban street, trying to get onto Ngong Road from another angle, and ran into another jam. He pulled out his phone.

'Charlie, it's me.'

'Mark. Are you all right?'

'I'm fine. And you?'

'Well, it's been kind of interesting.' She explained her situation.

'So, I don't think I'll be going anywhere tonight,' she added.

'I can't get through anyway,' he told her. 'The police must have closed off the whole area.'

'I'm okay at the moment. Joshua said it should be safe in the morning. Can I meet you on Ngong Road around eight?'

'I'll get there somehow, even if I have to walk.'

'Let's hope that's not necessary. I definitely wore the wrong shoes if we have to walk.'

'Charlie ...'

'Yes?'

'Please ... I want you to take care of yourself.'

There was a pause. 'I will, Mark.'

He felt he had to push the point home. 'It's very important, Charlie.'

'Yes, Mark. I hear what you're saying. Thank you.'

*   *   *

'This is Samuel Muthami of SKY FM at the Kenyatta International Conference Centre where the counting of the votes from Thursday's poll continues.

'There have been some startling developments in the last hour or so. Scrutineers from the Orange Democratic Movement have discovered irregularities in the votes tallied in the constituencies compared to those appearing here at the central tallying centre at KICC.

'ODM supporters are outraged — you may be able to hear them in the background. They are calling for a halt to the count until the discrepancies are investigated. Mr Samuel Kivuitu, the chairman of the Electoral Commission of Kenya, is refusing to budge, saying there is no reason to doubt the figures. He takes this stance in spite of his own admission that his telephone connections to the constituencies have failed for some strange reason. He's had no contact with the polling stations outside Nairobi since earlier today, yet he still maintains the counting is accurate.

'The police called for reinforcements and the General Services Unit have now arrived, but even they are struggling to hold back the crowd gathered outside.'

*   *   *

In his father's gloomy house, Joshua, who had returned shortly after sunset, sat in the flickering light of the tiny black and white TV, watching the Odinga victory sink from sight. He was numbed by what he heard. Odinga, the declared winner of the night before, had lost the presidency.

In the TV studio, the lights reflected off Kivuitu's thick spectacles, making his eyes look like those of an alien creature sent to earth with a death sentence for the human race. He smiled, he nodded reassuringly, but the words following his official declaration of the polls were unheard by Joshua. The margins, the percentages, the parliamentary seats, the electorates won and lost — none of it mattered. Only the presidential result mattered. And Odinga had lost. Behind it all was the charade of officialdom. The same officialdom that had ruled his life in Kibera since birth; the officialdom that Raila Odinga had promised to eradicate by making government more accountable. More human. More benevolent.

Joshua looked at Charlotte, her attention on the scenes filmed earlier outside the KICC. Clouds of teargas drifted on the warm afternoon air. Uniformed men charged into the crowd, violently smashing the heads and bodies of anyone unwilling or unable to get out of their way. What could Charlotte know of the real effects of this election on him and his fellow supporters? She was a *mzungu*, a European, able to fly away from whatever consequences might follow this travesty. Could he blame her and her countrymen for this debacle? There were many who thought the source of all Kenya's political woes sprang from the colonists' legacy at independence. Joshua couldn't see the connection. Not after all these years. Certainly not after this election, which had so obviously, so comprehensively, so callously, been stolen from them by some of their fellow Kenyans.

He found his father's sad eyes not on the TV, but on him. Despite the look, he thought it unlikely that his father shared his sense of loss about the presidential election. He wouldn't feel compelled to fight against the injustice of it all.

'Joshua, we must talk, you and I,' he whispered in Luo.

Joshua wanted to talk. He wanted to find some sense in what was happening; what had already happened. He was fearful for Charlotte, marooned in Kibera with a tsunami of trouble building around her. He was also afraid for Mayasa, who could be somewhere in the jungle of huts and alleys. Kibera required just one small spark to burst into violent flames. Anything might happen now.

From what seemed like a long distance away, but was probably not far at all, came a howling sound, a confusion of angry voices. Joshua felt trapped in the house while every fibre in his body screamed to be out in the night with the others, baying in outrage. The shameful theft of their election victory demanded immediate condemnation or else the government and their Kikuyu conspirators could celebrate a cheap victory.

He stood abruptly, needing to do something to relieve the feelings of guilt about his idleness, and bumped his head on the light globe, sending it spinning and the shadows with it. His father glanced at him but said nothing. Charlotte continued to stare at the TV screen.

Joshua fidgeted with his mobile phone. He checked how much credit he had and, hoping it would be enough, dialled the number. He stepped outside into the alley and felt a wash of relief when she answered.

'Joshua! Is that you?'

'Mayasa! I've been wanting to call —'

'Where have you been? I've been —'

'I had no credit. I've —'

'… worried to death about you. I love you. I'm at —'

'… I've been to … What?'

'I said I'm at my sister's house.'

'Before that.'

'I said … I said, I love you.'

'I love you too.'

308

'You do? Oh, Joshua, I'm sorry. I should have told you about my father when we first met.'

'It's okay.'

'I know it's a problem for some people.'

'Mayasa, it's okay.'

'He's been admitted into the antiretroviral program.'

'What's that?'

'A treatment program. He's getting better every week.'

'Good. That's good. But we can talk about this later. Where are you?'

'At my sister's house in Langata,' she said. 'I've been here since the trouble started. Are you safe?'

'I'm at my father's house. Stay there until tomorrow. Maybe it'll be all calm by then. I'll come for you and bring you home.'

'The market's safe. Why don't I meet you at Toi Market?'

'Yes. Toi Market. Tomorrow at nine. I'd better go, not much credit.'

'Okay. I love you, Josh.'

'Love you too. *Kwaheri.*'

Inside again, Joshua checked his texts. He had a dozen incoming broadcast messages rallying the faithful for a raid into the Kikuyu stronghold of Laini Saba, and others denouncing the government and the electoral commission in extravagant prose. There were texts from friends and team-mates demanding to know why he was absent.

He flicked through his various news feeds. There was one he'd set up while in the national park at Nakuru. He scanned the Nakuru headlines. An item caught his eye and he opened it:

Thugs Attack Local Driver at Londiani Roadblock.

A roadblock set up by outraged Odinga supporters stopped a local safari operator's car. The lone occupant of the car, Mr Maina Gatoto, a Kikuyu employee of Kenya Allover Tours, was savagely beaten and left for dead. A Good Samaritan stopped to give assistance, but he was also set upon by the gang and luckily escaped.

Mr Gatoto was dead on arrival at Nakuru General. He leaves behind a wife and four children.

Joshua was in Nakuru Park again, watching the dawn bursting through the umbrella trees; the wildlife in numbers unimaginable. He recalled Maina's fascinating stories of the Serengeti and its even greater wonders.

'The soft sounds of the Serengeti,' he whispered, just to hear Maina's words again.

Charlotte looked up at him. 'You must miss it,' she said.

He stared at her for a long time before answering. 'I have never been there.'

'What?' Charlotte looked confused.

'I'm sorry. I lied to you. All I know about the Serengeti is what a boy can learn from a poster in a travel agent's window. But I wanted so much to go. I was hoping to find work there so I could take Mayasa to live there.'

'I see. Mayasa's the girl we saw you with on Ngong Road?'

He nodded.

'But would you leave Kibera and take that risk?'

'I have no choice. We must leave Kibera. It will never be safe for us now that Mr Koske is angry. I know it.'

'Can't you go to the police if you're in danger?' she asked, then added, 'No, I guess not,' when she saw his expression.

He told her about Mayasa and her father's HIV, and how at first it had been a problem but now was not. He told her about their plans for the future. If they could get away … somewhere.

'Don't you have family in Luoland, near the lake?' she asked.

Joshua avoided glancing in the direction of his father. 'Yes. But I don't know them.'

Charlotte nodded thoughtfully. 'Even if you could get to the Serengeti National Park, or wherever else you might find work, how would you survive until you found a job?'

He said that Mayasa had family in Musoma, which was on Lake Victoria and quite near the Serengeti, but she said they were so poor she didn't think they could help them.

'Mayasa says there are few jobs in Musoma,' he added. 'I could try Kisumu. Maybe that's all I can do to feed us.' He smiled and fidgeted with his hands. 'To get a job in the Serengeti ... well, it's just a dream.'

'It's okay to dream, Joshua,' she said. 'I might have an idea.'

'What is it?' he asked with interest.

'I can't say just now. But maybe ...'

*   *   *

Simon sat quietly as Joshua and Charlotte talked. It was painful to know his son could reveal his hopes to a *mzungu* woman and not to his own father. He'd had no idea of Joshua's dream about the Serengeti. How could a son of his have such strange and unachievable notions?

Then Simon remembered he'd also had dreams at Joshua's age, and even younger. But he'd also learnt how disastrous it could be to pursue impossible goals. When Joshua started to show an interest in his Luo background, Simon had refused to share Luo customs with his son, afraid he would ultimately be disillusioned. There was no place for traditions and culture in an urban slum.

But Joshua had been a determined boy and when his father refused to indulge him with the stories from the past, he had found others who would. Simon, who had learnt Luo lore at his grandfather's knee — an elder enmeshed in the history and beliefs of the tribe — could see the flaws in Joshua's second-hand knowledge. The stories he heard, largely from disillusioned young Luos in Kibera, were tainted by an overlay of inter-tribal hatred.

Still Simon had remained obstinate, and by the time he'd realised that he and his son had erected barriers within their relationship, it was too late to change. The only chance he had now of breaking down those barriers was to tell his son the truth about 2002.

*   *   *

Simon stood at the open door, his steaming mug of tea cupped between his hands, and smelt the air. It was the best time of the day to taste the air in Kibera as the pre-dawn moisture seemed to clean it of the odours of the previous day. But although the stars were faintly present, this morning the air was not good.

Behind him, the kitchen light clicked on and his wife joined him at the door.

'Still there is smoke,' she said.

He nodded, taking a sip of his tea. 'You will be careful today,' he said. It was a reminder of their conversation the night before. They'd talked about the present troubles and the need for her to take care.

'I will,' she said, laying her head against his chest. 'When will this end?'

'Soon. When the elections are finished.'

They went inside and Patience closed the door on the acrid air.

The two little ones were curled together like a pair of kittens; Nellie was tucked under Faith's shoulder with a thumb stuck in the corner of her mouth. Charity lay on the fold-down, her head surrounded by long braids. Breathy gasps came from her slightly parted lips. The smoke was not good for her asthma. Simon struggled with feelings of helplessness and anger. Anger at his inability to improve his family's life; the helplessness of a father who had done all he could for an ailing child.

Joshua was asleep face down. At twelve, he had become a beanpole of a boy with long, spindly legs, large knees and broad feet, which he used to considerable effect on the football field. Simon had never been a keen supporter of the game, but he took vicarious pleasure each time his son slammed the ball into the back of an opponent's net.

'Are they with you today?' he asked, referring to the children.

'Yes. Except for Joshua, who is at football.'

Simon nodded. 'I will tell him to stay close to home today,' he said. 'He can run your errands and you can be with the girls.'

'Just let him sleep,' she said softly.

'The boy has his responsibilities.'

Patience was silent, but when Simon glanced at her, she had those eyes — the ones he simply couldn't disregard.

'He is a big boy now,' he countered, although his wife had said nothing.

'It is his only joy, Simon. Let him play football. I have few things that take me outside the house today.'

He rolled his eyes, but let it be. Patience was right. There was little for an energetic boy to do in Kibera. At least dirt football kept Joshua away from those who preferred petty theft and the risk of a beating, or worse, if caught.

Simon drained the dregs of his tea and put the mug on the table with a sigh. Moving quietly among the beds he kissed each of his children on the cheek.

Patience waited for him at the door and slipped her arms around his waist.

To her unasked question he said, 'Eastleigh today.'

'So far.'

'It will mean money for the *matatu*, but they say there is work in the timber yard.'

He kissed the top of her head and, with a final glance at his sleeping children, slipped into the smoke-sodden gloom.

It was a little after dawn when Simon arrived at the timber yard. Four men were at the chain-wire gate ahead of him. Simon recognised one from his days in Mathare.

'*Habari*,' he said.

The man, Nathaniel, replied, shaking hands in the African manner by clasping thumbs. They exchanged news.

Nathaniel was a Kamba, but Simon knew him well enough to enquire how the current election problems affected him.

'It is bad, *bwana*,' he said. 'Near my house, two boys beaten to death with sticks. Sixteen or seventeen years only.' He shook his head.

'*Kwa nini?*' Simon asked.

'Why? For nothing!' Nathaniel said in outrage. 'It is just this … this madness.'

'*Haki ya mungu,*' Simon muttered in sympathy. Then added, 'How is it with you? Any work?'

Nathaniel looked at the others standing with them at the gate, and drew Simon to one side. 'Work is difficult, *bwana*. Very difficult. The Kikuyus, ah? These days they are hiring only their brothers.'

Simon nodded.

The gateman arrived, irritable from lack of sleep. Without a word he put his hand out and the four men at the gate with Simon put a grubby fifty-shilling note in it. When he came to Simon, he took his fifty and grunted that it was not enough.

'More?' Simon said in disbelief. 'But from them you took fifty only.'

'A hundred,' the gateman said.

Simon looked at the others. Nathaniel pointedly averted his eyes.

The gateman was unmoved and, after waiting no more than a few seconds, turned his back on Simon while stuffing the notes in his pocket.

'Wait,' Simon said. 'Is there work here for us?'

Bribe money didn't guarantee work. That decision came from the foreman.

A shrug and nothing more from the gateman.

Simon fished out his last note and, after a hesitation that threatened to have the gateman turn his back again, he quickly shoved the fifty into his hand.

The gateman took a bundle of keys from his pocket and let himself in, putting a hand up to the others as they crowded close behind him. He snapped the padlock shut on the gate and ambled up to the site shed, scratching his backside. The men presumed they were in for a wait and squatted with their backs against the chain-wire gate.

Simon put his head back against the fence and stared into the clear sky directly above him. Clouds gathered in the distance, but he thought they would amount to nothing. *It's too early for the short rains*, he mused. A faint line of cloud in the middle distance stood in outline against the distant storm.

But it was more than cloud. There was also a line of smoke in the south-west; over Kibera.

Simon prayed he was wrong. Perhaps the smoke was from the more distant Ngong Hills. He stood and studied the line of misty grey, which was now joined by a filament of darker smoke. There could be no doubt. It was coming from Kibera.

He shifted his weight from one foot to the other. He knew his unease was because he and Patience had been discussing the crisis only last night. And it had been foremost in his thoughts for days. He was simply more conscious of the matter than previously.

He turned to see if the gateman was returning, but he was nowhere in sight.

Even if the smoke came from Kibera, it could be from the fires set the day before. He tried to convince himself that if it was from new fires in Kibera, they wouldn't be in Kisumu Ndogo, but he failed.

He turned again to see if the gateman and his money were returning, then hurriedly walked away from his chance of work and the certain loss of his hundred bob. Almost an hour later, he entered the maze of alleys, breathless.

No *matatu* driver would agree to bring him from Eastleigh to home. It was popularly rumoured that most of these small minibuses were owned by Kikuyu politicians, and a driver daring to enter Kibera risked a bombardment of missiles. It had therefore taken Simon an hour to reach the city, and a further forty minutes to run the gauntlet of the rioting, pillaging mobs from Uhuru Park.

During this time, the storm he'd first noticed at Eastleigh had gathered its undoubted energy above the city. Simon wished it onward as it was likely to be the only power able to disperse the crowds and stop the pillage and burning he'd witnessed on his homeward journey.

'*Haki wa; haki wa,*' a gang of youths shouted as they rushed up the alley towards Simon, who stood aside to let them pass. He'd heard their voices from a distance but felt no need to hide as he'd done on the other side of Kibera when a mob of Kikuyu youths had come rampaging along the road. *Haki wa; haki wa* had been the rallying Dho-Luo call for all Luos since the announcement of the election results. *Our right; our right.*

Simon was disgusted with them. Violence was not the answer. Instead of voting along tribal lines, they should have chosen their candidates on their policies and performance. It was all over, it was too late to cry that the wrong party or candidate had won. But he had more on his mind right now than the ill-mannered louts or short-sighted electorate. He'd been unable to find Joshua at the place he played football with his friends. He prayed he was already at home, safe from the turmoil now clearly in evidence around him.

His anxiety heightened as he neared Kisumu Ndogo. Instead of it being a relatively peaceful island in the middle of a stormy sea, there was a pall of smoke rising from its centre.

He hurried on through increasingly familiar neighbourhoods. *Don't think it; don't think it*, he whispered to himself.

He had tried to reassure Patience during their discussion the previous night that although she needed to be vigilant, there was no need for undue concern so long as she and the children stayed near the house. They were in the centre of the safest part of Kibera. Even the most foolhardy and aggressive gang would not dare invade Kisumu Ndogo, the Luo stronghold.

The smoke ahead of him towered higher. *Don't think it; don't think it.* The Ongoros' shack; the Oukos'. He was now in familiar territory. The Ogwan'gs'; the Onyangos'.

Still the smoke loomed. He dared not imagine the unthinkable.

The Okellos'.

Radiant heat, hot on his face.

The burning house. His house. Consumed by flames. The roof sagging, then collapsing inwards, sending a cloud of red ash into the air.

A flash of lightning.

He slid down the Okellos' rusted corrugated-iron wall, a hand covering his mouth where a soundless scream had caught in his throat.

The clap of thunder.

Suddenly Joshua was beside him, staring at him through his tears, which streamed down his face. Simon could see his own pain in his son's expression, but in addition he found confusion and loss and incomprehension.

After friends and neighbours had carried away the blackened corpses that had been his wife and daughters, Simon held his sobbing son in his arms.

He knew this tragedy was the result of a tribal war. He didn't want to kill his son's interest in his Luo legacy, but he had witnessed the unspeakable evil of tribal hatred that morning and he took an oath that his son would never be drawn into a similar situation because of a misguided notion of pride in tribe.

CHAPTER 33

Acrid smoke mixed with the morning mist as Charlotte followed Joshua through Kibera to the place on Kibera Road where she was to meet Riley.

When she'd put on the ankle-length *kanga* and modest headscarf that Joshua had borrowed from a neighbour, he'd said she looked very much like a proper Muslim lady off to the mosque in Ngong Road.

'But I look like a bag of laundry,' she'd protested.

'That is very good,' he'd said. 'When we meet Mr Mark, and you are far away in the Panafric Hotel, then you can look beautiful again.'

Before they'd gone more than five minutes from Simon's house, they passed burnt-out *dukas*, the smouldering remains of which were scattered about the bare earth. Other *dukas*, with words like *No Raila — No Peace* crudely painted on them, had been spared.

Even though it was early, Charlotte thought it strange that the streets were almost deserted. When they had arrived the previous day, they had been buzzing with activity. Now, an eerie silence shrouded Kibera's streets, paths and alleys, as if the settlement had been shocked by what had transpired during the night.

Once over the rise near Kamukungi, they heard and then saw a large crowd of youths walking quickly towards them. Joshua led Charlotte into a side alley where they were hidden from the road. The gang passed uneventfully. After this, Joshua kept away from the wider thoroughfares; they picked their way through garbage-strewn alleys, avoiding the putrid water that meandered in rivulets or gathered in broad shallow pools in the eroded paths.

A woman burst from a house ahead of them, screaming as a man lunged at her from the doorway. She struggled with him for a few moments before managing to shake him off. She dashed down the alley, her bare feet splashing slush and filth around her. The man uttered a grunt and caught sight of Charlotte and Joshua watching him. Joshua stepped in front of Charlotte as the man made a threatening move towards them. Two men ran past him and, after a moment's hesitation, he followed. All three disappeared down another alley.

Charlotte's heart pounded and she clung to Joshua's arm. For a moment, she was back in the dark Nakuru night, surrounded by grunts of savage fury and squeals of terror, as unseen creatures fought to establish dominance.

Joshua took her hand, coaxing her forward, but she was reluctant to move. She was distressed by what she'd witnessed, but more than that, she was troubled that neither she nor Joshua had made a move to help the poor woman. It had happened so quickly, but was that her only excuse? And if they had assisted the woman, would they also have become victims of the anarchy that now surrounded them? She wanted to ask why the neighbours had not been alerted by the woman's screams? Where was the sense of community she'd witnessed just the day before? Where were the police?

But there were never any police. And even the support usually given by neighbours in times of trouble was tested when violence and chaos reigned. There was no law and order in Kibera that morning. These were the realities, and Charlotte became acutely aware that she was an outsider in this strange world, with only her disguise and Joshua preventing her from becoming yet another victim.

They quickened their pace. Soon they were scampering between the puddles and leaping the scattered rubble. Charlotte felt ashamed to be running, but she kept going as if her life depended upon it, and with scarce regard for the mud and slime that spattered her colourful *kanga*.

They emerged from a winding alley they'd followed for some time and arrived at Kibera Road. It was all but deserted of the frantic traffic that had flowed and jounced and tooted there only a day before. The cars, the buses, the *matatus*, all were gone and the silence that pervaded the near-vacant space seemed somehow sinister.

She and Joshua had a good view of the wreckage-strewn road in both directions. They were almost exactly at the place where Mark was supposed to be waiting, but it was already eight o'clock and he wasn't there.

'What will we do?' she said, the panic rising in her voice.

Joshua didn't answer. He held up his hand as he stared down the length of Kibera Road. Charlotte followed his eyes, then heard it too. It was muffled, like the distant rumble of thunder, but grew in power as she searched for its source.

A massive crowd, carrying sticks or clubs or other weapons, came swinging into Kibera Road. They fanned out to fill the road, overturning push-carts and the small kiosks along the verges of the normally busy thoroughfare. They swarmed like ants over a single small sedan that had turned into Kibera Road without seeing the oncoming mob. The car tried to make a U-turn out of their path, but was trapped.

The shouting mob began to rock the car, until it finally toppled over. Nothing could be seen or heard of the occupants. A cloth tied to a stick was set alight and in another moment the petrol tank was ablaze — the flames leapt from the rear of the vehicle, sending up billowing clouds of black smoke. The crowd roared as if with one voice, and then continued towards Charlotte and Joshua like a lava flow, unchecked by the temporary diversion.

Charlotte felt trapped. She didn't want to retrace her steps, but nor could they stay where they were. More men joined the mob as it approached, pouring from the alleys. She swallowed a cry of alarm as two young men pushed roughly past her.

Three others hurried in their wake, waving their arms as they ran towards the approaching throng.

'We have to go,' Joshua said.

'Where?'

He searched the upper end of Kibera Road, towards the city. 'He's not here,' he said unnecessarily.

Within a few minutes, the head of the seething monster would be upon them and they would have no more choices. It was either be consumed by the mob or retreat into the Kibera jungle behind them.

* * *

Riley felt confident about his plan. He'd reconnoitred Kibera Road soon after dawn. It was quiet and the carriageway was relatively clear, except for the shrapnel and stones that littered the tarmac, and the *dukas* and shops that smouldered like memorials to the previous night's turmoil. He had then retired to a siding near the Ngong Hills Hotel to avoid attracting attention.

At seven minutes before eight o'clock he started the car and drove towards Kibera Road. He didn't get far before finding the street blocked by police mobile units. In the middle of the line-up, a heavily built police officer leant against his gleaming sedan, running his sleeve over a blemish on the duco. He ignored Riley when he gave a short beep to attract his attention, continuing his work on the blemish until it was completed to his satisfaction.

He sauntered over to Riley, who asked, 'What's the problem, Officer?'

The cop regarded him for a moment before replying sardonically, 'There is no problem, sir. Just turn around and go home.'

'I can't. I have to pick up a friend down there in Kibera Road in five minutes.'

The policeman frowned at him. 'I said, go home. There is no access to Kibera today.'

'Look, Officer, I understand there are some problems in the area, and I relieve you of all responsibility, but I have to go into Kibera. There's a young lady in there who's expecting me.'

'And what is this young lady of yours doing in Kibera?'

'She was — What's that got to do with it? I have to get through. Now.'

The officer straightened to his full height and sucked in his belly. 'This is my last warning to you,' he said, slapping his truncheon into his hand. 'I told you to get your car back from the barricade.'

'But you don't understand ... My friend is in Kibera. And I need to speak to someone who can let me through.'

Without further comment, the officer stepped to the front of the Land Rover and swung his truncheon hard into the headlight, causing an explosion of glass shards that glistened in the morning sun.

Riley glared at him, his white knuckles gripping the steering wheel to suppress his natural reaction.

The sound of smashing glass brought other policemen from the barricade, who gathered around, chuckling and cracking jokes.

The officer smiled vindictively and walked slowly to the other side of the car where he again smashed his truncheon into the headlight, bringing a roar of approval from his colleagues. He then began to pound the bonnet until it had a series of golf-ball-size dents in it.

Riley slammed the car into reverse, swung into a U-turn and drove as far as the corner, where he stopped out of sight of the roadblock, seething with anger and frustration. He hated corruption, particularly by those in positions of public service, and vividly recalled the situation with the Indonesian police when he'd tried to access details of his wife's death. It was common for them to use bluster to cover incompetence. There was the usual hint that if a small consideration were offered, matters could be different. They destroyed whatever self-respect they had; abused the power given them by the people's representatives. But if he'd allowed his anger to show, there was always the implied threat of the gun at the hip.

Sitting behind the wheel of the Land Rover, glaring down the road to the police blockade, his eyes stinging with tears of rage, Riley slowly reined in his anger. He should have planned for this outcome. Now there was no time to take another approach. Once again he had failed to intervene in a dangerous situation that affected someone he cared for. He felt a stab of recognition in his anger. He realised now that only part of it had been directed towards the terrorists responsible for Melissa's death. He had been angry with himself for failing his wife. Maddeningly, furiously angry that he had failed to avert the disaster. If he'd insisted they leave the silly cowboy hat in the restaurant, she would still be alive. If he'd said, *No, honey, I want to take you home and make love to you*, she would not have been blown apart. Since then, he'd allowed that anger to grow and distort his judgement. It explained a lot about the many poor decisions he'd made over the last five years.

The insight spurred him into action. He started the motor and revved it before dropping the clutch. The Land Rover almost gagged on the power burst, but responded with a leap. Riley let the counter soar into the red.

The roar of the approaching vehicle had the desired effect. The police manning the barricade scattered in all directions.

He kept the power up to the diesel, and aimed the Land Rover's heavy-duty bull-bars at the police officer's gleaming car. The windows imploded as he rammed it in a full broadside, moving it a metre or two past the line of other vehicles.

Riley reversed, sending a squad of policemen who were about to pile all over him into retreat. He then revved and accelerated into the police car again, spinning it around and almost clearing the path. Again he reversed, again he smashed into the now twisted car wreck, and this time he was able to complete the breakthrough and dash between the line of trucks and buses.

Beyond the barricade was the barrow of an enterprising ice-cream vendor, who saw him coming and flung himself out of his path. The Land Rover hit the roadside kerb, which launched it, airborne, into the ice-cream cart, sending buckets of ice-cream and pieces of the cart in all directions.

Riley roared with delight and swung into Kibera Road.

His elation was short-lived. Coming towards him was a wall of people, and he could not see Charlotte at the place they'd agreed for the pick-up. He drove past, unsure if he had the right spot, but was soon almost up to the rioters' front ranks.

He made a swinging one-eighty in front of the marchers, which incensed them. The leading group charged after him, and in the rear-view mirror he could see that the remainder were quick to join them. A barrage of rocks flew past, some crashing onto the roof and hood.

He screeched to a stop at the alley he was sure was the meeting point and jumped out of the car. 'Charlotte!' he shouted.

The roar of the oncoming mob, now less than two hundred metres away, was deafening. He yelled again.

'Mark!' Charlotte ran to him and grabbed his outstretched hand like a drowning woman.

'Charlie! Thank God. Come on.'

She turned back to Joshua, who waved them away.

Riley pushed her into the car and scrambled in behind her. A rock hit the roof with a heart-stopping thud. Charlotte stifled a cry of panic.

Another rock hit the back window, shattering it, as Riley gunned the Land Rover down Kibera Road.

* * *

Immediately after Charlotte fled with Mark, Joshua felt safe. He was free of responsibility and once again in his element — a Kiberan among Kiberans.

The mob surged past him. One or two shouted a greeting,

others urged him to join them. But Joshua felt quite exhausted. His only wish was to find Mayasa and to make sure she would be safely in his care until the trouble had passed.

The rioters left devastation in their wake. There was barely a structure untouched. Every vehicle was burning or destroyed. It appeared that even supporters' homes and businesses had been looted and in many cases burnt.

Someone shouted to a friend standing near Joshua, 'Hey, bro! Come to Toi. It's our time to eat.'

'To eat' was code for the rewards — the corrupt spoils of office — that supporters of the political party holding government could expect for their support, or for merely being a member of that tribal group, since the major parties were mainly formed along tribal lines and allegiances. The man in the crowd who invited his friend to join him at Toi Market was saying it was their time to take what they considered was owed them by the predominantly Kikuyu stall-owners. In this case, it meant looting and probably burning Toi Market.

Joshua's heart thumped as he realised Mayasa was waiting for him at Toi Market. He sprinted down Kibera Road, darting through alleys and taking all the short cuts he knew, but he was too late. A dozen spear-carrying Maasai *askaris* were already in unruly retreat from the market, abandoning their clients and their goods in the face of a far superior and determined force.

As Joshua dashed along the narrow aisles, searching among the stalls, he knew he might not find Mayasa. He hoped she had fled at the first sign of the trouble. If she hadn't, she would be in serious danger.

The vast throng very quickly emptied the stalls of any worthwhile trophies and, as Joshua had feared, the organisers immediately started a fire at the far end of the market. He headed towards it to be sure Mayasa was not in the vicinity, but then he saw smoke rising from the opposite end. And then more at each of the remaining two quadrants. The looters were well organised; they wanted to quickly and comprehensively destroy everything in the market. Retribution on the Kikuyu stall-owners had been a long time coming. They meant to leave nothing for salvage. Anyone left behind would be trapped by the raging fires converging towards the centre.

Joshua dialled Mayasa's number on his mobile phone. In perfect Swahili, her soft voice thanked him for calling and asked him to please leave a message.

A shrill whistle pierced the pervading noise.

A gang of Joshua's Siafu friends rushed by him, yelling at him to run. '*Polisi! Polisi!*' they shouted as he stood, immobile.

Through the forest of stall racks and struts he could see a column of the dreaded GSU police — helmeted and with batons drawn. A sound like a shot rang out.

Joshua took flight, dashing after his Siafu team-mates until they were all clear of the market. They ran as a pack, crossing the last of the bitumen and dashing into the almost impenetrable density of Kibera, where they knew the GSU was unlikely to pursue them.

Joshua paused at the entrance to the alley. He could see his friends quickly disappearing into the maze, but he hesitated. Burning Toi Market while people were still about had been reckless, and because everyone in Kibera knew he was a member of the Siafu gang, he was implicated.

Joshua ran on, choosing to take another alley and an escape route of his own.

*   *   *

Mayasa stood among the crowd of onlookers watching Toi Market burn. Around her were stall-holders who had lost all their goods, and residents who had lost access to cheap food, second-hand clothing and household products. The looting was well underway, with many in the mob competing for the best prizes. They ran from the burning market carrying boxes of stolen goods. A boy of around ten emerged from the flames, carrying a puppy.

Joshua was nowhere in sight and Mayasa was pleased. She couldn't bear the thought of him being involved in an act of such mindless destruction.

With the heat of the flames on her back, she decided to make her way home. Her father would not be happy that she had gone against his wishes, but she needed to call Joshua, which she planned to do as soon as she got there.

Not far from Toi, where the strip of bitumen that had once been a public road petered out into a narrow, muddy path, two men rushed from the burnt-out shell of a *duka* and grabbed her from behind. She tried to scream, but one had a hand clasped over her mouth, while the other man grabbed her legs. They carried her back to the bitumen where they threw her into the boot of a car.

Her muffled screams barely made it out into the daylight.

CHAPTER 34

It was late afternoon by the time Riley parked the car. It had been a trial to find a way out of Kibera without risking another confrontation with the police manning the barricades. The Land Rover had proved its credentials as Riley forced it over a rocky rampart and onto a playing field along Ngong Road.

He locked the vehicle and examined the new damage to its door skirts and undercarriage. The steering had felt a little heavy and it was likely that the front end had been damaged during their cross-country detour. He would worry about it in the morning.

He took Charlotte's arm as they climbed the steps to the hotel. 'Are you okay?' he asked.

She nodded. 'Better.'

'Care for a drink?' He motioned towards the bar.

'Yes, but can we have it upstairs? I'm a wreck, and I just want to freshen up and be comfortable.'

Riley mixed the drinks, listening to the faint patter of water as Charlotte took her shower. It reminded him of his days with Melissa, when she would come in from the gym, sweating a treat. She'd shower and put on her white terry-towelling robe and join him for a sundowner on the deck. He loved her in that robe. His knowledge that she was naked underneath it generally meant they had only one drink before tumbling into bed.

Riley had finished his whisky and soda before the shower stopped. He was making another as Charlotte came from the bathroom, her hair wet, wearing a white terry-towelling robe.

'I hope you don't mind,' she said. 'I didn't take a change of clothes into the bathroom, and anyway … it's just us.'

'Yes,' he said, his drink poised halfway to his mouth. 'It is. Just us, I mean.'

She accepted the wine he handed her and touched her glass to his.

'You're still a little shook up,' he said.

'A little, but, oh, this wine is going to help.'

'Cheers.'

She took a sip and smiled at him.

He removed the glass from her hand and placed it on the bench top. He drew her to him and lightly touched his lips to the firm flesh at the nape of her neck. Her hair was wet against his cheek. He moved his mouth up to the line of her jaw, then to her lips.

Charlotte responded slowly, very slowly, to his kiss, but then she pulled back.

He took a moment to study her expression, which he found hard to read, but came forward again, finding her lips more open and inviting. She let his tongue touch hers, but again she backed away.

'Mark,' she said, 'I'm not at all sure about this.'

'I know, I'm sorry. You've had a rough day.'

'It's not that, it's ... Well, yes, I have, haven't I? Perhaps I should just call for a sandwich and have an early night.'

'You should. Yes, that's a good idea.'

He waited for her to say more, but she didn't. The silence grew and Charlotte tried to divert attention from her embarrassment by taking a mouthful of wine.

'Well ... I'll leave you to it, shall I?'

She nodded.

At the door he said, 'Night, Charlie.'

'Good night, Mark.'

* * *

As Charlotte closed the door, she immediately regretted letting Mark go. She wasn't sure why she had backed away from the moment, but now, with her dismissive tone still hanging in the air, it was impossible to undo it.

Perhaps it was the overwhelming circumstances of the day, as he'd suggested. It had been frightening, but Mark had been wonderful. She hadn't realised it at the time, but as soon as she saw him arrive in the Land Rover, she knew she would be safe. He had the ability to invoke confidence. It was a feeling that had been missing in her relationship with Bradley.

She wondered, too, if she was concerned about Mark not having recovered from the death of his wife. And there was Kazlana. She had no idea what existed between Mark and her, but she knew she was in no mood to enter into a contest for Mark's attention.

She took her wine glass to the seat at the window and watched the traffic crawl up Valley Road from the city, headlights reflecting off the wet tarmac. The office buildings and hotels beyond the gloomy space that was Uhuru Park sparkled in the darkness. The city seemed oblivious to the rampaging violence that was occurring just a few kilometres up the road.

She took a sip of wine and swirled the glass, admiring the various shades of red as the liquid caught the light.

The events of the last twenty-four hours had shifted her attention away from her main objective, which was to complete her research. She resolved to put the political situation and the violent protests from her mind until that objective was reached.

Anything that might develop between Mark and her would have to wait until the end of the trip; if it were to happen at all.

*   *   *

'Good evening, this is John Muya with the latest news.

'The President of Uganda, Mr Yoweri Museveni, has congratulated President Kibaki on his success in retaining the position of Kenya's head of state. The message comes as a *surprise to most commentators as the outcome of the elections is still a matter of some dispute. Mr Museveni is the first and only national leader to make such an announcement, and has infuriated members and supporters of the Orange Democratic Movement, who claim that Mr Raila Odinga received the most votes but has been cheated of victory.*

'Police are mobilising in the Kibera district, where there are fears of an escalation in the unrest that has been occurring over recent days. A number of people have been injured in violent attacks and there have been many accounts of property damage.'

* * *

The news swept through Kibera like wildfire. Supporters of Raila Odinga felt that the Ugandan president, by personally congratulating President Kibaki on his win, had stabbed Odinga in the back.

The Luos turned to the only manifestation of the neighbouring country within their reach — the Ugandan railway, which passed through Kibera on its journey from the Indian Ocean port of Mombasa to the landlocked country on the distant shores of Lake Victoria. The railway was Uganda's lifeline and everyone in Kibera knew it.

That night, a mob attacked the iron rails in a fury. They used iron stakes, poles and sticks, as if the lines were an incarnation of the foreign government.

Joshua received text messages to join them, but when he arrived on the scene he could see nothing but chaos. The efforts to tear up the tracks were uncoordinated and futile. He sent out a call for the Siafu to gather at Kamukungi, where the railway tracked through the only open space in its path through Kibera. About thirty young men assembled. Joshua took charge, leading a raid on the railway maintenance shed, which yielded tools to attack the rails more vigorously. Many others, who saw the footballers working with such purpose, joined their ranks.

Joshua organised his followers into smaller crews, then joined one that worked furiously for hours with one of the precious few pinch-bars. They had only ten keys to show for their work. After another four hours and with over a hundred helpers straining to prise loose the keys on each of the iron-hard wooden sleepers, they had managed to rip up just one rail length. They rolled it into the ditch at the side of the track and gave a roar of satisfaction that filled the night.

But Joshua was less than impressed. It was slow, dangerous and exhausting work, made more difficult by a drizzling rain that caused the pinch-bars to be slippery. The key his small crew had been working on for some time refused to budge. Joshua, exhausted, was forced to admit defeat. He wiped the sweat from his forehead and handed the bar to one of his team-mates to continue the struggle. He then walked along the length of the rail to see how his companions were going. He could see they too were making only slow progress.

Each rail had two keys to hold it to the sleeper. There were over two hundred sleepers to a length of rail. It would take the whole gang the remainder of the night to remove just one more rail. This would never do. He had seen the railway maintenance gangs, with their mobile cranes, power tools and rams, remove and replace a rail in an hour or so. The loss and disorder they wanted to cause Uganda would therefore be very short-lived.

Joshua studied the rail section more carefully and realised everyone had missed the obvious answer to their problem. At the end of each length of rail, a pair of fishplates bolted the sections together. Therefore, by removing just sixteen fishplate bolts, a whole section of rail would be detached.

He dashed back to the maintenance shed and found the long spanner he needed. Gathering his crew around him, he explained his strategy. They soon had the fishplates off, but couldn't budge the complete length. Joshua gathered more and more men to the task, until everyone who could take a hold was aligned along the length of track. With a mighty effort, they lifted the iron rail and sleepers — keys intact — from the bed of ballast and carried them away to the cheers of workers and spectators alike.

Soon they had two kilometres of line uprooted. Uganda was cut off from the Indian Ocean — her connection to the world.

As the cheers and whistles reached a crescendo, Joshua pulled his mobile phone from his pocket. He wanted to share the moment with Mayasa, regardless of the hour. Again he received her voicemail message. His euphoria evaporated and his concerns for Mayasa's well-being grew.

*   *   *

Joshua had always been the leader of his football-club cadre of Raila supporters, but his scheme to effectively demolish the railway line was so successful he became an instant hero to all those fighting for an Odinga victory. Mobile phone calls and texts expounded his brilliance. Those who were not present on the night but knew him came to congratulate him. Those who didn't know him sought him out. He added another score of contacts to his address list. Each new contact had his own long list of supporters, whom he could call upon in response to Joshua's communication.

Joshua received a flurry of text messages and, having given up on his attempts to call Mayasa, he searched among them for a response to his anxious text. He again received no word from her.

Shortly after the removal of the railway tracks, rumours spread through the mobile phone network that Odinga would be making a public appearance at Uhuru Park. Joshua sent out a broadcast text message to advise all his network of friends and supporters to gather on Ngong Road to march en masse to the park. The concatenation of networks — Joshua's and others — created an avalanche of text messages that flooded Kisumu Ndogo and beyond, so that very soon all of Kibera and most of

Nairobi were aware of the rumour and the call for numbers to attend the march.

Tens of thousands converged on Ngong Road, cramming it from kerb to kerb. They carried makeshift banners and placards with crudely painted slogans. Joshua had under his control over a hundred young men, but there were thousands of women, children and old people in the march too, keen to hear and see the man who would bring about the change in their lives that they so desperately wanted.

Awaiting them at the city end, above Uhuru Park, were the police with their water cannons.

A senior police officer addressed the crowd with a powerful loudspeaker. His voice carried into the heart of the huge column, appealing for calm and for the marchers to disband peacefully.

Joshua's group wanted a confrontation and tried to drown him out by loudly chanting 'No Raila — No Peace', but the loudspeaker blared over them.

'Attention, please,' the officer said. 'This is an illegal gathering and it is my duty to bring it to an end. There is no rally in Uhuru Park. I repeat, there is no rally in Uhuru Park. The media have confirmed this. It is a rumour. So I ask you all to go home or else I will be forced to break up this illegal rally by whatever means at my disposal.'

The majority began to waver, glancing at their fellow marchers in some uncertainty. Others used their mobile phones to confirm there was nothing happening in Uhuru Park.

Joshua and his group kept shouting that the police had never been trustworthy. 'He lies! He lies!' they cried. 'No Raila — No Peace!'

But slowly the crowd melted away, leaving only the angry young men to face the water cannons and teargas.

* * *

Joshua sprinted ahead of the slower runners fleeing before the pursuing police baton charge. There were many bloodied heads around him, but he dodged and weaved, avoiding the vicious blows until he and his followers were safely among another mass of protesters on the fringe of Kibera.

The GSU, a paramilitary wing of the military, formed lines along Kibera Road, with grim-faced, riot-ready men staring down the protesters.

A rock bounced off a policeman's acrylic riot shield. It was soon followed by a torrent of rocks and abuse.

Teargas canisters exploded and then, quite suddenly, there was the *crack* of a firearm.

As if as one, the rioters paused in their assault, listening; uncertain.

Joshua couldn't be sure where the shot had originated, but a second shot — more powerful than the first — came from the police lines.

There was a roar of enraged disbelief from the ranks of the protesters, who began to pelt the police with renewed vigour.

As Joshua stooped to gather more ammunition, his young companion, who a moment before had stood shoulder to shoulder with him, dropped to the road like a sack of wheat. He lay there motionless. Joshua gaped, expecting to see him leap to his feet and reveal his joke, but as he stared at him, a dark stain spread across his back. Joshua rolled the young man over. The bullet had hit his chest, making a gory mess of it and his Che Guevara tee-shirt.

The protesters fell into disarray as more and more shots were fired and bodies dropped or the wounded screamed in fear and pain. Joshua ran into the nearest alley as a bullet pinged through the air near his ear.

Small groups re-formed from among the protesters, but now there were others too — young men Joshua had never seen before, who came swarming from elsewhere in the slums. But these newcomers did not confront the police. They were more intent on creating chaos and the opportunity to plunder anything of value.

As Joshua, in shock, retreated further into the Kibera heartland, he saw scores of looters breaking in the doors of houses and places of business. The door of the *duka* where he used to buy small food items was smashed open and a young boy busily stuffed his pockets with chocolate bars. Packs of rioters were now running berserk — burning, raiding, looting.

In front of Joshua, a group of four men broke into a shack. In a few moments Joshua heard screams coming from within. He dashed into the house.

'What are you doing?' he screamed. 'This is not right! Get out!'

He saw the club, but couldn't dodge it in time. It came down on his head and his face hit the hard, earthen floor. He slipped into blackness.

* * *

Joshua awoke in gloom. His head ached and there was a crusty patch in the short hair above his ear.

A chink of light from a closed shutter allowed him to see the outline of objects in the room. A female figure sat at a table above which hung a naked globe. He crept towards it and ran his hand up the cable to click the switch on. The woman sitting at the table appeared stunned. She was dishevelled and, as his eyes became accustomed to the blinding light, he noticed her blouse was torn open, revealing one breast. She had a scrap of old towelling covering her lower body.

They were alone in the shack. A trickle of blood ran from Joshua's scalp to his collar. They had both been victims of violent crimes, but the gulf between them was total. She was a Kikuyu and he a Luo. The tribes were in battle as they'd been for centuries.

He asked her if she needed help.

She kept her eyes on the table and made no answer.

'Can I call your neighbour to come to assist you?' he asked.

She looked up at him. 'Get out,' she said bitterly.

Joshua reached the door, then pulled a twenty-shilling note from his pocket. Avoiding those accusing eyes, he put it on the table, not because she might believe he'd taken any part in the rape, but because he was a man and a Luo.

There was a feeling of unreality in Kibera as Joshua stumbled home that late afternoon. The sky was blood red and the air thick with smoke. A baby cried somewhere in the distance. Shadowy figures raced across his path. He could hear someone sobbing behind a wooden packing-case wall.

He passed the smouldering ruins of the *duka* of an elderly Sikh fellow who sold Joshua his Safaricom mobile phone credits. Joshua had found him cheerful and courteous, and wondered if he'd had the sense to let the looters have their way, or if the Sikhs' legendary fighting qualities had forced him into an unwinnable battle.

Parts of Kisumu Ndogo were also alight. The Kikuyu had struck back. Joshua felt a knot in the pit of his stomach as he approached his father's house. The past had returned to haunt him. Had Kenya not changed in five years? Had nobody learnt the lessons? Would he arrive home to find a parent among the ashes as he had in 2002?

He gathered pace as he entered the neighbourhood, his head pounding with the increasing strength of his heartbeat.

There was smoke above the rooftops.

When he rounded the last corner, the alley feeding into the little group of neighbourhood dwellings was intact.

Joshua leant against the wall and wept.

CHAPTER 35

Koske sat alone, contemplating the virtue of patience. He knew that later that night his willing helpers would work further mischief on his behalf, but those events were already in place. He was presently content to sit in the relative calm of the Kibera evening and wait while his latest plan, a plan that pleased him immensely, came into play. He felt that patience was a very desirable quality because ultimately it led to more satisfying rewards. He could have taken swift revenge on the impetuous Joshua Otieng for spoiling Koske's opportunity to impress his friends who liked to wager on football games for fun and profit. Instead, he had been patient, and his patience now offered a far more fulfilling reward.

He looked around his makeshift office. The orphanage was conveniently empty because he had despatched his latest consignment to the medical clearing-house en route to Wajir.

The sound of a scuffle came from outside. The door flew open and the girl was flung in. Her tight blue jeans were smudged with filth, probably as a result of the tussle with his men, and her breasts thrust perkily from her tee-shirt. She had a smudge of blood on her top lip. *A fighter!* The thought pleased him.

'Ah!' he said. 'Mayasa, isn't it?'

She said nothing, but he didn't mind.

'Welcome to your new home. I hope you find it —'

'Why am I here?' she demanded.

Koske stood and walked towards her, stopping an arm's length from her. He sensed her courage was waning. He flung a backhand at her, catching her on the side of her face and knocking her to the floor. She whimpered, but clawed her way to her feet. A fighter indeed.

When she faced him again, he said, 'You are here, my dear Mayasa, because I need ... What is it called? Security. No. An insurance policy! That's what you are — my insurance policy.' He laughed, feeling quite witty. 'A short-term insurance policy. And these two gentlemen are my insurance agents. Oh, maybe they're not really gentlemen, but they do their job. Don't you?'

The two men nodded.

'So I'll leave you with them until this is over.'

The men restrained her as he opened the door.

'Oh, and boys,' he said, turning back, 'make sure Mayasa is comfortable, but be sure not to touch her. That is, not until this is all over.'

It was a masterful finishing touch. Koske closed the door behind him, content that he had made a suitable impression.

* * *

'Good afternoon, viewers, this is John Muya of the Kenya Broadcasting Corporation in Nairobi. We cross now to Studio Two to hear an official announcement by the chairman of the Electoral Commission of Kenya, Mr Samuel Kivuitu.

'Regional stations, please stand by.'

'... and it is my duty as chairman of the Electoral Commission of Kenya to announce the details of the voting in the Kenyan presidential election conducted on Thursday, 27 December 2007.

'The results are as follows:

'Stephen Kalonzo Musyoka — 879,903.

'Emelio Mwai Kibaki — 4,584,721.

'Raila Amolo Odinga — 4,352,993.

'I therefore declare Mr Mwai Kibaki to be the winner of the presidential election. Mr Kibaki retains his position as president of the Republic of Kenya.'

* * *

The man who opened the door to Mayasa's house was tall and lean. Apart from his tired eyes, which might have been caused by lack of sleep, he appeared healthy.

'Mr ... Shaban?' Joshua asked.

The man studied Joshua before answering. 'I am David Shaban,' he said warily, then his eyes widened. 'It's Mayasa. She's hurt!'

'No, Mr Shaban. She's not — that is, I don't know. I've come looking for her.'

'She's not here. Are you Joshua?'

'I am.'

Mayasa's father looked at him more intently then, before his expression again turned to one of concern. 'Where could she be?'

'I was supposed to meet her at Toi Market, but there was a fire and —'

'Toi Market? But I sent her to her sister's house in Langata.'

'She was there, but she said she wanted to come home.'

He didn't add that he had encouraged her. The knot in his stomach grew with the growing panic that he might have contributed to a ghastly mishap.

The man leant heavily against the door jamb and slowly shook his head. 'Then, where is she?'

* * *

Joshua pushed through the huge glass doors and into Kenyatta National Hospital. The suffocating odour of antiseptic attacked the back of his throat. He tried to avoid swallowing his saliva for as long as possible, but this made matters worse. When he finally surrendered to it, he had to fight the hot flush of nausea. It was only his second visit to a hospital, and he realised that after seeing Kwazi here, he had developed an irrational fear of the place.

He approached the information desk with trepidation.

'Mayasa Shaban,' he told the nurse when she asked who he wanted to see.

'None by that name,' she said, and looked beyond him to the queue. 'Next!'

'Are you sure?'

She glanced at him. 'None by that name,' she repeated impatiently.

When he remained where he stood, refusing to move, she added, 'The unidentified patients are in Ward 6C. Next!'

The stench hit him as he came from the stairwell onto the sixth floor. The injured lay among the dead and dying, many on wheeled litters crowding the corridors. He could go no further as he fought his rising panic. Every molecule in his body shrieked at him to flee.

A male nurse, a fellow Luo, asked him why he was there.

'I am looking for my girlfriend,' he said. 'They have no record of her coming to the hospital, and they thought ...'

'Those we have here have no ID and are too injured to speak,' the nurse replied. 'You can come with me while I do my rounds. If you're lucky you might see her. Or maybe it would be luckier if you don't.'

Joshua followed the young man as he attended to the worst of the injured. He explained that most of the injuries were caused by blunt instruments such as clubs and hammers; others were slash wounds, generally caused by machetes or *pangas*.

'Many of our fellow Luos are attending with slash wounds to the penis and genitals,' he said.

Joshua stared at him. 'Why?'

'Forced circumcisions. Some of the worst cases have been emasculated.'

Joshua put the thought from his mind. He was already having difficulty concentrating on the faces he passed, hoping and dreading he would find Mayasa. The injuries he saw made him physically ill. Many of the victims were damaged beyond being recognisably human. How anyone could survive such physical abuse was unimaginable. Twice he had to fight the gorge that came to his throat in a rush. On a third occasion, at the bedside of a young girl so mutilated by burns that the skin hung from her limbs in sagging sheets, he was unable to contain it and threw up.

At the end of the round he was exhausted. The nurse agreed that Kenyatta National Hospital was the most likely medical facility for Mayasa to be at, and since she was not among the admitted patients nor those in a coma or otherwise incapable of identifying themselves, he tactfully suggested Joshua try the next most likely place to find her.

Joshua thanked the young nurse and walked from the ward on rubbery legs.

He had to believe Mayasa was alive, because he knew it was beyond his capacity to visit the City Mortuary.

*   *   *

Joshua heard the door bolt slide and a moment later Kwazi's face was in the doorway.

'You are looking even uglier than me,' Kwazi said as he caught sight of Joshua's drawn features.

'You got my text?' Joshua asked.

Kwazi had a mobile phone, but seldom used it or admitted to it when he did.

'I did. Are you mad to come out when the day is full of smoke and crazy people?'

'Mayasa was at her sister's house and she was supposed to meet me at Toi Market, but I couldn't find her.'

'And now your friends have burnt the market,' Kwazi said with disgust.

Joshua didn't reply.

'What makes you think she was at Toi?'

Joshua related their mobile phone arrangements.

'Then if she was not there, she must be safe. Did you call her?'

'Yes, many times. No answer.'

'Probably no credit. Did you go to her sister's house?'

'No. Her father called the sister and she's not there. I'm worried.'

'She must be on her way. She will come home when this madness ends.'

'It won't end until Raila is declared president. Did you hear that he has been arrested?'

'How did you hear that?'

'The texts. Everybody's talking about it. We will not allow it,' Joshua said.

'Rumours. Always rumours. There's nothing on the radio.'

'We're planning more for tonight. You'll see. We won't rest until he is declared the winner.'

'And more burning. How are we going to eat without the market? And the police are letting no one past Kibera Road. You and your friends are making big trouble for all of us.'

'Someone has to fight.'

'Don't you understand? While you and your mad friends are fighting, many others are dying.'

'In all Luo history, people have died. People die when they fight for what is right or for what is theirs.'

Kwazi's eyes blazed. 'Why have you come here?'

Joshua was ready for another attack, but Kwazi's question brought him abruptly back to his immediate problem. Nobody knew Kibera like Kwazi, and nobody had as many contacts within its serpentine streets and alleys.

'I can't find Mayasa alone,' he said as his shoulders dropped and the anger drained from him. 'Kwazi. Help me.'

*   *   *

Joshua returned home in long shadows, the sun red on his back. The air was still and smoke clung tenaciously to the jumbled line of rooftops that marked the western boundary of Kisumu Ndogo.

When he entered the house, his father seemed surprised to see him.

'Have you eaten?' he asked Joshua.

'No.'

'I have *irio* and *sukumaweeki*,' Simon said.

He turned on the gas bottle and put a light under the pots. Neither spoke until Simon dished out the cornflour mash and greens.

'Thank you,' Joshua said.

'There's more if you want.'

'No. It is enough.'

'Are you not well, my son?'

Joshua didn't feel well at all. At the hospital he'd seen sights that he knew would haunt him for a long time.

'I'm well enough,' he answered, unsure how much to share with his father.

It was only during his long walk home that he'd been able to identify the reason for the numbness he felt, and the need to share the pain. The trauma at the hospital had been bad enough, but the sickness came from the realisation that he had to take some responsibility for causing such a disaster.

He wanted to see a new order in Kenya that gave people opportunities to share in the wealth of the country rather than having it purloined and distributed among the few in positions of power. He truly believed that Raila Odinga was the man to deliver that. Now, even if Odinga did get into State House, the price had been too high. Many innocents had been killed, injured or had lost homes and properties. The fight to win Odinga his stolen presidency had sown hatred in the community. The cause for which Joshua had fought so hard was irretrievably lost.

He could now see that people like Koske had used people like him to grab even more for themselves. And if, as a consequence of his involvement with Koske, he had put Mayasa at risk, it would be a stone that would bear down on him for the rest of his life. The burden seemed too onerous to shoulder alone, and, although he'd often had difficulties understanding his father, he needed to share it.

He had to start by explaining his relationship with Mayasa. Simon listened sympathetically.

'I'm worried about her,' Joshua said. 'She hasn't called and she's not at her sister's house. I don't know where she is.'

'It's the gangs and the looting,' Simon said. 'It's the young men like you who are causing all this trouble! The police have gone crazy because of you.' As he spoke, his anger increased. 'You and your hooligans, running around, burning people's houses. Looting. Raping.'

'I don't do those things! I am not one of them.'

'You are a supporter. What is the difference?'

'Those people are not with us. We are supporters, yes. But our fight is with the government. We have no need to fight our own people.'

'Who do you mean when you say "our own people"? Are the Kikuyu your people?'

'Of course not. I'm speaking about our Luo people.'

'There! That's why there's trouble. Don't you see? We have nothing and yet we steal from each other. We loot and burn each other's houses. It must stop.'

'It can't stop. What about 2002?'

'What is different between 2002 and today? You say it is wrong to fight our own people now, but it was the same only five years ago.'

'No. The Kikuyus did terrible things in 2002.'

Simon took his seat at the table beside his son. 'What terrible things are you speaking of, Joshua?'

'The fire that killed my mother and my sisters, of course. How can you forget?'

'I don't forget. I live with that memory every day of my life. But you don't understand —'

'What don't I understand?' Joshua demanded.

'That night ... the night you came home from football ... the night of the fires. They were everywhere. Flames to reach the sky. *Haki ya mungu*. And Joshua ... I saw the men who started the fires. I saw them.'

'You saw them? You were already there when I arrived. You told me you didn't see anyone. That they were gone before you came to find the house on fire.'

'No. I saw them running away.'

'Then why were you standing there? Why didn't you chase them?'

'I didn't chase them, no. Instead, I tried to get into the house —'

'You didn't chase them! What kind of man are you? My mother, my sisters — burnt to death by those Kikuyu cockroaches. And you didn't want to chase them.'

'Joshua. Stop.' Simon held up his hand. 'Listen to me.' He took a deep breath. 'The looters were not Kikuyu.'

Joshua stared at his father. 'What are you saying? Of course they were Kikuyu. You have always said they were Kikuyu. Who else would burn down a Luo house?'

'Did I ever say they were Kikuyu? No. But I let you think what you would, because it was easier to let you, a young boy, believe they were the enemy.'

'Then if it wasn't the Kikuyu, who burnt our house?' Joshua demanded.

The tension in his father's face fell away. He suddenly aged in the dim light of the naked globe.

'We thought we were safe in Kisumu Ndogo,' he said. 'Your mother was a Kikuyu, but everyone in Kisumu Ndogo knew she was my wife and they respected that. But these Luo boys came from outside Kisumu Ndogo. They were headed to Laini Saba to loot the Kikuyu *dukas*. They saw your mother. They chased her. She ran into the house. They locked her and the girls in.'

Joshua's heart thumped in his chest. He didn't want to voice the terrible words that flew into his head. 'Are you saying …?'

'I didn't chase them. There was no need. The Luo boys came forward days later when they realised their terrible mistake.'

Joshua thought of a dozen questions. Who were these Luos? What were their names? Why did they do it? Where are they now? But he realised nothing — no information, no punishment, no answer — would change the terrible facts. He only had one question for his father.

'Why didn't you tell me?'

'The Luo were your champions. I couldn't make your sadness worse by telling you the truth. We don't have much in Kibera and I could see how important it was for you to believe there was a Luo homeland where everything was perfect. You even imagined your home was in the Serengeti, which to you was the perfect place for your perfect homeland. I wish I had been a part of your dream. I foolishly fought against it instead of joining you in it. When I was a boy, I had a dream about being a warrior. When I lost that dream, I gave up. I've been afraid to dream ever since.'

His father stood and put a hand on Joshua's shoulder.

'Joshua, why not go to the Serengeti? See it. Stay there if you can. If it's not the place you want it to be, you can come back to Kibera.'

CHAPTER 36

Mayasa had overcome her initial paralysing fear, but whenever one or more of her captors came close to her in the first few hours of her confinement, she had difficulty breathing.

The one she'd named the Lieutenant was of medium height and build and wore a large silver ring in his left ear. He had a soft, clipped voice and his eyes bored into Mayasa. She felt sure he could read her every thought. In Koske's absence he was obviously in charge.

The second was heavyset and had a wide, open face. She called him Bull, not because of his size and physical menace, but because of his placid brown eyes. When he was guarding her, she had few concerns.

The third, who seemed to be responsible for bringing food and drink, was a lanky, acned youth of about twenty with broken front teeth. He was slow of speech and unkempt, and he couldn't meet her eye each time she caught him smiling or, more correctly, leering at her. Mayasa named him the Jackal, and feared him the most.

The two older men passed the time teasing the Jackal with terrible stories of the demons that still inhabited Kibera. They said they were the ghosts of long-dead Nubian soldiers who had been horribly disfigured during World War I, their faces melted by noxious gases. Anyone who saw them was driven mad with terror, they said. They were merciless, particularly the Lieutenant, who whispered his frightful descriptions into the Jackal's ear until he was gibbering with fear.

The orphanage door was bolted and the windows had curtains that closed out the daylight. A TV set in an alcove adjoining the small kitchen droned on regardless of the time of day or night. Mayasa would have found it difficult to keep track of time without it, although she was occasionally able to catch a glimpse of daylight when the Jackal was sent out or returned from an errand.

When Bull was left in charge, Mayasa tried to elicit information from him. He was wary of answering her questions, but she soon concluded he knew very little about why she was there.

After becoming more accustomed to the situation, Mayasa only truly felt uncomfortable when the Jackal found too many opportunities to be near her. When occasionally he brushed against her, she felt her flesh crawl.

* * *

A hundred and ten heavily armed police wearing flak jackets and helmets piled out of trucks on the outskirts of Kibera in the morning hours. The alleys thundered with the sound of their boots as they jogged towards Kamukungi to fulfil the government's promise to restore railway services on the Mombasa–Kampala line.

Word quickly spread by mobile phone calls and texts. The gangs poured from the settlements and congregated along the policemen's path, to harass and throw stones at these representatives of authority.

The officer in charge despatched a squad of policemen to scatter the troublemakers who kept up a running battle in the surrounding alleys. Residents fled indoors as the sounds of combat drew nearer, slamming and locking doors behind them.

In the closely confined alleys, the crack of a crude home-made handgun panicked a member of the police squad, who released a burst of AK-47 bullets in the direction of the shot. The main police contingent, now on the high ground at Kamukungi, responded. As the panic spread, they indiscriminately fired high-velocity ammunition into the neighbouring Kibera dwellings, penetrating layers of timber-clad walls and thin corrugated-iron roofs.

*   *   *

Dede, the cobbler, squatted at his last with a mouthful of tacks, tapping at his customer's red high-heeled shoe. The shoe's owner, Linda, sat on a cement block, watching him work. Her parents had been customers for years and, like many clients, she had been having her shoes repaired by the grasshopper for almost all her young life.

Dede lifted his head when he heard the first crack of rifle fire. It took some time to realise what it was, but when Linda stood, hopping on one foot to see what was causing the commotion, Dede warned her to keep low.

Another sharp report sent a bullet twanging off the iron roof of his *duka*. The next passed straight through Linda, leaving a hole his fist could fill as it exited. Dede leapt from his stool to catch her as she fell. He bent over her as she lay in the mud beside the path outside his little shop, her lifeless eyes staring at him.

Dede wrung his hands in anguish and danced about from one foot to another.

Another weapon snarled.

'No! No!' he shouted, coming from under his corrugated-iron awning and brandishing a fist at the police on Kamukungi hill. 'Stop! You are killing us!'

The next shot hit him in the thigh, shattering his femur and cutting the femoral artery. Ten minutes later, his cowering neighbours found his dead body lying in a pool of blood and mud beside Linda, his sixteen-year-old customer.

*   *   *

A knock at night on a Kibera door was a sound seldom welcomed. It could mean a neighbour in trouble, or a friend or

350

family member struck down by a dangerous illness. It could be a disaster or a death.

After a day in which Simon had seen his innocent neighbours harassed and beaten, people's houses burnt, and had heard on national radio unbelievable stories of people hacked down for no other reason than that they were of the wrong tribe, the knock on his door stopped all conversation.

Simon searched his son's face for a sign that the caller was expected, but found no such consolation. Nobody would be about on such a night.

The knock came again. More insistently.

Simon stood and walked slowly to the door. He opened it a peep and, in the dim light coming from the bare electric globe behind him, he recognised Gideon Koske. There was another, larger shape in the background. For a few moments he couldn't speak; could scarcely breathe.

'*Nini nataka hapa?*' he asked. 'What do you want here?'

Koske said he would speak to Joshua.

'He's not here,' Simon lied. 'I haven't seen my son in weeks.'

'I said I will speak to him.'

The voice was menacing. The figure in the background moved forward so he could be more clearly seen in the light.

Joshua placed a hand on his father's shoulder. 'I'm here,' he said.

Koske gave Simon a withering look and jerked his head to indicate that Joshua should step outside.

Simon put a hand on his son's arm, an unconscious gesture born of fear. If Gideon Koske wanted to speak to his son — indeed, wanted to do as he liked to him — there was nothing, no law, no power in all of Kibera, that could stop him.

Joshua eased past his father and stepped into the darkness.

*   *   *

Joshua followed Koske's slow and deliberate steps as the man avoided splashing the slush over his beige suit. The other man, twice the size of Joshua, followed a pace behind. They stopped not far from Simon's house, where the moon cast some light at the crossing of two alleys.

Koske turned to Joshua. 'You know something, my young friend,' he said, stroking his chin and smiling, 'you have made me very unhappy. No ... Let me say you've made me very ... disappointed.'

Joshua tried not to swallow. The spit accumulated in his mouth until he was forced to gulp.

'Haven't I been your friend?' The edge had crept back into Koske's tone. His jaw tightened under a knot of sinew. 'Haven't I helped you so many times?'

Joshua wondered if it were worthwhile apologising, then abandoned the idea. He knew Koske's soft hand of friendship concealed an iron fist. He would know his fate soon enough, regardless of anything he might do.

'And ... the football match. My, my. Such a good goal. Oh-oh-oh. Yes, it was such a good goal I thought it should be your last. You see, I had in mind to end your football career soon after your big game at Moi International. Knee injuries are so painful. But I couldn't find you. Where did you go, my friend? Not even a word goodbye.' His coal-black eyes glared at Joshua from under his heavy brow. 'And in time I became soft. I know, it is a bad habit in business, but what can you do?' He pulled a handkerchief from his pocket and blew his nose loudly. 'No matter. You're here now. But I saw the good work you were doing in the protest march and the rallies — those young men of yours are very good — and I thought, why not give the boy one more chance?' He scrubbed his nose with the handkerchief and stuffed it back in his pocket. 'I have another important task for you. And this time you will not fail me. *Si ndiyo?* You are still a supporter of Raila, ah?'

Joshua wasn't sure any more. Yes, he supported Raila Odinga, and yes, he felt Odinga had been cheated out of his presidency, but he was now not so sure about the tactics being used by some to secure his victory. Perhaps the news commentators were right. Maybe the result could be tested in the courts? He'd seen too much violence already. Innocent people were being hurt.

'Yes, of course I support Raila. He should be our president.'

'Good. Then this is what I want. You will get your people together for another strong protest. I will get you *chang'a* and *bhang*, whatever they need to get them in the right mood. I want to see you and your men in the KICC. You know how to get around the police. I want to make a big problem for the police in there.'

This was the first time Koske had offered to supply the illegally distilled spirits and marijuana to Joshua's group. He wondered why they were needed now.

'When?' he said.

'Tomorrow night.'

He knew the parliament would be sitting in a special session the following evening to pass the motion for vice-president. From all accounts, it would not be Odinga. Security would be intense and any protest would be met with a savage resolve to prove that the government could still enforce law and order.

'How many others will be there?'

'I only want you and your team.'

Now Joshua understood the reason for the drugs and alcohol. It would be suicide to attempt such a protest with only the hundred or so whose support he could call upon.

'It is not a march,' Koske added. 'I will arrange to have a van parked outside during the day. It will look like it is owned by the security company, but it will not have security people in it. It will have fuel — something to show the parliament that we are very serious about our claim for Odinga. Your team-mates will distract the police. You will go to the van, you will unlock it and you will light the fuel.'

Joshua stared at him.

'Yes, it will be a difficult day,' Koske said. 'But it will be a big message.'

It wasn't the message that Joshua feared, but the backlash from the police.

'You can do it. Your followers will go wherever you lead them.' Koske replaced his hat and brushed an invisible speck from his beige sleeve. 'If you do this well, I may feel better about letting you keep your knees. And I may consider letting your girlfriend go home again. She is such a sweet young thing, *si ndiyo?*'

A steel band tightened around Joshua's heart. He looked into the cold black eyes and knew that Koske was deadly serious. He was lucky to still be alive after what he'd done to this man who controlled so many lives in the slums. And he had no doubt Koske would kill him and Mayasa if he failed to do exactly as he was told.

CHAPTER 37

Joshua slept badly. Early the next morning, he thumbed the text message to his team-mates and supporters, giving instructions about the time and place to meet. He set up the broadcast call but his finger hovered over the *Send* option. He had no heart for continuing the battle. He and his fellow Odinga supporters were not achieving what they wanted. While there were thousands legitimately involved in protests against the actions of the government, there were many more who simply used the confusion to loot, rape and destroy indiscriminately.

He knew his team-mates would follow him into the bloody situation that Koske wanted at the KICC that night, but it would almost certainly mean more deaths. For Mayasa's sake, he felt compelled to do as Koske demanded, but it would be a cowardly retreat for him.

He deleted the text message.

Once he had made up his mind, he knew he had to act swiftly. When Riley didn't answer his mobile, he called Charlotte.

'I must speak to Mr Mark,' he said.

'He told me he was taking the car to a garage for some repairs. But are you okay? I've heard terrible news about the riots and looting.'

'Yes. I am, but ...'

'Yes ...?'

'I am worried about Mayasa.' He told her about Koske's threats. 'We need to find somewhere to hide outside Kibera. Can you help us get out?'

There was silence on the line for several heart-stopping moments.

'I might be able to do something, but let me make a few calls first, then I'll find Mark and we can come and get both of you

355

out of there. Text me later and tell me where to meet you. Is Mayasa with you?'

Joshua sighed. 'No, and I don't know where to look.'

'Just be calm. Think. Where could she be?'

Joshua clenched and unclenched his fists. 'I've asked Kwazi to find where she is.'

'When will you hear from him?'

'I don't know, but if I don't find her before tonight, I don't think I'll ever find her.'

*　　*　　*

Mayasa was only half awake, dozing in the heat of mid-morning, when the mobile phone rang. It made her start. She'd not heard it ring in all the time she'd been confined in the orphanage. Somehow she knew the call would be about her.

Bull took the call and immediately sat up straight in his chair. Mayasa kept her eyes half closed and listened, but Bull made no comment other than an occasional nod and grunt of acknowledgement. She watched him scratch his head and wrinkle his brow. He turned in her direction as the call ended, but remained seated for a moment, still scratching his head. Then he stood, straightened his shoulders and went to the door.

The Jackal followed him back inside, and, as usual, his eyes went directly to Mayasa. She kept her eyelids hooded to feign sleep and listened as the two men began to talk.

Bull said he needed to go out and that the Jackal should remain inside until he returned. He took the long, naked-bladed *panga* from the younger man, who had apparently been using it to slash the weeds in the compound, and placed it on the meeting table. At the door, he turned back to glance at Mayasa, who now sat up, pleading with her eyes that he not leave her alone with the frightening Jackal.

Bull turned away and pulled the door closed behind him.

The Jackal grinned.

CHAPTER 38

Joshua unbolted the door and Kwazi entered, merely nodding to Joshua's greeting of '*Habari*'. He did, however, take Simon's hand in the respectful African way, his two hands encircling Simon's in an encompassing grasp.

Joshua noticed Kwazi's eyes. They were flint-hard, and he took time to move to the chair where, without waiting for the customary invitation, he took a seat. From years of observing Kwazi's almost impenetrable moods, Joshua knew his friend was in pain.

'Where's your wheelchair?' he asked.

'It's gone. Last night someone threw me from it and stole it.'

'Ah, ah, ah,' Simon said, shaking his head. 'They must be from outside.'

'Maybe, but the whole of Kenya has gone mad,' Kwazi said. 'Anyway, what good is a wheelchair in Kibera alleys?'

'There are so many of these young thugs running about, making trouble,' Simon added. 'I don't know who can stop them. It was lucky you had no money or it would be gone.'

'Did you hear anything about Mayasa?' Joshua asked Kwazi impatiently.

'Do you know the old building behind Toi Market?' Kwazi asked. 'The one sometimes used as an orphanage?'

'No,' Joshua said. 'Is that where she is?'

Kwazi nodded.

Joshua knew the implications. It was Kikuyu territory. He hesitated before asking the inevitable question. 'Will you take me there?'

'No,' Simon interjected. 'It is not safe. You know the Mungiki will be watching for any Kalenjin or Luo who enters there.'

The Mungiki, a largely Kikuyu group modelled on the Mau Mau, had been accused of beheading opponents in a number of well-publicised incidents.

'I must go,' Joshua said.

'No.'

'Don't you understand? I must go for Mayasa. It's Koske's men who have her, and now that I have defied him he will use her to make me pay.'

'I will go,' Simon said defiantly. 'The Mungiki will pay no attention to an old man.'

'The Mungiki have no respect for anyone,' Joshua said heatedly.

He wasn't angry at his father, but at himself. He had been foolish to think he could accept Koske's help without paying a price. How could he have believed he might win a position in the national football competition on his own merits?

He softened his voice. 'Thank you, but I must do it. I will go alone.'

'You will not.' Now it was Kwazi who spoke sternly. 'You don't even know where you're going. I will come with you.'

* * *

Kwazi was exhausted by the time they reached the burnt-out remains of Toi Market. He'd been forced to trot behind Joshua's hurried strides. Now, Kwazi's hip sent fireballs of pain down his leg and his back was in spasm.

'Is that it?' Joshua asked as they stood at the end of the badly potholed road. A hundred metres away was a cement-block building behind a stand of lop-eared banana plants.

'It is,' Kwazi replied, panting.

'I don't see anything. Maybe it's not the place?'

'It's the place. My friend has seen Koske's men coming and going, but there is never a time when there is no one here. They must be inside. With Mayasa.'

'Let's go!' Joshua said.

Kwazi grabbed his arm. 'Wait! What are you doing?'

'I'm going to get Mayasa, of course.'

'Look, my friend, I have heard about these fellows. They are Koske's thugs. They do the work that even Koske won't do. They are big, and very bad.'

'What can I do? I have to get her out of there.'

'Do you think you'll be invited in when you get there? No. So let's do this. We go down and ask if Mr Kirangi is around — he's the caretaker. We make like we're looking for a job. But we check to make sure Mayasa is there and see how many men are inside with her. Then we come back here and think before we do anything. *Si ndiyo?*'

Joshua hesitated for an instant, nodded and turned to go.

'Wait, wait,' Kwazi pleaded. 'Charlotte. You've forgotten to tell Charlotte where we will meet her.'

Joshua pulled out his mobile phone, thumbed in a text, then set off down the pock-marked bitumen to the hall. Kwazi hobbled behind him as quickly as possible, cursing his aching hip and back.

*　*　*

Charlotte hung up from her call to Dr Gilanga. Mark still had not returned from the garage. She called him, but received his cheerless recorded voice suggesting the usual options.

When she clicked off, her message alert peeped. It was Joshua, saying they would meet her in the Nakumatt car park in Ngong Road.

At the hotel reception desk she enquired about a courtesy car. The hotel clerk advised that, owing to the security risk, all hotel cars were temporarily unavailable.

She asked the concierge to call a taxi, but no one would agree to take her anywhere near Kibera.

In desperation, she walked to the lower section of the car park where the taxis congregated, moved boldly through the gathered drivers, found a driverless taxi with the keys in the ignition and stole it.

* * *

Mayasa avoided eye contact with the Jackal, but she knew he was watching her as he made much of sharpening his *panga* on the unpainted cement-block wall.

She alternated between concern about being alone with the Jackal for the first time and the reason why Bull had found it necessary to desert her. Both actions were unprecedented. She caught the Jackal staring at her again and decided to get off the camp stretcher she used as a bed.

She started to pace the length of the wall with the shuttered window. Each time she passed she carefully examined the shutter's slide bolts, trying to establish if the bolts she could see were the only ones that kept it locked.

'You must not look out the window, ah?' the Jackal said with a crooked smile from across the breadth of the room.

'I ... I'm not. I'm just ... walking.'

On the third pass, she decided they were not fastened other than with the two slide bolts. There was a chair further along the wall that would serve as a stepladder to reach the bolts. If she were quick enough, she thought, she could scramble onto the chair, slide the bolts and open the window before the dim-witted Jackal could react.

On the next stroll past, she casually reached down to the chair and lifted it.

Suddenly she felt a presence behind her. Before she could swing around, the Jackal grabbed her around the waist. She struggled to loosen his grip and in the process he spun her around, his twisted smile now inches from her face.

* * *

Joshua heard a scream when halfway to the orphanage. He broke into a sprint, leaving Kwazi in his wake. The door was locked, but he threw his shoulder at it with all his weight. There was a splintering sound and the door burst inwards.

Mayasa was on the floor. Straddling her was a young man, tearing at her tee-shirt. A *panga* lay on the floor beside them.

Joshua bellowed and charged across the room, but the young man quickly leapt to his feet with the *panga* pointed towards Joshua like a sword. He was grinning like a fool, his teeth yellowed and broken.

Joshua circled him, trying to get between him and Mayasa, but the man with the *panga* moved to block the only escape route.

Just then, Kwazi came stumbling and cursing through the door.

The Jackal spun about. In horror, he saw the face of a demon leering at him. He screamed and lashed out with his *panga* again and again until the ghost of the Nubian soldier lay bleeding on the floor.

In another moment, howling like a madman, the Jackal was gone.

* * *

Joshua stood frozen in the seconds it took for Kwazi to arrive and for the *panga* to fall on him. The first blow felled his friend where he stood, and now he lay almost at Joshua's feet, the blood still flooding from his mutilated body. His neck appeared to have been broken by the force of the *panga* blow, and his face, frozen in the moment death had laid its cold hand on him, was twisted even beyond the ruin he'd carried with him through life.

Joshua couldn't move. He couldn't bring himself to reach out to touch Kwazi in case the action confirmed his worst fears.

As Mayasa knelt beside Kwazi's body, sobbing, he felt an almost unbearable urge to flee the building, the blood and the *panga*, and the tragic sight of Kwazi's pitiful body.

At that moment, he was once again a twelve-year-old with eyes of ice and a stone in place of his heart, staring at the incinerated bodies of his mother and three young sisters.

* * *

Simon could not sit at home alone while his son faced such danger. He headed towards Kibera Gardens Road and as he dashed through the Nakumatt car park, he saw Charlotte sitting in a taxi. Oddly, she was in the driver's seat. She flinched when he tapped on the window.

'Charlotte,' he said when she'd rolled it down, 'what are you doing here? It's not safe.'

She told him about Joshua's arrangements and he hurried on. Reaching the orphanage, he spotted Joshua and Mayasa from the garden. They were standing in the doorway.

'Joshua!' he hissed from the cluster of banana plants. 'This way! Charlotte is there. She's waiting.'

He knew they would have precious little time to escape Kibera before the local Mungiki gang heard of the Luos invading their territory.

Neither Joshua nor Mayasa made a move.

He hurried to them. 'We must be quick!' he said, this time more insistently. 'They will be coming!'

He tugged at Joshua's arm, then followed his gaze to the body lying on the ground like a broken and bloodied shell.

'*Haki ya mungu*,' he whispered. 'What have they done?'

Simon stepped between Joshua and what remained of Kwazi and hugged his son to him fiercely. 'Oh, my son,' he said. 'What have they done to this poor boy? This poor, poor boy.'

Mayasa, tears streaming down her face, joined them. They

stood in silence until the clamour of voices from behind the first row of shacks alerted them to the approaching mob.

'Come, Joshua,' Mayasa pleaded. 'We can do nothing for him. The ... the gang. They're coming.'

Joshua stooped to Kwazi's lifeless body.

'No,' Simon said, stopping his arm. 'There is no time for that. We must run!'

'No time?' Joshua cried, his eyes now ablaze. 'I have caused all this. How can I leave him here?'

'It will do nothing to help Kwazi if the Mungiki catch us,' Simon responded.

Mayasa tugged at his arm. 'Joshua! We must hurry!'

He stared at her, conflicting emotions twisting his face.

'Please,' she added.

'My son, we must leave. For Mayasa's sake if not for your own. You know what they will do to her.'

This time Joshua understood. He grabbed Mayasa's arm and, with Simon following, dashed up Kibera Gardens Road.

The voices followed them, but they made it to Charlotte and the taxi. She threw the car into gear and they fled down Ngong Road towards the hotel.

Simon sat in the back seat beside Joshua, tightly holding his son's shoulders. Nobody spoke. They were driving through what could have been a war zone, and Charlotte, who still knew nothing of Kwazi's death, was absorbed in avoiding the debris and piles of burning wreckage that littered the road.

Mayasa, red-eyed, sat on the other side of Joshua, who held his clenched fists in his lap.

She reached for his hand to hold it close, but he kept his fingers tightly closed. Mayasa persisted, prising at his fingers. Joshua finally let them uncurl and tears fell on his bloodstained palms.

* * *

'Good evening, this is "The Week in Revue", with Jephta Maraga.

'The violence that has swept Kenya in recent days has shocked us all; indeed, it has shocked the world. Not since Rwanda have right-minded people been so outraged.

'This week's story is from Kiambaa — a small community about four hours north-west of Nairobi.

'A dispute arose in this village between two groups of people. I won't resort to the common practice of defining them by their tribal group. Let's just say they were from opposite ends of the current political spectrum.

'The dispute might have been solved by the elders in the usual peaceful manner, but the community split along political lines. A member of one group wounded a person from the other with an arrow. The others retaliated. Reinforcements came from neighbouring towns, and the violence escalated.

'One group, overwhelmed by superior numbers, fled to safety in havens such as churches, police stations and mosques.

'We now know that the people who fled to the church at Kiambaa on 1 January 2008 were not safe at all.

'The assailants piled petrol-soaked mattresses and blankets at the doors and windows of the church, then set them alight. The flames quickly leapt to the roof and the church became an inferno. Men, women and children screamed for mercy. Those who tried to escape were forced back with clubs and spears. People who came to their rescue were hacked to death with machetes, shot with arrows, or pursued and then hacked to pieces. The death toll for this horrific incident stands at twenty-eight. Fifty-four others were seriously injured.

'Sadly, this is only one of many tragic stories that have happened throughout Kenya this week. We don't know the extent of the deaths and injuries as yet, but early estimates say there are somewhere between one and two thousand people already dead from this post-election violence.

'I imagine we will hear the phrase "post-election violence" quite a lot during the coming weeks and months. It will become a euphemism for the type of atrocities that happened at Kiambaa this week — atrocities committed by Kenyans against Kenyans.

'Ladies and gentlemen ... what is happening to our country?'

CHAPTER 39

Kazlana returned to her bedroom and sank onto the bed. She had no energy to go to the office; no heart to pretend she could go on as she had. She felt as if she'd been in mourning during the days since she'd learnt the true details of her father's murder. The fact that a man like Koske had murdered him compounded her grief. It was as though he had died a second time. Even with her most determined efforts, how could she bring a man like Koske to justice? It was simply impossible.

The telephone rang. It would be her secretary again, trying to keep the office functioning in her absence. She was prepared to ignore it like she had many other calls, but in an effort to restore herself, she took the call.

The male voice on the other end of the line was unrecognisable. He was a foreigner with almost indecipherable Swahili.

'English?' she asked in desperation.

'English, *si*.' He used the Italian word, but he wasn't Italian. Perhaps an Arab, or a Somali.

'Miss Kazlana?' he said.

'Yes. Who is this?'

'I am ... I am Antonio's ... friend.'

Her heart leapt in alarm. 'Antonio? Is he all right? Who are you?'

Silence.

'Can you hear me? Is Antonio safe?'

'Antonio ...' The voice cracked. 'Antonio ... he is finished.'

With her heart pounding, she listened as the foreigner told her the details in a mixture of stumbling English and Swahili.

Antonio had left Wajir, making haste towards the Somali border in his old truck. He was stopped just over the border by a contingent of the al-Awaab Resistance Army. He had no need to fear them, because of his friendship with Faraj Khalid Abukar. Unsuspecting, he had driven into a fusillade of bullets. The caller's brother had seen the assassination first-hand.

'But why? Abukar had so many opportunities to deal with Antonio in the past ...'

'Maybe his love for Antonio is not so strong as his love for winning the war.'

Kazlana instinctively trusted the man. It was the way he'd hesitated before saying the word 'friend' that gave her the impression that he was more than a friend to Antonio and therefore likely to be telling the truth. But she had to be sure and, as the tears streamed down her cheeks, she asked why she should believe him.

'It not only Abukar who love Antonio. Antonio, he love me, but it finish even before he ...' His voice broke and it was some time before he could resume. 'I know he love you, Miss Kazlana. That is why I call.'

She thanked him.

Now she understood what was happening to the children, and Koske, who must have convinced Abukar to ensure Antonio remained silent, was now responsible for the deaths of the only two men she had ever loved.

Even before she replaced the handset, she knew what she had to do. Tears still rolling down her cheeks, she threw on her clothes, grabbed her car keys and in the space of five minutes was charging through the unusually light traffic in her red Audi R8.

She mounted the gutter outside her office and, to the consternation of the building's security guard, left it there and dashed inside. She ignored her secretary's pleas to take some urgent messages.

The office safe was secluded behind a fake set of shelves. She spun the dials and opened it. The handgun sat ominously in its velvet-lined case. It was an item from her father's Mombasa office.

Kazlana thought it ironic that it would be her father's gun that ended the life of the man who had killed him.

*　*　*

Riley's mobile phone rang. As he answered it, he noticed he'd missed a call from Charlotte.

'Could I speak to Mr Mark Riley, please.' The words were clearly enunciated and the voice carried a slight accent.

'This is Riley speaking.'

'My name is Hoffman. Bernhard Hoffman. You left a message for me to call.'

'Judge Hoffman! Thank you for calling back. It's about your committee hearings. I have some information that may help you in your investigations.'

'Go on, Mr Riley.'

In a lowered voice, aware of the garage staff close by, Riley told Hoffman about Koske and the adoption racket he operated through the Circularian orphanage. He said that he had documents linking Koske to medical supplies delivered to a safe house in Nakuru from where he believed children were kept until taken to Wajir.

'What happens to the children in Wajir?'

'Actually, I don't know,' Riley said. 'Although we believe they are taken into Somalia where they are sold to Arab and Middle Eastern families.'

'Do you have evidence of this?'

Riley's heart sank. He could see where the judge was going. In his enthusiasm to get things moving, he'd overlooked a key fact. All he had so far was evidence that children were being moved around the country. If the committee were to take action against Koske, it would have to have proof that the children were being sold, or that they were sent for adoption against their will.

'No,' he said.

After a moment's silence, the judge said, 'Well, thank you for your concern, Mr Riley. I will have the Circularian orphanage added to our interview list. However, while you obviously believe that children are being treated badly there, and I don't doubt your integrity, for the committee to take any action we must have substantiating evidence of abuse and preferably a first-hand witness.'

Riley thanked him for his time and hung up.

* * *

Kazlana sped down Kenyatta Avenue with the wind whipping her hair and without missing a traffic light. She had the riots to thank for the clear run.

On Valley Road she came upon pockets of angry young men carrying placards, heavy clubs and various home-made weapons. She avoided them by swerving to the opposite side of the road, narrowly missing a barricade of burning car tyres.

The billowing black smoke blinded her for a moment. As she blinked to clear her eyes, a rock flew from the black cloud and smashed into the side of her head.

As she fought to regain control of the car and her senses, an oncoming *matatu* side-swiped the R8, sending it spinning across Valley Road. It hit the kerb, pirouetted on a front wheel and, with a crack like a rifle shot, sheared off a white hardwood post at the edge of the pavement before finally coming to rest on its side in Uhuru Park.

The roof had been torn off. Kazlana, senseless, hung suspended by her seatbelt across the gear lever console.

* * *

The young man who had found the handgun in the Audi whooped with elation and, holding the pistol aloft like a sporting trophy, danced around the overturned car to the cheers and jeers of the marauding mob.

Minutes later, they had stripped everything portable from the vehicle, including the spare wheel and jack, and continued on their journey of destruction to the parliament buildings.

The teenage boy who had arrived late on the scene could not believe his appalling luck. Here was yet another opportunity lost because of bad timing. In hope born of desperation, and risking the imminent arrival of the authorities, he combed the vehicle in vain for valuables. He even lifted the woman's crumpled body so that he might check the small compartment between the front seats, but again without luck. The mob had stripped the car like a plague of locusts.

He was about to continue on into the city when he heard the woman moan — a soft sound like the mewing of a trapped kitten. It was an effort for her to turn her head, but when she did so, a tumble of dark brown hair fell from her face and she lifted her mist-blue, unseeing eyes to him. Her beautiful face became distorted with pain and she slipped back into unconsciousness.

A *wahindi*, he'd thought when he caught sight of the dark brown hair, typical of the people of the Indian subcontinent who had come to East Africa soon after the whites decided to build their railway. But, no, when she turned her face to him he realised he had no idea of her origin. She was different.

Somehow, her being different changed the way he thought about her. He had always felt he too was somehow outside the crowd, and knew that being different would make it difficult for this woman. She was a rarity even among the many different colours, customs and beliefs in their country. He suspected that in their land of huge diversity, her uniqueness and beauty would make her even more vulnerable.

He'd taken little notice of her inert figure until she'd moved.

Now he studied her more carefully. The terrible wound to the side of her head oozed blood, matting into her hair. He knew nothing of the prognosis following severe intracranial injury, but he believed an ambulance would soon arrive and therefore the beautiful young woman would have a good chance of surviving. But the head injury alone could not explain the blood pooling in the seat well, spilling over the console and falling in dark, clotting dollops onto the passenger-side door below her.

He reached over her and moved her arm, which had somehow become trapped against the driver's door. A split piece of white-painted hardwood projected from the jagged flesh on the woman's side. Pale, shattered ribs protruded. The boy, although accustomed to the sickening sights in the refuse dumps of Kibera, felt his stomach lurch.

Her right arm, now freed, fell across her chest, revealing a ring with a large solitaire stone set on the thick gold band. The stone was blue; bluer than the dry-season morning sky.

The ring would not budge at first. He tugged more forcefully. The woman stirred and uttered a faint sob. She clenched her fist with surprising strength, resisting his attempts to remove the ring from her hand. He had to prise her fingers open to claim it. He walked swiftly from the wrecked car, his trophy — the symbol of his changed luck — tucked safely away in his pocket.

The boy had crossed Uhuru Park before the image of the dark-haired woman became too much to carry any further. He pulled the ring from his pocket, turning it this way and that. The blueness flared. It was the most beautiful ring he'd ever seen, but it weighed heavily in his hand.

He peered back in the direction of Valley Road. The police had not yet arrived, but he could hear a siren approaching from beyond Nairobi Hill. He must hurry.

As he neared the wreck, he could see that the car was as he had left it. The traffic jam extended up the hill and beyond, but only a few of the morbidly curious had dared to come from their cars to study the victim. It was foolish to be found loitering in the vicinity of a crime when the police arrived. They would crack a few heads and arrest a handful of 'suspects' for looting, which was usually enough to appease their masters.

The sirens were quite close now and the bystanders had already begun to disperse. He had only a few precious minutes to do what he must. He'd hoped to find her alive so he could tell her of his error and ask for forgiveness, but as he lifted her right hand he knew she was already dead. The ring with the beautiful blue stone slid easily over the knuckle of her thin and cooling finger.

The sirens were almost upon him. He could see the police car picking its way through the traffic jam. The boy took one last look at the serene face, the cold grey-blue eyes staring through slightly parted lids. Perhaps a policeman would take the ring, but the crime would then lie in that person's heart and not his.

CHAPTER 40

Riley was having a bad day. After spending most of the morning and too much money in the Land Rover repair centre, he now faced an impenetrable wall of traffic on Valley Road. Halfway up the hill, and blocking him from the Panafric's driveway, was a traffic accident. He could see the police cars and others banked up in both directions. It was too much. He drove the Defender up onto the footpath beside Uhuru Park and abandoned it.

Ten minutes later, he was abreast of the accident scene, forcing his way towards the hotel through a crowd of onlookers, TV cameramen and newspaper photographers.

At the top of the hotel driveway, the crash scene came into view. For a moment, he tried to convince himself that the red Audi R8 could belong to anyone, but Kazlana had told him it was one of a kind. *Like me*, she'd added.

Riley ran down the driveway and forged his way through the crowd until he was at the police lines, with the mangled Audi lying on its side in front of him.

Through the glare of TV camera lights, Riley watched grim City Mortuary staff remove the body from the wreck. A slender arm slowly slipped from beneath the grey shroud as it passed, and a ring set with a large blue stone glinted momentarily in the sunlight.

Riley pushed back through the crowd and walked up to the hotel, feeling empty. In the hotel garden he sat for some time, thinking about Kazlana and her mysterious, disturbing aura. Although she was an exciting woman, he knew the consequences of making love to her would have been remorse and emptiness. He had retreated from her because she was not someone who could engage the heart. As she herself had admitted, tragedy had stifled that part of her emotional composition and she shunned love. The idea saddened him and he felt he should have had more compassion for her. He felt grief for her death, but only as he might grieve the loss of any young life. The admission troubled him and made him feel somehow unworthy.

*　*　*

Riley stood in the shower, his arms propped against the tiled wall and his head under the stream for a very long time. He stayed there when it ran out of hot water, and stayed even longer until he was chilled to the bone. When he eventually climbed out and buffed himself dry with the large, soft towel, his toes and fingers were white and wrinkled.

He rang Charlotte's mobile phone and was worried when she didn't answer. He decided to retrieve the Land Rover from its emergency parking space and risk another excursion into Kibera.

He was too involved in his own thoughts to notice the buzz of excitement among the taxi drivers outside. It was only when Henry, the doorman, intercepted him to say he was worried about Miss Charlotte that Riley paid attention.

'She did what?' he asked.

'She wanted to go to Kibera, but the drivers, they just refused. So she, she … stole one of the taxis, Mr Riley.'

Riley felt a sinking sensation in his gut. Why was he always so completely out of touch when he was needed? His mind went into a spin as he tried to think of a way to find Charlie in the enormous maze that was Kibera.

A taxi pulled up in the hotel driveway and the drivers gathered around it, yabbering in excitement. He saw Charlotte in the driver's seat with Joshua and two others in the back. She climbed out and gave him a tired smile.

Riley could only shake his head in disbelief and, in spite of his annoyance at her impetuous act, had to concede admiration.

While Simon and the taxi drivers engaged in a heated political debate, Joshua and Mayasa retreated to the stone steps to talk.

'I feel bad that it was my fault this terrible thing happened,' she said.

'It was my fault. If I had listened to Kwazi, I wouldn't have run into the room when I heard you scream. I would have ...'

Mayasa placed her hand on his knee. 'What would you have done?'

'The same,' he said. 'When I heard you scream, what else could I do?'

She leant over to kiss him gently on the cheek.

'But it is still my fault,' he added. 'If I hadn't worked for Koske, this would not have happened.'

'How could you know?'

Mayasa was right. He'd had no way of knowing the consequences of his relationship with Koske. At the beginning, it was football boots and the excitement of helping Raila Odinga to victory. By the end of it, he had caused, directly and indirectly, the death of many of his followers and friends; his hands were soaked in the blood of innocents, no more so than that of his Kisii friend, Kwazi.

'He refused to admit he was a Kisii,' he said to Mayasa, sitting with her knees pressed together on the step. 'He would only say he was Kenyan.' Joshua smiled, remembering the arguments they'd had over tribal loyalties. They all seemed so trivial now. 'And he would never admit to voting for anyone, although I know he voted for the ODM and Odinga. He said that all politicians were corrupt thieves.'

'Everyone is talking about corruption these days,' Mayasa said. 'Even I have to pay the postal people if I want them to search for a missing parcel. What do you think we should do about it, Joshua?'

He was about to offer his standard reply, that the ills of their society were always the fault of the other side, but it no longer had the ring of truth.

'I'm not sure what I think,' he said. 'All I know is that I am sick of this tea-money business, with people like the admin police putting their hand out so I can sell papers on Kenyatta Avenue. It always made Kwazi so angry.'

'I think Kwazi was always angry.'

'Not always. Before his accident on Uhuru Highway he was always happy. After that, his face made me feel bad because it was so ugly. I was ashamed for him when people stared. But then, after some time, I forgot he looked different to everybody else. He was just Kwazi. It never bothered me again, but I think it always bothered him. After Gabriel became Kwazi, I began to see his anger when people whispered behind his back.'

'Gabriel?' Mayasa said. 'I thought Kwazi was his real name.'

'No, it was Gabriel Michael Maraga,' he replied. 'I had almost forgotten it. Gabriel Michael Maraga. Kwazi was just his nickname.'

'Gabriel ... Isn't that an angel's name?'

'It is,' he smiled, then added, 'He was.'

'Maybe he'll look after us,' she said wistfully.

Her words brought him back to the moment. Koske's threat was very real. He had to find a way to get out of Nairobi with Mayasa.

'Mayasa, we can't go back to Kibera. Ever.'

'But where can we go?'

'Charlotte says she has a plan, but I have a better one.' He squeezed her hand. 'You will come with me, wherever I go?'

She hesitated before saying, 'Yes.'

'Even if it's far, far away?'

'Of course. My sister can care for Papa. But where are we going?'

'To the Serengeti.'

CHAPTER 41

Charlotte's knees turned to rubber when she climbed out of the taxi. Mark came to her, offering his open arms for comfort. She hesitated, and then leant against his shoulder and let the tension drain from her body. She'd forgotten how reassuring a man's embrace could be. In Mark's arms, she took a deep breath and then released it, letting the anxiety of Kibera escape with the sigh.

He led her away from the excited taxi drivers to a quiet bench seat in the garden adjoining the restaurant and bar. He held her hand as she told him about their flight from Kibera with a mob in hot pursuit.

When she'd finished, she added, 'Thank you for rescuing me.'

'Did I do something right?'

'You knew what I needed.' She gestured to the excited cluster of drivers. 'I don't think I could have handled any more of that.'

He seemed unusually quiet.

'Mark? Is there something wrong?'

He hesitated. 'I'm wondering how much additional weight I should burden you with, but I guess it's best to be rid of all the bad news in one clean sweep.' He sighed. 'It's been a tough day for both of us,' he said, and told her of Kazlana's death.

Charlotte was shocked by the brutality of it and, illogically, ashamed of her recent feelings of petty jealousy.

He related his last conversation with Kazlana, in which she'd seemed reconciled to the fact that she would never see justice done for her father's death. She sensed something in his voice that was more than mere sadness.

'Did you love her?' she asked, before considering how intrusive the question was.

He took a deep breath. 'No. I don't think anyone could. Kazlana was on a mission; a predator with a predator's obsessions. I don't believe she had room in her heart for anything but that driving urge to avenge her father's murder.'

Mark didn't dwell on the details and she didn't press him further. He was obviously deeply troubled by the accident. Instead, she asked him how Kazlana had become involved with the Circularian organisation, and he told her about her father's suspicions regarding the medical supplies he flew to Nakuru.

'She was a strange lady,' he said in summary. 'I thought at one point that maybe I was caught up in a Hollywood plot: Kazlana, the vengeful daughter, and Riley, the amateur detective.' He shook his head to dismiss the thought. 'I should have stayed the hell out of it, but I had no idea what I was getting into. How can a guy like Koske run a business that so flagrantly ignores the law? And how can a bunch of religious nutters be allowed to spin their own version of happiness at the expense of the kids they claim to help?'

He pointed at Joshua and Mayasa, sitting on the steps, then to Simon and the taxi drivers, still engaged in animated conversation. 'Do you see those guys down there? They're the ones who suffer from the Koskes. They all want change, but change has to come from above. Nobody can defeat corruption from the bottom up. It has to imposed, top down. The parking-ticket inspector taking tea money to rip up a ticket has a boss who's on the city council and creaming bribes from the big developers, and his boss is the minister dealing with land releases that favour his benefactors, etcetera. The country needs a ruthless cleanskin at the top to root it all out. I don't know if Odinga could have done a better job than anyone else, but you have to wonder how long this country can survive while it's being bled dry. There is no way Kazlana could have trapped someone like Koske. She never had a hope. And I had no hope of finding Jafari. I guess there are dozens of corrupt, high-level officials out there who remain undetected. Scores more further down the line. Thousands of others on the take. Nothing will change if it doesn't come from the president. The incoming one has a lot to do.'

'Presuming he has the will to do so,' Charlotte said. 'Time will tell. And speaking of time, what do you think we should do? We have to make some decisions ...'

'We do,' he said. 'I need to get into my orphanage story. I'm more determined than ever to complete it now.'

'Oh ...' she said, flustered. He had misunderstood her question. 'And I need to revive my plan to go to Kisumu. It doesn't appear I'll be able to go back to Kibera. What about your book?'

'That'll have to wait. I'm running out of money. And time. There's been a lot of newspaper coverage of the UNICEF investigation into Kenya's compliance with the Convention on the Rights of the Child. It's an ideal time to expose Koske's whole rotten game.'

'What are you going to do?' she asked.

'Kazlana knew Koske was responsible for her father's murder, and that's as far as she wanted to pursue it. She believed it a waste of time to go to the police. She gave me her papers linking Koske with the Nakuru safe house, but if she knew what happened to the children, she wouldn't have told me.'

'Why?'

'I don't know. But I can't rest until I find out.'

She nodded. 'I know it's important to you. So you should do what you must. I'm running out of time too. Maybe we both need to do our own thing for a while,' she said.

'I suppose so.'

Regardless of their work, Charlotte thought it made sense to spend time apart following the emotional and physical stresses they'd been under. It would give them an opportunity to sort themselves out.

* * *

As they walked out of the hotel garden together in silence, Riley reflected upon the conversation they'd had. It was clear that Charlie had no plans for them to continue their friendship beyond Kenya. He'd been a useful partner in her research, but it was obvious that she was focused on the completion of her thesis and nothing else.

He looked at her; beautiful in spite of her ordeal. There was no way he could ask what she thought about the plan to go their separate ways.

For his part, he knew he would miss her company. He wondered if, when it was all over and they left Africa, she would want to meet again.

*　*　*

The waitress brought white coffee for the three Kenyans, who dosed them with packets of sugar, and a black tea for Charlotte. Mark ordered a double whisky soda and drank a good portion of it in a swallow.

Charlotte sipped at her tea and retreated to her thoughts. When Mark had agreed they should split up to pursue their individual assignments, she had tried to keep the disappointment out of her voice. She'd hoped they could continue to work together.

It had taken years to come within sight of her PhD thesis, but since arriving in Nairobi those few short weeks ago, she had found herself riding an emotional roller-coaster — firstly with the post-election violence, and then with Mark being so attentive and kind. And close. There had been occasions when she and Mark had connected, and once or twice had even stood on the threshold of intimacy. For one reason or another, each of them had taken a step forward, only to draw back.

On the Rift Valley escarpment, it was Mark who had begun to open up to her, but then retreated. Maybe he'd seen something in his past that he was not yet prepared to let go. And on the night when they both stumbled around in the darkness of her bungalow, it was she who'd drawn away. Not because of her past, but because of the present and future. She wasn't sure of Mark's state of mind. The death of his wife was obviously still raw. And there had been Kazlana. The atmosphere had almost pulsated with magnetism whenever she came near him. Charlotte wasn't sure if Mark had been in love with her and didn't realise it. She would have to give him time to work things out.

She looked at the others — they were an odd assembly. Simon was clearly uncomfortable in his surroundings, holding his sweetened coffee within his entwined fingers as if to absorb reassurance from its warmth. The young couple, Joshua and Mayasa, were oblivious to all else, communicating with their eyes as only lovers can and holding hands like their lives depended upon it.

'What are you two going to do now?' Mark asked Joshua, breaking the silence.

'I don't know,' he said. 'But we must leave Kibera.'

'Mark,' Charlotte said, 'I meant to tell you when we were talking in the garden. I think Joshua and Mayasa should leave Nairobi.'

All eyes were on her, waiting for her to continue, but she paused, realising she could have handled it better.

'I'm sorry, Simon, I should have spoken to you first, but I haven't had a chance. And now time is so important.'

'Please. Go on,' Simon said. 'I agree they must leave, but how?'

'Dr Gilanga, my supervisor, has given me a contact for Joshua in Kisumu. It's a long shot, but he said his son-in-law, who works in the Serengeti National Park, may be able to find him a job.'

'In the park?'

'Unlikely. But he has other contacts.'

Charlotte turned to Joshua and Mayasa. They were like two high-school students, their eyes wide. They exchanged glances.

Joshua was the first to speak. 'You think we should go to Kisumu?'

'Yes,' she answered. 'Are you two up for it?'

They nodded in unison.

'Of course. There is even a night train,' Joshua said enthusiastically.

'I have another suggestion,' Charlotte said, throwing a glance at Mark. 'Why don't I go to Kisumu with you?'

'I can see what you're thinking,' Mark said. 'But will you be okay on your own?'

'Joshua kept me out of trouble in Kibera. How hard could it be in a hotel in the very heart of Luoland?'

He nodded thoughtfully. 'It should be all right, I suppose ...'

'We will find somewhere to stay,' Joshua said to Mayasa. 'Until I find work.'

'I can help.' It was Simon who spoke. 'I have family in Kisumu,' he said to Joshua. 'No, *we* have family there.' He pulled a folded sheet of paper from his pocket. 'I prepared this when I decided I must tell you of our family. Here are the names of all those I can remember. There are also the names of the estates and villages where they lived. From then you just ask. Everyone knows the Otieng family.'

Joshua took the list and glanced down at the names. 'So many,' he whispered. He looked up at his father. 'And you? What will you do? Koske will want to take revenge on someone. You won't be safe.'

'I have thought about that also,' Simon said, and pulled another page from his coat pocket. 'I will find somewhere to stay here in Kibera until I can follow you there. Here is a letter I want you to send to my uncle before you go to our village. I have asked that he arrange the cleansing ceremony for me.'

'You will do that?'

Simon nodded. 'I will wait until the arrangements are settled. Then I will join you in Kisumu.'

Joshua looked back at the list of family names and showed it to Mayasa who sat moulded into his side.

'Look, Mayasa,' he said, shaking his head in disbelief. 'So many. These people are my family.'

* * *

'Wait,' Riley said as his passengers were about to alight at Nairobi station.

'What is it?' Charlotte asked.

Joshua, seated with Mayasa in the back seat, turned when he saw Riley's eyes intently studying the car in his rear-view mirror.

'It's Gideon Koske's car,' he murmured in a sinking voice.

'I thought so. It's the same blue Peugeot that nearly ran me down at the bus station,' Riley said. 'There are two men in it, and they've been following us since we left the hotel.'

'What can we do?' Charlotte asked.

Riley was struggling for ideas. He'd already ruled out the police — too unreliable under the circumstances. Keeping Koske and his man under close attention until the train departed would be tricky. It seemed they'd have to find another way of getting Joshua and Mayasa out of Nairobi.

'Koske's not in the car,' Joshua said after a closer look.

'Doesn't want to dirty his hands,' Riley muttered.

The train whistled a warning. Departure was imminent.

'Kikuyu village,' Mayasa said.

'What?'

'In Kikuyu village the train almost comes to a stop,' Mayasa said. 'Near my aunt's house. There is a big bend and a hill. The Kisumu train goes slowly. The children run alongside it and climb on for a short ride.'

Riley checked his rear-view mirror again. The Peugeot had not moved.

'It's not far,' Mayasa added for reassurance.

'Okay,' Riley said. 'Which way?'

As he followed Mayasa's directions, he kept an eye on the following car. It remained persistently in his rear-view mirror.

He would still have the problem of getting Charlie and the two young people on board without Koske's thugs joining them uninvited.

About thirty minutes later, as they approached the town, Riley was pleased to see the turn-off to Kikuyu was a narrow road with deep embankments. He told them his plans.

'Mark, are you sure?' Charlotte asked.

'Let's just say I'm short of other options,' he answered. A screech came from the distance. 'Is that the train?'

'It's coming,' Joshua said, pointing into the darkness. 'It's not far.'

The road-crossing lights began to blink ahead of them. Riley slowed the Land Rover to a crawl, then, just as the boom gates came down, he gunned the motor and slipped under. The train was only a hundred metres away. The boom clunked on the rear of the cabin roof, but they were through.

'Yahoo!' Joshua yelled, but Riley was studying the Peugeot in the mirror.

'He's rammed through the gates!' he said. 'Shit!'

'There's another crossing,' Mayasa said. 'Just around the next bend. It's where the train begins to speed up.'

'Plan B,' Riley said, powering the diesel through the gears.

The blue Peugeot followed, a hundred metres behind.

'You guys get ready. When I say go, you jump out and run like buggery to the train.'

The next set of booms loomed before them, blinking and clinking their warning.

Riley swung the Land Rover to a screeching stop, quickly reversing and making a U-turn at the wide section near the level crossing. The Peugeot swung through ninety degrees, blocking their expected retreat.

'Beauty,' Riley chuckled. He could see the men's faces in the Land Rover's headlights, grinning smugly. '*Go!*' he said to his passengers.

Joshua and Mayasa leapt from the car, but as Charlotte was

about to leave the seat beside him, he caught her hand and turned her to him. Reaching over, he kissed her. 'Now run!' he said.

She did.

The big man in the front seat of the Peugeot spotted them running for the train and swung his door open. Riley dropped the clutch and lurched the Land Rover towards the car, forcing him to retreat inside. There was a crash as the Defender slammed into the Peugeot.

The man's face filled with poisonous anger, and he turned from Riley to his driver, pushing at him to get out of his door. Before either man could alight, Riley again gunned the motor, rocking the Peugeot onto two wheels.

Again the man pushed at his driver, but Riley crunched the four-wheel shift into low range and applied the power again. Smoke billowed from the Land Rover's screaming rear tyres. The blue car shuddered, rocked, and edged inexorably towards the deep culvert running alongside the road. With a final abrupt jerk, its rear wheels lost grip on the bitumen and, with a gathering pace, the car slipped from view. An enormous crash and the sound of shattering glass signalled the end of its plunge into the rocky ditch several metres below road level.

Riley turned the Land Rover towards the crossing, shining its headlights onto the three figures trotting beside the last carriage as the train passed through. Joshua stepped onto a foothold, opened the carriage door and climbed in. The train began to gather speed. He pulled Mayasa up and into the doorway. Charlotte stumbled in the loose ballast, nearly falling under the wheels, but gathered herself and scrambled into the carriage.

'*Yes!*' Riley whooped, and gave a blast on the horn.

*   *   *

Charlotte couldn't see the hands on her little diamanté watch, but she thought it must be beyond midnight. The carriage was quiet and Joshua and Mayasa were asleep, curled together like a pair of otters. She felt alone in the carriage that she shared with a dozen others. She wondered if Mark was thinking of her.

She'd been unable to get him out of her mind since leaving him behind at the road crossing near Kikuyu village. He'd kissed her as the train whistled closer. The lingering touch of his lips on hers had been tender; it might have been the start of something significant, had they had the opportunity to pursue it. Or so she imagined. Then again, it could have been merely an expression of the friendship they'd shared during trying times.

Her uncertainties troubled her. Until she was back in a more familiar environment, she couldn't know for sure what had enchanted her over the last few weeks. Was it the new sense of freedom she felt after leaving Bradley? Was it Africa? Or was it Mark?

*   *   *

As the train began its climb out of the Great Rift Valley towards the heights of the Mau Escarpment, Joshua began to contemplate what reception he might receive when he reached his father's village near Kisumu. He tried to reassure himself that they were his relatives too, not only his father's, but it was difficult when for so long he'd thought his father the only family he had.

Mayasa and Charlotte were asleep. Charlotte was slumped against the window with her head on a pillow fashioned from her padded leather handbag. Mayasa's soft warm breath caressed his neck as she slept with her head on his shoulder. The gentle rocking of the carriage and the mesmerising *clatter-da-clatter* as the train rattled over the rail joins almost lulled him into sleep too, but his mind kept returning to the imminent meeting in Kisumu.

It was more than twenty years ago that his father had left his family's home near the lake. Twenty years during which the family and the community might have blamed their misfortunes on the runaway Simon Otieng. Joshua could imagine a hostile reception awaiting him. Perhaps there would be reprisals. After all, it was unimaginable what twenty years of bad luck could do to a person, and how simple it would be to blame an absent culprit. He began to doubt the wisdom of bringing Mayasa with him, but then, he'd had no alternative. To stay in Nairobi was to invite serious trouble from Koske.

A crescent moon flew through the silhouetted trees, disappearing for moments behind a ridge, then chasing the train again as it dashed westward through the dips and bends. The mournful cry of the train whistle bounced off the railway-cutting walls. Opposite him, Charlotte stirred in her slumber, adjusted her position, and was soon sound asleep again.

What could he say to appease his relatives? What excuse could a son offer on behalf of his father? He carried a letter from his father requesting the cleansing ceremony, but would that be enough after twenty years?

Joshua was on the point of discovering who he was; who his real people were. But would they accept him under these conditions? In spite of his excitement, he was filled with fear and apprehension.

CHAPTER 42

Immediately he'd seen Charlotte and the two young Kenyans safely onto the Kisumu train, Riley headed for Nakuru.

The narrow bitumen road from Kikuyu station, dotted with earthworks and perched atop deep culverts, was the first but the least of his difficulties. The line markings on the main Nakuru road were faint, making them difficult to see when heavy semitrailers — concealed behind the blinding glare of their high-beam headlights — swooshed past, jolting the Land Rover with the force of their air wake. At times he wasn't sure where the road edge ended and the precipitous drop into the Great Rift Valley began.

White eyes appeared along the roadside as hawkers ventured into his oncoming lights to tempt him with their roasted corn, peanuts or drinks. The smoke from illegal charcoal-making fires wafted among the folds in the escarpment, concealing hopeful hitchhikers thumbing a ride. He nearly collected a small crowd edging into his path and had to blast a warning when an oncoming lorry narrowed his available bitumen.

Exhausted, he gave up after an hour and slept in the cabin somewhere off the highway. He awoke soon after dawn with the wide eyes of four small children staring through the windows at him. They ran off giggling when he lifted his head.

He drove directly to the national park, arriving at the front gate around seven. As he was paying for his entry pass, the canvas-covered truck from the Circularian clinic drove out the gate.

Riley hurried to the Land Rover and followed it.

The truck was slow and easy to find in the traffic. Riley's problem was keeping it in sight without arousing the driver's suspicion. He was following in the hope of linking Koske's Kenyan operations with the adoption racket in Somalia, but soon after leaving Nakuru, the truck appeared to be heading towards Nairobi, rather than to the east, and Somalia. However, south of Naivasha it made an unexpected turn onto a road through the Aberdare Forest.

By mid-afternoon, it was obvious that the truck was not heading to Nairobi after all. Then, seventy kilometres past Thika, he checked his map and his confidence soared. At that point, the A3 had only two real destinations: Kismayo on the coast, or Wajir.

*　　*　　*

Dust and heat filled the cabin. Riley had a difficult time keeping his eyes open. He had been following the truck at a snail's pace for ten hours with only one break, back in Thika when it had stopped for fuel. The A3 had long ago lost its veneer of bitumen and now the lorry's dust plume was like a beacon leading him relentlessly into the dry country of the north-east. Stretches of spindly grey plants and granite boulders filled the flat plains between small volcano-shaped hills. It was stupefyingly monotonous.

He lost concentration in the Galla Hills beyond Garissa where the road climbed and twisted among the rock piles. As he took the Land Rover through a high cutting, a flash of reflected sunlight from an opening door about two hundred metres ahead caught his eye. The truck had stopped by the side of the road. He swung the Land Rover into the cover of the cutting and climbed out to see what was happening up ahead.

Two men were at the back of the truck, letting down the tailgate. Under the high canvas cover, Riley could see figures stirring in the shaded interior. He counted six boys who climbed wearily from the cabin, lined up along the edge of the road and urinated into a culvert.

It was the first evidence that he wasn't on a wild-goose chase out there in the limitless expanse of the Northern Frontier District.

*　*　*

There was less than an hour of daylight remaining when Riley saw the truck turn off the main road. He had stayed well back until now, as he had no difficulty keeping it in sight in such open terrain. It would be a different matter after dark, when he would face the double trouble of either losing them or, should he be forced to use his headlights, signalling his position to them across many kilometres.

The side road, heading east, was nothing more than a track, which meandered through rock piles into the only set of hills as far as the eye could see. He estimated they were about a hundred kilometres north of Wajir. They had just passed through a blindingly white patch of country surrounding what he'd assumed to be the small village of El Wak, which would place him very close to the point where the Somali border almost intersected the road north. He thought it possible the track might even lead him across the border, but there would be nothing to indicate it in that remote part of the country. He began to wonder how he would respond if a gang of the notorious Somali *shifta*, or raiders, appeared.

The truck disappeared over a ridge and shortly thereafter its dust plume evaporated in the breeze. Wherever they had been headed, the boys had now arrived.

*　*　*

Riley plodded up the road towards the place where the truck had disappeared from sight. The powdery dust rising from each step convinced him he'd done the right thing leaving the Land Rover on the road below.

The sun dipped below the horizon as he crested the rise. There was a number of indistinct shapes in the shadows of the shallow valley below him. He could just make out the truck and what might have been tents and other vehicles. It looked like someone had established a camp down there.

He sat on a rock, wondering about his next move. Having come so far, it was heartbreaking to retreat so close to what he believed would provide the answer to the missing children. He stared into the gloom, then had to admit defeat. He would have to return again at first light.

*　*　*

It was a cold night and Riley dozed fitfully until, around five, the eastern sky began to brighten.

He took one of the three hard-boiled eggs from the cool box and peeled it. He washed it down with a Coke, and stuffed one of the cooked corn cobs he'd bought from a roadside vendor into his pocket.

There was just enough light to pick his way up the rock-strewn slope to the vantage point he'd occupied the previous night. He pulled the corn from his pocket and ate it while he sat to await the dawn.

The grey shapes he'd seen the previous day began to take shape.

Five minutes later they looked like clumps of vegetation.

After a further ten, when the sun came up, it was clear. There were no tents or vehicles. There was no camp where the boys could be photographed in confinement.

What he'd seen in the gloom of the previous dusk was, in fact, a cluster of stunted shrubs.

*　*　*

Riley came upon the boy stumbling along the dirt road about twenty kilometres north of Wajir, an automatic rifle on his shoulder. He unslung the rifle and took a position behind a boulder as the Land Rover drew nearer.

Riley stopped short of him and climbed out of the cabin, a plastic bottle of Coke in his hand. '*Habari*,' he said, guessing the boy understood Swahili.

The boy, who looked about fourteen and was wearing heavy boots and mottled khaki trousers and shirt, made no reply. He jerked his rifle towards the vehicle.

'Okay,' Riley said, smiling. 'I'll leave you alone.' He raised the bottle beading with condensation. 'Just want a chat before I go.'

He thought the boy's determination wavered a little at the sight of the Coke. The rifle's nose dipped slightly towards the dirt.

'A drink?'

The boy glared at him. Said nothing.

'I was looking for a camp, which I thought was out past El Wak,' Riley said, indicating the road behind him. As he was speaking, he edged slowly forward. 'I'm looking for a boy, about your age. His name is Jafari. Do you know him?'

Riley had long ago given up hope of finding his sponsored child, but he thought it a useful ploy to overcome the boy's obvious animosity.

'My wife and I used to send money to him while he was in the Circularian orphanage in Nairobi.'

There was a hint of recognition in the boy's eyes. Riley thought he understood English, and, from his expression, might even be familiar with the Circularian orphanage.

'Are you sure you don't want a drink?' Riley said, holding the bottle up. 'It's nice and cold. And I have plenty more in the car.'

The boy stepped forward a couple of paces and took the bottle from his hand, gulping the Coke down while keeping his eyes fixed on Riley.

Riley squatted at the edge of the road. The rifle snout was uncomfortably close.

'Do you know a boy named Jafari?' he repeated.

The boy gasped as he lowered the Coke. His eyes watered from the build-up of gas from the drink. He burped loudly.

Riley smiled. 'Finish it. It's yours.'

'This boy,' he said. 'This boy with the name Jafari. What is his father's name?'

'Su'ud. Jafari Su'ud. Do you know him?'

'Why you send him money?'

'For whatever he needed. Food, school fees. Everything.'

The replies seemed to puzzle the boy. After a further moment he asked, 'You know this boy, Jafari Su'ud?'

'Never met him. That's why I'm here in Kenya. I was hoping to find him. Say hello. Where are you going?'

The boy shrugged, indicating the general direction of Wajir with a nod of his head.

'Why?'

He refused to speak, looking at Riley with sullen eyes.

Upon reflection, Riley thought the boy was probably closer to eleven or twelve than to fourteen. His brown face was angular, his eyes slightly sunken, with what might be the legacy of a fever in the dark smudges beneath his lower lids. His shirt was torn and his trousers too short by half a shinbone. His boots were laceless and the soles turned up at the toe because they were several sizes too large. The hatred and determination that had been apparent upon Riley's arrival were flagging. Clearly, the reason for Riley's visit — to see a boy he'd sent money to but had never met — had fascinated him.

It took Riley an hour, and much of the food and Coke that remained in his cool box, to elicit his story.

His name was Hamood, and he'd been in the Somalia border district for about two years. He was born near the beachside town of Malindi, where he'd lived with his only surviving relatives, his aunt and uncle. When they died of cholera, he started to steal food to survive. He was caught and sent to the Circularian orphanage in Mombasa. He then followed the trail that Riley now understood very well: from Mombasa to Nairobi to Nakuru to Wajir. What Riley hadn't known, and could even now scarcely believe, was that this boy, and several more like him, had been handed over to the al-Awaab Resistance Army. They were given rudimentary weapons training and then sent to fight a militia war along the Somalia borders. Now Hamood had decided to leave, but he wouldn't say why. He did say that if he were caught he would be severely punished.

Riley's original intention had been to try to find the camp where the children were handed over to the foreign adoption agency, and to get a photo of it or some other form of evidence. It was always going to be a long shot, and dangerous. Now he thought that if he could convince the boy to return to Nairobi with him, he would be living proof of Koske's trafficking of kidnapped orphans to serve as soldiers in Somalia.

Riley decided to press his luck.

CHAPTER 43

Nairobi: UNICEF Judge Calls Local Politician to Account
By Robert Wintergreen (AP)

Thursday, 3 January 2008

In what has become a very embarrassing string of allegations, Judge Hoffman, the UN-appointed investigator into Kenya's compliance with the Convention on the Rights of the Child, has pointed the finger at one of the country's prominent businessmen and politicians.

Judge Hoffman repeatedly asked Mr Gideon Koske to answer questions regarding the mysterious disappearance of children from his orphanage in Kibera, the continent's largest slum.

Mr Koske continually replied that he could not remember any details, but that the children had been sent to good homes.

Judge Hoffman, recently retired from the Austrian Constitutional Court, has made it clear that he regards Mr Koske as a hostile witness, but, without any substantive witnesses to any wrongdoings or a plaintiff, his hands are tied.

Under the intense scrutiny of the world's press, there is no doubt that the Kenyan government would be forced to respond appropriately should such a witness or plaintiff appear.

However, it seems that Judge Hoffman will have no alternative but to dismiss the allegations against Mr Koske unless there is a dramatic turn of events very soon.

* * *

Hamood sat resolutely still in the front passenger seat as the *mzungu*, who said his name was Riley, drove the Land Rover through the outer suburbs of Nairobi. The city had changed since he'd left it as a boy of around nine years old. He had no evidence of his true age, as the orphanage had no records other than an estimate of his birth date when he entered their care. *Circa 1996* was all the papers said regarding his birthday.

When Hamood left Nairobi two years ago, he was travelling north on an unknown, but exciting, adventure. He had not enjoyed life in the orphanage, where he was given food but very little freedom. He soon found it was not exciting to be a boy soldier in the al-Awaab army, where the discipline was severe and life was hard. But it was only after the latest, most vile incident that he had finally decided he must leave the al-Awaab camp. He was confused and sick at heart.

He believed the *mzungu* about the money. He'd heard tell of it from others over the time he had been at the orphanage. There was nothing of that sort in the camp, of course. Only hunger and the terrifying possibility of a violent, painful death.

Hamood could never admit, even to his fellow child-soldiers, that he was scared of pain and death. He'd seen many die on the Ethiopian border while fighting for the land that Faraj Khalid Abukar said was theirs. Hamood couldn't understand how he could have any claim over such a place. He was born to an unknown father from a forgotten mother. How could he lay claim to land so far from his home? Nobody seemed to have the answer; and they had stopped discussing it after one of their number was savagely beaten for daring to question the theory.

At first, Hamood was only frightened in the camp. Then he saw the way his friend Jafari had died. Jafari's screams still haunted his nights. He couldn't say if his friend was the Jafari Su'ud the *mzungu* searched for. If they had ever exchanged family names, Hamood had forgotten it, but it was possible his friend Jafari and Riley's boy were one and the same. Jafari had been about Hamood's own age, just as the *mzungu* said his boy was as he talked and talked on the road to Nairobi.

The mines were the worst, and it was the younger boys, like Hamood and Jafari, who were sent across the mine fields first, leaving a trail of frightened piss in their steps. Once Hamood had felt the hard edge of the mine canister with his bare feet. The soldiers celebrated, saying Hamood enjoyed the Prophet's good luck as he'd not set off the trigger mechanism. It won him the prize of an extra piece of goat's meat, but he was regularly chosen for the mine searching after that, and life became even more terrifying.

Jafari stepped on a mine, but didn't die. Instead, he lay where the explosion threw him and screamed for a long time, so long that Hamood wanted to run from it. All day Jafari cried for help but no one would go to him. The soldiers would never think of such a thing. It was far too dangerous. Hamood did, but he was too afraid. Later in the night, when Jafari's voice had been silent for an hour, Hamood shed tears of shame for himself and tears of sadness for Jafari.

The *mzungu* thought that it was he who had convinced Hamood to leave the camp, but he couldn't know that the decision had been made by Hamood days before Riley saw him on the road. Hamood had sworn an oath to seek revenge against the men who, six days ago, had stood over him and argued who would be first to use him. It had taken that long to find the opportunity to escape, particularly since the men had kept a close eye on him, knowing he might take flight at the first opportunity.

Riley was also wrong in his belief that it was he who had convinced Hamood that he should go to the authorities in Nairobi. Hamood wanted those men dead, and he wanted the man who had sent him and all the other boys to their fate to be dead too. All Riley had contributed to that plan was to offer transport and the best means to make the man in Nairobi pay for sending him to such a place.

Hamood knew that neither the police nor the government would help. No, Riley had explained it clearly enough and Hamood had instinctively understood. It could only be someone from outside Kenya who could fix the problem. The *wazungu* from the UN could do this, and Hamood needed no convincing that he should try to stop the flow of more children into the border war.

Riley had spent considerable time assuring Hamood that he would support him in the investigation; that he would be at his side when he stood to tell his story. But Hamood needed no one to stand with him. He'd stood in the long Ogaden grass and turned his Kalashnikov on the swarming enemy. He would need no one with him when he did what he had to do next.

He did not know the name of the man who had sent him into the desert; the man who had received him in Nairobi from the orphanage in Mombasa. But he would recognise him whenever he saw him again.

* * *

Judge Bernhard Hoffman rapped his gavel on the table. 'I must insist upon order from the press gallery,' he said. 'I remind you again, ladies and gentlemen, that I can dismiss you from this hearing if you cannot exercise decorum.'

He looked over the half-lenses of his reading glasses as he ran his eyes around the ground-floor meeting room of the Kenyatta International Conference Centre. He seemed satisfied with what he saw in the packed gallery.

'Very well. Now then, I will repeat the question, Mr Koske. Do you have the destination addresses of these children who have departed your care at the Circularian orphanage in Kibera Gardens Road?'

'I do not, Mr Chairman,' Koske said. 'As I said earlier, I have the address of my partner organisation in Mogadishu. They place the children in loving homes throughout the Middle East. I have no information on the destination addresses. You would have to ask them.'

The chairman frowned. 'As I am sure you know, Mr Koske, that is quite impossible. Somalia is a failed state. The legal government of Somalia resides here in Kenya and has no recourse to business records or, indeed, any of the instruments of the law in its own country.'

Koske let his smile spread. 'I am sure that if it did, it would find that my children have been well-treated and placed with suitable families.'

The chairman sighed and glanced at his fellow panellists. A couple raised their eyebrows. One shook her head in annoyance.

'That, I am afraid, Mr Koske, we may never know.' Hoffman closed the folder before him. 'I rule that claim number 4a, which is that the orphanage formerly run by the Circularian organisation and now owned by Mr Gideon Koske is alleged to have colluded to illegally move children across the Somali border, be suspended pending further evidence.'

Koske stood, smiled at the panel and turned his back on them to face the milling crowd of newspaper reporters and well-wishers in the gallery.

A lone figure stepped into his path. A dirty boy with tangled, matted hair and bedraggled clothing of mottled earth colours that looked like a camouflage uniform. It was clear from his bearing that he had no intention of moving to allow Koske to pass. His feet were planted firmly in the aisle and his intense, coal-brown eyes did not flinch as they took in the imposing figure of Koske in his immaculate beige suit and striped tie.

The judge, who had stood to vacate the bench, noticed the silence that had fallen over the conference room and turned to find the cause. When he saw the boy at the centre of the crowd, he indicated the situation to the other panellists.

Koske made a comment about how ridiculous the boy appeared among such a well-dressed crowd. A number of his supporters sniggered.

The boy ignored the taunts. He raised his arm towards Koske and pointed a finger.

'*You*,' he said. 'You are the one.'

CHAPTER 44

'Otieng ...' Joshua heard his name whispered by those he passed as he made his way towards the most prominent house in the village. 'Otieng ...'

Many of these observers were too young to have been alive when his father had fled to the anonymous vastness of Nairobi. Others, with flecks of grey in their crinkled hair, studied him with interest. He felt uncomfortable with all this attention. These people gawking at him were his people, but no one had come forward to greet him. No one had said they knew his family; knew his father. But they knew his name: 'Otieng ...' And they watched with the detached disinterest of a group of witnesses at a hanging.

He had not brought Mayasa or Charlotte with him for this formal meeting with the chief. It was impossible to know how he would be received, and for a Sukuma woman to be present when important matters of tribe were to be discussed would have been unforgivable. To have a white woman present would have turned the event into a circus.

The house at the end of the path was a modest affair by Nairobi standards, but compared to the surrounding dwellings, constructed from mixtures of traditional and contemporary materials, it was substantial.

The large man standing at the front of the house was also imposing. His arms were folded, resting on his belly, and he watched Joshua approach with unfathomable eyes.

Joshua's knees grew weak. Depending upon the chief's reception, Joshua and his father would be condemned forever or welcomed back into the bosom of the tribe.

The chief wore a crumpled pair of black pants and a white shirt with sleeves rolled up to his elbows. Joshua wished he owned a shirt with a collar to wear for the occasion.

When Joshua stood before the big man, heart thumping and ears ringing in the silence that now surrounded them, he suddenly realised he had no idea what he was supposed to do or say.

The chief raised an arm, gesturing Joshua towards him, his face solemn.

Joshua moved forward until he was within reach of the man, who raised both arms above his head.

He closed his eyes, expecting the worst, then felt the chief's large fleshy arms embrace him.

*   *   *

Joshua was surrounded by people — members of his extended family. They gathered on a small patch of bare earth, which in better days might have been called a garden, to celebrate the reunification of the Otieng family in Kisumu with the Nairobi branch as represented by Joshua.

He had sent for Mayasa and Charlotte to share his joy, and they joined him among the cluster of people in the shade of three enormous mango trees.

The older folk wore the bright cotton prints typical of the Luo. The younger men, true to their generation, wore tee-shirts bearing names known only among their peers; while jeans and long rat-tail braids were the popular fashion with the girls.

Running around and under the feet of the adults were the children, with smiles to challenge the Nyanza sunshine. As Joshua had suspected, Charlotte's fair skin and hair were of instant fascination. The little ones stared round-eyed at her, some bursting into tears at her approach. Once or twice, tiny hands probed her white skin to find any differences.

There weren't quite enough people to warrant the slaughter of a bull, but there were several *kukus* — chickens — and two goats barbecued for the popular *nyama chosa*. The family members piled Luo favourites onto the tables under the trees: *ugali*, sweet potato, chapattis, cassava, samousas and yams. There was Nile perch — or *mbuta* in Luo — from Lake Victoria. Tilapia and herring bubbled with aromatic curries in huge *sufuria* cooking pots.

And there were drinks. The elders drank *buzaa* — a traditional fermentation of finger millet, barley and sorghum. One of Joshua's uncles insisted he try some. Joshua took a tentative sip. It was sour, but he drank it all and his uncle laughed and clapped him on the shoulder. For the stronger constitutions, there was *chang'aa* — the fierce, illegal distilled spirit. Children and most of the women drank tea and *ujii*-porridge.

Joshua was the guest of honour and, being at the centre of a crowd of family and friends, he somehow became separated from Mayasa. When he saw her standing alone, he caught her hand and, against her protests that she was too shy, drew her close to him.

All he needed now was to have his father accepted back into the community and his happiness would be complete.

*   *   *

Before the cleansing ceremony could begin, all the cattle belonging to the village had to be driven from their grazing grounds past the hut where Simon was waiting and into a holding pen on the outskirts of the village.

Joshua joined the men and boys in the task. They wore only leaves and vines to cover their nakedness, while running behind the herd, shouting and whistling. He could see no other reason for it than an excuse to make a lot of noise, which they did enthusiastically. They also carried clubs and spears to be used in the *tero buro*, which his father told him was the part of the cleansing ceremony called the 'battle with death', during which death was driven from the village.

As the herd neared the village, others helped by blowing horns and whistles. A cloud of dust hung in the air, along with the smell of cattle — a new scent for Joshua, who had never even seen a herd before.

The men returned from the holding pen and a chorus of voices greeted them with sonorous dirges. When the medicine man entered Simon's hut the singers began to dance and the songs changed to those of praise for past heroes. The women ululated and the men whooped in celebration.

The medicine man led Simon from the hut. Joshua hardly recognised his father who was wearing a long cloak over his shoulders and white ash on his face. Joshua thought he looked like a ghost.

The medicine man held up his hands for silence, then began to chant a story about two high-spirited boys, friends, who played spear-throwing games in the dust. The boys had travelled a great distance to prepare for their *muko lak* and they stole black feathers from the male ostrich's nest to beautify their ceremonial headdresses. But in their games to improve their spear-throwing, one boy cast his spear through the other's eye, causing his friend's death.

'He is a brother Luo,' the medicine man said, raising his voice to be heard by all, 'so he cannot leave this hut until he is cleansed. If he does, he will cause a terrible curse to descend upon this whole village. The women will fall barren and the crops will fail. There will be no milk from the cows and they will throw their calves before term. This man says he is sorry. He says he begs forgiveness of his friend's family, and of all of you. He says he has never committed another such violent act, and he promises never to do so.'

Joshua caught his father's eye. He could see the anxiety in Simon's wavering smile.

The wizened medicine man looked out over the assembled village. 'I have cleansed this man for the death of his friend, Nicholas Odhiambo,' he said. 'How say you? Do you accept Simon Otieng back into our community?'

The roar sent a rush of relief through Joshua.

MARCH 2009

'Isn't this great?' Riley's publicist whispered as he entered London's largest bookstore on Charing Cross Road. 'I Googled you this morning. Your gig here is top of the sites. And look at that.' She indicated the queue at the register. 'You're selling like hotcakes! Now, take a deep breath — I'm going up to introduce you.'

Riley had arrived late for the lunchtime launch after spending the morning working the phone and searching the internet for Charlotte Manning. He cursed his foolishness. It had been a hectic time since leaving Kenya, but he'd never doubted he would make contact with her when he was done with his commitments. But it wasn't as easy as he'd thought. What had possessed him to believe he only had to call the Oxford anthropology department to find her?

When the applause subsided, he began his launch speech.

'I went to Kenya in 2007 for a few reasons, including to research a historical novel set there at the beginning of the twentieth century. But historical novels can be such a pain. One never knows where the history ends and the novel begins. So, instead, I decided to write a book about contemporary Kenya, inspired by the events of the 2007 post-election violence that erupted along tribal lines. Over thirteen hundred people were killed during that violence, many thousands more sustained terrible injuries, and almost half a million became what are called "internally displaced persons", that is, refugees in their own country. Many of these are still too afraid of retribution to return to their hometowns and villages.'

There was not a sound as he paused to survey his audience. The faces raised towards his lectern were attentive. Apart from his beaming publicist, they were all strangers.

'This is a damning condemnation of the country's political leaders,' he continued, 'many of whom have been identified as instigators and supporters of the violence. Yet they continue to hold office and positions of power and influence.

'The Kenyan people are friendly and welcoming to visitors. The country has much to offer the tourist. Some say Kenya is beautiful, while others might describe it as magnificent rather than beautiful —'

He could see the Great Rift Valley escarpment. He was there with Charlie.

The audience exchanged glances as the silence persisted.

'I'm sorry, ladies and gentlemen, just lost my train of thought for a moment. As I was saying, Kenya has magnificent scenery, friendly people and is a great holiday destination, but there is an underlying ugliness that we must challenge in every way we can. I encourage you to press our government and those of other countries to ... to demand accountability ...'

Again, his thoughts faltered, and suddenly he'd lost the energy to continue. This morning's lack of success had affected him more deeply than he realised. He looked around the room and decided to wind things up.

'Um, I'm sorry ... it's all explained in the notes on the signing table. Thank you.'

Riley stepped down from the lectern amid generous applause, and was led by his publicist to a stack of books on the signing table. After half an hour, his mind was numb and his wrist ached. Still they came, book in hand and itching to chat.

'Who would you like me to sign it for?' he asked for perhaps the fortieth time.

'You could make it out to "Charlotte", please, Mr Riley.'

The voice. Her voice.

'Charlie!' he said, looking up at her in disbelief.

'Hello, Mark,' she replied. 'Congratulations.'

'Thank you,' he said, standing to take her outstretched hand. 'I've been looking everywhere for you and ... well ... How've you been, Charlie?'

She smiled. 'Nobody's called me Charlie since Kenya. But I'm fine. And you?'

He nodded. 'I'm okay.'

A snug-fitting black dress — too light for the weather that day — hugged her body underneath a tan leather jacket trimmed along the lapels with fake fur. The burgundy scarf tied loosely at her slender throat gave her face a healthy glow of colour — as he remembered she'd looked after a couple of weeks in the Kenyan sun.

'You look great,' he added.

'Thank you.'

'I didn't see you in the crowd.'

'I was passing and, well ...'

'I can't believe it! Just as I'm giving my talk.'

'It's a small world,' she said.

He remembered their last night together. She was fresh from the shower in the white terry-towelling robe, her hair wet and with pearls of water glistening on her skin, his lips on the firm flesh of her throat.

She caught his eyes on her and flushed. Her fingertips fluttered over the silky smooth skin just below her ear where he'd kissed her.

'How's your doctoral thesis going?' he asked.

'It's Dr Charlie now, if you don't mind.'

'Congratulations! That's great news.'

She smiled. It was the same smile as on the inside cover of her book.

'You look great,' he said.

'Thank you. Again.'

He struggled to think of something to fill the void his mind had become since her sudden appearance. He moved from behind the table and took her hand again.

'It's just that … I'm so amazed that we've bumped into each other here today, out of all of the millions in London. It just proves my point about synchronicity, don't you think?'

She raised a shaped eyebrow. 'Maybe. If it wasn't for Google.' She wore that I-know-stuff smile.

'What!' he said, then laughed as he understood.

He drew her to him, holding her body close.

Charlie wrapped her arms around his neck, smiling into his eyes.

He kissed her.

* * *

A soft breeze played over the stony, dry earth of the Seronera parade ground. The short rains were yet to bring the verdant flush of new grasses, but Joshua loved the fragrance of dry grass and dust. It was hot, but he didn't mind. He stood to attention with his ten fellow recruits while the chief game warden made a speech about conservation, park management and the park's history.

'The Maasai call this place *Siringitu*,' he said, 'which means "the place where the land moves on forever". The Maasai have always appreciated the beauty of the Serengeti; and it is you new recruits, gathered here today, whom the Maasai now entrust to protect that beauty. If you complete your training to become game wardens, you will have the skills necessary for the task. But it is how you use those skills that will determine the success or failure of your mission.'

Joshua glanced towards Mayasa, who stood with her hands clasped beneath her swollen belly as if to hold the weight of their unborn child. She had been determined to attend his induction, regardless of his pleas to avoid the heat. But his father was at her side, holding a large umbrella to shelter her from the Serengeti sun.

Joshua filled his lungs with the scent of the Serengeti — dry grass; dust; the peppery organic fragrance of growth, death and rebirth — and looked above the semicircle of government huts to the endless, clear blue sky.

He blocked out the chief game warden's voice and listened instead to the voices playing on the breeze: the twitter of birds, the rustle of tree leaves, the distant bark of a zebra. The sounds of the Serengeti.

Perhaps the call of the Serengeti had always been present in his mind, but it was a call too soft to be heard over the din of Kibera. Now he could hear it. Every sweet soft sound of it.

ACKNOWLEDGEMENTS

In August and September of 2008, I spent a month in the Nairobi informal settlement area of Kibera while researching this novel. Although the vast majority of Kibera's residents are law-abiding, I was warned that to attempt to go unescorted into many parts of Kibera would be dangerous. I was therefore very fortunate to have the assistance of a number of people to enable me to spend time in Kibera and complete this research.

I wish to thank Michelle Osborn, who at the time was a doctoral student in Nairobi, Kenya, for her advice and her assistance in arranging for me to meet a number of individuals who agreed to act as my guides in Kibera.

The assistance of Jared Nyamweya during my visits to Kibera is gratefully acknowledged. Jared is one of the many private citizens of Kibera who selflessly devote their time and limited resources to provide community assistance programs within the settlement.

There were others who offered information and opinions on the political situation in Kenya but who have asked to remain anonymous. Their contributions are gratefully acknowledged.

Many thanks go to my editors, Nicola O'Shea and Kate O'Donnell, and my publishers at HarperCollins, Anna Valdinger and Linda Funnell.

As always, my agent and friend, Selwa Anthony, has been a constant source of encouragement and guidance, which is gratefully acknowledged.

Finally, I also acknowledge Wendy Fairweather and James Hudson for their support and feedback on my early drafts.